Fearless Warrior

THE ROYALS
BOOK FIVE

C. R. RILEY

Created with Vellum

Hermosa Islas

This book is dedicated to all my readers who have stuck it out me while I wrote this series.

Thank you.
I hope you it lives up to your expectations.

Prologue

The Royals

22 Years Ago

Something is amiss. There's an electric current charging the air. My gut aches and sending up all these warnings to stay alert. I may only be a kid, twelve to be exact, but I know when trouble is closing in. While the adults held hushed conversations, doing their very best to keep my sister and me out of the loop, their efforts didn't work. These last few weeks I listened in the shadows.

I'm constantly aware, on guard. It's a trait my father swears will make me a powerful man. One who recognizes danger before it sneaks up on him. I'm not sure why that's important, but I trust him to know.

My father is a wise businessman who dabbles in politics. I overheard someone call him Your Majesty the other day, which I thought odd. I assumed the man was joking until my father's eye caught mine and I realized there was more to it than I understood. I haven't had the chance to speak with him about that. Men who are acting more like prison guards have overtaken our home.

We've always had security. Today, however, it feels different.

My mother looks more stressed than usual. She tries to conceal it, but I pinpoint every forced smile and false pleasantness she bestows upon us. I notice how she never lets a few hours pass without checking in with father. She's never been so involved with his business. Not to mention, I've overheard her crying this past week when she assumed she was alone. I even caught my father comforting her, telling her it would be fine. That he would make sure of it and keep us safe. But it became obvious she was worried and didn't believe him.

A few hours ago, my sister Giovanna and I were sent to the study. It was after my uncle stopped by for a visit. Something felt off about his unannounced social call. I cannot explain it, just that I'm not sure I trust him. It's not the first time I've had that uneasiness around him. Over the last several months, a tension began building in the air between Father and Uncle Dracul. It's as if hatred now stands between them.

An armed guard of my uncle's steps inside the room and snaps his fingers at us. "Come."

I recognize him from earlier. His eyes are wild and a deep scar marks his left cheek. When we hesitate, he grabs the back of my neck, squeezing hard, making me wince in pain. Laughing at my reaction, muttering a response in a language not commonly used around us. A mixed dialect of Hungarian, Slovak, and Romanian. The language I read about in the book my father keeps in his office. It's not one I've actually heard spoken until now, though.

"Don't fuck with me, boy." The guard turns an eye on my sister who has tears streaming down her face. "I have no problem taking out my frustrations on a little girl. Keeping her until she comes of age, even."

I'm bigger than a boy of only twelve should be. Many times, I've been mistaken for older, often thought to be sixteen. My father trained me well on how to defend myself and my little sister. He always proclaimed a man should know how to fight, so he can protect those he cares most about. He taught me not only to use my brain, but my muscles as well.

"Over my dead body," I spit out as my fist connects with his face, catching him off guard. The man's body crumbles and lands with a loud thud. His head bouncing when it hits the wood floor.

"Simion!" Giovanna screams my name as she watches the jerk drop.

I spot the earpiece in his ear. Yanking it out, I place it in mine, allowing me to eavesdrop. Immediately, I realize the situation is worse than I'd imagined. We only have seconds to hide before more of these assholes show up and do God knows what.

One I can handle. More than one? I'm not sure.

"Gia, I need you to listen and move quickly. We have to get out of here." I remove the gun from the holster strapped to the guard's side and check it. Again, my father taught me how to use one. He wanted me to always feel comfortable enough to respect them. I'm beginning to believe he did so for a time such as this. "Through the back passage, hurry." The passages hidden within the walls were often our playground. Only a few of my father's most trustworthy men even knew they existed.

At only seven, she's scared, but my sister has always trusted me. We've only ever had each other, more so these last three years. Our parents claimed it was too dangerous to continue attending private school, too many uproars in this country we called home. We've only interacted with tutors, our parents, and each other.

We run for the bookcase. Gia enters first, me close behind her, latching the lock just as my uncle's men storm the study. I place a finger over my mouth, signaling Gia to remain silent. Since I'm still wearing the earpiece, I hear what they're saying. They're assuming we fled the room before they could get to us, and that's to our advantage.

I flip the extra padlock that will keep them out and motion for Giovanna to lead the way. When we reach the safe room—another hidden secret—I order her inside and instruct her to stay while I check on our parents. She doesn't want me to leave, but at the same time, she wants our mother.

We have a signal, a knock we've used more than once over the years. Child's play that will come in handy now. I remind her of it and promise to use it when I return, so she knows it's me, ensuring her it is safe to open the door. I hate leaving her, but right now she'll only get in my way. In this space, no one can get to her, and it puts my mind at ease.

When I reach my father's office, I listen through the comm still in my ear. The other voices have stopped speaking. Only my uncle's pierces my ears now. "Dragos, where are your children?"

I slide the concealed panel open carefully so I can see inside. It's behind a vent. No one will notice, and while it obscures my view, it allows me to assess the room and see what I need to.

I don't miss it when my father looks directly at me. "How am I to know that, brother? And even if I did, I'd not tell you."

My uncle curses in Russian, a language he often uses, as he stomps out of my view. When he steps back into it, he has my mother in an agonizing grip. She's crying, a gag over her mouth, a fresh bruise on her cheek. I cover my ears when I watch him lift his gun to her head and fire without so much as a warning.

Red is all I see now. Crimson takes over my vision. I can't be sure if it's from the blood now pouring out of her or the fury building inside me. My heart is pounding in my chest so hard I can hear it. I want to pound my fists into the wall but can't, so I clinch them to hold back my rage and not give up my hiding spot.

I hate him, will forever hate him.

My father has tears streaming down his face, but remains strong. I can tell he's dying inside, but refuses to let my uncle see him physically crumble. It takes all the strength he has to not collapse at the sight of my mother executed in front of him.

His last words will forever stay with me, haunt my dreams for many nights. "Fuck you! I'll never tell you or forgive you for what you just did. We may have once shared a womb, but today we are no longer brothers. You will never achieve the prize you are hungry for. You will never rule or wear the crown."

An evil laugh flows from my uncle before he lifts his gun and shoots his twin the same way he did my mother. I can only stare at my parents' lifeless bodies as my world disintegrates in front of my eyes. There is so much I don't understand. The hatred building inside my soul, for the man I once thought was a good person, will drive me now. He will one day pay for what he stole from me.

It isn't until I hear my uncle speak that I come to my senses. "Locate those brats. Do not kill them. I may allow the girl to live. We could certainly sell her for a profit to the right man. The boy, however, he must die, but I want him brought to me first. My brother should have told me where to find them. Torturing his son will now give me great pleasure. Revealing who he is will be my reward for all I've been through living as the second best, under Dragon. Simion's fate is now sealed, and it only makes this so much sweeter. Find them so we can get this over with. We've wasted enough time here already."

I close the panel and collapse to the floor, not sure I'm strong enough to do what I know I must. How the hell am I supposed to break us out of here? I know my uncle will eventually discover the passages, even though it could take him hours to do so. Which means I need to sneak us out sooner rather than later. But where will we go, and who can we trust?

I wipe the tears off my face while I devise a plan. If Giovanna and I have any chance at all, I need to remain strong, like father. I'm not sure why our uncle murdered our parents, and at this moment I don't care. We have to get out of here first. I'll deal with the reason why later.

Once I return to the safe room, I've composed myself enough to keep Gia from becoming suspicious. As soon as the door opens, I inform her of the plan I've come up with. I lie, of course. I tell her mother and father will meet us later in the forest. That we are to make our way to the east garden and then head for the woods. Find a good hiding place and stay there until they come to get us. I don't know what I'll do once we get there. It's important I get us out of here first, I'll figure out our next move once we're safe.

Forty minutes is how long we take to make it down the interweaving passages. The comm I'm wearing keeps me updated. No one's onto us yet. Once outside, that could become a different story. My uncle and his men are doing a perimeter check, searching the grounds frantically for us. As soon as we leave our safe hiding spot, we'll have to climb the enormous stone wall, possibly exposing us.

We wait until the men move past the garden. I offer up a prayer, hoping I don't get both of us killed.

"I'm scared, Simion," Giovanna admits as I do my best to help her scale the wall. "How am I going to climb down? It's too high."

"I'll help you, promise." The wall is taller than I remember, but I trust I can do just that. "Sit here while I climb down. Once I'm on the ground, jump to me."

She nods, but I see the fear in her eyes. As soon as I'm on solid ground, I scan the area to make sure no one is near. "Now, Giovanna."

"I can't," she cries as the concern of getting hurt mares her face. "I can't do it. I'm scared."

I rub my hand across my forehead, knowing we are pushing our luck the longer we stay here. "I'm scared too. I promise I'll—"

Before I can say more, rapid gun fire assaults the air.

Giovanna screams.

I watch in horror as she topples forward off the sixteen-foot wall and pitches over. My legs have never moved so fast. Before she hits the ground, I catch her, not perfectly, but enough to break her fall. "Fuck."

"You aren't supposed to say that word," she reminds me.

I snort squeezing her tight to my chest. "Forgive me. I'll try to do better the next time you topple off a wall and nearly give me a heart attack."

She giggles, although it sounds forced. "I'm glad you move fast. Thank you."

We don't have time for chit chat. "Can you walk? We need to make it to the woods."

She nods, and we run. We run together the fastest we can. When the yelling starts, I fear we've been spotted. I stop and order her onto my back so we can move faster. It works until a sharp bite tears through my thigh and knocks me to the ground. One more rips through my back and everything goes black.

———

"SIMION, DON'T MOVE." A male voice breaks through my fog and the pain. "Hold still, son. I need to stabilize you so we can get you in the chopper."

"Giovanna. You have to help her." I force my eyes open and stare at the face covered in black, concealing his features. His blue eyes, however, are plain as day looking down at me. The sadness in them tells me all I need to know. "Let me die. I have no reason to live. My family is gone and I want to join them."

"You have thousands of reasons to live. You just don't know it yet.

One day, you'll see the light." He ties something tight around my thigh and then tosses me over his shoulder. "We cannot let a future leader die before his time. I have my orders. While we failed to save the others, we will not fail to save you, and you will appreciate why that is when the time comes. It won't be easy, but one day you'll return to this land and understand why God chose you to survive. Trust me. Now let's get on that chopper so we can take you to Hermosa Islas. Your father, King Dragos, has arranged everything to ensure your safety. Time to get the fuck out of here and secure the future for you and so many others."

I don't fight him. I let him load me on the chopper and watch as five others dressed like him join us. As we lift off, the world I once knew disappears. I have no idea what I'll face, but I swear then and there that before I die, I will avenge my family's unwarranted deaths. My uncle will pay for what he has done.

Chapter One

GINO

16 Years Later

Ilie low in the shadows, trying not to overreact as I watch her sneak out once again. We've played this game a few times already this week. I've lost track how many times this month she's dared to test my ability to stay ahead of her. She's only slipped past me once, and in my defense, it was because I'd been away for the evening. I was, however, waiting for her when she returned. I didn't miss the snarky expression in her copper brown eyes as she passed, knowing she won that round. It was a sport for her now. Could she slip past me or would I be there waiting to send her back?

Tonight, I decide it's time to handle this another way. I'm not sure why. Maybe it has more to do with me understanding her motive for sneaking out. At her age, I'd done the same thing, snuck out because I could, without the knowledge of my new family. I appreciate the pressure of being trapped, not yet recognizing your place in a world you didn't understand. Always feeling lost and confused about why you were here and not somewhere else, someone else. Wishing you could be like others your age, but unable to change who you are. It's out of your hands, so you choose to steal a moment here and there when you can.

I'll never forget the day my eyes were opened to a world I'd never known existed. Waking in a hospital next to a man with piercing blue eyes. The same one who promised to keep me safe when I wanted nothing more than to die. He'd saved me from certain death and swore one day I'd see the bigger picture.

I didn't feel like he'd saved me. I felt betrayed. My entire life had been one lie after another. At twelve, I didn't comprehend why it was so important for everyone to keep my identity from me. Why my father pretended to be someone he was not, instead of proud to be the man he was. Or why he never once shared who we were, how important we were, even. I was confused on why he'd refused to explain after he'd placed us in danger, even though his reason sounded like the right thing to do. For so many years, I questioned why, with no real answers. As I grew older, I saw matters differently, but that didn't mean I agreed with his choices. In the long run, it would've been best if we'd known, so we were prepared, but he'd obviously felt different about that.

The world I was raised in collapsed after he sided with *the people* when they declared a revolution was necessary. They'd sought him out for support, the only kind a man like him could offer them. Why? It turns out they wished to overthrow the government that was holding the citizens in our country down. They expected my father to lead the way. Once he'd accomplished that, they looked forward to him accepting his rightful place as sovereign leader, one his family once controlled. They desired a king who would lead them, not another dictator who ruled over them.

My father was the rightful heir to a throne that hadn't held power for almost two hundred years. Many wars were fought since the day his family lost sovereignty. Governments were erected and later removed many times over.

When the current government of Kosonia learned he was backing those fighting against them, they sent my uncle to resolve the issue. Dracul vowed to annihilate the problem, starting at the top and then working his way down. In cold blood Dracul murdered his own brother when the dictator, a close friend of his, promised a seat next to him after proving his loyalty.

My father had seen through his brother's corrupt plans. The reason the unit of covert men showed up to save me in the end. They'd arrived too late to protect the leader of the revolution, but not too late to rescue his successor who was unaware he was an heir. The plan was to keep him —me—far away from the war until the time was right. Hide me inside a country often overlooked as an influential one.

After they explained my heritage the best it could be to a twelve-year-old orphan, the man who saved me took responsibility to raise me as one of his. I no longer could be known as Simion Kelemen. It was important everyone believed the Prince of Kosonia was dead, so I constructed a new name. In honor of my family, I'd chosen Gino Luka Leblanc, a way to remember those I'd lost. Gino to honor my mother Gianna, and sister Giovanna. Luka for my father, Dragos Lucian, a man I couldn't decide if I respected or hated. Only time would reveal if I'd accept father's reasoning for why he'd done this to us.

My new father, Sergeant Kyle Leblanc, recognized my potential and continued my training the best he could. Encouraged me to learn all I could about the royal family of my new country, to study them, eventually accept my assignment as one of their most trusted guards. To be a man who stood by the king of this land, ready to do what needed to be done while also learning how he ruled over his people. The irony did not escape me. That, in reality, we were more equals than I led any of them to believe. The only ones who knew the truth were sworn to secrecy. The respect I held for this family was deep, making me determined to not let anything happen while I was a part of such a vital team.

King Ramon finally introduced me to Princess Gabriela, his young daughter. I was drawn to her instantly. At first, it was a protectiveness I couldn't explain. She reminded me of Giovanna. That feeling changed rather quickly when she was no longer a young girl, but turning into a feisty young woman. It was then I noticed how beautiful she was inside and out, and refused to acknowledge why.

The fire she possessed to never let her position hold her back had me toying with her. It started as a fun game between a guard and a child, but when she moved back into the palace with her mother, it turned into something else. She was determined to slip away, breaking all the rules meant to keep her safe, and I enjoyed catching her, sending her back to her quarters.

It wasn't until I'd stepped in a few months ago, after some arsehole tried to take advantage during her first after party, that things between us grew even more interesting. She'd awakened something entirely different inside of me that night. An emotion I've been fearful to let spark. I thought it risky, and I didn't take those. Now I'm in knots over her and more protective than I was before.

She's merely eighteen, a baby in comparison to my twenty-eight years, and yet she dares to challenge me like no one else ever has. Not only does she challenge me as one of the guards, testing my skills, but also as a man who knows it is wrong to be so attracted to this fireball.

When it comes to Ela—her nickname she acquired that night, and the only one I use when I think of her—it seems I'm willing to risk it all, even the job I love. If we get caught, both our heads will be on the chopping block. But it's become clear she needs to learn a lesson on why there were rules, why she's assigned guards. I've accepted the task of being the one who will teach her this, all because I understand all too well what happens when danger closes in. It wasn't my choice really, Sir Edward, my captain, has requested I help keep an eye on her.

Bloody hell.

Had I known she'd give me heart failure the second she suspected she'd left the grounds undetected, I'd have stopped it sooner. Thankfully, I'm parked right outside the gates so I can follow her. The entire drive, I'm cursing her recklessness and myself for thinking this was a good idea. All the while promising to disable or even steal the damn death machine she's riding like she's been doing it her entire life.

How the fuck has she kept this a secret? When did she learn to ride and take the corners like a pro?

My damn cock is so fucking hard watching her dart through traffic on the sexy midnight blue Ducati. She's guiding the beast like it was custom built for her. The machine glides through the street with ease. As she takes a corner, the sight of her thighs, gripping tight, make my mouth water. She's not even following the traffic laws, forcing me to break them while attempting to keep her in my line of sight. It's a good thing my Porsche can keep up with the speed demon. When I catch her, she's getting one hell of a lip lashing from me. I'd spank her arse, but something inside warns me that could lead us to a whole other kind of trouble, and there's no way we're ready for that.

I remind myself she's only eighteen, a child inside one sassy body that screams woman. She may be legal, but that does not make it okay for me to pounce like I might if she were older. Her innocence is still intact, and I'm a complicated man. My demons are specific. I'm here to teach her a lesson. Not drag her off and educate her on what her behavior does to a man attracted to her. I am a man who has been watching everything she does closer than he should. And she tempts me like no other woman ever has.

Fuck.

My heart settles slightly when Ela parks her Ducati outside a popular nightclub. I pull over and watch as she joins a group of her friends. They appear to have been waiting on her before heading inside.

It's then I make a phone call to have the motorcycle confiscated and taken back. "I need a team to pick up a motorcycle and deliver it to the palace. Park it next to Sir Edward's precious vehicle. I'm confident he'll have questions about who it belongs to, and I'll be more than happy to share that with him when he does. You can even leave him a message to contact me in the morning about it." He has a unique relationship with the princess. She often seeks him out for fatherly advice, even though he's the man sworn to protect her family, and nothing more. I've watched them interact enough to appreciate how important their relationship is and hope to use that to my advantage. "No, that's all. I have something else to deal with or I'd do it myself. And make sure you tell them that if they put one scratch on it, heads will roll."

Once I hang up, I decide it's time to establish my point and move this evening along. I flash my badge to gain access into the club, locating the princess almost immediately. I watch and wait for the right moment to strike. If anyone knew my plan, I'd be fired and tossed in jail. But until someone is willing to show this young woman why we have established protocols, she will continue to carry on like this, never understanding that putting her life at risk for a good time is dangerous. Her negligence for her own safety affects all our jobs.

Watching her is always one of my favorite pastimes. It allows me to get to know her better, observe a side she keeps buried when she knows I'm watching. Tonight, she believes no one has followed her, so she lets her guard down just a little.

Ela's laughing with her friends, having a good time. Unless you know who she is, it would be hard to recognize her dressed the way she is. Her makeup is even different from how she wears it when portraying the flawless, prestigious princess. The dark eyeliner, the bolder colors that define her cheekbones, all conceal the sweet princess she is when standing next to her family. I hate I notice the difference and like it. I hate that her laughter encourages me to smile, and how the sway of her hips when she dances affects my body. It even stirs me when I realize she's aware of her surroundings, like we have trained her to do. All of those little things bother me because I shouldn't let them affect me at all.

A few hours pass before I acknowledge the time to act is now. I almost second guess myself on what I'm about to do. If she wants to report me after it's all said and done, she could. My job as a guard would end, and for good reason.

What pushes me to carry out my reckless scheme has more to do with the man I notice now stalking her. He's watching her just as closely as I am. A sick unknown stalker who has nefarious intentions for her, even if he doesn't recognize he's tracking someone who could cost him his life. The twat is up to no good. I'm not about to take a chance with him getting his turn to carry it out, with her or anyone else. Before I can deal with her, I need to handle this fucking bastard.

"Little old for this crowd, aren't you?" I close in on him from behind.

The arsehole doesn't even hear me approaching. He startles at my voice and drops something. It makes a clanking noise when it crashes to the floor, catching my attention more now. I collect it before dragging his arse out the backdoor.

"What were you going to do with this?" I shove the switch blade in his face, pressing it against his cheek just hard enough to draw blood. "I should gut you with this. Open you up and let the rats feed on you."

"I-I h-h-have kids." Wide-eyes turn on me, the light of the alleyway making his skin ghostly white.

"And yet here you are, ready to do something extremely stupid." I shake my head and glance down, where I notice the stain on his pants growing wetter by the second. "You fucking piss yourself and somehow thought you were going to be man enough to grab some badass chick? She'd have your balls before you saw it coming. Do us all a favor, man, stop pretending to be a tough guy and get a life. Go home to your kids and do better for them." I yank his wallet from his back pocket and flip it open. "I'll be checking in on you, Dorian Helms. I never forget a face or name. If I so much as catch you anywhere near her again, you won't be walking away. Do I make myself clear?"

Dorian nods and then runs off like the chicken shit he is. Never once looking back or waiting for me to return his wallet. I close the knife and shove both in my waistband. My level of anger is tenfold now. Princess Gabriela is about to meet her match and learn a lesson she will never forget.

I'm done. Tonight, she's about to see a side of me that can't be ignored, and I know once I do, things between us will change.

Chapter Two

GABRIELA

The Royals

It is such a relief to finally escape that stifling palace. To breathe and hang out with others my age without someone always hovering.

No one understands what it's like growing up the way I have. While a few of my friends have security, it's not the same. Theirs are mostly drivers who double as body guards when one is required, but even then, they are often left alone to do as they please. My guards never leave when they're around. They stick close by, scrutinize everyone who attempts to approach me, and always object to letting me visit places like this one. If I'd asked to come here, they would have told me no. Informed me, the crowd inside couldn't be vetted properly to ensure my safety and blah, blah, blah.

Instead, I did what I started perfecting when I was ten. I snuck out. I've only gotten caught a few times, well not true. Recently, I've been stopped more and sent back, forced to plot out my next escape.

Damn, I hated living in the palace. It was way harder sneaking past the guards and staff than it had been when we lived in Prieto. Especially since a certain guard of my brother's has made it his life's goal to guarantee I fail.

Gino Leblanc is quickly becoming a pain in my arse. It's as if he possesses some type of radar that notifies him when and where I'm going to make my next breakout. Like he always knows what I'm planning before I even do it, and it is so fucking irritating. The only time I was able to sneak past him had been when I overheard him speaking with one of my guards. He was warning the other man to stay on top of me, to watch me closely. I knew then I could slip past everyone, finally have some fun with no one being the wiser.

What I hadn't expected was the disappointment I felt by not getting caught that night. Freedom was great and all, but the way Gino stood there waiting, like he'd been anticipating catching me long before I even made my plans to escape. I'd sickly grown to appreciate him spotting me.

I once again suffered disappointment tonight when he wasn't there ready to send me back. To hear his voice, with the deep sexy tone that made my stomach do weird things while melting my insides. None of the boys I'd met elicited that sort of physical reaction. They had to do a hell of a lot more than just open their mouths, and even then, it didn't hold a candle to how he affected me. I'd taken advantage of him not being around, disappointment be damned, and made a run for it so I could feel slightly normal.

I think what I enjoy more than an evening out with my friends, is jumping on my baby and experiencing the power of it vibrating between my legs. My Ducati is my freedom, my way of giving life the middle finger and taking charge.

I learned to ride one while at boarding school. A local boy would drive his motorcycle around town, attracting my attention. One day, I stopped him and then convinced him to take me for a ride. Later, I persuaded him to teach me how to drive it.

He'd taught me more than how to drive this exhilarating machine. He also showed me what it was like to be female. Even though he never took my virginity, we'd done more than I had with any boy before him. He differed from the guys I went to school with. A little bad, but still one of the good guys. It would have been only a matter of time before I let him take that too. But the kitchen fire at the citadel happened, and my time with him ended abruptly.

A year ago, I ran into him at a club in Aragon, the capital city of

Hermosa Islas. I convinced him to help me purchase a badass motorcycle, one I could park in a garage near the palace under a false name I paid dearly for. He knew I loved the thrill the speed stirred when I rode, and only agreed to help if I secured a proper license and proved I could handle the dangerous machine like a pro. Once I'd done that, he bought it with my money and then warned me to be careful.

What was the fun in being careful? I wasn't stupid, but I also refused not to enjoy life. I liked the edge, the thrill of adventure. Not following all the rules drilled into my head since birth kept my blood flowing. I've faced death enough times to know it would come when it was ready. Childhood cancer sucked, and dying no longer scared me. Until it was ready to take me, I vowed to not sit around and play it safe, but to live a full, adventurous life.

I wasn't stupid. I also took the proper precautions to make sure I remained safe. Learned how to defend myself, because I knew there were people in this world who would assume I was easy prey. Not because I was a princess, but simply because I was female. I made sure I wasn't defenseless, by training with some of the best guards assigned to us, soaking in anything and everything they were willing to teach me.

Sir Edward was eager to confirm that even a small framed woman could do serious damage if she knew how. He seemed to enjoy it as much as I did. Never once suggested I didn't need to know how to defend myself because I had guards. My enthusiasm to learn, to take it seriously, brought a smile to his face. He would beam at me the way I'd always wished my own father would have when he was alive. And when mine died, Sir Edward was there to pick up as many pieces as he could, stepping in to do his best to be that for me.

So now when I go out without guards, I know I can take care of myself. Even when no one else believes it, I know, and I'm not worried.

My evening has been interesting so far. Mercedes, my best friend and cousin, is with me. We don't go anywhere without the other. On the nights I'd not been able to sneak past Gino, she'd come and sit with me, help me plot.

Five others join us. They aren't my favorite people—but to be fair, I'm not fond of most—but they are pretty cool. Not snobs like so many others we often find ourselves forced to hang out with. These five would never make it inside of the socials hosted at the palace. They weren't part of high-class society, but from middle-class families, who weren't bothered by my princess status—not that they know who I am. We've never once told them, and we both look very different on nights like this. You can do amazing transformations with makeup to alter yourself, and Mercedes and I have perfected that. At least we've never been recognized, or if we have, no one has said anything.

"I'm so glad you made it tonight." Mercedes hugs me as soon as we find a table. "I needed this."

"Me too. I'm so tired of being stuck behind those guarded walls. I can't wait to move out and make my own way. It's suffocating." I grab my drink we ordered moments ago, letting the burn slide down my throat.

"How do you drink that hard stuff like that? It tastes like cough syrup, worse than that, even." My cousin makes a face that has me laughing. "I like my alcohol to hide under the sweetness of fruits and sugar. Then I forget I'm even drinking, which isn't always a good thing."

I sip my bourbon through the tiny straw and let it wash the day away. "Why drink if you can't taste it? It's all about the flavors, the taste of the barrels it sat in, the hints of vanilla or cinnamon. They all have something unique about them, and when you mix them in fruity drinks like that, you ruin all that."

"You sound like your mother." Mercedes shakes her head.

"Who do you think taught me about savoring a good bourbon?" I lift my glass to hers and click it. "To good drinks, great company, and a night free of overbearing men."

She laughs. "How long before you think he tracks us down tonight?"

"Hopefully not for several hours. I need time to drag some guy off into a corner and have my way with him." I glance around, because I'm not so certain he's not already here. It's as if I can feel his eyes on me, but I don't see him, so I assume I'm being paranoid. I brush it off and continue with my night, determined to have a great time.

A guy with us is doing his best to hit on me. It's kind of cute. I mean, I'm flattered. He's a decent bloke, one of the good ones. If I were hoping for a good guy, he would fit the bill just fine. And because I'm a nice person and don't want to hurt his feelings, I'm doing my best to let him down easily.

The thing people don't know about me, is that I'm not looking for love. I'm not even hoping to find a boyfriend. I don't want one. Never plan on falling in love or getting married. I'm just hoping for a good time. I have a lot of personal issues that I consider make me less than whole.

My mother would argue with me about it, but I know what others expect. A royal wedding and babies. It's all anyone expects from a princess, and I don't plan on falling into that trap. I have other ideas about how my life will play out. And since this is my life, not theirs, I'm determined to focus on me and do it my way.

So, while I'm flattered, it will never happen. I mean, I guess we could have some fun. He's probably never gotten to second base or even attempted to since he's on the shy side. I'd be more than willing to fool around with him, but guys like him aren't usually about good times, they want the complete package. And he deserves that, the real deal, not someone like me who has too many flaws.

Which is why when I see my chance to dance with someone else, I do. I don't miss the disappointment in his eyes, I even feel a little guilty. But better to let him appreciate the real me now than to lead him on and break his heart later.

Plus, the guy I'm dancing with is exactly what I'm searching for. He wants to have fun, no strings, a good time that will last one night. It's not hard to differentiate those guys, they give off a vibe I can relate to.

"I think it's time we blow this joint," he whispers in my ear grabbing my arse. "Damn. These leather pants you have painted on this little sexpot body are killing me. My place is only a few blocks away."

"Do you have a car?" I slide my hand down the front of his shirt. "I'm not sure I can wait that long."

I could go home with him. I've tried that a few times, and it didn't work out the way I'd expected. Plus, I'm not sure I want him to get the wrong idea of what it is I'm looking for. I want to fuck quickly. Get this done with so I can go. I have no expectations on it being amazing or mind-blowing. All I want is to finally do the deed. Give it another shot to determine if my body will fail me again like it has the last couple of times, or if maybe this time will be different. The last two guys I tried this with didn't get that far. I have an issue they weren't prepared to deal with—like I said earlier, childhood cancer sucks. This time I have it covered, but that means we have to do it fast and quick so this guy never catches on to why. It's not a conversation I wish to have.

"Whatever you want, baby." He drags me closer and rubs his hard length against me.

I grind into him, hoping that will jump start a reaction, something. But like always, nothing happens. I refuse to let that stop me, though. "I need to use the ladies' room first. Give me ten minutes, I'll meet you right outside."

"I'm Caton. Thought you should know that so you can thank me later." He drags his teeth along my ear, proving he's done this before. "Hurry up."

I do just that. I'm prepared. Leather pants aren't exactly the best for a quickie and skirts aren't ideal for riding, which is why I shoved one in my small backpack. I'd planned to change as soon as I got here, but then became distracted. I'm pretty sure Caton won't complain, easy access and all.

Once I've changed, I dig for the other item I know I'll need. My body isn't like others. It can be stubborn at the worst moments, and like I've learned from past experiences, will require lube. The other guys didn't have any and refused to go there once they were aware of my dilemma. It was embarrassing, and I'd left quickly once I knew it was a no-go.

I should be thankful, right? That they didn't want to hurt me or make it painful. It sucks having a body that doesn't work like it should. This time I'm adding the lube first and praying that works. It's also why I wanted to do it now and not wait until we got to his place. If we go to his place, I'll have to explain, and I didn't fancy having that conversation with a complete stranger. I know that's weird since I'm okay with fucking one, but talking about the mechanics of sex when you only want a quick fuck is way too personal.

The door to the washroom opens and I think nothing of it. There are two other stalls not being used. What gets my attention is when I hear the lock engage.

"Hey, I'll be out in a minute if you prefer privacy," I holler and sigh when I realize I won't be finishing my task.

When the lights go out, I become pissed. I toss the tube in my backpack and jerk it over my shoulder. This bitch is about to get an earful.

Yanking the stall open, I step out. "Did you not—"

I'm grabbed from behind, shoved forward until my front slams into the wall. I try to squirm free to no avail. The person trapping me is way bigger than I am, easily overpowering me. So instead, I relax, giving this individual the illusion they're in control. Except he doesn't seem to buy into it. My hands are seized and wrenched behind my back, as my body is pressed harder into the nasty washroom wall.

"Look, my boyfriend is waiting on me. He'll come looking for me soon. Not to mention, I'm someone you don't want to mess with." I do my best to announce it with confidence.

The only response I receive is a snort and the pressure of plastic zip tie cuffs being slipped over my hands. I can get out of those easily if given the chance, although it makes things interesting now.

I bang my forehead against the wall and try to focus. Something is oddly familiar. Why am I not freaking out? Why do I feel at ease instead of panicking?

Closing my eyes, I allow my other senses to kick in. The noises around me start to center. I block out the background club hums and focus on those that will help me figure this out. Like the breathing of the body behind me. It's rhythmic, calm, not pumped up with adrenaline the way I would expect it to be. Everything is too composed for this type of situations.

I don't want to breathe in the surrounding scents, but I do. The stenches of the washroom are strong, almost overpowering. But there is something else I recognize. It's subtle, but it's there. I smile inwardly, knowing I'm going to kill him when he lets me go.

His breath tickles my ear, causing me to shiver. "You are in so much trouble, Princess."

I fucking hate it when anyone calls me princess, even more so after the incident at the after party a few months ago. Jerking my head away from him, I grumble, "Fuck you, Gino. So, you followed me instead of stopping me this time? What do you think my brother would think of that?"

I'm spun around so fast I almost lose my balance. There's barely any light for me to see him properly. The only available is coming from the tiny window, making it difficult to take him in. Not that the dimness makes his features any less impressive.

Goddamn him for having such an effect on me. Why is he the only man my body dares respond to? It's not fair and only pisses me off. Mostly because I know there's no way anything will ever happen between us.

Gino leans in and gets so close I can almost feel his lips on mine. "I should—"

"You should what?" I snarl as I raise my chin, tempting him. "I'm too young and innocent, remember? Although I wouldn't be so innocent if you'd stop interfering with my life." I'll never forget him saying those words after discovering me with a boy I'd taught a valuable lesson to—don't fuck with a princess. He'd leaned in and warned me I was too young.

He bites his lower lip as he directs his gaze at the ceiling. "That only makes me more determined to continue, Princess."

I shift my body forward into his, giving him a solid shove. "Stop calling me princess. Call me that one more time and I'll make you pay."

He takes another step away, giving me more space, or him, maybe. It's a good idea no matter, because I was having difficulty focusing with him that close.

"Do you know how close you came to getting into some serious trouble? I mean, my plan was to scare the shit out of you, but I had no idea I'd find a real twat who thought he'd have a go."

"What the hell are you talking about? Caton is not a twat." I take this chance to get out of the cuffs cutting into my wrist. It's almost too easy, he didn't tighten them like he should have.

Spinning on his heels, he stomps like a disgruntled child, flips the light back on while tramping around. When he turns to face me, I've freed my hands. I drop the cuffs on the floor before crossing my arms, waiting for him to explain.

"I have no idea who this Caton guy is, and I dare not ask. I meant the twat I caught stalking you, watching and waiting for you to separate from your friends. He had this and intended to use it. I'm sure he was hoping to scare the shit out of you." He flashes a switch blade, and I'll admit—to myself—that could have been a complication, although I'll never tell him. "Now granted, I'm sure you'd have taken it from him and then cut off his balls, but that is neither here nor there. The point is, if you'd stop being so fucking stubborn with all this sneaking around crap, guys like him wouldn't be a problem."

There's a knock on the door interrupting us. "Did you change your mind, baby?"

Gino's eyes grow dark for reasons I'm not sure I want to know. They go even darker as he listens to my response. "I'll be there in five. Sorry, I got a call I couldn't ignore. I didn't change my mind. I'm eager and—"

Before I know it, Gino is throwing the door open, surprising Caton when he comes face to face with him. Caton's eyes shift to me and twitch when he notices I've changed, making Gino groan out a warning. "Who the fuck are you? Ela will not be joining you tonight or any other night."

"You don't get to..." I raise my voice and attempt to storm past him.

He steps in front of me, keeping me here for now. "Princess, I swear I will—"

I warned him.

Without so much as a second thought I perform a maneuver I learned a few weeks ago. It's one I know will knock him on his arse.

When my foot comes in contact with his face, two things cross my mind. First thought is, *take that you wanker*. Then another immediately washes the first away. I just flashed both these men with that stunt, since I left my knickers at home. Probably explains why Gino is dazed and Caton is blushing. At least it allows me to get the hell out of there before he can retaliate.

Chapter Three

GINO

My hand drags down my face as I blink, unable to get the flash of her sweet, wet pussy out of my mind. I don't even care she dared to execute a perfect hook kick and landed it. I watched Amanda, Queen Larkin's guard, teach her how to execute one while sparring. If I could actually think, I'd be impressed, but I can't. All I can focus on is what she flashed us the moment she lifted her leg straight over her head and kicked.

Us.

"You will forget everything. You saw nothing." I grab the shirt of the prick who was banging on the door. "Nothing."

He nods, but I can tell he's planning to whack off to that image later.

"Who are you again? Caton, is it? I see you anywhere near her again and we are going to have a problem. Understand?" I tighten my grip to get my point across.

He raises his hands in defeat. "I didn't know, man. I don't fuck around with someone else's chick. I assumed she was free game."

I don't correct him about her being mine. She's not, but hell if he needs to know. "Maybe tell your cronies to steer clear as well. That one's off limits."

When I loosen my grip, he takes off quickly, glancing over his shoulder once to make sure I'm not about to follow. Now that he's gone, it's time to go after her.

I no sooner step outside than to catch her staring at the spot where her Ducati was parked, except it isn't now. The fury on her face is way sexier than it should be. When she notices me, that fire behind her eyes ignites, and I prepare myself for the inferno I'm about to walk into.

"What did you do?" she yells, her anger rising fast. "You had no right!"

I don't bother responding. It doesn't matter what I say, she's not in any mood to hear me out. Plus, she's right, not that I'll admit it. Instead, I walk toward my car, sensing her close behind. When we're next to it, I open the passenger door and wait.

"No." Ela stops short and glares at me. "Where's my bike?"

"Get in," I order, my grip on the door tightening. "Now."

I should've realized that was the wrong thing to say, that she'd not follow a direct order. I watch her straighten her spine and begin walking, just not in my direction. Well, she can think again, I'm done playing tonight. I've sat back and studied her all night while I fought my attraction to her. I'm on her in five strides, tossing her fine arse over my shoulder before she protests.

"Enough," I grunt, not happy with how her body provokes mine. As soon as we're next to my car, I set her feet on the ground and point at the seat. "Get in. Buckle up. Please."

"If there is one scratch on my baby, you are paying for a new paint job. You," she snarls right before she yanks the door closed.

I walk around, adjusting my cock that is way too fond of the little minx who thinks she can give me orders. Not that I wouldn't gladly do that. I would, but fucking hell, this cannot happen.

When I get in, she's digging through her purse frantically. In the process, a few items spill out, so I reach over to pick them up. As soon as I recognize what I'm holding, all the resolve I've been holding on to so dearly dissolves, and I see red. In my hand is a vape and a tube of lube.

Her eyes meet mine as she pulls out her phone and shrugs, as if daring me to object to her choices. "What?"

I lay the tube in my lap and wave the vape at her. "What the hell are you thinking?"

"That's not mine. And don't even start with that shit. I've seen you and a few other guards enjoying a cigar after a tough day." She types on her phone as if her explanation should cut it for me. "What?"

"Have you ever tried it? And whose is it then?" I toss it into the backseat because that piece of shit is not going back into her purse.

"I don't remember. Someone gave it to me a few weeks ago to hold for them and then they forgot to take it back. I've been holding onto it until I remember who." She glances at my lap where the lube is resting and blushes. "Can I ask you something and you promise not to overreact?"

"No." I start the engine and shift into first so we can get out of here.

"Okay, then, can I have that back?" She points to my lap, still blushing. I don't miss how it darkens when the light from the streetlight shines in on us, making my predicament more visible.

"Tell me why you have this and I'll think about it." Clearly, I'm provoking a fight throwing those words out there.

She burrows through her purse again. As soon as she finds what she is searching for, an evil grin forms on her face. My grip on the steering wheel tightens when she opens up her hand.

What the hell is she doing with a butt plug? It's a small one, very small, but fucking hell. Is she serious? Does she dabble in that kind of shit? She's fucking eighteen. How the hell does she even know about butt plugs?

"You know, it's not sanitary keeping that in there." I snarl, doing my best to not imagine what it would be like to watch that toy disappear inside of her right before I fucked her.

"Thanks for the info. I'll make sure to thoroughly wash it before letting some guy shove it up my bum." Ela rolls her eyes like she's done so many times. It stirs an urge inside of me that has me fantasizing about them rolling for other reasons.

I'm not sure what I'm thinking or why I do what I do next. It doesn't matter because I don't regret it one bit. My hand snags the offensive toy, and just as quickly, I hit the button to roll down the window, tossing it out as it lowers. Now I can think without having that sex toy around to distract me.

"You're an arsehole. You know that, right? And for the record, before I let some guy shove anything up my arse, I probably should let him fuck me first. Which was the plan tonight before you once again stuck your nose where it does not belong." Ela directs her eyes away from me, so she's looking out the other window, not allowing me to see her face. I do, however, notice when she lifts her hand and wipes something off her cheek.

The rest of the ride is quiet. As soon as we park, she starts to jump out, no concern about getting caught when walking back in. I reach for her arm, firmly holding on above her elbow. There is a reason I've always avoided touching her. Every time I do, a jolt of energy races through me, awakening the man I do not believe I'm capable of being.

I try my best to make her feel better. "There is nothing wrong with you being a virgin still, Ela. You should wait until you find someone who will—"

"I'm not like my brothers, Gino. I have no desire to find love. I'm not sure I even believe in it." She tugs on her arm, encouraging me to release it. "And don't act like you're some saint waiting around for the love of your life to drop into your lap. Why is it okay for guys to fuck about, but when a girl decides she's not into flowers and happily ever after's, she's a slut?"

I release her arm so we climb out at the same time. As she walks away, I have one more fact to reveal. "I never said you were a slut for wanting to have sex. You are very right about what you said. But Ela, you'll have to forgive me for wanting only the best for you."

"Why do you even care, Gino? I'm nothing. Not really. There's so much no one knows and for that reason alone, it's best I don't drag some unsuspecting soul down with me. Some of us are better off alone. I believe you understand what I mean? Isn't that why you've remained unattached at your age?" Her insight into my life surprises me. "Goodnight."

"Ela." I jog after her and almost laugh when she sighs and slumps against the gate leading to the garden.

I'm not sure why I do this. Call me stupid.

We're hidden in the shadows when I lean in, placing one hand next to her head, while letting the other trace her cheekbone. I catch a glimpse of a future I never deemed possible and hear the truth in my words as I admit, "No one should have to settle for a life alone. We all eventually need someone to share our lives with. Maybe one day our paths will allow that." Then I bend forward ever so briefly and let my lips brush hers before stepping back and briskly walking away.

What the fuck was I thinking? That brief contact was more intense than it should have been. Moving forward, I'll need to be extremely careful or I'll forget why we are a bad idea and let my selfish cock get his way.

Chapter Four

GABRIELA

The Royals

2 Years Later

I can't believe my speedy exit after Lorenzo's unexpected cage fight against our cousin Rueben went so well. I came to the arena to watch a few good rounds and ended up having to sit there and watch those two go at it. My mind is still trying to wrap itself around how it came to be. I'm not sure why Violet let him step inside a cage with a man we knew wanted them both dead. My loud protests were ignored, no one listened to me. They had a plan in play, and no matter what I said, the fight was happening. It ended in Lorenzo's favor, thankfully. I'd sat there and worried my asshat cousin would play dirty and my brother would be carted off in a body bag. Instead, it was Rueben being dragged out of there after getting his clock cleaned.

That wasn't the worst of it, really. I mean, sure, those two—Lorenzo and Violet—had serious stuff going on, and it was hard to wrap my head around all of it. But I had my own problems weighing me down. One of those being the man determined to be a black thorn in my side.

Once I left for university, I was granted a little more freedom. Living in Hermosa Islas, allowed me to live in the dorms with everyone else. The only stipulation was those on my floor had to be approved. I had my own room with no suite mate. Meaning, I basically had two rooms. One I set up like a living space and used the other as a bedroom. And my guards had free roam of the entire floor, always present to ensure my safety. They could go on any floor they wanted, check any room, deny access to anyone they felt a threat, even if they lived there. It was over the top, but I didn't complain because at least I had some independence.

This new freedom made it easier to explore my sexuality. I didn't go wild or anything, but I finally got laid. We were university students who preferred to have our fun. No one cared who I was. Maybe they bragged later about it. I don't know or care. I've heard no rumors, and I'm certain I would have by now. I wasn't trying to hide here. I was living my life, how I chose to live it, as were my classmates.

The sex wasn't great, but I could at least check it off my list. Mercedes kept encouraging me to give it time, to write that experience off as a first-time encounter. So that's what I'd done, and quickly learned after the second, third, and fourth times, I still wasn't impressed and came to the conclusion it was the guys who weren't doing it for me. A completely different brand of fella is what I required to test the waters. Someone who'd lived a little, with skill. Older, not too old, just old enough to have been out in the world longer than me or these college dudes. A man who was now out in the real-world living life. I'm not picky, really. Something different was what I was in search of.

The problem I had now was every time I tried to get away from the guys I went to school with, I found myself with an unwelcome escort. If it wasn't the thorn—Gino—who I thought I'd scared off when he'd left me in a daze after a brief kiss two years ago, then it was this other prick who was equally annoying. Both men were the biggest cock blockers out there, and I was tiring of their games.

Earlier at the fight, it surprised me when Gino stepped out of the shadows to let Lorenzo see he was the man pissing me off. The alcohol I consumed made my lips looser, and it didn't help that Violet and Karina were egging me on. I was confused about why he kept hovering and not prepared to deal with his timing on making a public statement. When his brother, Bruno—the other guy following me when Gino wasn't—

suggested it was because he cared about me, I called bullshit, then tried to leave.

I will never forget what Gino said for as long as I live.

"Now you listen to me. You will put an end to this nonsense. Stop with these foolish games. No more sneaking out, putting yourself in danger. The next time I catch you without your guards, I will spank your arse. Fuck, Ela. Why do I get the impression if I do, it is going to lead to so much more?"

I didn't know what to say to him after that. Like always, when he spoke or displayed his concern for me, my knickers felt damp. He was the only man who inspired my body to react when he spoke. The boys I'd fucked couldn't coerce it to do what came naturally—or so I thought —to other women, during foreplay. We were required to use lube, and even then, it never seemed to be enough. I'd learned to tolerate some discomfort and was always thankful when it was over.

The rest of the night I sat there confused, turned on, and pissed off. The crowd fell far away in my head while they cheered on the fighters. And after my brother's win, we were moved to the back staging area, which is when the opportunity for a quick escape presented itself, and I acted.

The friends I came with were pumped after watching Lorenzo kick some serious arse. They suggested we go to a local club and celebrate. I'd gone along because, why not? I was up for more fun in my life and pretty sure before the night ended my shadow would be on me again.

He always eventually located me, but I don't know how. I'm guessing he's tracking me somehow. When I discover how, I'm not only destroying it, but using it against him. Turning the tables on him for a taste of his own medicine.

The air in the club changes after we've been there an hour. I can't help but roll my eyes as I recall the threat he made earlier. I must be one deranged woman to find his threat of spanking me a turn on. If any other man implied that, I'd slap him and leave. But Gino is not just any man. Everything about him is different, and maybe it's time to find out why that is.

His hand grips my forearm when he realizes I'm ignoring his

presence because I'm talking to someone that isn't him. "Time for you to go home."

With little effort I twist out of his hold. Once free, I decide to push him a tad more. "I'm not ready to leave yet."

I've been flirting with this bloke for the last ten minutes. He's not really my type, but at the moment, I don't care. He'll do what I need him to do—irritate the brooding jerk acting out next to me.

I'd leave with Gino if he'd simply ask me nicely, instead of giving orders like he expects me to follow them. I'm not a woman he can order around, or one who will thank him for acting like my protector. I don't want one, and I don't need one. Even if no one else appreciates that fact yet, I'm more than capable of protecting myself.

I grab club guy's arm and start dragging him behind me. When he slips one around my waist, I go with it. I let him slither one hand under my cutoff t-shirt and don't protest when his other skates up my thigh, where his finger brushes against my knickers. I almost wish I didn't have them on, but after I flashed Gino and some poor bloke, I decided it was better to always wear them.

Just like I'd anticipated, club dude gets yanked back by a very growly male. "You don't touch her. You don't look at her. You don't even breathe the same air as her. Because if you ever do any of those again, it will be your last day on this earth. Do. I. Make. Myself. Clear?"

Even though I expected it, doesn't mean I'll let Gino get away with acting like a neanderthal. As soon as he turns, I slap him right before I shove him hard enough to make him take a step back. "If you ever do that again, when you're too much of a chicken shit to act, you'll never get the chance. I'll end *you* first."

While he is immobilized by my braver than I'm really feeling move, I spin and make a beeline for the dance floor. Any minute now I expect him to stop me in that dominating manner that radiates off him in waves. I know he's not one of those men who exploits his power as an alpha male, but I also get the impression he gets pleasure from control, requires it, even. Which could be very interesting since I'm not one to relinquish mine to anyone.

One interesting fact I've learned about myself since becoming sexually active is I don't mind letting a guy do his thing. But if he's not doing it right, then I'm not afraid to takeover. And since the ones I've been with aren't exactly those who demand control, it's worked. But it has also taught me I wish they'd want to be in charge. Hand it to me briefly, but not fully. It was another reason I've been out prowling, trying to figure out if I could discover someone like that. Only to have the man now following me get in my way each and every time.

I reach behind me and seize Gino's arm, pulling him with me. If he's interfering, then it's time to see what he's made of. "Either man up or leave me the fuck alone. It's been weeks since I've enjoyed any dick and since you keep cock blocking me, you will step up." The man growls at my words, exactly the reaction I was expecting.

Man, I'm on a roll with the brave talk tonight. For some reason, I seem to believe the only way to get what I want is to poke Gino enough to force a reaction. That thought alone has my body heating and melting like it only does when he's around. And because he's still trying to process my boldness, another guy on the dance floor moves to take advantage of his mistake. I'm finally seized by the waist and yanked against Gino's rock-hard torso before the daring soul can fully step in. That move has both of us breathing harder as we stare into each other's eyes.

Damn.

These last several years we've been toying with the other, and until now I've never been this close to him. He's only hovered, never once letting our frames actually touch. Even when he dared to brush those intoxicating lips against mine, he never allowed our bodies to come in complete contact. Only brief touches here and there. A hand on one of my arms. His knuckles running along my jawline. A palm pressed to the small of my back. The exception being when he tried to scare me in the bathroom, but even then, certain parts of ours never touched.

Tonight, he's not holding back. My body is secured to his and I'm learning quickly what I've been missing. Gino is all man. One hundred percent. He's not growing into a man like the guys at the university. He is fully grown. Solid in all the right places. And when he moves, he knows how to do it, how to make me move so we fit even better together. There's none of that awkwardness that always happens with the others. We're immediately in sync. Now that I'm aware of this, there is no way I'm letting him dismiss me later. It's time to see if I can tempt him enough to give me all I've ever desired.

Just as I'm settling in, enjoying a dance with a man who knows how, I hear him whisper in my ear. "When have you had time for dick?"

I fling my body back so I'm now arched over his arm while I grind against him, letting his hard length rub my clit perfectly. "There is always some guy willing and ready on campus. The university is flooded with them. Most of those, however, have no idea what the hell they're doing. It's why I sneak off to places like this, eager to uncover at least one who does." He asked, so I should be honest if I wish this to go farther.

The words no sooner leave my mouth when he yanks me closer to that perfect chest of his. "Fucking hell, Ela. You should not be—"

My hand covers his to stop him from saying something that will only piss me off. The feel of his hard body against mine is all I crave from him right now. "Oh no. You don't get to tell me it's not okay for me to be sexually free when I know for a fact you're no innocent. I have just as much right to experiment with sex as anyone else. Do you look down at the women you entertain? Guys are the biggest shitheads with their double standards."

I watch him close his eyes, not enjoying this conversation. "I can't think of you like that."

I snort as my hands fist his shirt so I can make sure he doesn't pull away. "I believe you've thought of me like that more than you're willing to admit."

He growls and places a hand behind my neck, squeezing it just hard enough to grab my attention. "Do you think that's what I want? You experienced? It's not, so stop fucking little boys who are only disappointing you."

I do my best to shake my head as I tell him a truth I'm not sure he wants to hear. "Is that why you assume I'm fucking about? Because of you? Sorry, Gino. While you intrigue me, and I wouldn't mind finding out what you have to offer, my plans for my life don't include me having a man in it. I don't need one. I don't have any use for a relationship. Plus, a man would only get in my way."

"Correct me if I'm wrong, but if you ever plan on becoming a mother..." He halts his thoughts when I release his shirt so I can step away from him. "You don't want to be a mother?"

Reaching behind me, I remove his hand, rolling my eyes at his assumption that is what all women want. "Every woman does not yearn to be a slave to raising children. Thanks for killing my buzz and the vibe we had going. You are now getting your wish. I'm leaving."

I don't wait for him to ask me to explain more. There are some subjects I don't enjoy talking about. Even if I wanted to be a mother, it's not possible. That dream was stolen from me years ago when I was fighting for my life.

My childhood cancer caused most of my issues when it comes to sex. My mother tried to make me feel better once we learned what those aggressive treatments did to my body. While I was *cured* and deemed a *healthy* female, one who would live a long life, it was a load of bullshit, because I felt nothing like a woman at all. Other complications when I got older had us making some hard choices. I understand it doesn't make me any less female because I'm barren, missing key parts of my anatomy. But until you've walked a mile in my shoes you have no clue how that knowledge makes you feel.

My personal issues ran deeper. I have a less than feminine figure. It has nothing to do with the treatments, that is good old fashion DNA. My tiny breasts, however, only developed after they prescribed hormones. My body needed a kick-start, and that issue was because of the medications that once flooded it. That little fact certainly didn't help me, it only added to the way I saw myself, a damaged female. I don't have to suffer through monthly cycles or fully understand how inconvenient one is. Just another point to add to my list of why I felt less than adequate. My estrogen levels are high enough now a low dose of progestin in the form of birth control is all I'm required to take so my bones and heart and other vital organs will remain healthy. I find it insulting that those pills force my body to *act* female, that I have to be on birth control, even though I'll never need it. The pills make me moodier like other women, I guess—at least I'm blaming them for those mood swings.

Never once have I felt like I'm a woman. Instead, I feel damaged, inadequate, and abnormal because I require assistance to keep my body in check. According to my doctors, it functions more like a post-menopausal woman than one of barely twenty and in her prime. Meaning, I'll always require aid to ensure sex is comfortable and probably should invest in some great toys to help me finally achieve an orgasm.

I've yet to have one, even a self-love one. I've almost given up on it being achievable, until rubbing up against Gino a few minutes ago, and he ruined it by opening his mouth.

Now all I want to do is escape. I could use some time alone to think, or maybe not think. It's time to get my mind off what I cannot have and focus on the life I will have. Because let me be clear, I will have a life, an amazing one. It's just going to look different from what so many would have predicted.

Chapter Five

GINO

The Royals

The night I let Princess Gabriela see behind my well-placed mask, no longer a faceless guard, was the day our relationship changed. For years, I'd kept to myself, not letting anyone outside my immediate family appreciate the man behind the guise. It was better that way. If they uncovered the truth, my life history would come across perilous and unbelievable to most. Keeping my distance, maintaining my cover, not disclosing who I really was, kept everyone I cared about safe. Should anyone ever discover who I am, it could all come falling in around me. They would force me to return. It wouldn't matter that I wasn't interested in that life, only that it was my destiny.

It was ironic my alias was assigned to protect a family also born into duty, one many treasured and revered. Because I completely understand how important the members of this family are, I perform the job well. The world needs the Reyes family safe to rule and maintain the peace. It's why I give it everything I have, praying the good I do while I'm here will one day atone for the sins of those whose blood runs through my veins.

On that night, when I let my mask slip, a war began brewing inside of me, one I wouldn't win. I stopped viewing the young princess as another royal under my protection. She grew on me, stirred a fire inside, that, if left to burn, would consume us both. And I knew how important it was to keep that from happening. I couldn't afford to start any fires.

I thought it would get better when she left the palace for university, but I'd been wrong. I was a man who couldn't let go and allow those who protected her to do their jobs. Probably because I'd learned how good she was at slipping past them. So, I'd done something that would permit me to know where she was, always. If she ever found out, there would be hell to pay.

It's how I locate her for a second time tonight.

I thought after the arena fight she went home. Ela seemed torn up about her brother taking Rueben's bait and jumping in the cage, and that gave me a false assurance about her next move. Instead, she used me helping the other guards with crowd control to make her escape before I could stop her.

I'm in no mood to play games. Personal experience has taught me how dangerous it can be when you let your guard down. Each time she slips away without alerting her guards, she is putting herself in danger. If I've learned anything during my stint here, it is that there's always someone ready to strike. It's time to stop this and take her home before something else happens.

I don't bother hiding. I march up to her and try to drag her out, only to have her fight me on it.

Why does she always have to be so goddamn stubborn? The banter between us is so fucking confusing to me. I don't know if I should drag her out of here and give her some dick like she is demanding or do what I've always done and drop her off safely at home after calling her guards.

That isn't a decision I have to make after saying something that upsets her. She storms out, leaving me scratching my head, unable to understand why she'd not want to be a mother.

Why had that comment sent her over the edge? I have no doubt she'll do something that isn't typical for a princess, and I support that fully. There is no way Ela will ever sit in some stuffy office and organize fancy balls or events for those who only attended to kiss royal ass. That isn't who she is or will ever be.

I can clearly see her in a courtroom—pre-law is her major. I am even capable of picturing her taking over her mother's job one day, forcing those who saw her as less to listen and never once bow down to them. I believe she can do anything she sets her mind to, and that includes being a wonderful mother, one who is resilient and teaches her children to be equally as strong.

After I pull my foggy head back from the unknown, I take off after her. She's long gone, so I pull out my phone and open the tracking app disguised as a game. It alerts me she's heading back to her dorm, and for some stupid reason, I follow. I have to see for myself she's made it back and not just dumped her phone on some bus heading that way. I wouldn't put that past her at all.

It takes me ten minutes to drive there. I park on the street and stare up at her window. It's been reenforced with special glass to keep her safe, but she refused to let us black it out. I've never been more appreciative of her stubbornness than I am right now.

There for me to admire is the woman I can't get out of my head. She's wearing only a small tank top with knickers and they hide nothing. Not her flawless breasts, slim waist, or those legs I've dreamed about wrapped around me while I get lost in her. My cock swells, and I know later I'll think about this perfect image while relieving myself before sleep will come.

I make a stupid decision and text her. Glutton for punishment.

> ME: Close your blinds and go to bed.

Glancing down at her phone, Ela scowls before she glares out the window. Glaring back at her phone she rapidly lets her fingers fly. I know she's responding to mine, and it's bound to be epic.

> ELA: Perv. Why are you sitting outside watching me? Shouldn't you be somewhere else? Don't you have a job to do that has nothing to do with me? I'm home. I'm safe. You can leave.

ME: Part of that job is looking out for you. Please make mine easier and stay safe. Take your guards with you when you go out. If something happened to you, I'd...

ELA: You'd what? Have nothing to do with all your free time?

ME: That too.

ME: I'd be lost. You give me something to look forward to. A reason to keep going.

ELA: You are so confusing. I have no idea what that even means. Are you saying I'm your purpose for being a stalker? That's creepy.

I chuckle as I respond. She never gives up, and I have to admit I like that about her.

ME: Something like that. Now go to bed so I can leave.

ME: I'm sorry I upset you earlier. I didn't mean to.

I watch her shadow in the window, don't miss when she spots my car. We both stare, even though we can't really see the other person all that well. That doesn't stop the electric pull that passes between us. It charges the air and sets my skin on fire. It takes all I have in me not to climb out of this car, walk through the door, and up to her room. That wouldn't help matters, only complicate them more.

The dots appear and then disappear a few times before a message pings through.

ELA: Goodnight. Now go home.

She tugs the curtain closed before her shadow moves away. The lights go out shortly after, and I try not to imagine her climbing into bed.

Will she think of me, like I know I will be thinking of her?

> ME: Goodnight.

I start my car and pull away. I'll jack off in the shower once I get home, because my dick is so hard it won't let me rest until it gets some relief. And something warns me from this day forward the only one who will ever satisfy it again is the one I need to stay far away from.

Life sure knows how to fuck with me. It has me coveting something that can never be. It's asking me to fight a war that will put me on a battlefield I swore to avoid. Destiny is a bitch, and it'll be a miracle if I'm able to stand when this battle is all said and done.

Chapter Six

GABRIELA

The Royals

The rest of my weekend was quiet. I holed up in my room and studied. I need to ensure I have the best grades, so when it's time to apply for the Elite Forces Academy, they'll have no reason to decline my application. Grades are high on the long list recruiters focus on first. I'm at the top of my class for now, in a pre-law bachelor's program that is considered one of the toughest in Hermosa Islas.

Once I make it past the initial round, I'll have to pass a physical, and a PT test. Then come the interviews. After I slide through all those, it's up to the military's highest ranks running the intense bootcamp, to decide who will be accepted.

And just because I'm Princess Gabriela doesn't mean I'm a shoo-in. In fact, it may be to my disadvantage. It's a risk they might not wish to take. My brothers performed their duty in the military as weekend reservists. I want my chance to do the same, but I desire the full experience, so I'm not letting who I am stop or discourage me. I'll do whatever I have to do to prove I'm not only the best woman for the job, but the best.

When my week starts, I do what I always do, stay focused. I never permit myself to become distracted during the week. I go to class, spend a lot of hours in the library, and attend as many study groups as I can. The only time I let myself to relax is on the weekends, but only after everything is done that needs to be done. I've put in the hours and study time this week and now that it's Friday, I need to escape the grueling pressures surrounding me.

I have a plan. I've been thinking about Gino way more than I should. Not just about how he affects me, but what I know about him, what others even know about him. The more my mind focuses on him, the more I realize he's very much a mystery, not just to me but to everyone. No one has provided me any real answers about who or what his story is. I've asked around. The guards who work with him, those who serve me, even Sir Edward are very elusive on the subject of Gino. It only makes me that much more curious on why that is. Why does no one seem to know him?

It's why I decide to make a trip to Homero and see if I can uncover more of the mystery surrounding him. I have a few questions for those who should know him better than anyone else. It's time to put the same pressure on him he has enjoyed torturing me with. See how he appreciates it when someone digs into his life, both professional and private.

As soon as class is over, I inform Yvette, my guard on duty, where I'm heading. It took her all of five minutes to get the car and team ready to make the trip. I could have done what I've been doing lately, drive myself and alert my team after the fact. But since I'm visiting my brother, the king, it's best to not push my luck.

I arrive an hour before supper, just in time to help Larkin and Isabel start dinner. This is what I love about this sister-in-law, she insists on keeping her family as normal as possible. Cooking as a family, when feasible, is something she enjoys and refuses to give up just because of her new title. It has taken those who work for her time to accept the changes she's introducing, but because Antonio supports her, they are doing their best.

"Gabby!" Isabel, my half-sister, squeals when I step inside the large kitchen. "I didn't know you were coming for dinner."

I toss my purse and phone on the counter before I open my arms to receive her. "It was a last-minute decision. What are we making tonight?"

Larkin doesn't miss a beat, "Wash your hands and you can peel the potatoes. I'm introducing them to chicken fried steak, mashed potatoes, and green beans with bacon. You picked a good night for a surprise visit. I even invited the staff on duty to join us."

I try to feign disinterest in who that might be, but the grin on Larkin's face informs me I fail big time. "Who do I owe the pleasure of dining with? Antonio is around, correct? Not that I care, but he would be upset if I stopped by when he was out of town on business."

"He's here. As is Gino. They returned a few hours ago after spending the day in Aragon. I'm sure both will be thrilled to see you." Larkin rubs her belly that is now in full bloom. "Isabel, why don't you let Antonio know Gabby's here?"

It should surprise me that my family seems okay with me and one of the guards skating on thin ice. It's taboo, a big no. And while I think they are taken aback, they also trust we know what the stakes are. To keep it low key and not get caught until we're ready to go public. And I love them so much for that, even if I have no fucking clue what, if anything, will ever come of this.

"You just don't want me to hear about why Gino has been grumpy all week." Isabel makes a face that lets us see she's not oblivious to what goes on around her. "Are you two going to figure this out soon? I like Gino, but lately he's been very moody."

Larkin grips my sister's shoulders and squeezes. "You are almost as sneaky as this one." She points a finger at me. "Now move before I decide to talk about a certain—"

Isabel's eyes widen. "You promised."

"I did. Just like I'm sure Gabby does not wish to discuss what she herself doesn't understand yet. Now go. Be a little girl for a few more years so your brother doesn't get any more gray hairs." She kisses the top of Isabel's head, and I catch the affectionate respect they share. Larkin has stepped in as a mother figure for my little sister, not at all shy about it. I know how hard it has been on Isabel growing up without her mother these past six years. My respect for Larkin sprouts even more.

"So why are you really here?" Larkin batters a piece of tenderized steak and drops it into the hot grease.

"Has he really been moping around?" I have a tough time believing that, although he can impersonate a brooding man well. But the Gino he is here is not the same man who shows up and interferes with my good times. He's much more relaxed, provides comic relief when it's called for, although I've never experienced that side of him. Around me he's extremely serious, a man determined to prove some point I have yet to completely figure out.

"Something is definitely on his mind. I think there's more to it than whatever you two have going on, though." Larkin presses her lips together before she asks, "Are you planning to tell me what took place between you two the other night after that crazy fight?"

"Nothing happened. Nothing ever happens," I explain as I peel potatoes, doing my best not to mutilate them thinking about how true that is. "Did you get this frustrated with Antonio?"

"Yes. So even though nothing has happened, you'd like something to happen? You realize Lorenzo had a heart to heart with him?" The smirk on her face tells me that probably went over like water poured into a corridor. In one ear and out the other where the man receiving said lecture is concerned. "When he left, Gino volunteered to do a perimeter check. I think he needed time to cool off."

"My brothers, all three of them, need to mind their damn business." I roll my eyes knowing that will never happen. "I just don't understand what he wants, what his angle is. Well, besides making sure I don't hookup with anyone." My cheeks warm. "I know you were different, and that's great. But that is not me, I'm not looking for Mr. Right or Mr. Forever. That kind of life doesn't interest me whatsoever. But that doesn't mean I plan on being some spinster who owns twenty-five cats and never has any fun. I don't need a man holding me down, telling me I cannot do all the things I hope to do one day."

Larkin places the lid on her pan and crosses her arms. "Good for you. I mean, I'm happy that you know what you want, Gabby. I'm not thrilled about the part where you don't think you can find a partner who would support you, though. That you're willing to settle for a good time instead of something more. That being said, this is your life and you may live it how you choose, with all of our support. Every one of us has a journey only we can travel, and we have the right to do so without judgment."

"Thanks," I feel the need to express as I fill the pan with water. "I'm really glad Antonio followed his gut when he found you. You're the woman he was always meant to be with."

"You're still young, Gabby. No one expects you to have all the answers yet, or know what you want, even. At twenty, I was very unsure what the future held. If you had told me this would be my life, I'd have laughed in your face. No way would I have ever imagined I'd end up falling in love with a man like your brother. That he'd be a king and make me his queen. Which is why I don't enjoy hearing you're not open to something you never thought possible. Who knows? Your Prince Charming could be hiding, just waiting for you to realize you can have him along with the life you crave. Anything is possible."

I shake my head. She has no clue how wrong she is, no clue. "Sorry, Larkin. I have no desire to find a prince, even if he is charming. If I could throw my title away, I'd do it in a heartbeat. I love my family, but I have never once loved all the attention, obligations, or even wanted to use my royal ties to make it in this world. I just want to be Gabriela, a woman who can get lost in the crowd and go unnoticed, not a princess who stands out."

Larkin places her hand on my arm. "You are so much like Antonio."

"No, I'm not."

"Yes, honey, you are. All he ever wanted was to find someone who didn't see him as a king. He sought to be just a man who could be loved by someone who never focused on those other parts of his complicated life. But like I told him, throwing away the other part of you is impossible. You have to learn to live with yourself, who you are, before you can expect someone to see you. Once you do that, Gabby, then the life you were always meant to have will fall into your lap. Everything you have gone through to get there will become very clear. Don't settle for less than you deserve. Reach for the stars, and trust your instincts to guide you." Her eyes sparkle as she looks past me, and I know then we are no longer alone. Only one person brings that gleam to her face—my brother.

Not to mention the flutters that take flight the moment I sense someone else nearby. It only confuses me more and has me excusing myself. I need air, and I need to figure out how I want to deal with him all the way around.

Chapter Seven

GINO

The Royals

"Gino." Queen Larkin addresses me while I stare after the woman who hasn't left my thoughts since she ran out on me a little over a week ago. "What are you going to do about that?"

King Antonio's low rumbled laugh catches me off guard and has me glaring at him. I sort of expected him to disapprove of such an affair between me and his sister. It is, after all, against protocol, not to mention I'm ten years her senior. I never predicted he would find anything about this comical, but it seems I was wrong.

"Don't look at me like that," he orders, strolling over to his wife to plant a gentle kiss her on her cheek. "Your queen asked you a question."

"Don't drag my status as queen into this," Larkin scolds, and now I'm chuckling. "But I do expect an answer. She's my sister-in-law, someone I care about, and from what I've been able to establish, she's confused about what game you're playing."

That quickly stops my amusement, and I turn serious, more serious than I imagine I've been in a long time. "No game, madam. I don't play games when it comes to women. I would never play them with Princess Gabriela."

Larkin shakes her head as she turns her eyes to the ceiling, displaying how she doesn't believe me. "Okay, so tell me this. Do you like her?"

"Princess Gabriela is a very lovely woman. Smart and witty. Brave for a girl." I don't know why I said the last sentence because as soon as I do, I regret it. "I mean, she is brave, not just for a girl. One day, she'll have a man all tied up in knots over her."

King Antonio shakes his head in that way that warns I'm about to receive an ear full. He walks over to the stove and opens a pan, only to get swatted away. It's fascinating to witness these two. They carry on like any other couple I imagine out there does. He lifts his hands and steps back, not willing to mess up her dinner.

"Does she have you in knots? And don't try and skate around that answer. A simple yes or no will do." Larkin flips something in the pan and then places the lid back on. "Or are you what she claimed?"

"What did she claim he was?" King Antonio must not have heard the entire story, like his lovely wife seems to have.

"A chicken shit," Larkin blurts out, raising her eyebrows. "I never took you for one, but maybe she's right."

"I'm not a chicken shit. I just don't believe either of us is ready for any sort of relationship." I'm not lying. She as much told me that, and my life is a big clusterfuck. Everything about my life is up in the air, waiting for the right time to get here. Bringing a woman into my chaos seems cruel.

"Bullshit." Larkin points her tongs at me. "If you ask me—"

I don't know why I interrupt her, but I do. "I didn't though."

King Antonio glares at me over his wife's head, but Larkin only grins as if my response pleases her. "True, but this is my kitchen, and I'm about to give you my thoughts anyway. I believe the universe brings people together for a reason. It has decided you and Gabby need each other right now. I'm not sure why, and maybe it's only for a season. That is for you and her to decide. But denying it will only bring you more grief. One day, you may regret not acting. Trust me, I know how that feels. I appreciate the pain it causes the person who is left behind." Her husband lays a hand on her shoulder and squeezes. "It's better to act and fail, then to never act and have regrets."

I know her story. As a young woman, she had a friend who never acted. He later admitted he cared, but by then it was too late, and he killed himself only hours after confessing. I don't want Ela to ever have to deal with anything like that.

Dammit all to hell.

My feet are moving before I can stop them, heading in the direction Ela disappeared. I follow the worn path that leads to the natural spring, knowing where I'll likely find her.

Summer is in full bloom, hot enough to make my clothes stick to me. It's a hike to get there, but a favorite of Ela's. She never misses a chance to stop at the secluded natural spring pool when she visits.

The moment I clear the trees, I stop and stare at the most magnificent sight set out before me. I catch Ela emerging like a mermaid, water rolling off her long hair as she surfaces. Without a care in the world, she lies back. It is then I realize just how perfect her body is. The peaks of her breasts stand out like islands made to be worshipped. She drifts on top of the cool water's surface as if she is a treasure waiting to be claimed.

I'm a lot of things, have been able to control myself for the most part. But a man can only take so much before he gives into desire. The sight of her laid out in front of me snaps the last string holding me back. I decide right then and there, Larkin has a point. If this never happens between us, we will both always wonder what might have been. I'm not expecting any more than a fling. A season where I'm allowed the pleasure of knowing this amazing woman.

My clothes fall from my body almost on their own. Landing next to hers before I dive into the cold spring. The coolness against my overheated skin feels unbelievable, but it does nothing to calm the fire burning inside of me.

Ela is no longer floating when I surface. She is treading water, eyeing me attentively. It's difficult to read the thoughts running through her lovely head. Over the course of her life, she has perfected how to keep those repressed. Years of faking it for the crowd, has taught her to never permit anyone to see her. We are very much alike in that respect, although I didn't start burying mine until I was twelve.

I maintain my distance for now, knowing should I get too close, everything between us will change. Not that it isn't about to change, but before it does, we need to come to an agreement.

"Why are you here?" Her voice echoes off the rocks surrounding us. There is a tinge of concern in it, distrust, irritation. "I came out here to be alone so I could think. Like always, you seem determined to interfere with my life and time."

"Is that really what you believe I'm doing?" I swim a little closer hoping my actions speak volumes.

"Honestly? I have no idea. That's the thing, Gino. When it comes to you, I have absolutely no clue what it is you want, or why you show up, or even how I feel about it. I'm not sure you know, which only makes it that much more confusing. Now here we are, both literally bare and exposed, and it only adds perplexity to a situation neither of us can figure out how to handle. My body wants one thing, while my mind, heart, and soul are all over the fucking place." She sinks further into the water, keeping her nose above so she can breathe.

As I approach, I watch. "I know the feeling. I know in here," I tap my head, "that you are a bad idea."

"Fuck you." She moves her arms, slipping farther away from me. Anger over takes her face, a sign she's misunderstanding what I'm trying to say.

I move with her, not letting her distance herself from me. "You'll get to do that if it is really what you want." My words escape before I can stop them, and they only annoy her further.

"And if it isn't?" she challenges, unaware that challenging me when I know what she wants is a mistake. The way her eyes sparked when I suggested we'd get there gave her away.

"I'll never take something you aren't willing to give me, Ela. Not your body. Not your freewill to choose. Not even your heart. But you need to understand a few things about me before you can make a fair decision about what you want to happen." I move closer, so we are only an arm's length away. "How many people have you slept with?"

Like I suspected, she assumes I'm asking for one reason. "I don't see why that matters. That's personal and none of your goddamn business."

"I was sixteen when I lost my virginity to a nice girl I went to school with. Like any young man, I fumbled around and it was over before it really began. I had no clue about the different ways a woman's body reacted during sex in comparison to mine. I assumed, like so many others, that her body worked much like mine did. I continued down that road for way longer than I should have. It wasn't until I was in my early twenties that a woman was brave enough to complain about me not knowing." If I want her to be honest with me, I need to be the same with her. "I got better about it after that, I guess. Or at least I tried to be better. Then when I was twenty-five, I met a woman who knew what she preferred, how she wanted it, and wasn't afraid to share it with me. We weren't together for a long time, but she awoke an entirely different sexual hunger I didn't appreciate until her. So, I'll ask again, how many unexperienced arseholes have you been with?"

"Two, but we had sex more than once. And there was a third guy, one who would have been my first, but he couldn't stop firing off early. We did other things, tried some oral stuff." I have to lean in to hear her clearly. When I do, I don't miss the blush that takes over her face and slides down her neck. "How many women have you been with, since we're sharing?"

"Not as many as you might think." I'm now even a little closer, so close that when she kicks her feet, they brush against mine. Chills, that have nothing to do with the freezing water, travel up my spine, and I watch in awe as goose pebbles break out on hers. "And it doesn't matter, not really. They were all only there to provide me some release. None of them meant anything to me. I wasn't friends with them, didn't chase after them, nor did I care about who they fucked. It was just sex."

"What are you saying?" Her voice is breathy and the uncertainty in her eyes has me wishing I could, that we could, be more. "I told you I am not—"

I lift my hand and place two fingers on her warm lips. "Yes, I know what you said, Ela. And I'm not asking for you to give me more than you are capable of. But I will not share you. While you are with me, you will only be with me. When you are no longer interested in being with me, then you only need to tell me and I'll walk away."

Her eyes narrow so she can study me. "Why don't I believe you? If that were true, then you wouldn't be here now."

Her willingness to call me out turns me the fuck on. Even in this icy water, my cock shows signs of life. "Are you going to lie and say you aren't the least bit interested in what I can teach you?"

"Is that what you want to do? Teach me?" She swallows but refuses to look away, boldly holding my gaze. "What if I'm not impressed by your talents? So far, no man has done more than make me wonder what the fuss is about."

I smirk, knowing the young males she's been with had no clue how to handle a woman like her. They were missing out on all she could give them. It's going to be my pleasure to watch her come apart. "I'll have you begging me before the night is over."

Ela turns to swim for the rocks so she can climb out. "I don't beg." Her voice has that hint of heat that doesn't match her glare, and it provokes me to act.

I snag her arm before she gets too far, yanking her to my lips. She fights me at first, refuses to acknowledge that this kiss is more than any of the others. I release her, only to grip her jaw and try again. Within a few seconds, she gives in and I claim her mouth like a man possessed.

When she whimpers, I growl. "Watch out Ela, that could be mistaken for begging."

Her hand presses against my chest and she pushes me away. This time I allow her to climb out, follow her. She spins to say something, but the moment her eyes land on my body, her words dry up.

I'm not a small man. And even after being in a spring-fed pool, my dick is long and semi erect. Giving her an idea of what she'll be getting as soon as I get her some place more private. I would love nothing more than to have her here and now, but not this first time. No, the first time I need a bed where I can lie her down and worship every delicious inch that is her.

"Get dressed, Ela. I will not fuck you here this first time. One day maybe, but not today." I toss her the pile of clothes next to mine.

She shakes her head, bringing her out of the daze as she steps into her knickers. "You don't have to show off by proving the others were lacking. There is no way that will... I mean, is the plan to ruin me for all other men who come after you?"

I tuck myself inside my briefs and jump into my pants. As soon as we are dressed, I extend my hand for hers. When she takes it, I drag her into my arms and let our foreheads touch. We stare for a few seconds before my lips lower to hers. This time she lets me kiss her, really kiss her. She tastes good, better than any other woman before her. But it's not just that, it's the way she kisses me back, how she seeps into me as we let our mouths enjoy each other.

Once I've gotten a good taste, I moan against her mouth. "Are you sure about this?"

A wicked grin takes over her face as she licks her lips. I can't help but watch, imagining what they would feel like wrapped around my cock. "Yes, plus now I'm curious. You've been holding back on me, Gino. You can't show off like that and not—"

I stop her words by kissing her hard. Hell, if she keeps talking, I'll rip our clothes off and forget about taking my time. I'll shove her up against these rocks and fuck her until she can't think or walk.

Chapter Eight

GABRIELA

The Royals

Wet, hot, and turned on are not the best combination. I take care of the first two not long after returning to the house. I have my own room, like I do at my other brothers' homes. Which also means I have spare clothes, meaning I don't have to bring extras.

I shower quickly, like ordered to do, and then make my way downstairs. My plan was to head for the dining room, where I know the others were now eating. It's better to be late for dinner instead of not showing up at all. That would certainly draw more attention than being tardy. Disappearing is a skill of mine, but it always gets me into trouble with my brothers. Antonio is the worst of the three, constantly letting me appreciate his thoughts when he disapproves.

Once my feet land on the main floor, large arms seize my waist, dragging me in the opposite direction. "Don't you think we should at least eat the dinner Larkin fixed?"

"No." Gino responds, as if he's not the least bit concerned about disappointing his employer for skipping dinner. "We can pick up something along the way if you want. But I'm not wasting an hour chatting it up with your brother when all I want is to get you home, naked, and in my bed."

"Well, isn't that romantic?" I mumble, annoyed for some odd reason. "I feel honored." He disregards my sarcastic remark and his non-response only allows my mind to play catch up. "Hey, wait. Aren't you on duty tonight?"

"My shift ended two hours ago. I was only sticking around because Larkin asked me to." He guides me into the garage and stops in front of a beautiful machine that makes my heart pound a little harder. I now understand why he told me to wear jeans and anything but girly shoes. "There's an extra jacket hanging over there."

I find the leather coat and slip it on. It's big on me, but better than getting road rash should we crash. "How long have you owned a bike?"

He beckons me to come to him. Gripping the jacket, he tugs, making sure it's tight enough, I guess. Then he places a helmet on my head and adjusts the strap so it's snug, not that I need him to do it, but I let him. I revel in him taking charge, looking out for me. I'm not sure why, because normally I'd hate it.

There's a mischievous gleam in his eye as he explains. "I bought my first when I was sixteen, against my father's wishes. He found out about it and threatened to sell it. I told him if he did, I'd just buy another behind his back."

"You were a rebel?" I mock, feigning shock. "A rule breaker?"

He straddles the bike and waits for me to climb on behind him, giving me that look that says hurry up. I do, but that doesn't mean I do it without rolling my eyes first. Once I'm on, he kicks the stand and starts walking backward. "It's why I'm so good at catching you, sweetheart. I know all the tricks. Been there, done that. There isn't much you can pull I didn't pull ten years earlier. Now hang on tight and enjoy the ride."

The engine roars to life as I slide my arms under his jacket, placing my hands on his stomach. I feel his muscles flex and holy hell. The sight of him as he climbed out of the natural pool flashes across my mind again. Gino is the textbook version of a man. Every inch of his body is male perfection. It was impossible to not take note of the beast that hung between his legs.

I've heard the expression *hung like a horse*, and because I grew up around horses, it always made me laugh. When a stallion lets his hang out, it's difficult to miss. I'd even watched as the stud mounted his chosen mare and wondered how she took all he offered her.

The guys I've been with were a little shy. I never got the chance to inspect their packages. Even though I'd given one of them a blowjob, I hadn't taken the time to examine his thoroughly. I was only doing it in hopes he'd stay hard long enough for me to jump on, but the poor bloke was less experienced than me. Another fell asleep soon after we finished, so I hightailed it out of there to avoid a second round of not so good sex. And the other barely got his pants past his arse before he was suiting up and humping me. Now maybe you understand why I decided I needed a real man who differed from those boys I'd played with before.

"You like gyros?" Gino's voice comes through the speaker in my helmet, sending a tingle of heat straight to my core. I clench my thighs around him to make it stop, not that it helps.

"Yes." I shift my hands and come in contact with skin. It is warm and inviting. "Or we could just skip dinner altogether."

Gino's deep chuckle invades my ears. "You in a hurry?"

"How far away do you live?" I notice we're almost outside of Homero and heading down the highway back to Sevilla. "I thought we were heading to your place? I'm not sure it would be wise to go back to the dorms."

One of his hand's lands on my thigh. "Ela, I live in Sevilla. We'll be there in twenty. Once we get there, we'll grab the gyros. There's a deli just around the corner from my place and then we'll carry on with our evening."

I want to ask him why he lives in Sevilla, but refuse to do so. It explains why he keeps showing up like a bad penny. That information only confuses me more and has my mind trying to figure him out.

He parks his motorcycle outside a brick building. Shops line the street and I know for a fact there are apartments above them. I thought about asking my brother if I could move into one, but knew he'd say it wasn't safe, so I let it go. This neighborhood is nice, an area my friends and I visit a lot. Lots of businesses to explore, where I can easily get lost in the crowd.

I climb off and reach into my pocket for my phone, only to realize it's not there. "Shit."

"What?" Gino has unzipped his jacket and I almost forget what I was doing. His t-shirt sticks to his perfect body, one I cannot wait to delve into.

"My phone. I left it at Antonio's." I normally text Mercedes in a situation like this, so if something should happen, someone would know who I was with last. "Can I use yours?"

"Why?" He hands it to me before I answer.

"I need to text my cousin." I glance up as I'm typing the number in, somewhat surprised when her name pops up. "So, should I be worried you have her number stored on your phone?"

"I have all your friends, family, and acquaintances' numbers on my phone." He admits unfazed. "It's my job to look out for you."

I press send and pass it back before I do something stupid, like bounce it off his head. "Your job? Is it also your job to teach me how to fuck? I mean, do you get a bonus if you get me to orgasm, or maybe extra for each one? Your fucking job? You know what, I think I'll—"

I'm upside down and over his shoulder before I can finish my rant. And I'm not being silent about what I think about his little stunt. "You buffoon. Put me down. Are you hoping to get your arse kicked before the night is over? I will not be manhandled like some weak woman you order around."

The people around us are watching, unaffected by my protest. They may recognize me, or they may not. I'm not in my typical princess wear, currently looking more like everyone else, making it easier to blend in.

He strides past them, nodding while I seethe. I even hear him say hello to the gent manning a flower stand as he stops to do God knows what.

"What the hell are you doing?" I do my best to peek around his side when I feel a smack on my backside. "Did you just spank me?"

"Just ignore her. She's not used to knowing when to shut up and—"

Oh, hell no. I reach under his arm and twist that spot I know hurts like a mother. It works like I anticipate. I soon find my feet on the ground again and am about to bolt. The only thing that stops me is the sight of what he's holding out for me to take. He must have purchased them from the cart and the smiling chap behind him. A bushel of yellow daisies, like the ones I used to pick when I was a little girl. No one has ever given me flowers before.

Okay, not true. When I was sick, I received a ton of flowers, all kinds. I loved them. They made the room I had to spend so much time in less gloomy. I often pretended I was outside in a beautiful garden, lying in the sunshine. But after I got better, the flowers stopped coming.

No man has ever bought me flowers before. Not even when I was a teenager. And the fact Gino is the one presenting me with flowers, that also happen to be daisies, makes me pause and wonder if he knew or just got lucky. Has he been watching me? Does he notice I stop and buy them for myself whenever I pass a flower shop? Surely not.

"Peace offering." He shoves his hands in his pocket. "I didn't mean that literally, Ela. Fucking hell, what kind of man do you think I am?"

"That's just it. I have no idea what to even think." I bring the bouquet to my nose and inhale. "Did you know daisies are my favorite? You read that in one of those dossiers you keep on all of us, didn't you?"

The pain on his face shows me the vulnerable side to him, one I have to admit I understand more than I wish to let on. "You have no idea how close I've kept an eye on you since that night so long ago. Fuck, Ela. I think about you all the goddamn time, even when I'm doing my damndest not to. I tried to keep my distance. I have. Powers beyond my control seem to push me toward you, pulling you toward me. Tell me you don't feel that. Tell me and I'll walk away."

I can't lie to him. "I feel something. I'm not positive what it is or what it even means. But Gino, I meant it when I said I'm not interested in a relationship. I know how that sounds, but that isn't the future I see for myself. As long as you understand, then I'm willing to have some fun. Just don't get attached." Now if only I can make sure I don't become attached as well.

"How about we agree to take it one day at a time? When one of us is ready to move on, the other agrees here and now to let them go." He says the words, but I get the impression he doesn't actually mean them.

I put out my hand. "Deal."

He takes it and jerks me into his arms. "Let's seal it with a kiss instead."

I don't get a chance to object. His lips are on mine, and I become lost in his kiss. This is more than a kiss that seals the deal we made. This is a kiss that will change my life forever.

Chapter Nine

GINO

The Royals

We pick up the gyros before we head to my place. Ela keeps sniffing the daisies I purchased. Funny thing about that purchase is I'm not sure why I did it. I've never once bought flowers for a woman until now. Never thought about it, even.

You know what else I've never done? Invited a woman back to my place. I was the arsehole who always suggested we go to hers. That way, when we were finished, I could leave. I had no desire to stick around and cuddle. Didn't want to talk about her life or know more about who she was. I only wanted to fuck and go.

I've never once considered only fucking Ela. Even in those fantasies my mind constructed, we don't simply fuck. We also talked, cuddled, recovered, ate meals together, even spent time outside the bedroom.

I know that means trouble for me, that what I told her I'd do should she decide she's done will be impossible. Not to mention there's still so much I've not shared. Stuff I'm afraid to share. If she knew who I was, what my life would one day likely be, what she could become if things turn out to be different for us, my time with her will end before it begins. And for selfish reasons, I'm keeping tight lips so I can at least have her here and now. I'll deal with the rest later.

My place isn't huge. A loft above a bakery. Two small bedrooms and one bathroom that can be an uncomfortable fit for a man of my size. We walk in and I motion for her to have a seat at the small table while I grab plates and a few beers. In companionable silence we eat, and when we're done, she scrounges around my kitchen, searching for something. I don't think she's ignoring me on purpose, or maybe she is, but I assume it has to do with what will come next. She's trying to decide how to ask for it without sounding eager to jump me.

I smile when I notice the glass she's filled with water, her daisies arranged inside. To brighten up the room she sets them in the center of the table, wearing a beautiful smile.

Ela drops into the chair, tapping her nails. "So, now what?"

I bring my bottle of beer to my lips and drink the last few drops. "Now it's time for dessert."

Redness blooms on Ela's cheeks and quickly spreads. "Before we get started, I need to make sure you have lube and condoms."

I stand and extend my hand to her. "I have a new box of condoms on my nightstand and we won't be needing lube. Not planning to do any anal play tonight, babe."

She doesn't accept my hand as her eyes drop to the floor. "That's great, but if you don't have lube, then we aren't having sex."

I'm missing something here. "Ela, look at me."

Of course, she doesn't. My stubborn woman slides her chair back and darts past me, heading for my door. "Guess I'll be going, then."

I only let her grab the knob before I flatten my palm against the metal surface to keep her from running. "What am I missing?"

Dropping her head against the door, she shakes it while mumbling to herself. I cannot make out her words, but I get the impression I'm not intended to.

"Ela, what am I missing? Is that why you had lube with you the other night? Are you saying no man has got you so worked up you didn't need... assistance? What kind of fucking pinheads have you been sleeping with?" I form a fist and slam it into the door frame.

Bringing her own fist to the door, she pounds it three times before spinning around with hurt and anger scorching her eyes. "Look, Mister Perfect. It isn't their fault my body doesn't work like every other female. You can blame that one on the big C."

I stare down at her, confused. She's too young to have had cancer. What the hell is she talking about? When the fuck did she have that horrible disease? And why didn't I know about it? "I'm sorry, but what the fuck do you mean?"

Ducking under my arm, she heads for my living room. Walking up to the window facing the street, she stares out as if remembering. "I was only three when I got so sick the doctors thought I might die. After some extensive tests they realized I had leukemia, an aggressive strain that wasn't reacting well with normal treatments. Eventually I required a bone marrow transplant, which changes the body and causes all types of other issues. It saved my life, but it also altered how mine developed. Add in a few other complications and together, they all impacted how my female parts reacted as I got older. I basically have the body of a fifty-some-year-old post-menopausal woman at the ripe age of twenty. I don't care how talented you think you are, or how my lady bits come to life when I'm around you. You are not coming near me with that oversized snake you hide in your pants unless you have lube. Good lube and aren't afraid to use it."

When she was three, I was thirteen. I was adjusting to my new life here and hadn't been introduced to her father yet. That came a few years later, around my eighteenth birthday. It was an encounter I will never forget, and one I wish sometimes I could. But that's a subject for another day.

When I don't move, she mistakes my silence for something else. I hear the cracking in her voice, the certainty that my silence reveals something unintended. "I get it. No man wants a woman who won't respond to him. One who is broken and requires more work. It's why I've kept my mouth shut and prayed no one noticed. You don't need to worry, Gino. I won't hold you to anything. I'll walk away, and we will never talk about any of this ever again."

Like hell am I letting her walk away. As soon as she spins to leave, I crack my neck and stand firm in my spot. "I don't know where you think you're going. I never said a word about you being less than anything. I have lube in the bathroom. I use it regularly—"

"I don't want to hear about your sexcapades." Ela covers her ears.

Gripping her wrists to tug them away from her ears, I hold them gently but firmly in mine. "When I'm choking my snake, thinking about your tight pussy and how it will strangle it if I ever get the pleasure of fucking you."

"Oh." She blinks slowly. "But seriously, it's okay if you—"

I release her wrists and grab her tiny waist, lifting her easily. I drag her body up mine so I can kiss those soft sweet lips to shut her up. While I'm doing that, I spin and begin walking. Time to teach her the difference between a man and a boy. A man doesn't give two fucks if he has to work harder to get inside the woman who has captured his every thought. A man who desires to worship her until she can no longer stand and will gladly do whatever it takes. Then once she's lost in the pleasure only he can bring her, that is when he joins in on the fun and brings them to heights unknown.

I drop her on my bed and rip my shirt over my head, tossing it to the side as I snag the box of condoms and chuck them at her. "Open those and place a strip on the pillow. I'm going to grab the lube."

My feet move as quickly as I can with an enraged cock that is ready to escape the prison it's trapped behind. I locate the lube and am back in less than a minute. When I glance up, I have to close my eyes and count to ten. "What did I tell you to do? Did I say anything about taking off your top or bra? No. I said place a strip of condoms on the pillow. Next time you don't listen to me, I'm spanking your arse."

One thing she needs to learn is that I prefer control. In my life and in the bedroom. It is why I don't go to just any bar or club to pick up women. I have a very specific taste, or I did. Everything inside warns me Ela isn't ever going to be like those women I once settled for. Women who like men to take control and order them around. I'm not a true dominant, like I don't expect complete submission or envisage a woman getting on her knees for me. I simply prefer to be the one calling the shots.

And to be clear, I've never spanked a woman as punishment. I've spanked them while pounding into them when they've asked me to. And I've only done it a few times. It isn't my kink, I have other fetishes I enjoy more, stuff I will do to Ela once she trusts me. Just the thought of her allowing me to do a few of my wicked pleasures is making my cock throb and weep.

"The only way you will ever spank my arse is if you tie me down so I can't move. Otherwise, I'll fight you with everything I have." She scowls while attempting to roll off the bed.

I toss the lube next to the pillow and catch her foot, crawling until I'm on top of her. "You can't run away every time you get upset with me, Ela. That's not how it works."

"And you can't expect me to be some weak female you can order around. I'm not weak. I can kick your arse. I believe I've proven that once already," she snarls over her shoulder, her eyes filled with fury and lust.

I surprise us both and roll onto my back, bringing her sweet body on top of mine. Her thighs straddle my hips as she glares down at me, her dark hair making a curtain around us when she places her hands on my chest to steady herself. My fingers dig into her hips before they skim up her sides and settle just below her breasts.

"I don't want you to be anything other than yourself, Ela. I adore your fiery attitude." I let my thumbs brush the underside of her breasts. "But tying you up, with your permission to do so... fuck, sweetheart, that is one of my greatest fantasies. I, however, would never tie you up without your consent, that's not who I am. And I would only spank your arse to bring you pleasure, I'm not into punishing a woman, not really. But fuck me, if I wouldn't love to watch you squirm while my hand reddened your bum right before I fucked it."

"Gino." My name falls from her lips in a hoarse whisper.

"What do you want, sweetheart?" I tug her closer. "You only need to ask and I will do it."

"And if I were to say I don't know what I want? That I want you to show me all you know, all those things no one else has been able to offer me?" She leans forward and kisses my lips. "I just want you."

Her words cause the fire inside me to spread and rage. I take her mouth and let my tongue spear its way inside as I own it. No woman has ever tasted so good or felt like she was made for me the way this woman does.

Chapter Ten

GABRIELA

The Royals

The warmth of his mouth against mine has my body reacting. I thought he drew out wicked responses from me previously, but I had no idea. My stomach is taking flight, sending all these strange flutters between my legs. I'm aware my knickers are becoming damp, but not soaked the way I've read can happen in those stupid romance novels Mercedes loves. There is definitely moisture seeping slowly from my core as a result of what this man is doing to me.

I sense us moving and end up under him again. I'm not a big fan of having a man loom over me. The others I've been with I requested they not completely cover me with their bodies, moved them with ease when I felt uncomfortable. Even took over when it was an issue and settled on top, so they didn't trap me. Not that any of them could trap me, not with the skills I had. If I'd wanted to, I could have easily taken any of them, but I didn't care to embarrass those guys by showing them up.

The sensation of being under Gino does something completely different to me. I don't feel trapped at all. He would never hold me down against my will. If I protested even slightly, he'd move and let me up. Although I don't wish to be anywhere else. I long to be right here with his powerful form pressed firmly against mine. The strength he possesses can be felt with his every movement.

Gino breaks the kiss and immediately relocates those amazing lips down my neck. He licks and sucks his way to my collarbone where his teeth rake along it until a sharp sting hits me when he clamps down.

"Oh, God!" I barely recognize my voice as I cry out. "Why did you do that?"

His tongue soothes the sting before he buries his face, nuzzling in, and sucks harder. I swear if he marks me there as well, I'll make sure he pays for it. "Shh. 'Tis the price you pay when you taste like a treat made just for me."

I was about to say something but swallow my words when his left hand covers my breast and squeezes. It's not the same as when others have played with them. What they did was play. He isn't playing at all. It has a gentleness that proves he knows what he's doing. That he has done this before and understands the correct way to manipulate a woman's breasts to bring the blood to the nipple, making it extremely sensitive. When he flicks it with one of his fingers, I shiver.

The second his hot breath surrounds the tip—before his mouth—I forget to breathe. I watch him instead. Admire how he suckles, like he is doing his best to draw something from inside of me. The pull and squeeze with each hard tug has me holding on until I have to fill my lungs so I don't pass out.

Our eyes lock, and I swear there's a blaze behind his, warning me we haven't even touched the surface of the oasis he is taking me to. With a pop, he releases the one only to bring the exact same pleasure to the other. Making me whimper at the sensation, knowing I'll be begging him to do more if he doesn't move on.

Thankfully he does, meaning I don't have to eat my words. He kisses his way down my center, dipping his tongue over a small scar on my stomach and then into my belly button. I can tell he has questions but leaves it for now to not ruin the moment. His rough whiskers scratch my stomach as he lets his lips caress along the waistband of my jeans.

"I'm peeling these off of you now, Ela." He groans as he undoes the snap and releases the zipper. Then he groans again, sending a shiver through me before announcing, "Then I'm feasting on this pussy."

I swallow and blink, lifting my hips. His blatant words aren't something I'm used to. His dirty talk, holy hell, it's doing miraculous things to my body, and I'm learning I like it very much. It's fucking hot when he talks filthy to me, and I'll do whatever he wants me to do. Yes, please.

I watch him stare at my exposed flesh and feel the need to offer him an out. "You don't have to do that. I'm not sure it will make much of a difference. I mean, others have tried, but in the end, I still require the lube."

Gino shakes his head just enough to display he disagrees. Once he's tossed my jeans to the side, along with my socks, he places his palm over my center. Running his middle finger slowly over the top of my knickers, the area he will later enter, while he presses against a very sensitive nerve that craves more. Leaving his hand to continue his torture, he leans over me and presses his body into me again, suspended just above my face while he watches closely.

"Have you ever had an orgasm?" His eyes bore into mine as he asks me directly, forcing a response.

I want to look away but don't. "No. Or maybe I have, but nothing momentous, small, insignificant ones. It's fine. I realize you're ready to do something else besides trying to wake up this sleeping body of mine. I've already felt more than I ever have before." Even though I'm disappointed when he slides down my torso, I meant what I said.

I know what's coming next. He'll slide off my knickers, suit up, spread some lube on me, and then get his jollies on. At least this time I've experienced more pleasure than in previous encounters, and maybe each time after this I'll learn something new.

My legs are stretched wide. I close my eyes that are stinging with unshed tears while I wait. His fingers run along my thighs first. They trail over my sex and along the outer parts of my slit. I nearly levitate off the bed when his thumb presses against that bundle of nerves hidden behind its hood. He presses and rubs firmly against it, waking my clit enough to expose it even more. Then, to my surprise, he lowers his head and places his mouth there. I practically come unglued when he sucks on it the same way he suckled my nipples. The man doesn't let up until he's drawn it out of hiding and has me gripping the sheets, struggling to calm the fuck down. He sucks, nips, and licks it, making me react like I might explode. I swear my vision gets spotty while I fight my way through the unknown.

While I'm trying to figure out what the hell is happening, he lets one of his thick fingers slip inside my warm center slowly. I gasp for air as he stretches me, waiting for the pain to soon follow. To my disbelief, it slides in way easier than it should have without lube. I turn my head to check if maybe I'm wrong, if maybe he grabbed it when I wasn't looking. It's still next to me, unopened, and I'm so confused.

Gino lifts his body off mine and undoes his pants. Slides them off his hips and down those amazing thighs. Leaving him in nothing once they are removed completely. I can only stare at the twitching angry erection targeting me. I watch him fist it tightly as he runs his thumb over the tip, gathering the beads of moisture dripping from the head. I've never witnessed a man do this before. Those before Gino weren't as comfortable as he seems to be.

"Touch yourself." He growls while he moves up and down his shaft slowly. "I want you to touch that delicious pussy while I watch."

"What?" I've touched myself before, but it's not something I do regularly. Nor is it something I've let anyone watch me do. I'm not sure how I feel about him watching.

Gino kneels between my legs, presses his thighs against mine to open me even more. Still gripping his amazing male package, he turns his heated gaze on me. "Take your hand and rub the spot I exposed with your fingers. Show me how you like to be touched, Ela. What you do when you want to bring yourself pleasure."

When I don't do as he suggests, he leans over me. The length of him brushes my thigh and glides across my belly as he seizes my wrist and then sits up again. With my hand in his, he places it on that spot and moves our hands in sync until he's satisfied. I now understand what he wants me to do. "Like that. Fuck, Ela, that is hot. I want to watch you come undone before I fuck you."

My hand stops moving as tears threaten to fall. How do I explain this isn't working like he hopes it will? I'm not like other women. My touch does jack shit for me. I remove my hand and cover my face with both so he cannot witness me falling apart.

The bed dips, and I'm engulfed in powerful arms before I know what's coming. That doesn't help keep my emotions at bay. It sends me right over the edge, and I cry. I hate crying. Acting like one of those emotional females who uses her tears to grab a man's attention. I'd rather stab myself with a rusty dull knife than let anyone see me cry. I detest feeling vulnerable. The only time I ever allow myself to cry is when I'm alone and in the shower. I only permit myself to let go for the time it takes me to wash up, fifteen minutes at most. So, it really pisses me off that I'm losing my shit now while I'm the most exposed I've ever allowed myself to be.

"Are you going to tell me what is wrong?" Gino's deep, smooth voice surrounds me from above. He kisses the top of my head as his hands caress my back and he pulls me into his chest. "Why are you crying?"

"I don't know." I do, but I'm not telling him. My body is an electric current right now, on fire like it has never been, making my emotional side open to new experiences as well. I hate feeling this way. There is no way I want to explain it to him. Not now, maybe never. "Just ignore me."

We roll until I'm on top of him again. His erection pressing into my belly, not at all ashamed to remind me why we are here. Strong hands grip my arms and drag me up enough so we're staring into each other's eyes.

I sigh and then sit up fully, so I'm now straddling him. His large cock trapped between my folds, wedged against my sensitive pearl. I shift back, but his hands land on my hips to hold me firmly there.

Once again, my hands find my face so I can hide. Embarrassed that all I want to do is rub against him while we are like this. I gasp when he reads my mind and drags me forward and then back along the length of him. Letting my hands drop as I pitch forward and use them to brace my body while he plays me like a violin.

"Fuck, Ela. That's even hotter than watching you touch yourself. Keep rubbing your pussy on my cock like that, baby. Use me to get yourself off and let me watch you come."

He releases my hips and grabs my breasts again. Begins massaging them, encouraging me to move faster. When he pinches and then twists both my nipples, something happens. It's like an explosion goes off inside of me, and I have the urge to cry out as it takes over my body and mind.

Hot spurts land on my stomach, forcing me to glance down and watch. I've never seen a man fire off when he reaches the point of no return. It's a sight to witness. Before I stop to think about it, I wipe it off my belly, rise enough to spread it where I know I'll need lubricant, then shift forward and line my entrance with the still oozing tip. In one swift move, I spear myself with it and moan.

"Fuck." Gino groans as I settle on him. "Fuck. Ela. What are you—"

His words halt when I rise and fall on the largest dick I have ever seen or taken. I can feel him stretching me, making me burn in a good way. It isn't painful, not like it's been before when I've not used lube or not used enough. It is only uncomfortable enough for me to notice. I keep moving, trying to make the explosion building inside of me go off again.

My hand slides down my body to locate my clit. I rub it while bouncing like a wild woman on him. Within seconds I reach the cliff I'm searching for and moan as my insides seize tight around him. Not able to stop myself, I collapse forward.

I'm on my back again soon. Gino is above me now. My legs are placed over his shoulders, bending me in half while he pounds into me. It's as if he's doing his best to impale himself so deep inside of me I will always and forever remember him. Right as my muscles seize up again, he explodes, sending hot semen into the depths of my core, making his movements even easier until he slams in and holds me there. I can feel his body shaking all around me, and I fall apart in his arms once again, not sure I'll survive this or him.

Chapter Eleven

GINO

What the fuck just happened?

I stare down at the woman who encouraged me to do the unthinkable. I've never been so careless. It was bad enough I was letting her rub her pussy against my throbbing, unsheathed cock. I've always wrapped it the second it was out and loose, making sure something like this never happened. I wasn't worried about STDs, not as much as I was concerned about an unplanned pregnancy. I understand who I am and what it would mean if that ever happened.

Her expression has me regretting what I'm about to do. I don't want her to assume I didn't enjoy what we did, because that was by far the best sexual experience of my life. I've never felt more connected with anyone, or been so lost I couldn't think before I acted. So many thoughts are running through my brain right now, and a few of them should have me concerned.

I should be freaking out. Should be angry with her and myself for being so stupid. The very thought we could have created life, a life that will not only be an heir, but a target, should anyone learn my true identity.

My time to come clean is drawing closer. I've been watching everything closely, know exactly what is going on in the country I once called home. And while it scares me to think what that will mean for me, I refuse to let the man who betrayed my family lead them should it reach that. I will reveal who I am when the moment is right, while taking him down in the process. And when that happens, anyone connected to me will be in danger, especially a child, my child.

Her voice breaks through my thoughts, bringing me back to the present. "What's wrong? Why are you not smiling after that? Was I that bad?"

I slowly and carefully slip out of her. I'm still surprisingly hard, even after I've fired off twice. Once I'm free, I grab her hand and tug her with me as I stand. Thankfully, she follows without hesitation.

We need to clean up after that. Sex without condoms is way messier than it is with. I've always been the gentleman and never left a woman a sticky mess. Before I escaped, I either handed her a washcloth or started the shower for her. What I didn't do was drag her into the shower with me, where we could get into even more trouble. The kind I wouldn't mind doing again with Ela, even if it's risky. Fuck, I'm willing to take all those risks with her.

As soon as we enter the bathroom, Ela releases my hand and steps away from me. "I should get out of here."

I flip on the shower while I inform her what I know she needs to do. "You need to use the toilet before we clean up."

"What?" She crosses her arms defensively and is glaring at me. "You want me to pee in front of you? No. And why the hell are you being so quiet? Are you that disgusted—"

"Shut up." I groan when I glance down and notice my cum on her leg, dripping slowly from her. My hand runs over my face while I do my best not to capture her then bury my face between her legs again. I'm a man who would have no problem finding out what my cum tastes like mixed with hers. Hell, it takes everything inside me not to bend her over the counter in here and fuck her again. "You need to pee so you don't get an UTI. How do you not know this? Then we'll wash me off of you so you'll sleep better. And sweetheart, my face was between your legs, my cock inside of you, so there isn't any reason for you to not take a piss while we wait for the water to warm. Actually, I'm going to grab us some water. Piss while I'm doing that, but hurry because it's getting late and we still need to talk about what we are doing now."

I leave and grab the waters to give her a few more minutes. When I return, she's washing her hands, which I find comical since we'll be showering soon. I place the cups on the nightstand and wrap my arm around her waist when I step back into the bathroom. Guiding us into the shower that is a tight fit for just me.

"I know how to wash up." She smarts off as my hand smacks her bare arse. "Ouch."

"Did you ever think I might want to wash you off because I helped dirty you up?" I grab the clean washcloth I hung on the shower door earlier and add soap. "Or that maybe I like it, even?"

She shakes her head and shivers when I run the cloth over her breasts and down her torso. Fuck me. My body will never calm with her this close. I try to keep it quick, but when I start to clean her pussy, her whimpers have me slowing down and taking my time. It's cruel, I know, to play her again after what I did earlier, to coerce another orgasm out of her when I should be doing my best to bathe us both so we can talk.

"Gino," she whimpers. "Oh my God. Gino, please."

I drop the washcloth and let my hand finish the job it started. My thumb rubs against her sweet spot while my fingers reach back and sink into her again. It's a good thing I'm holding her up with my other arm, because it doesn't take long for her to fall this time. She rides my hand like we have been doing this for years, pressing her arse into me, my cock enjoying the times it slides between her cheeks.

"Fuck me again, Gino. Please. I want to feel your cock inside me again." She reaches behind her, sliding the devil along her arse, guiding it between her legs. "I'm so close."

I bite her neck. "I don't have a condom, Ela. I made that mistake once. I won't do it again."

Her body stiffens, but because she is so close, she can't stop her orgasm from escaping, even though I can feel her trying. What she can do, however, is elbow me once she recovers, knocking the wind out of me long enough for her to make a quick exit.

I don't bother with a towel when I follow behind as she drips her way through my bedroom to retrieve her clothes. I catch her right as she picks up her jeans and fall back onto the bed with her in a tight hug. She's slippery and doing her best to get free, which is why I end up rolling over and pressing her into the mattress. Even like this, it's difficult holding her down with us both still drenched from the shower.

"Let me go. I'm a mistake, remember?" She shouts from beneath me as she bucks and squirms.

"I said fucking you without a condom was a mistake. There is a difference, Ela. I will gladly fuck you again using a condom. I'll do it now." I tighten my grip to keep her where I can control her. "You are not a mistake. Not now, not ever will I think of you as a mistake. Even if you end up pregnant because of what we did, I wouldn't believe it a mistake, just bad timing."

She goes slack under me, and I can feel the fight in her fade. "Can you get off me, please?"

I do as she asks, ready to stop her from running if I have to. "I mean that, Ela."

Her sad eyes turn on mine, and I don't understand why she looks so sorrowful, lost. "You don't need to worry about me getting pregnant. That won't happen."

"You're on the pill?" I don't know why I didn't think she might be. I'm sure her mother put her on it as soon as she realized her daughter was a little wilder than her boys.

"I'm not going to get pregnant. I can ensure you it will not happen. And I don't have any STDs. I've always used condoms." She picks up my t-shirt and slides it over her body. Pulling her legs in, she slips it over them so she is tightly wrapped up inside.

I stand and walk back into the bathroom, grab two towels, wrapping one around my waist. The other is for Ela's hair, which I keep with me until I sit behind her. I then do my best to get the excess water out. She lets me without fighting, proving something is off. My girl likes her independence, and I realize I've hurt her somehow with my words.

"I wouldn't want to trap you, sweetheart. You seem to know what you want out of life. I would hate to be the one who derailed you from that." I try to fix this by telling her half-truths. I think I'd like nothing more than to derail her of certain plans. But neither of us is at a place where we would be ready to handle all the things children bring with them. I have my own fears to face and she has a lot of growing up to do first. "One day maybe, though."

"I don't want a family, Gino." Ela's expression is sad again. "You have to stop believing I do. This, what we are doing, is no more than just a good time. Please don't get attached and start thinking it will ever be more than that."

I want to tell her she doesn't have to worry; I don't get attached to women. But that would be a lie. Since the day this woman jumped onto my radar, before then, even, I have attached a part of me to her.

"I believe we agreed to that already." I track a finger down her arm. "I care, Ela. I'll always care. But I'll never ask you to do or be someone you don't choose to be. I understand how it feels, and that is the reason I only ever want the best for you."

With that being said, I stand again, make my way over to my dresser and slip into a pair of boxers. I set the strip of condoms back on my nightstand, next to the tube of lube. Crawling into bed, I pat the spot beside me and am pleased when she slides over and gets comfortable. We say nothing else. We do nothing but stare into the other's eyes until they get heavy and sleep takes over.

Chapter Twelve

GABRIELA

I've spent most of my weekends at Gino's. At least the ones when he's been off. Because my brother's baby is due in only a few short months, traveling out of the country has halted. This week, Antonio moved his family back to the palace to be ready when the moment comes. It is still months away, but he wanted to be closer to the doctor in charge of Larkin's care, which means Gino has been gone more as well. Everyone is focused on the next heir's arrival. No one has had time to worry about what was happening with me, which I'm totally fine with.

It's been almost six weeks since this thing started between us. I spent the entire weekend with Gino after our first sexual encounter. He certainly showed me what I'd been missing out on. Never rushed and made sure I had at least one orgasm before him, usually more than one, but sometimes he couldn't wait.

It wasn't only about sex, there was so much more to it than that. He would sometimes show up at my dorm with dinner. Hang out with me in my room like we were dating. Not just to make out or fuck me—even though both of those also happened. He would come and sit with me while I studied. He'd rub my feet while he read and I finished my homework, or quiz me when he knew I had an exam. While he was there, he'd dismiss my guards, grant them a few hours to chill without worry I'd once again give them the slip. I wouldn't say we were flaunting our relationship or out in the open about it. We were, however, two adults who enjoyed being around the other person, even though we didn't always agree. I'm sure others knew it was more than a friendship, but no one dared to ask.

We also didn't skip the condoms like we'd done that first time. Not that it mattered. I wouldn't get pregnant. His concerns about it happening were both touching and something else. I couldn't quite put my finger on it, but it came across as if he was almost terrified about it. His reaction was unlike him and put me on edge, making me very uncomfortable whenever he brought it up.

It's been a few days since we've seen each other. I had a long weekend, so I thought it might be nice to surprise him. It wasn't the first time I'd stopped by his place to do so. After a trying day, sometimes I wanted to get out and away from the chaos of the university. He gave me a key after he found me outside his place alone, waiting on him to make it home. Said it was safer inside than it was sitting exposed on the streets, because of course I'd ditched my guards. Funny how he stopped lecturing me about slipping past them when I did it to be with him.

There's yelling coming from inside his place when I arrive. I recognize his voice over the other two. I probably should knock, but I have a key, so instead I let myself in.

Gino is standing by the window, holding a folder tightly in one grip as he throws his fist in the air. "What if I don't want to take my place and claim it back? Maybe it's time to let this go and move on. Enough blood has been shed."

One of the men speaks with an accent that sounds Slavic, not quite Russian, more of a mixture between those and the Latin speaking countries.

I love languages. Ever since I was a little girl, I've been interested in them. All my siblings speak Spanish, Portuguese, and French fluently. I also speak Italian, Latin, and Romanian because I'm double-majoring in linguistics to make me stand out in a few years. Once you learn the basics of one Latin based language, picking up on others is easier. Eventually, I hope to learn Russian, Arabic, and Mandarin Chinese. I appreciate how important it is to communicate with those all over the world, to understand what others are saying when they don't expect. It's why I work so hard in school. That skill will add value to what I offer a team in the Elite Forces and help me get accepted into that program.

"It is your birthright as the Kelemen male heir." The other man starts to say more, but stops when he notices Gino's eyes are now focused on me, standing there, listening.

I don't know what emotion I witness as his stare bores into me. He clearly isn't happy to find me here, overhearing whatever this is. The vein in his forehead is pulsing the way it does when he's unhappy about something.

The other man stands and stalks toward me. His expression is smug and I'm not sure I like him. "You didn't mention—"

Gino cuts him off before he can finish. "There is nothing to mention, Cezar."

Cezar eyes me carefully before he turns back to Gino. "But it was arranged long before—"

"I did not agree to any arrangement, even if others did. Now leave. I have company." Gino tosses the folder at the other man, who is still seated. "Beni, please inform them they need to find another way. I'm not the man for the job. I have no desire to ever be that man. Birthrights do not make a leader."

Beni stands, straightens his jacket, and follows Cezar to the door. When he passes me, he smiles brightly and in very clear Romanian calls me the future to a lost kingdom, the one who will heal the land and many souls. He doesn't voice it loud, only enough for me to hear. I want to ask him more, but Gino is shoving him out the door before I can.

"Who were those men?" I don't expect him to give me an answer, not the way he's acting. Whoever they are, he wasn't happy to see them and wanted them gone. More so after I showed up, but why?

"No one you need to be concerned with. What brings you here in the middle of the day on a weeknight?" He doesn't sound delighted to see me, like I'm an inconvenience he has to deal with.

I adjust the backpack on my shoulder, irritated about how that makes me feel. "Maybe I'll go, since you're in rare form. I've got some reading to catch up on, anyway. You may not want me to know who they are, but it seems Beni does." I wave the folder the older man slipped in my hand on his way out. "Do you have secrets, Gino?"

He yanks it out of my grip faster than I can pull it back, then storms off to the office located in the spare room. I hear the shredder kick on and then watch him place the contents through it quickly. His eyes display how unhappy he is about whatever was inside as he watches the machine destroy each page. My curious nature spikes at his actions, and I know later I'll be digging into it on my own.

"Big secrets it looks like." My mind is working faster than I can process the information. I know what I heard, and I can't help but wonder why he doesn't want me to read those pages. What's he hiding? "Do you want to talk about it?"

Gino glares at me, but says nothing.

"You realize I might be able to help. I'm pretty good at knowing how to handle tough situations. I've been dealing with men like those two most of my life. And you aren't fooling me, Gino. Whoever they are, they've put you on edge. Why not tell me what it is they want you to do so we can figure out the best way to get them to back off?" I drop my backpack and take a seat in the chair by the door.

"You want to help, do you? Sure." He reaches inside a white paper sack and pulls out a box. I sense the anger building when I catch what it is. "Take this and prove once and for all we have nothing to worry about."

"My word isn't good enough?" I cross my arms so I don't punch him in his smug face. "Fine arsehole. Give me that damn test so I can prove you didn't knock me up."

He tosses the box at me with no emotion. "I just want to make certain, Ela."

I roll my eyes, knowing this is a fucking waste of time. I sense him behind me as I stomp down the hall to his bathroom so I can piss on a stick. I might very well shove it up his arse when I'm done. Not once did I think I'd have to do this. I seriously want to scream at him for making me.

I can't really be mad at him for being an idiot, because I haven't exactly been honest with him. Which is why I'm now peeing on a pregnancy test when I'm as sterile as they come. At least he didn't follow me into the bathroom to watch. He had the decency to stand outside the door and wait.

I slap the useless test in his palm and attempt to make my escape. "Thank you very much for trusting me. I think we're done now. You can go fuck yourself and leave me alone. I have never in my life been more humiliated."

He holds the stick between his fingers as he follows me. I know he's watching it closely, praying it will be negative. "I just need to make certain, Ela."

"It's Gabriela from this point forward. I'm done with you." I sling my backpack over my shoulder, refusing to look at him so I don't make this any harder on me than it already is. "Have a nice life."

Gino isn't about to let me leave, though. He blocks me with his large body, breathing in a rhythm I once found soothing. "Where are you going? Why are you mad at me for wanting to make sure? Most women would be equally concerned and thankful to have a man so bent out of shape."

"Newsflash! I'm not most women!" I shove him, but he doesn't even budge. "Move, you big buffoon. I have a life to get back to."

"Like hell you do. You're going to tell me why you are so mad about this. Did you already know it was negative? Were you hoping it would be positive? I thought..."

My fist slams into his chest. "No, you fucking moron! I don't need a goddamn test to tell me I'm not pregnant. It's hard to get pregnant when you have useless female organs that never worked to start with. That's why I knew! I can't get pregnant, Gino!"

"I thought you said you were on the pill?" He sounds so confused, and I can't blame him.

"I believe my exact words were, 'You don't have to worry.' And before you point out you've seen me taking the pill, the pill I take is to help my body pretend it is a functioning female body instead of a dead useless one." I duck around him while he's dazed, struggling to figure out what I just told him. I toss the key he gave me on his counter and run out the door, slamming it behind me.

My feet lead me to the nearest train station that will take me far away from here. It wouldn't be the first time I took one to get away. I have one of those passes that allows me to board without a ticket. One pleasant convenience in this country is the public transportation we have that will take you almost anywhere.

Gino won't expect me to board a train to take me home. He'll assume I'm headed to the dorms and likely show up there. I need to get away from him and hideout for the next four days with the only person on this earth who gets me. We've been leaning on each other all my life and her love and strength are what I require right now. My mother is the only rock I can count on. She's been there through all the good, bad, and tough times. One look at me and she'll understand.

I need time to pull my shit together and forget all about these last six weeks and the dreams it awakened. Dreams are best left to the sleeping. I'm awake now and I need to move on.

Chapter Thirteen

GINO

The Royals

I punch the wall the moment the door slams shut, making a sizable hole in the sheetrock. All that does is piss me off more. I have to be the biggest arsehole who ever walked this earth. I deserve the hatred reflected in her eyes after pressuring her to take a test that hurt her more than it eased the worry I've been carrying.

What's worse is how I wished the lines to change. I wanted her to be pregnant so I could coerce my way into her life forever. Make her mine and only mine for the rest of our lives. Share who I was and what her father had done for me, despite the fact he'd carried it out for selfish reasons. I need to tell her what he'd asked of me where his daughter was concerned. Even though I know she'll be pissed, and I also thought it a horrible idea, I realize part of her will wonder if the only reason I continually went after her had to do with an agreement others encouraged me to make long before we met.

I drop to the floor, resting my tired arse there while I do my best to figure this out.

When I came to this country, I had no clue why. Barely a teenager, I wasn't ready to face my fate that had been decided the day I was born. Not to mention it had been kept a secret to protect me and my family. But like most secrets, they find a way to surface and then destroy those who keep them. Secrets, I've learned, are poison, waiting to do their worst the moment they are spilled. I lost three members of my family, and now it wanted my life as well. It would take out anyone who stepped in its way to get to me. I'd seen it happen, heard the rumors about what my uncle had done to those he thought were harboring me. As far as most people were concerned, I was dead, but a rumor compelled him to doubt. I saw the photographs of the war being fought in a country that hasn't known peace since long before my birth.

Legend claimed that peace would only come when the rightful ruler took the throne back and led the people into the light. He would return when his warrior, the one who strengthened him, finally found him. Together they would heal the land and souls of the people, restoring hope and a future everyone could be proud of for many years to come.

My father established a treaty to keep me safe when he saw trouble heading his way. King Ramon and he agreed to unite forces and fight for the good of the country he loved. Those two had taken it so far as to set up a union with King Ramon's young daughter and me when the time arrived, an arranged marriage. A royal bond that would forever unify our two countries, strengthening the powers both nations had as the last sovereign born rulers. A burden I'd been carrying with me since the day I learned about this arrangement shortly after turning eighteen. The same day, they accepted me into the academy to be trained as a soldier. It seems that my father prearranged that too. He wanted his son to appreciate what it took to keep a royal family safe. A suitable approach for me to watch how it worked, keeping an eye on the inner circle, while surrounded by men like King Ramon. His thought was that it would better prepare me when the time came to take my place as the future ruler of Kosonia. To say I'd been upset about the prearrangement was an understatement. It was another deceitful blow to how secretive my family had been and how those secrets were poisonous to the soul.

My protectiveness over Ela started the day I learned what these two kings had formulated. I never planned on acting on the selfish acts of two men who'd done it in secret. Nor did I believe in the act of arranged marriages. The ones I'd seen only caused issues later. What I hadn't expected was to fall for the young, spunky princess when she was barely eighteen, and I much older at twenty-eight. I'd only meant to keep her safe from those who wished to harm her. But while I'd been doing that, it seems my heart and soul were admiring hers.

Six weeks ago, it came crashing down around me and my worlds collided. I realized she was the only woman who could calm the demons inside of me. It wasn't as if I hadn't tried other ways, but until my Ela, I'd felt lost in a world I didn't belong. Her fiery spirit matched mine. Her desire to be something other than what her birthright demanded mirrored my own. It honored me to be the man who brought a smile to her face, a genuine one. To be the only man who could touch the deepest parts of her and show her she wasn't a broken woman. That she only needed a partner happy to learn how to play her body, enjoy it, even, lighting all kinds of fires while doing so. Not just the sexually sensual sides of her, but a companion who was eager to feed all her desires.

My girl was smart. Not mine, she's not mine, can never be mine. Not fully mine at least, since I have secrets I'm determined to keep from her. She is way smarter than I ever realized, and one day she'll take this world by its balls and soar high.

What I wasn't willing to do, however, was drag her into a world she wanted no part of. It's the reason I shouldn't have gotten involved with her to begin with. Kept my distance, like I intended. Although, I don't regret the time I was allotted. I will forever be grateful to have been given the chance to love her, to know all of her like no other man before me had. That doesn't mean I'll forget about or stop protecting her. My life's goal is to look out for her, ensure she stays safe no matter what.

I glare at the test still in my hand and want to kick my arse. Pulling out my phone, I bring up the tracking app and make a face. Something isn't right. It says she's here, in my apartment, when I know very well, she isn't.

I shoot her a text and hear the muffled ding it makes when one goes through. After a frantic search, I find it buried behind the chair in the corner. It must have fallen out of her backpack, and during her rush to leave, she never noticed.

I call Milo, one of the seasoned men on her team. "I need Gabriela's location now." I don't give him much time to make excuses, when he answers.

"Last I knew she was—"

"She just ran out of here fifteen minutes ago. Her phone was left behind. I need you to see if she has one of her other trackers on her." My anger rises with each word. I cannot fault her team for always allowing her to slip past them. She was able to sneak past me a few times. Even Sir Edward had trouble keeping up with her. Which is why they haven't been reprimanded whenever she snuck out without their knowledge.

"All three show her still in my apartment." His voice is winded, meaning he's likely running to her room to check. There's a harsh knock and a different voice announces they are entering. "Fuck. It's empty."

I want to respond with no shit, but instead I say, "Check the campus. It's very reasonable to assume she is returning and might head to another building. I'll call in reinforcements."

"I'm sorry, Gino. We've been doing better, I thought, but you know the princess." He chuckles, but I'm not laughing.

"I don't need your apology, Milo. I need her found and safe. Just find her," I grumble into the phone before I hang up.

Pinching the bridge of my nose, I make another call. Again, I don't wait for more than a hello before I speak. "I need a location on the princess."

"Don't let her hear you call her that," Sir Edward clears his throat. "I thought you two were getting along better lately."

"We were. Then I stuck my foot in my goddamn mouth and she ran off. Her phone was left behind and now she's God knows where. Please tell me you surgically implanted a tracker in her." I'm pacing, my anxiety rising.

This time, he outright laughs. "Do I look like I have a death wish? No implant. But I did slip one on the beaded gold bracelet I gave her for her birthday. If she has it on, I can activate it."

"She never takes it off." I know the one he's talking about. Ela's always toying with it, but never removes it. It wouldn't surprise me if she's aware it has a tracker, but because she trusts Sir Edward, knows he would only activate it in an emergency.

"Interesting." I'm assuming he's had success locating her with that comment. "Please don't make me regret this. I've worked hard at keeping my relationship with her honest."

"I need to fix this before it's too late. A few people came to visit me today. My mood wasn't the best after they left, and instead of trusting her, I acted. Now I need to correct it, because if I don't, I may never get the chance. Please, Edward. Please." I run a hand down my face and try not to panic.

"She's heading home. Maybe you should come and speak with me while you're in town. Sounds like it's time we have that talk we've been putting off for several years. King Antonio needs to be brought into the light, and it appears you have a hard decision to make." He is one of the few who knows my true identity. It's hard to keep something like that from a man in his position.

He's right. No matter how much I want to ignore it and wish it would go away. It won't. I am who I am, and as soon as others figure it out, I'll have no choice but to leave my position here and move on with my life. The hardest thing about that will be leaving the one person who has given me a chance to hope and dream again.

"I'll contact you tomorrow, and we'll talk then. Thank you."

"Don't thank me, Gino. Fix what you need to fix and don't be a chicken shit. She's a lot smarter and stronger than I imagine you are giving her credit for."

I don't get a chance to respond. He hangs up, leaving me plenty to think about during my three-hour drive to Aragon.

Chapter Fourteen

GINO

The Royals

I arrive in Aragon shortly after midnight. Now that Esteban has moved out of Castile Vicente, Her Royal Highness, Angela — Ela's mother—quickly moved in. I'm sure the palace held too many ghosts and never offered her any peace. It was as if she couldn't escape its walls fast enough once the Castile became available.

I'm waved through the moment the guards spot my Porsche approaching the gates. Sir Edward has obviously alerted them to be on the lookout. It makes me wonder if he also forewarned Gabriela to expect a visitor.

Before I can make it to the front door, it opens, and I brace myself for the battle I believe will occur. Instead, I'm greeted by an older, yet stunning woman, who's holding a tumbler of bourbon with maraschino cherries floating around. "Gino. I was informed you might stop by tonight."

I grip the back of my neck, uncomfortable having this particular conversation with her. "Madam, I hope this isn't a problem. I need to speak with Gabriela, if you don't mind."

Angela waves me in and gestures for me to follow her into the office, where it looks like she's been waiting. The fire is roaring, and a book is laid open next to a throw. Heading straight to the bar, she grabs a tumbler and lifts the canter of bourbon, pours two fingers, and shoves it my way as I approach her cautiously.

"You might require that first. I love my daughter dearly, but she doesn't always keep a level head when pushed beyond her comfort zone. You confuse her and have for a very long time. I'm not sure what the hell happened, she won't say, but I'm guessing you're here to fix it." She prods a finger into her drink to snag a cherry. "I'm going to bed now. You know your way around here and her from what I understand. I'm not holding judgment. You are both adults and know the price for getting caught. Just be careful, the way you've both been, unless you're ready to take this public, then do what it is you must. There's a bottle of tequila somewhere, you might require it later. I hope to see you in the morning and find her in a more agreeable mood. Good luck."

As soon as she gathers her book, she's gone, leaving me alone with my drink and thoughts. I've never once done what I'm about to do. I shouldn't do it now, either. What I should do is finish this drink and walk right back out the door and forget all about the minx who has me in knots. However, when it comes to this woman, what I should do and what I do are two entirely different things.

I down the alcohol and wipe my mouth with my sleeve. Before I overthink this, I step out of the office and stroll down the hall to the room she claimed as hers after Esteban married Winifred. The way her brothers all have a designated suite in each of their homes for both of their sisters says so much about how close they are. I pause outside the door, knowing once I step inside, it could very well be the last time I ever do so.

The room is dark, making it hard to see anything. I sense her before I notice her and barely get out of the way before she makes contact. The grin that takes over my face has more to do with the fact I know how close she came to knocking me on my arse. If I'd been an average bloke, I'd be on the ground right now with a very pissed off female ready to do her best.

"Calm down, Ela. It's only me." I spin to face her and nearly go weak in the knees at the image she's presenting. Not only does it look like she might have knocked me on my arse, but gutted me as well once I was down. "Damn. Remind me to warn your guards to never sneak up on you while you're sleeping."

The light flicks on and it's then I notice her knife is to cut the apple she's slicing into tiny bites. I've seen her eat an apple like this many times, mentioned how hot it was to watch her cut and then place the piece in her mouth using the sharp blade. It always made my cock rock hard, knowing she never once feared bringing something so dangerous to her lips.

I walk over and challenge her. "Are you going to share?"

She slices off a piece and offers it to me with her knife. I don't even flinch. I open my mouth and wait for her to bring it to mine. Once she's close, I lean forward and take the bite off slowly, being careful not to get cut by the sharp blade. The smirk on her face alerts me her mood has shifted since we last spoke.

"I'm still mad at you." She cuts another slice and slips it in her mouth. The fire in her eyes is still there, but the flame has calmed some. "But I'm high, so my anger has lessened slightly because of that. Now I have the munchies."

"High?" I sniff the air to determine if I smell the distinct aroma of marijuana.

"I forgot about that stash I once hid inside the torn velvet of my jewelry box. I wasn't sure it would be any good after all this time." Her glossy gaze proves she isn't lying. "Guess that shit doesn't go bad."

"You shouldn't smoke that shit. You could get in a lot of trouble for even having it. Maybe I should take it so you don't..."

Pointing the knife at me, she snorts. It isn't a laugh but more a noise that suggest I get over myself. "I had one fucking joint. It's not like I had this massive stash or anything. And for the record, that's only the second time I've ever tried it. I was fourteen, or maybe it was thirteen, somewhere around that age, right after my father's untimely death. Sir Damon and I smoked it out in the barn's loft. I do believe that may have been the first time I let a boy kiss me. I think he wanted to do more, but I still hadn't developed and there was not much for him to mess with. I only wore a bra because I didn't want anyone to know I was different. He did, however, get a hand over my clothes and squeeze the extra gel pads I shoved inside. Moaned about it, even, which made me giggle in my state of highness."

I run my hand down my five o'clock shadow and don't miss the way she gets that hungry expression. Even though she is pissed, there is that longing, that electric charge that lingers in the air. It takes all I have inside of me to not give her what I know she desires. Taking advantage of her now would be wrong, even though I want nothing more than to get lost in her and forget the rest of the world. "We need to talk."

Ela shoves another slice in her mouth, folds the blade into itself, and tosses the core into the trash. After she flings the cased knife onto her dresser, she stalks toward me. It reminds me of a hungry lioness getting ready to pounce on the prey she's about to devour. It doesn't help my state when she licks her lips and drops to her knees in front of me, her hands immediately flying to the snap of my jeans. "Talking is overrated."

I step back, only to discover myself trapped between the wall and the charming temptress. She doesn't slow down or give me a second before she rips my jeans open and has her soft hand wrapped around my throbbing cock. "I'll miss this very large serpent of yours. It definitely brings me pleasure, and I doubt I'll ever be able to find another like it."

Her words hurt. They make me feel like all I am, all I've been these last six weeks, is no more than a cock for her to ride. It explains why I lift her off the floor and turn the tables on her. Trapping her against the wall, with one hand seizing her wrist while the other applies pressure to her delicate neck. I'm not hurting her, because I could never do that. The heat resonating in her eyes, however, makes me wonder if she'd like it if I fucked her while holding her just like this. I know I would.

"Is that all I am to you? A large cock? Or am I more, and you're just afraid to admit it?" I ask through clenched teeth, a breath away from her tempting lips.

"Why do you care?" Her eyes are dilated, revealing so much. I see the anger, pain, and the unwelcome desire that she's experiencing for me. "You don't trust me. Without trust, there can be nothing more."

"Do you wish there could be more?" I growl, not really sure why I'm pushing this. "Tell me. The truth. If we could be more, would you want that?"

Sadness washes over her, and it guts me to the deepest parts of my core. "I don't know. I never wanted more before. I'm not clear I want it now, even. Can there be more for us? I have plans, Gino. I'm not sure how you fit into those." Admitting that is killing her, if she weren't high, I'm not sure she would have.

I have the answer I need. She may not have all the information she needs, but I cannot drag her into a world she hopes to escape. My breath catches in my throat as I swallow the words I crave to say. Now is not the time to share who I am. She has the right to live her life how she wishes without some fucked up arsehole throwing her off that course.

Releasing her, I spin and tuck myself back in my pants. I need to go before I can't. Over my shoulder, I apologize and pray one day she forgives me. "I'm sorry. What happened earlier, I was wrong. I should have trusted you. Good luck with your plans. I hope you get everything you want, Ela."

One arm winds around me from behind, gutting me. "Why does this feel like goodbye? Not just the end of us, but a forever goodbye?" Then she pounds against my back with her other hand, her anger coming out.

I place my hand on hers and soak in all she is and was to me. Take her punishment blows, knowing I deserve them. "Forever is a long time. Nothing besides death is forever."

"You aren't telling me something. Why?" Her hand slides under my shirt, her skin on mine sends a jolt through my body. "I think... I think you're scared too. Afraid to admit the same thing I am. It was never supposed to happen."

Spinning in her arms, I grab her face and look deep into her eyes. "What was never supposed to happen?" She doesn't say it, but I see it reflecting at me in her eyes. Goddamn if I can stop what happens next. Not when I know I feel the same way she does.

I scoop her in my arms and carry her to the bed. Drop her there and fall on top of her, our lips colliding hard at first then turning soft as if trying to say the words we cannot. I'm in no hurry to move this along. I want to take my time, to love her like only I can. She's not being as patient, so I stop her, doing my best to kiss the anger and urgency away. It seems to work, so I release her and take my time again.

Soft hands tug at the bottom of my shirt, and I let her help me remove it. We undress each other leisurely—Ela still trying to speed it up from time to time. With my encouragement we take our time to kiss, touch, and adore the skin exposed little by little. Each caress burns, making permanent unseen marks to my soul and hers. This will be a claiming that will forever bond us.

My breaking point comes when I spread her out before me. I stare down at her alluring figure and wonder how I'll survive without her. She is the air I want to breathe, the nectar I desire, the blood life that keeps my heart beating. My soul from this day forward will be entwined with hers. And my heart, my heart, will never beat for another.

I do my best to show her. Feast on her body slowly. Eat her sweet pussy like I'm starving. Her cries, moans, screams, and trembles only encourage me to keep going. Only her words stop me while I'm doing my damndest to drain every last ounce of her orgasm out of her.

"Fuck me, Gino, please." She is still determined to make this a fuck and no more, but she's begging and knowing I caused that makes me smile. "Please. I need you inside of me now."

I grab the bottle of lube from her top drawer and flip it open. Squeezing an ample amount into my palm, I apply it to my throbbing dick. "I'm done fucking you, Ela."

Her eyes find mine, confused. "What?"

"I said I am done fucking you. Tonight, I don't want to fuck. Tonight, I choose to make love to you. I'm taking my time and not stopping until I have nothing left inside of me. No more fucking." I grip my member hard. "No condom, either, if that's okay."

I watch her process my words. It takes her a second or two before giving in. Letting her true feelings take over, pushing the anger aside for now. She sits up enough to wrap an arm around my neck and tugs me to her. "No more fucking and no more condoms." Her lips are on mine, dragging me on top of her as she falls back onto the bed. "Make love to me, Gino. Make love to me until we are both unable to move or think, please."

And that's what I do. I slide into her slowly while kissing her. Wait for her to accept all of me and then I make love to her. I don't rush us. Even when I crave to pound into her, I force myself to take it slow. I need to draw this out for as long as possible. I do it until I can no longer stop the inevitable. When my balls draw tight, I explode inside of her. It pulls another orgasm from her as well, one that drains us of all our energy and has us collapsing on the bed.

I'm not sure how long we lay there. I think we drift off more than once. When the life in my limbs returns, I climb out of the bed and grab a washcloth to clean us. Her moans that escape, as I gently wipe off my cum leaking out of her, have me in knots. She's swollen and still throbbing. I can feel it against my palm.

Tossing the cloth onto the floor, I crawl in next to her and drag her into my arms. Kissing the top of her head, I wish we had more time. I wish we had forever.

"I love you," she breathes out quietly, as if trying to say it soft enough for me to not hear. I'm not sure she wanted me to, that it slipped out after I softened her up.

I lift her chin and stare into her copper brown eyes, letting her know she didn't get away with it. Then vow to be just as honest. "I love you too. Don't you ever forget that, no matter what. I love you, Ela."

She blinks back the tears threatening to spill from her eyes. The anger is still there, and I see her processing those last words, only letting them go when she yawns. "Same. Sleep now. We'll talk later."

We fall asleep gazing into each other's eyes. Me taking in every moment we have and wishing I could explain. Her trying to read my mind and getting more frustrated that she can't.

A few hours pass when I hear my phone buzzing. I crawl out of bed to retrieve it. The message flashing across my screen has my heart sinking. Glancing over my shoulder, I put the sight of her lying there to memory. I hope she forgives me. I pray she understands why I'm about to do this.

I get dressed and know this will probably be the last time I ever lay eyes on her. What I have to do, where I have to go, it is no place for her. I will forever love her and never forget this night or what we've shared these last six weeks. But it seems the moment has come for me to take my place far away from here and step into a battle I'm not sure I will win.

Chapter Fifteen

GABRIELA

W hen I woke that next morning, I knew he'd left me. That he wasn't coming back. I tried to hide that his action gutted me, ripped my heart out of my chest and left me bleeding out.

The ache in my chest grew with each passing hour without so much as a word from him, though I hid it well. I cried in the shower, only for the allotted time it took me to clean up, of course. Returned to Sevilla before my mother could see the pain that only she'd notice reflecting in my eyes. I made my way back to the dorms and went on with my life, the numbest I'd been in a very long time.

He made one attempt to explain, but it was clear I'd not be given the full story. I wasn't interested in half-truths or excuses. So, I'd opted to let him go and hopefully live the rest of his life with a huge open wound as large as mine. I replay it in my head way more than I should.

> GINO: Please don't be mad at me. I'd like to see you one last time before I have to leave.

> ME: The time for explanations was a week ago before you left my bed.

GINO: Where are you? I'm not playing here, Ela. I need to see you.

ME: Lorenzo's. Don't care. You made your choice, Gino, now I'm making mine.

GINO: We can do this in front of them, hash it out there or in private. That is the only option I'm giving you.

GINO: I'm twenty minutes out. On my way now. Decide.

ME: The nightclub where you stole my bike. It's there or nowhere. That is your only option.

GINO: Outside of the nightclub. I'm not having a serious conversation like this, shouting over loud music and annoying patrons. If you don't show, I'm hunting you down and you'll be sorry.

My phone rang five minutes later. His name flashed across it, so I picked it up and he doesn't wait, he just starts talking. "I'm not playing games, Ela."

"First and foremost, you are no longer the one calling the shots. Tell me what's so damn important it couldn't have waited another day. You've waited this long to reach out, so if you want me to meet you, then you need to tell me the truth. The truth, Gino. No excuses or more unclear explanations." My voice held a warning he should have taken seriously.

"I'm leaving. I'm not sure if and when I'll be back. I can't leave without telling you goodbye." He wasn't telling me the complete truth, only what he thought would work. It wouldn't.

The silence was worse than having me yell, or so I'd thought. He tried again, only giving me the smallest amount of information, hoping it would be enough to satisfy. "Do you like your social status, or would you rather be rid of it completely? It's your turn to be honest, too."

"I can't change who I am even if I wanted to. So, I don't see how that matters. You're only avoiding telling me the truth. Which also gives me

some insight into if you'll bother explaining at all. I think it's best we just end this now. You said we could do that once, call it quits when the time came. You're leaving. I'm not interested in half-truths about why. It's been fun, and you've certainly proven to me that love sucks and happily ever afters aren't for everyone. Goodbye, Gino." There was no anger in my voice, only hurt. I kept it soft, and made sure he had to really listen to catch every word.

That was several months ago. I'm not any better now than I was then. I hate him. Refuse to even speak his name. He taught me something, though, a lesson I'll never forget.

Love sucks. It only causes pain, and I'm not strong enough to deal with more heartache. Never again.

Thankfully, no one in my family dares to bring up his name, either. He resigned and then left the country and was all but forgotten. Good riddance. Have a nice life, cocksucker. If this is the man he is, then I'm glad it ended instead of dragging out.

Larkin and Antonio had their baby a few days ago. The princess is adorable. I'm so happy for them. But that fucking arsehole made this cute baby thing even harder on me. I stared at the new heiress to the throne, taking in all her cuteness, and all I felt was an emptiness inside. He'd woken a longing inside me I'd done my best to avoid. No matter how bad my heart might long for this one day, my head and body know it to be impossible.

My nights are filled with dreams of a baby with dark eyes, like his father. The kind that when he looked at me, pierced me to the depths of my soul. They would change instantly to those of a little girl with her father's curly hair, bouncing as she ran through the fields. When I'd wake, the sadness hit my core and crushed me more and more each day. Making me desire something I knew I could never entertain. Forcing me to hate him even more for being such a chicken shit who ran off without so much as a word.

No matter how badly I desired a baby, my safe place to grow one is no longer. I was one of the unluckiest females ever to walk the earth. Not only had it forced me to face leukemia as a child, as a teenager my doctors discovered small tumors growing in my uterus. While they turned out to be benign, even after being removed, they would regrow faster than any of us were comfortable with. And because no one wanted to take a chance—me included—on those turning into more, they performed a partial hysterectomy. The only thing left behind were my ovaries, because at sixteen, a still developing female, I needed them to help my body produce the estrogen required to keep me healthy.

We once again kept this new development quiet and out of the media. This was a choice mother and I made. My father was no longer with us to voice his concern. I had the surgery in Spain at a private facility under an alias. Everyone thought I was on holiday at an exclusive resort with my mother in Belize. We eventually visited the resort, but not until after my surgery. We stayed a month while I recovered—not only physically but mentally as well. Rage, sadness, worthlessness flooded my thoughts during those dark days. Mother did her best to help me forget how my life once again had forever changed. She was suffering right there with me. We healed together.

A couple of weeks ago, I was asked to stop by Dr. Wilson's office. She wanted to discuss a research program being conducted on fertility studying women who were like me. Clearly, there was no way a woman with my condition could carry a child without her uterus. What they were researching was the retrieval of mature eggs that could be frozen and later used for in-vitro via surrogates.

I had no reason to consider a surrogate, not at twenty, not at any age, really. But I might let them harvest eggs, not to keep, but to study, nothing more. Being a survivor meant mine may not be as healthy as they once were, and even if they were, there could be issues in the development once fertilized. Those eggs could allow them to determine how certain treatments affect the female reproductive system. I wanted nothing to do with the fertility side. That was more than I was ready to deal with. Once the researchers finish analyzing my unfertilized eggs, they would be destroyed.

The team would send a report through Dr. Wilson to inform me of what they learn. All of this would be anonymous, meaning no one would know they were royal eggs. I would be a number, one of many. The results would either be the final blow or offer me a trickle of hope.

Dr. Wilson thought I should do it for two reasons. She believed it would benefit the way young girls might be treated and possibly save them from the same fate of infertility I've faced. The other had more to do with me and the age I was. Because I was so young, she hated that I'd written off ever being a mother. Said that one day I might change my mind about wanting children. She'd been encouraging me to harvest my eggs and have them frozen now while it would be easier, instead of waiting. With the advancements in fertility constantly changing, she never wanted me to believe a child of my own was impossible. I, however, wasn't agreeing until I discussed it with my mother.

Which is why I'm back in Aragon now, to sit down and talk with her about what she thinks. My mother and I have always been close. We've had several heart-to-heart discussions about my life and how I planned to live it. She doesn't always agree with my choices, but never once has she told me I couldn't do something. My mother offers her advice and then lets me turn the information over in my head until I've made a final decision.

"Are you going to take classes during summer session or do some traveling?" Mother asks after we've caught up and ate our breakfast.

"I might travel after I have a few treatments done. Dr. Wilson told me about a research team she's working with. She'd like me to be a part of the study. It would be anonymous, of course. She's not part of the team in charge of what I'll be donating to. She's handling the surrogates." I go on to explain the entire program.

My mother nods and listens carefully. "That sounds interesting. So, you're thinking about joining it?" She pours us more coffee. "It will certainly help others like you."

"That's the plan if I join, to help others. I'm not comfortable being a part of the other side, though. They can study my eggs, but I don't want it to go further than that. I mean, what's the point? The likelihood of my eggs being healthy enough for fertilization is slim. I've been doing some reading on my own. Even if that were possible, the risk of birth defects is greater. That would be an unfair decision for me to make for a child. Taking a risk like that, knowing he or she would face a life that could be inundated with complications, would be selfish on my part. Life is hard enough as it is. I know more than most what it's like to not be like the other kids. I wouldn't want to put a child through that." I pause as a look passes between us, showing she disagrees. "What?"

"There is always a risk no matter what, Gabby. Every parent takes a risk when having a baby that things could go wrong. I'm not disagreeing with you, but I'm not agreeing either. It's your choice, of course. But if you're putting your body through all the prep work, why not also let them keep a few eggs in case you one day change your mind?" Reaching over, she takes my hand. "One day, you might decide you feel differently. I'm sure you could go through it all again if you did, but would it hurt to plan ahead?"

"I'm never getting married, mother. That's not in the cards for me. I tried this love shit, and it sucks. I'm not putting myself out there again, sorry. And I'm not doing it how you did the first time. I'm better off alone. Not everyone is meant to have a family or even fall in love." I lift my hand when she starts to speak. "Please, just know I've thought long and hard about this. I've got a plan and that other shit will only impede the life I want."

"It's your life, Gabriela. Your body and your choice. I'm only offering my opinion that you came here to hear." She stands and kisses me on the cheek, a gesture I've always found comforting. "I know you will make the best decision for you. I trust you to do that. You have to trust yourself now to do the same."

She's right. This isn't an easy choice. I need to give this some more thought, but no matter what, I think I'm going to join the study. It's my duty to help those who can't help themselves. Maybe what they uncover will make another child's life better. I just wish I knew what the hell I was supposed to do about the other. If this had happened before the chicken shit showed up in my life, there would be no question about what I'd do. Now all I can think about are those damn dreams that keep me awake at night. The family I come across as soon as my eyes close and sleep takes over.

Chapter Sixteen

GINO

One Year Later

It has been an agonizing year since I left my love alone in bed after we made love and opening my heart to her. The memory of that night, our first and last time to say those words, her body soft against mine while I loved her deeply, it all haunts me nightly. After this long, I thought the emptiness inside would lessen. It hasn't. Each day it grows and makes me one moody son of a bitch and more determined to make my uncle pay with his life for taking another from me.

I'm sitting in the home office of the place I've lived since leaving. It belongs to Beni. He's lived here most of his life. We've been trying to hunt down the missing pieces that brought me here. It started with a rumor that the once assumed murdered Princess Giovanna Luisa Kelemen, my precious sister, was alive.

I want it to be true. But find it difficult believing Kyle Leblanc would lie or leave her behind if she were alive when he rescued me. That he would allow me to suffer so many years from the loss of my family, when all this time she was alive somewhere far away from me.

So far, the rumors are just that. Every time we think we've found her, the girl is too young, too old, the wrong look, just all around, not her. It's as if we are chasing our tails, like someone is hoping to lead us on a wild goose chase to distract us.

I've yelled at everyone, broken a few glasses and one chair, and even punched one of our men when he looked at me the wrong way. The longer it goes on, the angrier I become.

Moments ago, we hit another dead end. I'm beyond spent. Ready to give up and tell them to go to hell. My demons are back, and they are dragging me slowly to the pits of hell. Without my angel to ward them off, their attack has my brain working overtime. The next person who delivers bad news very likely may lose his or her life.

Not even, Emoni, the woman Beni brought in to help—how I'm not sure, although I think it's obvious—is capable of warding them off. She clearly wishes to be a distraction, but I'm not interested. Lord knows she's tried. If I hadn't sent her on her way earlier with the others, I'm sure she'd offer to suck my dick—not that I'd let her. She's offered to do so much more, but I'm not interested. I've turned her down so many times I thought she'd get the message, but it seems she hasn't. Something about her warns me not to trust her, but Beni does, so I've left it for now.

I open the laptop and log in so I can check in on the one woman who never leaves my mind. My connections back home—Hermosa Islas will always feel like home—have helped me keep tabs on her. The men I made friends with, those who once worked with me, send me photos through Kyle and Bruno regularly. They drop those into an untraceable account. Keeping both of us safe from those who would harm her if they ever learned of our connection.

There's a special present waiting for me when I log on this time. A rare video of Ela with her niece. I even get the pleasure of hearing her voice as she talks to the little angel sitting on her lap. It's one she's taken herself, probably so she can later watch or share it with Nicolette when she grows up.

"Who's a big girl?" Ela is making a silly face and leans in to kiss the little one's chubby cheeks. The light in her eyes is missing and it kills me. "You are."

A sad expression washes over her face when another voice speaks in the background. I recognize it as Queen Larkin. "One day you will have one of these and I can tell you'll be a pro at it."

"I doubt that. I think babies are cute and all, but they are not for me." Ela picks her niece up and cradles her.

She seems to be watching someone. I'm guessing she's waiting for the other woman to walk away. Then once again she puts Nicolette in front of her and smiles, but it doesn't reach her eyes. "Shh. You promised you'd keep my secret, and a princess never breaks a promise. It's okay that I'll never have a little girl like you. It just means I'll have to steal you more so I can spoil you. Give you all the things your mommy and daddy won't." Then she leans down and kisses her cheeks before the video stops.

Fuck.

I should be there. I should be with her to comfort her when she gets sad like this. Take her in my arms and do whatever I have to do to make sure she doesn't get blue about any of that. It's clear her family is unaware she can't have children. I'm not clear why that is, but she's kept that a secret. If I were there, I'd share how damaging it is keeping secrets. I'd make her see secrets, destroy those keeping them and seep poison, slowly destroying everything around them.

I should know, right? My secret destroyed the most precious thing I had. Now I'm stuck here in this hellhole, waiting for what, exactly?

I flip through a few more photos before I log out and grab a drink. It's looking to be another long night of restless sleep. The strong alcohol helps me pass out eventually, but it doesn't stop the dreams that slip in when I close my eyes.

Drink in hand, I head for the large staircase, and, like always, Emoni is lurking and waiting. "Going to bed?"

I don't bother responding. I sip on my glass and ascend the stairs.

"I could help, you know? Take your mind off whatever is eating away at you. I'm okay with only fucking. We all need a good fuck sometimes to clear our heads." Her hand lands on my arm, and she squeezes.

I react. She never sees it coming. My tumbler drops to the floor, and

I have her pinned against the wall, my hand around her throat. "It wouldn't work."

There is fear in her eyes, even though she does her best to not show it to me. "If you like it rough..."

I squeeze harder, getting right in her face. "It won't work because you are not her. My dick won't even get hard for you because you aren't her. Could never be her. So stop trying to seduce me. I'm not interested."

"Is there a problem?" Beni asks behind us with concern in his voice.

I release Emoni slowly and shake my head. "Nope. I was just telling Emoni to go find someone else to bother. I'm going to bed."

Beni's eyes meet mine, and I know he understands I'm on the edge of losing my shit. "Emoni, maybe it would be best if you left."

"You're dismissing me?" She sounds pissed.

"I think it would be better if we reassigned you," Beni tells her as I leave him to handle this.

I don't bother sticking around to hear her protest. I'm done being nice. Fighting off her advances each time she senses I'm on the edge is getting old.

Stepping into my bedroom, I lock the door behind me and head straight for the bathroom. I need a shower and to whack off to the image burned in my brain. Emoni may not get my dick hard, but the thought of Ela does. My hand will offer me the help I require, letting me release some tension. It will never be the same as having her, but neither would Emoni. No one will ever be the same, and I've decided if I can't have her, then I'd rather suffer.

Had I dared to pin Ela against the wall out of anger like that, she'd have laid me out flat. Then, after I'd picked myself up, I'd have dragged her upstairs and buried myself so deep inside her she'd never be the same. Instead, I'm cursed to let my hand do the best it can, which sucks and only offers a small amount of relief.

I grab the bottle of bourbon and don't bother with a glass this time. I tip it to my lips and guzzle, letting the burn drop into my gut and pray when I pass out, I'll not dream tonight.

The dreams are worse than my reality. Because they are about the life I could have had with her if everything were different. The life we could have shared had I just told her the truth. And what kills me most is the fact I did this to us. I'm a chicken shit, and now I have to live with myself and this miserable life I'm doomed to live.

Chapter Seventeen

GABRIELA

The Royals

Present Day

I only have a few months left in the academy, which means soon it will be time for me to train in the field. My time here has taught me a lot about who I am. Not only that, but also what I'm made of. I've had to prove my worth more than once, show these twonks who think I'm just a pretty face why they don't want to fuck with me.

Only a few minutes ago, I had one of the worst twonks on his back, begging me to let him up. It happened for a few reasons. The reason most assume he ended up on his arse is because he volunteered to spar with me when our instructor challenged the group. None of whom have been able to keep me pinned. The real reason had more to do with what occurred a few nights ago when he approached me at the bar.

"I'm on to you," Jae baited while I enjoyed the rum and coke I ordered before heading home.

"Is that so?" I raised one eyebrow, not at all impressed by this piece of shit.

"You can't fuck your way out of a real situation, Princess. Spreading

your legs in the real world doesn't work the same as it does here." He ran *his sleazeball gaze down my body, making me want to throw up. "You're going to get someone killed."*

"Just because you are fucking your way through the academy doesn't mean I am." I narrowed my eyes and kept my face emotionless. *"Not all of us have to give free BJs to pass the classes. Any day, any time you want to test me, just say the word."*

I've learned that one must be able to talk the talk if I hope to get the other recruits to take me seriously. I'm not afraid of verbal banter and can go head-to-head with the best. When the women show the men up, most of those poor chaps don't like it. A few try really hard to intimidate and single out the weaker females, harassing them until they're crying or doubting themselves. I witnessed a real S.O.B grab a female recruit inappropriately. His hand ended up broken and his balls may never fall back out of his throat.

Jae hadn't learned his lesson outside the bar, apparently. One arse kicking by me wasn't enough for him. That night, his not so surprise attack to put me in my place backfired. He ended up on his back with a knife to his throat. It appeared he required another one with witnesses this time. Accompanied by a second black eye to match the one I gave him three days earlier. He was lucky I didn't cut his balls off with the switchblade I carried with me. Although, I believe he won't be using his pathetic, tiny dick anytime soon, either.

"Princess!" It takes all I have in me not to rage at that name, even when it's an instructor using it. "You are to report to the main house in ten. Seems they have an assignment for you. Don't disappoint me or I'll be the next one on the mat with you."

"Yes, sir." I try my best not to smile as I jog off to keep from showing up late.

I don't bother changing out of my workout clothes. When I enter the main building, I'm escorted to a conference room where a meeting is already underway. I enter and listen, not really understanding what's going on. As soon as I'm spotted, they ask me to take a seat.

As I'm about to sit, a familiar voice speaks. It's been a few years, but I never forget a voice. "It is lovely to see you again, Princess Gabriela. I'm Beni Kelemen, in case you forgot. How have you been?"

I stare blankly at the man I once saw inside Gino's apartment. "Why are you here?"

"We need your assistance. It is past time, really, but Simion is as stubborn as they come." When I shake my head, not understanding or knowing who he's speaking of, he goes on. "Gino."

I do my best to remain calm and not let that name affect me or rub me the wrong way. Should I ever lay eyes on him again, it will be too soon. He walked away and refused to give me an explanation. I hated him for it, because I knew he was hiding something, and after our late-night confession, I expected more from him. He disappointed me and now I've moved on.

"Find someone else. If I see him again, I have plans that probably won't help you." Like kill him with my bare hands, or better yet, gut him slowly while I watch him suffer.

"Tell me what you know of him." Beni smirks, sitting tall in his chair. Head held high, he maintains eye contact, not intimidated by who I am. And that makes me leery of him. I don't trust him at all.

"He's a chicken shit who isn't worth my time." I push my hands against the table and stand. "He can rot in hell as far as I'm concerned."

The older man covers his mouth with his fist to conceal his smile. "Hell would be a reprieve for him, I'm certain. Nevertheless, he needs you. Even if he won't admit it, he requires your help. If you cared for him at all, I ask you... no, I beg you to think long and hard about how you would feel should he die at the hands of a madman. I plead to the woman inside of you to listen closely. Wishing you would come to understand, deep within the depth of your soul, that he did not leave you behind because he had a choice. He left hoping to save the life of someone he thought he'd lost many years before. Now he's locked in a prison controlled by his enemy, who, should he ever learn of Gino's true identity, would execute him immediately. Each day he remains there, the chances of that becoming a reality grows. Are you saying you have no problem letting him die, when you could save him and keep his true identity protected? Are you that angry with him? Do you hate him so much you would—"

"Enough! I get it. Are you going to bother telling me who he is or are you using his mysterious identity to pique my curiosity, hoping to get me to agree?" I see the answer shining in his eye before he opens his mouth.

"It is not mine to tell, Princess."

"Never call me that." I warn him.

"Are you not a princess?"

I pop my knuckles by pressing my fingers hard against each other to maintain my cool. "If I had my choice, I'd not be one. Being born into a family of nobility does not make a person deserving of that title. I was never meant to be some pretty princess who kissed everyone's arse and smiled on demand. I was born a warrior. A woman who has fought every day on this earth to have a life worth living. A life I will choose, not one someone else demands I choose. So, drop the princess and call me by my given name."

"Gabriela, it is not my story to share. When the time is right, I hope Gino will do so. Until then, however, since you are determined to have choices, will you choose to aid me or will you force me to find another way to save him?" He slides a picture across the table, an older one of a young boy standing next to a girl who is smiling up at him. I recognize those eyes so black they appear to be staring right through me. "Will this boy get his chance to shine and be the leader we have all been waiting on?"

I don't understand what he means, and I know if I ask, I'll only get the runaround. "Will I get my chance to kick his arse for misleading me?"

"That will be your choice, of course. I'm not sure he misled you, though. I think he only wanted you to have a choice as well." Beni rubs his chin slowly. "But it is hard to make choices when not given all the facts, isn't it?"

Not that I'll be given a choice about helping him, not if I want to be a member of Elite Forces. So I accept that fact and nod, although I'm not happy about it at all. Maybe I'll finally learn something about the man who still haunts me.

For the next several hours, I am briefed about the situation Gino seems to have gotten caught in. There are a ton of holes I know I'm missing. But if I've learned anything during my time here, it's that only those in charge know the details. The rest of us are only given what we need to know to get the job done. I'm certain this is a test on how well I take orders and follow them without asking more questions. So, I don't bother asking, I only listen.

Before the night is over, I'm boarding a plane with Beni and two of my personal guards, Yvette and Ashton. I'll be forced to play the dutiful Princess Gabriela Angela Reyes once we land in the newly established Federation of Kosonia. As her I'll demand they release one of our citizens, Gino Luka Leblanc, one of the King's Guards and a protected soldier. Claim he was acting on his king's orders to hunt down the men responsible for helping Viktor Del Markov escape Hermosa Islas. They've given me three more names to drop, one at a time, should they refuse to hand him over to me. All three names ring a bell. One of them sends chills down my spine for some odd reason.

My plan is to do a little research of my own once in the air. I may not have asked questions, but I know how to investigate better than most. My hacking skills served me well when I was younger. It is one reason I was so good at sneaking out of a place as secure as the palace. When you hack into such a secured system, like the one used at the palace, without leaving evidence behind, it makes things so much easier. Cameras, door locks, and alarms all needed to be manipulated so I'd go undetected. I never shared my ability with anyone, even to get accepted into the academy, because I still use it to get past those guarding me. It's my little secret. Funny how no one suspected a princess could also be a hacker, but I was one of the best and not afraid to get my hands dirty.

Chapter Eighteen

GINO

The last person I expected to come rescue me out of this Kosonia prison was her.

I'd gotten myself in a jam and arrested by the corrupt police, who were paid to look the other way. Set up by Emoni, a woman who had her eyes on me once she suspected I might be someone important. For the last few years, she's been trying to worm her way into my bed, only to fail. I had no interest in bedding anyone other than the one woman I was sure I'd never get the chance to bed again. So instead of settling for meaningless sex, the kind I knew wouldn't bring me release, I'd opted to abstain.

The truth is Ela has always been on my mind. The day I walked away from her is the same day everything in my life changed. I'll never forget our exchange or her spoken words a few days after I left her alone in bed, still warm from our lovemaking. Her words still gut me and make me wish everything, including us, could be different.

I play those last hours over and over again daily in my mind. Remember the conversation word for word and wish I would have handled it differently. The tracker on her phone disappeared immediately after she hung up. I waited as long as I could wait at the nightclub. She never showed up. I never got the chance to tell her more lies or partial truths. What we had was done, and now I was a man with an even bigger hole in my heart.

The last four years, I did my best to not think about her. Had plenty of other business to handle while I tried to understand the dynamics of a country I once called home. Spent my days and nights trying to be the person they wanted me to be. Feeling lonelier than ever and lost most of the time, annoyed by women like Emoni who thought they could take the place of the woman I gave my heart to. The only thing that kept me from tossing it all away was the intel we'd received about my family. It is why I left her to come here. Finding out if what they claimed was true has proven to be nearly impossible. I couldn't just walk away, knowing there might be a sliver of hope my sister Giovanna was still alive.

That is why I'm here in prison as well. I'd been trying to pinpoint the men tracking her down. If she is alive, I need to find her first, protect her like I should have when I was twelve. Instead, I got caught setting a trap for those men.

I know it was Emoni who turned me in. I might have led her to believe if she helped me with a certain problem, I'd give her a chance to win me over. She'd been able to get me exactly what I needed faster than I'd expected, which sent up several red flags. It was then I had to wonder where her loyalty truly laid. I began suspecting she was playing both sides and tested her. Sure enough, my gut had been correct. When Cezar learned of her ties to the very man he despised— more than I did—he fired her and kicked her out from under the protection of his organization.

Cezar Kovaloff's family was one who still had a lot of pull in the New Federation of Kosonia. A country trying to form a new government inside the corrupt system that poisoned everything it touched. Weeding out the old to bring in the new was not easy. It took time and lots of money, blood, and patience. Not to mention trusting other leaders of the world to aid in the process. It all was taking way too long.

Until the dragon, who was determined to not let the new settle in and start fresh, got his head cut off, the battles would continue. More corruption would seep in, destroying all the progress being made. Hunting dragons wasn't as easy as it sounded, and each time we felt close, something always got in our way.

I'd been this close to getting the answer to where the leader of our enemy was hiding. Only to get picked up by the local police, accused of being a traitor plotting an attack. Thrown into the worst prison Kosonia had, hoping I'd be taken care of by the felons once they caught word of the charges being brought against me. A traitor on the outside was considered one on the inside as well, and they hated traitors.

Beni Kelemen was a man of many resources. His connections on the inside have kept me alive while he bargains with the best to get me released. Eleven months I've sat in the pits of hell. A place where I was forced to kill or be killed a few times. No one cares about the prisoners in this underworld; they are left to govern themselves. It was survival of the fittest, and the rest be damned.

I'm a mess at the moment. My nose was broken a few days ago and set by the inmate paid to protect me. I have cracked ribs. Each time I move my stomach revolts due to all the other shit wrong with me. There are cuts and bruises on top of cuts and bruises, some of which are infected. I'm dehydrated, malnourished, and God only knows what else. If I'd spent one more day inside, I'm not sure I'd have made it out alive. I'm uncertain I won't die still.

The guards didn't bother cleaning me up. They drag me behind them when my feet give out, and then toss my weak body on the ground once we are a few feet outside the doors of Hades. Freedom and fresh air have never smelled so good.

There is yelling. My head pounds harder as the sound gets louder. The guards are shouting at someone as they kick me hard in the side to make some point. One of them yanks on my dislocated shoulder, making me roar in pain, just because he can. It was his parting gift to me before telling me someone paid a hefty price for my release. One last beating on the other side of the cell block I'd called home, where I'd thought my grave would be.

"Get your hands off of him. What the hell is wrong with you?" A female voice breaks through the fog crowding my brain. I know it all too well and can hardly believe she would come for me.

My arm is yanked harder and I suffer a punch to one of my angry ribs. Pain shoots through me as bile rises in my throat. Just as quickly, my arm is released. I hear a loud thud followed by an *uff*. I don't hit the ground like I expected. Soft feminine arms catch me, holding my larger body up easier than they should be able to. My heart speeds up when it recognizes hers. Her strength has always been one of her greatest features, not just her physical, but her mental.

"We have him now. You can go. Unless you want more, then, please, stay. I believe I might be in the mood to kick your arse. It's been a few days since I've gotten to practice my skills." She stands her ground, never once flinching when the second guard dares to come at her. Without releasing me, her leg sweeps out to the side, catching him in the chest. The heel of her stiletto ripping his shirt and making a visible mark he will be feeling for a few days. "We can do this all day. I believe it might be fun, even."

"Stop showing off." I cough when she adjusts me so I can stand taller. Looking at the guards, now clearly pissed and ready to have a turn at her, I give them a salute using my middle finger. "I truly enjoyed my stay. It was unlike any experience I've ever had. Maybe I'll come back for a visit."

Ashton, a man I trained several years ago, steps between us, letting them know to back off unless they want to look like me. Yvette joins him, along with two of Beni's men. After some verbal exchanges, the guards turn and head back inside, knowing when they are outnumbered and out skilled.

"What are you doing here?" I try to stand on my own, but I'm too weak. "Are you going to kick my arse too?"

Yvette takes flank on my opposite side and wraps her arm around my waist, aiding Ela as we slowly walk toward the caravan of SUVs. It should embarrass me that these two women are easily holding me up, but they're not your average women, either.

I moan as they guide me into the backseat. Every inch of my body aches, and my head feels like it might explode any moment. When the door closes, I use it to help me sit upright. Moaning again when the sweet scent of her invades my space as she tugs the seatbelt over my shoulder to strap me in. "Fuck. Is that really necessary?"

Her hand lightly brushes against my cheek as she studies my face. "You look like shit."

Our eyes lock, and I recognize the pain in hers. I can't tell if it is because I look that bad or if maybe it has to do with how I hurt her. "You look like—"

"Nope. You don't get to be nice to me. Don't think I won't kick your arse as soon as you can stand on two feet." Her hand cups my face, and I soak in the warmth.

When the vehicle moves, she drops her hand and takes mine. I know I have no right to enjoy her touch. I gave that up the moment I disappeared without telling her the truth. Hopefully she will forgive me, but I don't expect her to ever forget.

When we stop, I'm once again forced to walk. I don't miss the armed guards watching us with fierce intent as we board a plane. They aren't here to keep us safe, they are the enemy and I'm guessing would love to be given the order to shoot me. "Is this what it is like to get the royal treatment?"

Ela shakes her head, not amused by my jokes. "It seems you've made a name for yourself. They've ordered us to leave as soon as they released you. Warned us that should you return, they will charge you with treason and execute you immediately."

I nod, knowing I'll be returning one day. My business here is not even close to finished. And when I do return, it will be me giving the orders. The question is, will I have mercy on those who did this or will I want my revenge?

Stopping at the top of the stairs, I turn and wave at the men ready to take me out. "Thanks for the escort. I'm so glad you care."

"You really are something else." Ela pushes gently on my back, encouraging me inside before they decide to just shoot me.

When I go to sit in the first chair we come to, she doesn't allow it. "Not happening. We are heading straight to the stateroom."

"I've missed you too, sweetheart. But I'm not sure I have the strength to even get it up." I groan when she pokes me in the side, pain shooting through my entire body. "Fuck! Be careful."

Three others try to join us, but she cuts them off. "I'll call for you when we're ready. As soon as we are in the air, I'm helping him clean up. I think it will make the doctor's job easier."

I drop onto the bed and fall back, closing my eyes as I relax. The last time I laid in a bed was almost a year ago. I haven't had a decent night's sleep since then.

Actually, that isn't true. I haven't slept well since the last time I slept next to her.

"Gino." Her voice is soft as it says my name, and it takes all I have to focus. "Come on. Sit up."

I try but fail.

Slipping a hand behind me, she does her best to bring my weak body to a sitting position. It's then I realize my pants are gone, my arse bare before her. I didn't even realize she'd removed them. I also don't miss the tears streaming down her face as she inspects me while removing the tattered shirt sticking to my body, dried blood holding it in place. She shoves it inside a plastic bag and tosses it into the corner.

Leaving me momentarily, she heads to the lavatory. I hear the water run, a shower, I assume. She's back, and it's then I notice she has changed out of her power suit and into a tank and shorts. The body I once worshipped is different. Every curve more defined. Her arms toned, letting me appreciate why she could support me with ease. The legs that once gripped my waist while I power drove into her tight body, makes my dry mouth water. Her thighs are firm and powerful, sexy as fuck. Amazing calves flexing when she walks.

"I can explain. All of it. Everything." I take her hand and do my best to stand without relying on her. "Why are you being so nice to me?"

"Explain later." She helps me walk, or more like shuffle my feet, into the bathroom.

There's a mirror over the sink. It is the first time I've taken in my reflection for months. I look like death. My hair is a matted, mangled mess. My thick, unkempt beard is no better. Dirt and blood cover my skin, making it difficult to recognize the bruises I also know are there. I've lost weight, more than is healthy in such a short amount of time. I look nothing like the man I was. The shame I feel about some of the incidents that happened while in hell hits me hard.

"You can leave. I got this." I head for the shower and step inside. A bath would be better. I'm weak and it's hard to stand. However, we are on a plane and this is all that is available, so I'll do my best not to land on my arse in my state.

"I think—"

"I don't want you here. Leave." I let the water wash over me and close my eyes. It feels amazing. I've not had a shower since they tossed me in that prison. I can barely stand the stench. It's embarrassing to know she and everyone else had to suffer from it.

"I'm not leaving. You are too weak to do this alone. It's me or one of the others. I figured given the choice between me or Beni, I'd win. His hands are old and he'd not be nearly as gentle about it as me." She steps inside with me but I refuse to look at her. "Are you going to be an arsehole, or will you let me help?"

I don't answer, not until her hands start to wash me and it becomes too much. My vulnerability hits me; my shame, my anger all come out at once. "Stop! Don't touch me! Don't touch me!" I glare over my shoulder, trying not to give too much away on the new secrets I'll take to my grave. "Don't. Touch. Me. I got this."

She crosses her arms and steps back as far as she can, which isn't far. Thankfully, she isn't naked. She's still wearing the tank and a pair of black silky knickers. Not that it helps, but at least I'm not forced to witness her perfection and unable to touch her.

I wash off the best I can. It isn't easy, but it's better than having her hands on me. When I'm done, she steps out first, dries off, and then offers me a towel. Once back in the bedroom, I head straight for the bed. She watches, but doesn't touch me again.

Her reaction, the pain in her eyes, warns me she knows more than I wish her to ever know. "I'm going to get the doctor now."

"Gabriela," I growl as I fall onto the bed. "Only the doctor. You are no longer welcome. Thank you for your assistance, but our business is done."

"Fuck you, Gino." Her chin is high, but I don't miss the hitch in her voice. She knows I'm dismissing her, disconnecting from her by addressing her by her full name, and now she's pissed.

As soon as the door closes, I let out the loudest roar I am capable of. I hate myself for hurting her again. This has nothing to do with her, though. Not really. It is me. I've got shit I need to deal with that she will thankfully never understand. It's better to let her despise me than it is to drag her down into the pits of my newest hell. I cannot let my sins taint her, and I have more sins than ever before now. There is blood on my hands, a darkness to my soul, and a new hatred for those who did this to me. I will one day have my revenge, and I won't take the only light left in my dark world with me when I do.

Chapter Nineteen

GABRIELA

The Royals

I haven't seen or spoken to Gino since I walked out of the stateroom on the plane. Seeing him so distraught, frail, and distant broke me in ways I never knew I could be. I was mad and angry with him, but that didn't mean I wanted the man to suffer the way he had. What I aspired to do after seeing him was to go back to that fucking prison and make them pay.

I appreciated what on the verge of death looked like. I'd stared at it more than once when I was a sick, frightened little girl who sometimes wished for it. My body often resembled a beaten one, felt like it too. Every movement was painful and I remember I tried not to cry because it hurt. The only person I allowed to touch me was my mother, and I did that because I believe she needed to as much as I needed her to.

What was worse than me catching how awful I looked was watching my mother sympathize with me. She suffered right alongside me. Her face aged daily while she sat by my side and witnessed me slowly slipping away from her. So many nights she refused to sleep, afraid I'd pass while she rested and didn't want to miss a single moment, just in case. I'd had some very close calls, and I trust that to be why we are as tight as we are now.

I hated thinking about that stage of my life, but seeing Gino like that brought every single memory back to the forefront of my mind. I was so shaken by his appearance that the nightmares and the fear of the unknown have returned. They always center around the time I lost when they medicated me because the pain was so unbearable. I never knew what day it was and would wake up in a panic. All those scary memories once again flood my brain and keep me awake at night.

I dream about being horrified when my hair fell out. Crying as clumps came out in my hand. Eventually, I was left with a bald head. All three of my brothers visited and I was embarrassed my pretty long hair was gone. Lorenzo asked mother to shave his head so we matched. Esteban and Antonio followed his lead. They kept their heads looking like Mr. Clean until mine started sprouting again. My mother had wanted to shave hers as well, but I told her no. I loved her hair, loved running my hands through it, playing with it when she would lie next to me.

Then I dream of the day when the doctors realized I would need more than chemo. The treatments weren't working the way they expected. I would get better and then relapse very quickly. It was then they decided I required a bone marrow transplant to save my life.

My parents were already divorced. My father visited only when mother guilted him into it. I'd overheard them fighting, heard him more than once claim I wasn't his. When the family was tested and the only perfect match was him. Which is a rarity in itself, family members are usually the best match, not a perfect one. I witnessed the shame he felt. Until then, he'd been an absent father, keeping his distance and treating me differently than he did my brothers. After that day, things between us changed. He wasn't perfect by any means, but at least he tried from that point forward to have a relationship with me. We weren't close, but we shared a bond after having gone through my sickness and recovery together.

I still bear a few of the scars left behind. There was a port inserted into a main vein so I didn't have to be poked so much. That scar is just below my collar bone. Because I had so many mouth sores, making it hard to convince me to eat, a feeding tube was implanted. When I was at my worst, it was what helped keep my body alive and as well-nourished as possible. That scar is small but can be found on my stomach. There are also the ones left behind when my hysterectomy was necessary. Thankfully, the doctors performed it laparoscopically, so I only have tiny incisions.

My experience differs greatly from what Gino went through, or is still going through. But I feel like maybe I understand some of it, at least. Needing space to recover without the sympathy of others reminding you of a time you'd rather forget. That is why when he'd asked me to leave, I did it and then kept my distance. For him and for me.

When I overheard Gino was one of the private body guards Sir Edward hired to protect my mother, I'd done my best to avoid him. It wasn't difficult to do the week I was on leave. He also seemed to not want to have any contact during that time. He would stay outside or hide in the designated guards' area, absent from anywhere I might be. Not ready to face me, and that was fine. I wasn't ready, either.

The times I ran into him were intense. He wasn't the same man I once knew. The light that had previously been there was missing from his eyes. He was angrier, colder, and possessed a sadness about him that made me want to fix him, even though I realized how impossible that would be. It also hurt knowing he didn't seem to welcome me to be part of his life anymore. I certainly wasn't one to push someone to choose what they didn't appear to want.

Each day that passed, I'll admit, turned me a little more bitter. It had me questioning what had transpired between us during those months before he disappeared. But I wasn't about to force him to explain himself or to put myself out there, only to get my heart ripped from my chest again. Never again would I allow someone in. I'd set it all behind me the best I could and was trying to move on. Not that moving on was easy, or that I was ready to let a man into my life. It seemed easier to just focus on my career and invest in a vibrator or two to take care of the rest.

That didn't mean I stayed home and didn't have fun. I was still a woman who remembered what it felt like to be held. Sometimes I craved physical touch and tried to determine if there might be another who could make me forget about a certain someone. It seemed I wasn't alone in that particular quest.

It's the first time I'd run into him in months. We're at one of those places you go when you're looking for a very explicit kind of hookup. I'm here with my brother's friend, Lord Crispin Oliver. We've grown closer these last couple of years. He's fond of my cousin Mercedes, but she's not so fond of him. So, when he visited Sevilla or I was in Aragon, we went out as friends, no more.

At the moment, he is a little downhearted. Mercedes just got engaged to the man she's been dating for the last year. Both of us believe it's a bad idea. I don't know why, really, there is just something about this guy I don't like. Crispin, on the other hand, hates him because he obviously thinks he would make Mercedes happier. And because she is also pregnant, he realizes he's lost his chance to prove otherwise.

Thus, the reason we are at this establishment. I don't even know what to think about this place. It's a unique marque strip club designed for everyone who dares to enter. There are topless waitresses and male servers wearing mesh thongs that do nothing to hide their packages. I've watched male and female dancers perform on stage. One couple danced a duet, and it felt like I was a voyeur to a private moment between them. The only thing they didn't do was the deed itself. Although they had their lips and hands everywhere, and I mean everywhere.

It undoubtedly isn't my scene, although Crispin is having a good time. He's enjoyed a few lap dances, slipped off with one waitress—I'm pretty sure she blew him—and flirted with so many female patrons, offering a few promises of meeting up with them another time. The man was not ashamed of his freeness to all things sexual, and we are here because he suggested it. I'm not sure I'll let him drag me back anytime soon.

I've been hit on more than once myself. One fella is being very persistent, but I'm handling him fine on my own. However, it seems someone disagrees and suffers the need to step in. I might have been grateful if it had been anyone but him to do so.

"She's not interested." The deep rich tone announces from behind me. My body defies me and reacts, pissing me off.

"And you would be?"

This man must have a death wish mouthing off like that.

I nearly jump out of my skin when a finger traces the length of my arm as his lips land on my bare shoulder. "The only man she wants."

I cough into my hand as I slip out of my seat, away from the only one who has ever had any effect on me. "Not anymore." I try to sound convincing, but even I don't believe my words.

"Seems she disagrees."

Mr. Death Wish attempts to touch me, but before he can, I bend his wrist back, bringing him to his knees.

"What the hell?"

"Did I ask you to touch me? No." I release him and head for the exit, needing to leave before I get caught up in Gino again. "Don't follow me, either of you."

Crispin is dancing with a woman, so I tap his shoulder when I pass him. "I'm leaving."

He leans forward and kisses his dance partner on her cheek, whispering in her ear before he follows. "Where are we going now?"

"I'm going home. You're welcome to come with me if you dare," I inform him as we step outside, glancing over my shoulder, knowing we are being followed.

Crispin chuckles as he slides his arm into mine. "Is that a proposition?"

I start to answer him, laughing at his playful banter. But before I can, he is being dislodged from my arm and about to get a face full of fist. The rage in Gino's eyes has me very worried. I've never seen him this mad before, and Crispin has always joked around inappropriately with me. He means nothing by it.

"Stop! What the hell are you doing?" I step between them and pray he doesn't finish the punch that is about to collide with my cheek. Unfortunately, he's unable to pull back, and I end up taking the full power of that blow, making my vision blur. "Fuck. Goddamn you."

Strong arms catch me before I hit the sidewalk. Two sets of them, actually. They are accompanied by foul language and male voices yelling at each other. Both men accusing the other for making my face feel as if it is on fucking fire. Arguing who's going to take care of me while I try my best to shake off the fuzziness and both men.

"How about you both shut the hell up?" I manage to finally scream. "I don't need either of you to take care of me."

While I get my bearings, I lean against the brick building. Before I walk to my bike and ride home, I need to catch my breath. It's not the first time I've gotten punched in the face, but those other times I'd been expecting it. Sparring can be very physical, and in the academy, we didn't have the option of using protective gear. Recruits have to learn how to take a blow and keep fighting, part of our preparation.

Hands grip my face and I hear Crispin's softer voice. "That's going to hurt for a few days."

I cringe, because it hurts like a son of a bitch already. "No shit, Sherlock."

"Get your hands off of her." Gino's harsher voice roars as he bats Crispin's hands away.

"Would you stop already? Cris is a doctor or at least has a medical degree. You're just a brute with one hell of a left hook." I go to bring my hand to my face only to have it seized by a rough, hard palm.

"Fuck. Don't touch it. Goddammit. Why did you step in front of him?" Gino shoves Crispin to the side and lifts my chin with his thumb. The moment makes my head spin. "Fuck."

Knocking his hand away, I urge him back and push my body off the wall. "I'm going home."

"I'll take you." Gino grabs my arm and tugs me in the opposite direction of where my baby is parked. That does nothing to help my head, it's making me dizzy. "You're in no shape to drive."

I break free of his hold easily and flip him off. "I don't need you to take me home or even take care of me. I've managed just fine these past four years without you."

I make it five steps before I stumble, wobble, and then puke all over the sidewalk. My head is spinning, my shoes are like bricks on my feet, and my stomach is churning from all the pain and change of direction. I'm sure them jerking me around like I was some fucking toy, didn't help.

"This is what we're going to do." Crispin's voice echoes in my ear, like he has it all figured out. "Big guy there is pulling his vehicle around and then we're taking you home. I think he may have given you a concussion. Which means we need to monitor you all night. And since I'm a little on the not so sober side, and he's far gone on the I'll kill anyone who dares to touch her side. It will take the two of us to do it. No arguing."

Gino must have listened, because in a few minutes I'm being led to the passenger seat of a nice Porsche, a familiar one. Before I can sit, Crispin slithers into the small space between the boot and seat. Not really a backseat, but he fits. I notice Gino shaking his head as he helps me take my seat.

"You still own this piece of shit," I bait once he climbs in and speeds off.

"My sister kept it for me." He shifts gears. "Where do you live?"

"You mean you don't know?" I have a hard time buying he doesn't know this; he always knew it all before.

"Surprisingly, no." He sighs and rolls his neck.

I'm not sure I want to take him back to the apartment I moved into a few weeks ago. I like the place, and I don't want to hate it because it will now hold memories of him. "Maybe you should just take me to Fort Serna. My guards stay there. They can look after me."

Crispin chuckles in the backseat. He's onto my real reason for not wanting Gino in my place. We've talked a lot over these past four years. He knows more than most do. Just like I know how he feels about Mercedes.

"Address or I'll take you back to mine," Gino threatens, and his tone warns me he's not joking.

I rattle it off quickly, because going back to his place can't happen. I've avoided the area entirely since he walked out of my life. Why do I get the feeling he's once again aiming to be a colossal pain in my arse?

Chapter Twenty

GINO

The Royals

Everything I've worked so hard for since returning to Hermosa Islas went to shit the second I walked into one of my old haunts. I once frequented places that allowed me to find a certain type of woman. Those who were fine with a quick hookup and never asked for more. That is exactly what this place is and there was a time it was what I craved.

I am no longer that man.

The only reason I'm even in Sevilla is because a contact of mine said he had information for me. We always meet in places that are less than stellar and a little rough around the edges. It keeps matters between us private. He suggested this place, and for some stupid reason, I agreed.

The last place I want to be is in a joint like this. The farthest thing from my mind is sex. And this place promotes it in a way that no longer interests me after living in hell for a year. It reminds me of when the guards would punish the female prisoners by throwing them in with the males. It was one of the most disgusting punishments I'd been forced to witness and listen to—twice. Even though everyone was here because they chose to be, the grabbing, groping, and open sexual acts brought all that shit back to my mind and sickened me.

We are sitting in a booth where I can keep an eye on the room, not allowing anyone to sneak up behind me. Which only makes it worse. I can't ignore the activities around us. I feel edgy, have been ever since I got out. That's what happens when you're forced to be on alert every second. The only thing that brought me any peace while there were the memories I have of her. The ones I focused on when fire and brimstone fell down around me.

Sending her away the day she came for me saved her from the devil who now lives inside me. I feared what would happen if she stayed. What I would do when I eventually asked her to help me ward off the darkness. So instead of dragging her into my turpitude, I sent her away, suffered the nightmares, and plotted my revenge.

"Are you even listening to me?" Mika taps his shot glass against the table. "You need to get fucked."

I glare at him. "What I need is for you to find the person we've spent four years searching for. If you can't, I'll hire someone who can."

While his eyes follow the waitress passing us, he shakes his head. "I'll find her. We have another problem that needs our immediate attention."

I'm so sick and tired of problems. It seems all we ever have is problems. "What?"

"Someone figured out Simion Kelemen isn't dead." Mika has my full attention now. "They haven't worked out who he is, from what I've been able to learn, but it's only a matter of time. It gets better, so hold your questions until I've finished."

I close my eyes, knowing I won't like this at all. "Continue."

"The rumor states the young boy fled his home in Kosonia after murdering his parents and sister. Hid in the woods until his uncle showed up days later to determine why he couldn't get ahold of his brother. He claims Simion left with a tactical team who was led to believe the boy was fleeing a massacre lead by the revolutionists. He's offering a hefty sum for any information that will help him hunt down the now dangerous man." The sides of his lips curl. "Here's a photo of what they suspect he looks like."

I tilt my head and stare at the photo and struggle not to laugh. "You're serious?"

He scoffs and throws back another shot. "Apparently Simion is a large, short, stocky man who hasn't aged well. Balding, even. Loves to gamble and drink while he hosts sex trafficking parties. A real menace to society who needs eliminated. It's all in the report attached to his new contract on the dark web. It will do what he wants it to do, keep everyone's ears open to anything that points them in the right direction. Don't look so worried, I've got it covered. Cezar and Beni are sending everyone on a wild goose chase, and I'm keeping a very close eye on Dracul."

"I'm not buying he believes this." I point at the ridiculous photo. "This is only a distraction. He's up to something, and I don't like it."

"I agree. Which is why I'm watching him. Tracking every breath he takes. You need to be ready to move soon. Which means you need to get your shit together, so when the time comes, we can cut the head right off the dragon and end this once and for all." Mika rubs his chin and clears his throat. "Don't hate me. But it's time to form that alliance you've been fighting. She's the warrior you need. Even if you cannot see that, the rest of us can."

I turn just in time to notice Ela sitting at a high table with some tattooed, pierced, very eager male, eyeing her like a piece of fresh meat. I can't blame him. She's the sexiest woman in the joint. Dressed in tight leather pants, a red silk blouse, and six-inch heeled boots that make her arse pop. The high ponytail only adds to the fantasy too many men in this rathole have. She's a walking wet dream in a sea of lust hungry males who assume every woman here is theirs for the taking.

I'm not really sure what happens after that or how we end up outside. All I know is I see red more than once and somehow my fist ends up landing on her face instead of the pretty face of Lorenzo's friend Crispin.

I recognize the man, remember him well. I watched the way his eyes traveled down her body the night of the fight. I've seen them together more than once since my return. He isn't good enough for her, and I act without so much as a thought.

Mayhem is what I feel now as I drive to the address she spouted off after getting her into my Porsche. Twat face is with us, and I'd love nothing more than to get rid of him.

"Where can I drop you, Cris?" I glare in my rearview mirror, hoping he can read my warning.

He doesn't. Scooting between the seats, he smirks. It would be so easy to break his face now.

"Do you know what signs to look for that could be very dangerous when a person is concussed? No? Shame, cause I do, fuck face. Plus, if you think I'm leaving you with her after the shit you pulled last time, you can think again."

I take the corner a little harsher than necessary, sending his unbuckled arse all over the back. I'd chuckle at the thud and *ugg* sound he makes if it weren't for the unamused expression on Ela's.

We walk into her small studio fifteen minutes later, and she tosses her purse in a chair. "I'm going to change. Don't kill each other while I'm gone."

Crispin moseys over to the couch and falls onto it dramatically, getting way too comfortable. "You can go. I'm the one with medical training."

I don't, of course. Instead, I drop into a chair and cross my arms. "If you think I'm leaving her with your drunk arse, you're fucking crazy. She can do better than you."

The arsehole laughs. "Really? You mean like you? I believe that ship has sailed, and you sank it all by yourself. I may not be the best man out there, but at least I'm man enough to not leave without so much as a fucking explanation. You broke her heart and spirit. I'll be damned if I sit back and let you do it again. Over my fucking dead body."

I crack my neck and don't even blink. "That can be arranged."

"What can be arranged?" Ela walks into the room wearing an oversized t-shirt. I really pray she's hiding a pair of shorts under it.

It's then I recognize the shirt instantly as the one she stole after our first night together. It has Great Britain's flag on it. My sister, Heidi, bought it for me when she visited their country the year I turned nineteen. It was well worn the day she slipped it inside her backpack. The dang thing is so thin now you can almost see through it. Those dark areolas of hers can be seen if you look close enough.

The smirk on Crispin's smug face tells me he also notices.

"You need to change your shirt, Ela," I growl, hoping to embarrass her enough to get her to do just that.

In one swift move she has the shirt off and over her head flashing us.

"I hate that shirt, anyway. You should take it with you." Then she spins on her heels and heads back to the bathroom.

I glare at Crispin, who has his head thrown back, grinning like an arsehole. "Gotta love her charisma."

Before I can respond, Ela is back in a much more revealing lacy camisole. This is clearly her rebelling against my earlier complaints, proving the thin t-shirt was the better choice. Fucking hell, she's going to cause her friend's death, because there is no way he's not thinking what I'm thinking.

Standing, the prick grabs his crotch to adjust himself and strolls up to her. "You are so bad."

Rolling her eyes, she glances down at her outfit and shrugs. "This is way more comfortable."

I nearly shoot out of my seat when he kisses her swollen cheek and pats her arse. "I'm leaving. I have a meeting tomorrow afternoon. I can catch the train back now and still have time to sleep all this off. Plus, if I stay here, his head just might explode, making an awful mess."

Pointing his finger at me, he lowers as if talking to a child. "Don't let her have caffeine. If you can, try to keep her off her phone. Screen time is best if limited. She needs to ice her cheek for fifteen minutes before she goes to sleep. And make sure to check on her at least once during the night. Wake her if you are brave enough. Think you can handle all that?"

I nod, but don't speak.

Ela leads him to the door, and I hear them whispering, hear his laughs mixed with hers. It's the loud smack on her arse that has me whipping my head around, just in time to watch him plant one on her lips. Nothing sloppy, a quick and meaningless kiss, if her playful shove is any indication.

"You really don't need to stick around. I can take care of myself," she declares as soon as the door clicks.

"Are you dating him?" I blurt out as I stand, going directly to the freezer to find ice for her cheek.

"So, what if I am? It is none of your business who I date or fuck. You gave that right up the day you left." She rests her elbows on the high counter and blows out a frustrated breath of air. "I don't want to hear it now, either. The time for explanations has long passed. You made your choice Gino, now you are going to have to learn to live with mine."

Tossing her the bag of peas I found, I do my best not to breakdown and tell her everything. Because she's right, I made a choice. It may not have been the right one, it may not have even been a fair one for me to make without her, but I made it, and now I have to live with it. "Ice your cheek while I use the bathroom. I'm not leaving tonight. I wrecked your face, and I want to make sure you don't get sick again."

My feet carry me to the small bathroom in five strides. I shut the door and take a few minutes to glare at the man staring back at me. He's very disappointed in me and the way I've handled everything. If he had his way, he'd march out there and spill all my secrets, force her to understand I didn't really have a choice. That like her, I was born into a world I didn't appreciate or want to be a part of. The difference being my role was more like Antonio's, out of my hands, really, because there were people counting on me to make their lives better, end their suffering. If I refused, then their blood, the blood of their children, would forever stain my hands.

This time when I throw my fist, I do it at the reflection in the mirror, shattering it into a thousand shards. "Fuck!"

Chapter Twenty-One

GINO

The Royals

The darkness is what makes this place a living hell. When the night falls, there is no light, only thick black shadows. The cold, the screams of pain, the smell of death permeating the hallways.

Tonight is the worst it's ever been. New blood arrived earlier, those now sentenced to suffer in this prison. Nights like this are when conditions always go from bad to hell quickly. The guards turn blind eyes and ears to what is brewing and let the depraved have their fun.

No one is safe.

I took a beating only hours ago for not speaking when asked who I was and what I was doing in this country. They've labeled me a traitor, an enemy who was here to destroy those in office. It wasn't a lie, but I wasn't about to admit my true identity to anyone. That would be a death sentence, and I'm no good if I end up dead. I remained silent. Beaten repeatedly for being uncooperative until I collapsed unconscious. They tossed me back into my dirty cellblock for the animals inside to finish me off once night fell.

A few inmates look out for me. I'm guessing Beni paid them well to do so. In exchange, I'm sure he's sworn to take care of their families, or made promises of how life for them one day would be better when the corrupt got what was coming. But it's impossible to hold back the worst on nights like this, and when they come, it's every man for himself.

It is kill or be killed.

And these shitheads don't just kill you, they fucking torture you. The cruel acts they favor turn the stomachs of those forced to watch. And tonight, they are coming for me.

I know it. Those who stand by my side know it. We would be fighting for our lives and dignity as men. My weakened state makes me a much easier target, but I'll be damned if I'll let them hold me down so they can defile me, to make me carry shame or break me like that.

I'm prepared. A rusty chunk of metal is hidden in my dark corner, sharpened to cut deep and do as much damage as I can until either my time in this world ends or daylight breaks. All my training will help me survive this for as long as I can.

"Look at him. He's lying there like a secondhand whore ready for us." One of them snarls when he discovers my hiding place. "You hold him down while I enjoy him first."

Through slitted eyes, I notice there are only two tonight. The others must have decided they would have better luck with fresh blood than me. I've given them a few scares when they've tried this before. But these two have been after me since I arrived, and tonight it will be their last time to ever defile a man.

I allow the first bastard to get into position. He's a large bloke, but he's not strong. There is a difference. As soon as he's close enough, I strike swiftly, hitting my mark. Letting out the biggest battle cry I have in me, I roar. Blood from his neck gushes, and he gasps for air. He tries to stop it from spilling out of him with his dirty hands, but very soon all his blood will pump from his body and coat the ground.

The sight of his comrade wheezing and stumbling grants me enough time to attack the other shithead when he least expects it. His wound won't bring death to him quickly, but he will die from it within the hour. I watch him stagger as he does his best to keep his insides from falling out of the deep slash I implemented before he even saw it coming.

"Take that, you motherfucker. How does it feel to be gutted like a fish?" I roar as I wipe his blood on my shirt and yell loud enough that it echoes off the wall. "I will gut every last one of you if you try to fuck with me. Do you hear me? Come see for yourselves if you don't believe me. The next one who tries this shit will get his cock sliced off and then choke on it as I ram it down his goddamn throat."

I let out a piercing howl as my sanity starts to slip away. It is so loud I sound like one of them, deranged and driven, emerging from the depths of hell. I collapse to my knees, still roaring, coated in blood as the smell of death fills the air.

My body jolts as I wake. I'm covered in sweat and the taste of bile drenches my mouth. As I look around, I realize I'm no longer in the hell I once thought I would die in. I'm safe and in a warm home, with a soft blanket wrapped around me.

It was just a dream, a nightmare, of a time I wish I could forget. Taking a deep breath, I let my brain remind me where I am and why.

The second our eyes lock, I know Ela heard me. There is pain on her face and tears streaming down her cheeks, telling me she knows more than I ever wished her to. I'm ashamed of what happened, of the acts I was forced to do to make it out of there. We don't speak, but she makes it clear with just a look that my secret is safe with her.

Chapter Twenty-Two

GABRIELA

Apparently, I fell asleep shortly after lying down on my bed with a bag of peas pressed to my face. Getting punched by a two-hundred plus, solid brick of a man must take a lot out of a girl who only weighs a buck twenty-something.

I wake when my phone buzzes with that sound I dread most mornings, but on a Saturday, it's so much worse. Why do they insist on making us work seven days a week, up before the sun, and start with the physical, even on the freaking weekends? I guess they're preparing us for the long days we'll face once in the field. No rest for the soldier who sneaks behind enemy lines, or in my case, uses her status as a princess to gain access to areas others could never infiltrate.

That's the plan, at least. Use my sweet, vulnerable, single princess persona to my advantage. The parties I'll get invited to, the men I'll have access to, all because of the title I've been running from my entire life. Who would ever suspect me to be a member of the Elite Force team trained to steal intel and kill those who are a threat? It's the best cover to date, and the team we are putting together is going to kick arse and take names.

I ignore the man sleeping like an ogre on my couch. It's better this way. If I pay too much attention to him, it could be detrimental to all the progress I've made. I'll turn into this sex deprived female, rip that damn throw he has wrapped his upper body in, and mount him before riding him the way I dreamed about last night.

If he'd have left liked I'd asked him to, I could pull out my very special toy I only use when I'm really needy. Mercedes and I purchased it as a joke one night when browsing the sex toy sites, giggling like little girls. When it came, she rushed over and we stared at the size of it in awe. She jokingly said she'd know if I ever tried it out because I'd walk funny for weeks after. I didn't bother explaining it had nothing on the man who ruined me for all others, length wise maybe, but girth wise it wasn't even close. Although it did a superb job, reminding my body how much it missed the jerk who once claimed he loved me right before abandoning me.

When I walk into my bathroom and flip on the light, I glower at the shattered mirror hanging there. There's dried blood dead center. All I can do is shake my head, knowing exactly what happened. Instead of worrying why he did it, I strip and jump in the shower to wash the night off and hopefully get my brain ready for the day.

I'm so distracted by the warmth of the water relaxing my tired body, I completely forget I'm not alone until the curtain is yanked back.

"Get out!"

He ignores me, of course. "Do you know what time it is?"

Jerking the curtain back in place, I respond. "Yes. Now, if you don't mind?"

He yanks it open again, scowling like the crabby arsehole he has become. "It's fucking four in the goddamn morning. Nobody gets up at this hour."

I guess my peaceful shower is over, so I turn it off and snag the blue fluffy towel I hung on the peg. "I get up this early every morning. Roll call is at five. If I'm late, I'll be given the worst job they can think of. So, I try to be the first. Now move."

He backs up, scratching his head. I slink into my small closet for privacy and hear him taking a piss. Not much has changed there. He's still not ashamed about that stuff. I rush as fast as I can before he pops in the doorway to get a full glimpse of my naked form. I barely get my uniform on when his large body obstructs the light.

Grabbing my combat boots, I slip under his arm and flee to the main area. I locate a hair tie and bring it all to the top of my head, wrapping it into a messy bun and calling it good. Dropping into the chair, I shove my feet into my boots and lace them quickly.

"Why do you look like you're about to go join the army?" His frown makes the dark shadows of his beard stand out.

"Not the army. They wear that gray camo shit. All black is for the Elite Forces. You should know this. Before you joined the King's Guard, I believe you were a part of them." I start to head for the door, then remember my bike is still parked next to the club. "I need a lift since you wouldn't let me drive my baby home last night."

I expected a string of questions, not the silent grunts as he slips his shoes on and grabs his keys. He opens the door while he studies me with curious eyes.

When we arrive at the base, I thought he'd drop me off at the gate, not pull up to it. "I can get out here. It's a pain in the..."

The guard looks at something Gino flashes and waves him past. As he drives through the gate, he speaks for the first time since we left my loft. "Explain."

"I'm sorry? Did you just ask me to explain?" I don't, though. Once he parks, I jump out and jog for the field we meet at every Saturday.

I'm not the first, but I'm also not the last. Like I'm trained to do, I report in and take my spot front and center. Standing at ease while we wait for the others to fall in.

Once everyone arrives, our instructor explains the day's agenda. He halts in front of me and stops to ask the question I knew would come up. "What happened to your face, Princess?"

I hear a loud whistle and glare in the Gino's direction, where he stands, watching. "I stepped in front of a fist meant for one of my friends, sir. Don't worry, it won't affect my performance today. I'll still finish first and break another record."

The drill master smirks as he calls over his shoulder. "Hey, Wannabe, get your arse over here."

"You don't get to call me that any more, Drill Master." Gino, however, moves slowly, with a strut more than a walk. It irritates the man in charge of my team, visibly the reason he's doing it.

"Why are you here annoying me? You know I don't allow spectators." He eyes Gino up and down. "You're as pathetic as always. You okay with letting the princess break another of your records, or are you prepared to show her how it's done? I'm guessing she's all set to kick your arse since you look like you've been pussyfooting about. I bet even Hamilton over there could beat you. He finishes last each time. Good thing he's the brains of the operation and has that to fall back on."

Hamilton is our IT guy. He's not as lacking as the DM makes him sound. No one is on this team by mistake or considered a weak link. Everyone here could out course any other team by five minutes. Even Hamilton.

Gino smirks for the first time since we ran into one another last night. "I'd love to stay and show these rookies how it's done, sir. Unfortunately for them, duty calls. I've got to get back to my assignment. I was just dropping the princess off."

"Chicken shit," I mumble under my breath, making my team snicker.

Right on cue, his phone rings, and he waves it in the air with a bigger smirk now. "This is the boss calling, and we all know when the boss calls, you gotta go. Have fun and don't break a nail."

We waste no time getting started. The course record is just under an hour—fifty-seven minutes, and fifteen seconds, to be exact. My fastest time before today was sixty minutes and seven seconds. I'm feeling very confident I'm blowing it out of the water, especially now that I know exactly whose records I've been demolishing. Because of the top secrecy of this Elite Force unit, all record holders are given nicknames, and only those in the same recruit class are privy to those. Wannabe must be Gino's, since that's the name mentioned whenever I break it. The drill masters are always impressed, referencing how, if that recruit ever caught wind, he'd likely challenge me. Seems they were wrong about him, just like I was.

Before we start today, my DM throws out a challenge of his own. "Princess, I'll make a deal with you. You beat Wannabe's record today and this afternoon we'll skip the twenty-mile run up Hell's Peak, enjoy an ocean swim instead. I'll even join this sorry excuse of benchwarmers."

No pressure, right? I mean, one isn't that much better than the other, but then again, seeing the drill master fight the ocean with us will be fun. So, I agree with my team's approval.

Fifty-six minutes and fifty-nine seconds later, I cross the finish line with three others not far behind me. They won't break the previous record, but they'll make it on the board. I'm muddy, have a few new cuts on my arms, a nice bruise on my left thigh, and my cheek throbs like a bitch. My legs are burning and my head is spinning, but there's no way in hell I'm letting any of them know I'm about to pass out. This is how it is done here.

Never give up, never fail a challenge, and never let anyone see your weakness.

Especially the man lurking between the buildings. The one who's here when he shouldn't be. When my eye's lock with his, I don't look away. I stare him down until he blinks first. Watch him turn unhurriedly and walk away as if unimpressed.

Fuck him. Fuck him and his damn secrets. In a few weeks when I graduate, the first thing I'm doing is digging them all up and throwing them right back in his face.

Chapter Twenty-Three

GINO

The Royals

I've been running like a man afraid of his own shadow. Until now, I've used my job as an excuse not to return to Sevilla. It was a good excuse, too, because Her Royal Highness and Sir Edward were keeping me very busy making certain no one got close to her.

I'm back now with a list of questions. Though I have my doubts of getting them answered. So, I did something that will at least ensure she acknowledges me.

What did I do?

I did what any man in my position would do. I broke into her small loft and wait for her to return home. I expected her home hours ago. More than once, I've opened the new app that tracks her, but she's finally grown wise and disabled this one as well. Not a surprise. She's training to be in the Elite Forces. No one makes it into that unit unless they're up for the challenge, not even a princess.

This week, I've spent hours on the phone with anyone willing to talk to me. I may have dropped a few names to encourage them to tell me what I wanted to know. Not that I got any valid answers. It didn't matter I was working with them on other foreign matters. The questions I asked were classified. I wasn't on the privileged list to learn more than I'd learned by mistake. It became clear very quickly I was banging my head against a brick wall.

I've never been known to be patient, or accept answers I didn't like. When I was old enough to join the military, I did. It wasn't always part of my plan to be a military-trained leader. My country, however, required a man who was unafraid to fight. They deserved a leader who would go the distance and understood what had to be done, how to get answers, no matter the cost. Under the advisement of those guiding me, I decided the best way to do that was to apply for the Elite Forces. They turned me down so many times in those first four years, any other soldier would have given up, but not me. When they finally offered me a chance to fail, I soared so high it forced them to take notice.

The day I graduated is the day they handed my assignment to me. I almost walked away and left Hermosa Islas forever. I was an Elite Force member, not a Royal Guard. It felt like a demotion, like I was being punished for proving I had what it took to be a part of their best. I learned later that my job was anything but a demotion. It was exactly where I was needed. My training allowed me to see what other guards couldn't. As one of King Antonio's personal guards it offered me insight into the world I would enter one day.

I hated it for the longest time. Felt useless, like I wasn't allowed to use my training properly. Until the day arrived when those skills were essential at stopping an attack on the family. One I saw before anyone else, all because I had a talent no other guard did. I was not only learning what it took to protect a king, but from him as well. I soaked in as much knowledge as I could until the day came for me to step aside and move on.

So, my first question was why had they allowed Princess Gabriela to join? The only response they offered when I'd dared to ask was one day I might be lucky enough to know, but for now, it was none of my concern.

None of my fucking concern.

When it came to Princess Gabriela, they were wrong. She was my concern. It was all her passionate memories that saved me when I was locked in hell. There was no one else I was more concerned about than her. I had no right to be after walking away the way I did, but that didn't change a damn thing. My heart belonged solely to her, always would. No matter how hard I tried to not form an attachment and then pushed her away, deep inside, I knew what was coming.

After witnessing her run a course meant to break the strongest men, with a determination to defeat it, I was done fighting. I may not be ready to bring her into my world, but I was ready to mend the bridge I destroyed.

The lock to the door disengages, and I do my best to remain calm. She's late by several hours. It's nearly three in the morning and there's no reason for her to be out past midnight. Nothing good happens after midnight.

As the light from the outside shines through the now open door, I get my first glimpse of her in days. Even her silhouette takes my breath away. Her slow movements, however, have me rising to my feet. When the light flickers on as the door closes, dark rage rises inside of me.

"Who do I need to kill?" I growl and watch her flinch.

Dropping her helmet, Ela glares at me with blood-shot eyes. The jacket she's wearing is shredded. Her jeans are no better, exposing the skin beneath them, dirty and coated in blood. When she unzips her jacket, I catch the bright red wet stain soaking her white shirt.

"Ela, what the fuck happened?" As I move closer, it is then I spot the scratches on her helmet. "Tell me you went to the hospital."

In true form, Ela responds as she hobbles into the kitchen. "Does it look like I've been to a damn hospital? What the fuck are you doing here, anyway? Don't you have something better to be doing than breaking into my place?"

She groans reaching for a glass in her cupboard, abandons that thought and snags a mug turned upside down in the sink. After a shrug of her shoulder, she bangs it on the counter and limps to the freezer, where she retrieves a bottle of dark amber liquid. Using her teeth, she opens it, then spits the lid on the counter before tipping it to her lips and swallowing a few gulps. A cough stops her from drinking more, so she tilts the bottle over the mug and fills it completely before setting it down. With shaky hands, she grabs the mug and sips the liquid off the top until it will no longer spill over.

Once again, she hobbles into her living space. "Help yourself. I need this more than I need anything else at the moment." As soon as she's close enough to her large chair, she falls into it with a painful moan, spilling some of her drink. "Fucking hell."

I watch while she sips from the mug. It's easy to tell her mind is somewhere else. She's in pain and trying her hardest to hold it together. While I watch, a whole new string of questions fills my head. My feet finally move and don't stop until I'm kneeling in front of her.

Cup to her lips, she takes one look at me and mouths off. "I never thought I'd see the day when you'd be kneeling before me. Are you here to beg my forgiveness?"

"What happened?" I ignore her and attempt to get a few answers. She's trying her damndest to distract me from the truth.

"That all depends on who you ask." She sips from her cup again. "But basically, I'm pretty sure I totaled my baby. God, I loved that bike."

I snag the drink from her hand and almost get kicked in the balls again for it. "I need you to focus, Ela. How did you total your bike?"

"If I tell you, then you'll go all stupid alpha male on me. Do that thing you used to do and treat me like I'm some helpless female who can't handle her own shit." Exasperated, she points her finger at me. "And you are an arsehole. You can't have it both ways, Gino. You can't come back into my life and start demanding shit, pretending you care, when you have proven you're a sexy liar who runs the first chance you get. I don't have to tell you shit. You should go and bother someone who hasn't been ruined by you yet."

Her words hurt, while at the same time reveal a few things. She's not as immune to me as she'd like me to believe. Deep down, she's still very much attracted to me, as I am to her. And that gives me some confidence I can fix this after I fix her.

The mug in my hand finds its way to my lips. I take a healthy drink and then set it on the floor next to me. "Fair enough. I'll just use my resources to find out as soon as I get you cleaned up."

"Good luck with that." Ela places her hands on the armrest, pushing her broken body upward, doing her best not to show she's suffering. "Sometimes shit happens. All they'll find is my bike at the bottom of some ravine. No cameras in the area to prove I didn't just lose control, taking a curve too fast."

"Someone ran you off the road?" Even I hear my voice turn deep and come out sounding lethal.

"Why do you care, anyway?" She winces trying to make her way for the bathroom. "Fuck!"

I scoop her in my arms and hear her complaints as I settle her. "Why do I care? You can't mean that. I've always cared, Ela. That's the problem. What are you trying to prove? You aren't made of steel. You may be a badass, but you're not invincible. It's time to stop acting like nothing can hurt you, and you need to be more careful."

I carry her into her bathroom and gently deposit her on the counter. We stand our ground, staring each other down for a few moments. She's still the sexiest woman I've ever seen, even looking like she's taken one hell of a tumble. It's all I can do not to act on my desire. Now is not the time or place to make her mine again. We have so much to discuss, and until we talk, really talk, this can't go there.

Her next words tear my heart from my chest. "Did you ever love me?"

My hands cup her face as I step closer and press my forehead to hers. I can't lie to her. I'll never lie to her again. "I never stopped loving you, Ela."

"Then why did you leave me? Hurt me worse than anyone else ever could? I trusted you, and you..." Tears fill her eyes.

"I had to do something, and you couldn't help me then. I'm not sure you can now. It's complicated." Seeing her like this, my strong independent woman, broken and in pain because of me, is almost unbearable. "There are things you don't understand."

"So, the rumors are true?" She stares me in the eye and holds it so I can see the truth in hers.

"What rumors?" I try not to panic. Are there rumors about me? If there are, then we may have a problem.

"That you're part of the Kosonia revolution and know who the missing heir is. They say you're protecting him. That very soon you will help him make his appearance and then stand by him when he takes his place on the throne that was stolen from him." Her sad copper brown eyes are searching mine for the truth. I hate seeing her sad, thinking I lied to her. "Is it true?"

"Who told you this?"

"Well, no one told me, really. I may have done some snooping, overheard those in charge talking," she admits. "I'm pretty sure the plan when I graduate is to help. I won't know, though, until I receive my first assignment. With my influences as a princess, I can get close to those in charge. Help him learn the best ways to infiltrate their ranks by doing what a single unattached woman in my position does. I may finally get to use my title I hate so much. Who knew it would come in handy?"

"That won't happen. I'd never allow it." I pull back to remove her leather jacket.

She whimpers in pain, but that doesn't stop her from telling me how very wrong she believes I am. "Well, isn't that funny? It's a good thing they won't be asking you for your opinion on the matter, since you have no say in what I do or how I do it."

I was about to say more, tell her how wrong she was. The only thing that stops me is the large gash on her shirt I missed earlier. This one has something lodged inside and I'm not sure how deep it goes.

"So that's why my side feels like it's on fire?" Ella glares down, grabs the end, and yanks it out. "Goddamn motherfucker, that hurt."

I watch in horror as she pulls a wooden shard from her side before I can stop her. All I can think about is how that could be a horrible idea, but it's too late to stop her now.

Chapter Twenty-Four

GABRIELA

I tug on the wooden fragment. It must have jabbed me when I took my spill as my baby went off the road and over the edge of the small rocky cliff. It was bail or go over with the bike. Bailing seemed like the better option in the moment. But that meant I had to do my best to tuck and pray all ended well.

I landed just on the other side of the guard rail, in a wooded area, and tumbled down the rocky hill a few hundred yards. My bike went airborne and crashed into several trees on the way to the bottom. I couldn't see much in the dark, but I'm guessing it didn't make it there in one piece. And had I stayed on it, things would have been way worse than they are right now.

It all started when an arsehole cut me off, going way too fast for the curve approaching. He'd been riding my arse not long after I turned onto the road leading up to the hills where you could look down on Sevilla. It was one of my favorite rides, one that forced my mind to focus on something other than my problems. Tonight, it had been anything but relaxing.

Once he sped past me, I assumed I would be able to enjoy the rest of my ride. It wasn't until I was coming around a blind curve, I realized my mistake. He'd nearly caused me to wipe out, stopped in the road, forcing me to either go around him or try to stop. I'm experienced enough on my baby to know how to move her with ease. I shot past him while flashing the bird and shouting a few choice words he couldn't hear. I picked up speed to hopefully avoid another altercation.

It seemed to have worked until out of nowhere he came flying by me right before a sharp curve, cutting me off and forcing me to either hit him or swerve. I swerved and lost control. Unable to recover, I made a last-minute decision that probably saved my life.

My body was now paying for it, though. I wouldn't be surprised to discover I broke a few ribs. If they weren't broken, then they were severely bruised. Thank God I had my helmet on. I don't even want to think about what I'd be dealing with if I'd not been wearing one. People who ride without helmets are playing Russian Roulette with a fully loaded gun. They're just waiting for someone to pull the trigger.

"Fucking hell, Ela. Don't you know not to remove anything like that from your body? What if it had punctured an artery and you started bleeding out?" Gino grumbles as he slaps my hand away and inspects my newly open wound. "How the hell did you get home?"

I can't think with him so close, blasting his hot sexy breath on my oversensitive skin. So, I grab his hair and tug as hard as I can, which isn't that hard. "I walked. Would you stop? And it wasn't pulsing, so I knew it wasn't stuck in some place that would cause me to bleed more than I already am."

He removes my hands from his mane and holds them between his. I can't read his controlled expression, and it pisses me off more.

"What do you mean, you walked home? How far of a walk? Why didn't you call someone?"

"My phone is somewhere off of High Mountain Road. No cars on the road, and by the time I got into town, I wasn't stopping to flag someone down. Plus, I'm pretty sure you'd yell at me more if I got in a car with some stranger. And I was pissed, not in the mood to deal with another idiot. Seems I wasn't lucky enough to avoid that. Once I walked into my locked apartment, one was waiting for me." I'm not even attempting to be nice. I have no reason to kiss this man's arse. He's been on my shit list for some time now, and I'm in the perfect mood to say it like it is. "You should leave. I can take care of myself. I've been doing fine without—"

His lips land on mine, stunning me to silence. We haven't kissed since the day he left me, and it's better than I remember.

"Shut up. I'm not leaving," Gino grumbles, now that I seem more compliant.

"You will eventually. You're an expert at tucking tail and running." I'm on a roll tonight. Tired, pissed, and in immense pain is like throwing fuel on the fire.

"That is not what happened." He tucks a strand of my fallen hair behind my ear. Even that hurt. "You're a mess. We need to clean you up to make sure you don't need a doctor."

The only kind of doctor I need is one to examine my head. I shouldn't have tingly feelings in my stomach when I'm in so much pain, all because this man is here when I need someone more than I'm willing to admit.

As gently as he can, Gino removes my battered clothes. I don't stop him, because what's the point? I'm worse than I even realized. Evident to us once he gets me out of my top and pants. I have scratches—deep ones—all over my body. A large gash on my left thigh to go with the two on my torso. My ribs are black and blue, and it hurts to breathe anything more than simple, shallow, quick breaths.

I'm staring at my broken body in the mirror when I hear the shower turn on behind me. There is no way I can suffer the torture of him washing me. I'd rather stay dirty if it's the only way for me to become clean. Not that he's giving me a choice. Our eyes lock in the mirror, and I almost miss the fact he's standing behind me in all his magnificent glory.

The last time I saw him like this was not long after we boarded a plane and I helped him the best I could. He didn't let me do more than make sure he didn't fall on his arse in the shower. I may not look as awful as he did, but I feel extremely vulnerable, much like I'm sure he did.

I don't want him to see me like this, to think of me as a weak helpless female who can't take care of herself. I hate feeling weak. When I was little and going through treatments, I had no choice but to accept help. I have one now.

"Please leave." I whisper through the lump in my throat, needing time so I can regain my strength. "I can't do this right now, Gino."

His arms snake around my center, and I moan for two reasons, one being how much I've missed him. "I'm not leaving."

My bra and knickers are disposed of in seconds. Leaving me naked before him, in more ways than just physically. Exposed completely, afraid he can perceive all my fears and worries I've done my best to conceal.

He guides me to the steam filled shower. The water burns as it does its job to rinse my battered skin, forcing hot tears from deep within my soul as well. Tears I haven't cried in four years, all of it spilling out of me at my weakest moment. As gently as he can, Gino scrubs all the dirt and blood off me while I stand there and cry. It hurts being this close to him, knowing we are miles away from each other and may never find our way back to where we once were.

When I'm clean enough to satisfy him, he dries me off. Wraps my body in the soft robe my mother bought me for my birthday last year. Once he's dry and back in his clothes, he carries me to the main room and lays me down on my bed so he can study my nastiest lesions.

I'm not sure where he found the first aid kit, probably under the sink. Cris keeps one stocked here, not long after I took a spill on my bike and called him. It happens when you ride. You are bound to take a few spills and sport some road rash.

"Who did this to you, Ela?" Gino asks as he tapes a patch of gauze to my deepest cut. "And don't tell me you don't know. You are in Elite Force training. They train you to know these things. Who are you protecting?"

All the adrenaline coursing through my veins has diminished. I'm exhausted, in extreme pain, and an emotional wreck. "Can we not do this now?" I have a few ideas, but I'm not ready to share those yet. It's as if my brain is catching up now that I'm calming down. Maybe after a good night's sleep I can piece it all together and hunt down the arsehole responsible.

My body is only covered by the robe he slipped on earlier. It isn't doing much to keep me concealed from his hungry eyes. Each time he lingers, I feel the smolder deep in my core, proving I'm a mess and fighting a losing battle where he's concerned.

His fingers run down my thigh to inspect the gash, but does my brain register that? No. It goes all stupid and recalls every moment he'd touch me there for other reasons. My fucking nipples harden, and because one has slipped out from behind the robe, Gino immediately notices. Heat so intense scalds my skin as he stares, his desire evident.

I try to move, pull the robe closed, and slide away from him. The problem is my body won't move fast enough. Before I can make my escape, I'm gathered up into his powerful arms and drawn closer. Our eyes lock, and I give up fighting the pull that brings our lips together.

This kiss is the gentlest that has ever passed between us, but the passion behind it is as strong as it has ever been. I'm not sure what it means or if it is only a responsive kiss between past lovers.

"Ela." He whispers my name more than once between kisses. "God, Ela. I'm sorry."

"Please, don't. I can't do this right now." I break away and bury my face in his neck doing my best to hold it together. I fail miserably.

Tugging the robe tightly around me, he ties it before he arranges us on the soft pillows. As soon as we're just right, he settles in next to me. I can only sob as he wraps his warmth around me. This is all too much. My mind can't take his kindness. I refuse to let my heart out of the safe place I've stored it since he walked away.

"I'm here, Ela. When you're feeling better, we need to talk. But I want you to understand this. I love you. I never stopped loving you. I'll forever love you, even if you decide I'm not worth loving back. I hope that will not be the case, but until you know everything, like you should have known from the beginning, you can't make that choice." I hear agony in his words, his struggle to say them, and I have to wonder what the hell he's been hiding from me.

My eyes are heavy and words are impossible for me to form at the moment, so I nod. I have no idea what to say to any of that. He broke my heart once, and while I love him, I hate him for it. I guess in a few days we can talk and he can do his best to explain then.

It had better be one hell of an explanation, though. I had better get the truth, the story behind the story. If he doesn't tell me everything, I might be forced to do something I know will be the end for both of us. Walk away and never look back.

Chapter Twenty-Five

GINO

The Royals

I didn't sleep at all last night. Ela had a rough one, and my mind was racing, unable to shut down enough for a catnap here and there. Around three this morning I gave up even trying. I decided to see if I could get to the bottom of what really happened.

Did I get anywhere? No.

The only thing I accomplished was tracking down her phone. Which ultimately led me to where the accident occurred. Meaning there was a crew on its way up High Mountain Road to retrieve her phone, bike, and any evidence they could use to track down the asshat who ran the princess off the road.

She's going to hate me. Because the moment King Antonio learns about what happened, he will reassign guards to her detail. He won't give a damn about her being a member of Elite Forces. I have my doubts he knows shit about her being a part of them as it is. If he knows, I bet he doesn't appreciate the extent of her training or what unit they've assigned her to. Because if he did, he'd not allow his little sister to be in this unit. Those in this division of Elite Forces were the ones no one knew about once they graduated. The ones we sent to do missions we don't talk about.

And yes, there are other units in Elite Forces that are more well known. They even get the credit for the operations they manage.

I can only imagine what her other brothers will say when they discover what their little sister has been up to. Heads are likely to roll and Sir Edward may end up on the wrong side of it all. Her Royal Highness is a lot of things, but I doubt she'll support her daughter putting her life in danger.

When I tire of hearing and watching her suffer, I suck it up and call the one person I know she trusts. I don't like the guy, but he's her friend, and took care of her while I was gone. Plus, he'll keep this private and should she need medical attention, he'll make sure she gets it. In no way will he play around with her life.

I'm on the phone when he arrives, getting the full report from one of my contacts in the King's Guard. They located the bike, or what was left of it once it landed at the bottom of a very steep ravine. Her phone was discovered about fifty yards from the drop-off, thirty-five yards from where they determined she stopped her descent. That's how close she came from tumbling over the rocky edge and ending up a broken mess. I can't even let my mind ponder on what would have happened if she'd ended up going over.

Fuck!!

The smirk on Crispin's face disappears once he steps inside the small loft and glances over at her sleeping figure. I dressed her in something that covered her better than the robe I slipped on her last night. I was the only man who would get the privilege of seeing her naked form. Doctor or not, he would have to work around the sports bra and boy shorts her body was now cloaked in. There were no wounds or concerns in the areas protected. The areas that made my dick hard and mouth water even though she was in no condition to deal with my carnal desires.

"Why the hell is she not in a hospital?" Crispin grunts as he makes a straight line for her. "This is not some fucking tumble. She was in an accident that should have required an emergency call and a few nights and days in the hospital."

"You don't think I know this?" I grumble as I take my place on the other side of the bed. "She walked through the damn door like this.

Wandered from the top of High Mountain Road, because she's a proud woman who has one hell of a stubborn streak."

Pulling out his medical equipment, Crispin tells me as he sees it. "Stubborn goes both ways, man. You are as stubborn as they come. And who wears the pants here? I thought it was you, but it seems she's the one with balls so big she's running this show. I held more hope for you, Gino. I expected you could keep her under control better. All I've seen you do since the day you entered her life is confuse the hell out of her and make her feel like she has to prove herself over and over again."

"Leave him alone." A weak, gravelly voice chastises her friend. "What are you doing here? Did he call you?" Her blood-shot eyes turn on me and it kills me to watch her doing her best to hide the pain I know she has to be experiencing.

Slipping the blood pressure cuff on her arm, he glares at her. "You sure as hell didn't. Why is that, exactly? We had a deal, remember? No matter the time, you were to call when shit like this happened."

I perk up a bit, not liking what that means. "This has happened before?"

"No." Ela drags the word out. "I've had a few minor spills. It happens. But I've never had more than a few scrapes or a nasty headache."

"You're never getting on a damn bike again." I let the words fall and I mean it.

Calmer than I expected, Ela glares at me. "And you would be my what? Oh, wait. You are nothing to me, so you don't get to tell me what I will and will not be doing in the future. If I want to jump on a new bike tomorrow, I'll do it. In fact—"

I get in her face and pinch her lips together. "I'm the man who loves you, and I refuse to sit back and watch you—"

She slaps my hand away as her glare turns deadly. "If that is my reward for being loved by a twatwaffle like you, then I'll pass." Her anger turns to Crispin when he presses against her ribs. "Fuck. Stop that. Damn, that hurts like razors."

He doesn't stop, only presses harder and even starts in on the other side. When he's done, his expression is grim and turns serious. "I'm taking you to the hospital. You have three broken ribs, three. I suspect a few others may be cracked as well. It's a wonder that you didn't puncture a lung moving around during the night. Or walking home from the damn accident. It's one thing to be a stubborn woman, Gabby, but this isn't stubbornness. This is downright stupid, and I should kick both your arses for not taking it more seriously."

Gabriela lifts her chin defiantly as she protests. "I'm fine."

Crispin places his hand over a dark spot on her side I've noticed has grown darker and larger since the last time I looked. "Are you? Do you know what this is? It's blood pooling behind the skin." He presses against it and that nearly causes Ela to pass out. "You are not fucking fine! Get your arse dressed or I'm calling your brother. What do you think Lenny would say about this? I bet he'd drag his arse up here, kick lover boy's arse while he drags yours off to the hospital. Is that what it's going to take?" He yanks out his phone, ready to carry out his threat.

I respond before she can. "Find us a ride. I'll help her dress, and we'll meet you downstairs in ten minutes."

Crispin angrily shoves his medical supplies back in his bag while grumbling about dealing with shit like this way too much. Something about being tired of secrets and royals and dipshits who fall in love with impossible women. I get the impression I'm not the dipshit, or at least I'm not the only one. "You have ten minutes, that's it. I swear, Gabby, I will call in reinforcement and your mother will be one of them."

"Arsehole!" she shouts, which cause her to cough and whimper. "I'm fine."

I scoop her up in my arms as gently as I can. "No, you're not. He's right. I should have dragged you out of here last night kicking and screaming. If you fight me, I'll do it now."

That makes her laugh. "Fight you? Do I look like I'm in any shape to fight anyone? My nieces and nephews could take me right now with little effort."

I plop her sexy arse on the counter of the bathroom and walk into her closet. When I return, she has jumped off to use the commode. Her face pales when she spots blood on the paper, she used to clean herself. While it may be common for most women to see blood, it's not for her.

After I help her stand, tug up her knickers, and slip the only causal dress I could find hanging in her closet over her head, I wrap my arms around her. Not tight, but enough to hold her up and offer her some comfort. I read once that women need hugs, physical affection that isn't necessarily intimate. Even my strong, independent woman requires hugs from those closest to her. I may not be her favorite person at the moment, but we have a bond that is unbreakable, even though we're at odds.

"I'm sure it's nothing. Blood in your bladder happens when your kidneys take a beating sometimes. I've pissed my share after a good one. This is why it's important we get you checked out." I rub her back and feel her body relax against me the best she can right now.

"I was going to call him. But you distracted me last night," she informs me. "So, it's your fault I'm in trouble. Figures."

Pulling away, I scoop her back into my arms and do what I should have done last night when she walked through the door. "Let's go get you checked out."

Chapter Twenty-Six

GABRIELA

I hate hospitals. When you've spent almost five years in and out of them, even at a young age, you never want to go back. I'd been luckier than most, had a special ward set up for me in the palace infirmary. One that didn't look much like a hospital room. However, no matter how much they tried to make it appear homey and pleasant, it still smelled like a hospital. Nothing could take the sterile scent or cover the strong medicine pong. The moment I get anywhere near one it all comes flooding back, turning my stomach sour, making me anxious.

The only doctor I trust is Crispin. He has a mannerism about him that makes me comfortable. Maybe it's because he's my friend first, someone I've known since I returned to the healthy world. He always treated me the same, was kind and caring, respected me and the way I lived my life. I believe it also has to do with the fact he understands what it means to not live up to certain expectations. His family never understood why he turned his back on them. Or maybe they did. They just didn't think it necessary to dig up the dead to find answers. They believed the past was best left alone. Crispin's family had secrets they wanted to stay buried. I didn't know what those were, but I always got the impression one day he planned to uncover them, expose the truth too many tried to ignore.

I sit in the sterile white room, pissed at the two men, forcing me to stay until the surgeon comes to check on me. I've already protested to the nurse who checked my vitals. Complained to the physician about not needing or wanting to be here. Only to be threatened that if I kept it up, others would be called.

When Gino dared to call me princess, if I'd have been capable, I'd have knocked his teeth out. I stayed only because, as soon as I was cleared, I was leaving and doing so without either of my escorts. I don't need a damn babysitter.

When Crispin steps out to take a phone call, Gino decides we should talk. "Why are you being difficult?"

I don't respond, figure it's best to remain silent. If I speak, I don't trust my voice to work correctly, exposing more than I wish. I need to sound strong, even though I feel anything but strong right now.

Standing, Gino stalks over to the bed and does the unexpected. He brushes the hair from my face and opens up a bit, exposing a few secrets he's been keeping. "When you came to my rescue, I felt weak for not being able to save myself. Hated that I needed someone to step in and get me out of the depths of hell. It wasn't how I wanted you to see me. Weak and unable to do shit for myself. I was supposed to be strong in your eyes always, not some pansy arse who could barely stand on his own two feet. Seeing me so vulnerable, lost because of the hell I had barely survived, made me weak. I pushed you away because I knew it was going to be one horrendous battle to get my mind back on track. I didn't want to drag you down with me. It killed me to send you away. You were the only sunshine I had left in my life. I never stopped loving you, Ela. You don't believe me, I know that. I don't blame you. Somehow, I'll prove it and then it will be your choice what happens next."

This damn man knows how to get me to stop putting up more walls and allow him to knock a hole in it instead. "What happened in there, Gino?"

I realize something beyond my comprehension has broken him. The night he stayed with me. I woke to his cries. It was obvious he was having a nightmare.

He shakes his head and there is shame reflecting in his eyes. It breaks me. He has nothing, no matter what, to feel shameful. "I can't. Maybe one day. I'm not sure. I'd not wish my worst enemy to suffer an hour in that place. And if you understood what that meant, what my enemies have done to me, you'd know it was a hell beyond hell."

Before I can pull more out of him, the surgeon walks in with Crispin on his heels. "Princess, it seems you've gotten yourself into one nasty state."

"Gabriela, that is how you are to address me." I realize it won't work, but at least I let him know my wishes.

"I'm Dr. Alexander. I'll be the one performing your surgery this afternoon to repair those ribs. While we are in there, we are going to—"

"Hold up." I interrupt him while shaking my head. "No."

"Did you just say no?" He crosses his arms as if surprised. "This isn't an option. This is what needs to be done, so you heal correctly and don't undergo unnecessary complications." When I start to speak again, he holds up his hand to stop me. "I don't think you understand the severity of your injuries. Without surgery to repair those broken ribs, you'll be restricted to a bed for at least four weeks and even then, there is so much that could go wrong. You're a member of our armed forces, correct? If you refuse this operation, they could dismiss you for not being fit to serve. Are you willing to take that risk?"

My hatred for doctors just went up, this one hitting the top of that list. "Isn't there another way? I can't stay here overnight. I can't. You don't understand." Oh shit. Panic takes over and the walls close in all around me. "I have to... I have..."

Gino's handsome face appears out of nowhere. "Calm down. Breathe. In. Out."

I shake my head. "I can't. Gino. Hospitals. No. I hate them. My childhood."

"Dr. Alexander? Is there a way she can have the surgery and still leave the hospital?" Gino wipes the tears I didn't know were falling off my cheeks.

"It would be better if she stayed," the doctor tells him. "But as long as she's stable and has someone to stay with her for a few days, I could maybe be talked into signing off on it. It also depends on what we find when we do the CT scan. I need to determine if there is internal bleeding or major damage to her vital organs. The bruising around her abdomen that keeps getting darker suggests some, but we can't be positive until we do the scan or exploratory surgery."

"No exploratory surgery!" I shout. "I've had more than my share and I... I can't. Fuck. Fuck."

All my composure is now gone. I can no longer keep it together. Instantly, I breakdown and look like one of those weak-arse females. I'm not criticizing, but not showing weakness has always been a rule installed in me since a child.

Never show weakness, remain strong at all times. Royals aren't weak. They remain strong always, never expose you're vulnerable. Never let them see the areas where they can strike to take you down.

My father would repeat those words to me, even when I was three and facing death. Being weak was not allowed, not even then, not in front of those watching, at least. He only broke down when he believed he was alone. I witnessed it once when he sat by my bed and thought I may not make it through the night. That was the only time I saw my father cry like a baby. He assumed I was asleep, but even at four, I understood not to reveal I wasn't.

And here I am, being weak, and it pisses me off more.

Gino takes over, knowing I need him to take charge. "Schedule the CT. We will take this one step at a time. If she needs to stay, I'm staying with her. No exceptions."

Dr. Alexander nods. "I think we might be able to arrange that."

"Now leave so I can get her ready for what is coming and calm her down." Gino looks to Crispin next. "Can you give us a few, please?"

Crispin walks over to my bed and kisses the top of my head, making Gino growl. "I understand you hate this, but he's right. Please do as you're told."

I can only nod.

"You had better do right by her this time. If you hurt her again, I'm recruiting her brothers and dealing with you the way they would have done in the 15th century." He glares at Gino, and I almost laugh. "And keep in mind that my job has taught me how to use a scalpel, unmanning you would take seconds."

Gino runs a hand over his face. "I'll keep that in mind."

As soon as the door closes, his eyes land on me. I really wish he were an ogre-looking man, one that repulsed me. He is anything but, and the years away have only made his posture more dominant. Confidence rolls off of him. I envision him as a leader, ready to stand his ground while he makes a point. Until his eyes soften and all I can picture is him being mine. A man willing to hold me up when I'm weak, but not one who will control me.

"What can I do?" he asks as he strides toward me. "How can I make this better for you?"

"Sneak me out of here." I hiccup and try not to swoon when he drops to his knees and takes my hand. Damn, that's sexy.

"Besides that." He kisses my hand.

"I'm scared." I admit so quietly I'm not sure he can hear the words. Every cell inside me wants out of here. I'd do just about anything to escape. "I'm freaking the fuck out, and I'm so damn scared. Please, can we just go?"

"You know what scares me?" He kisses my hand again.

I shake my head. "What?"

"Never holding you in my arms again. Never hearing your voice. Never making love to you again once you're better. Never getting the chance to prove my place in your life. That is what scares me, Ela." He rises to his feet and leans over the bed, grabbing my chin with his firm hand. "Losing you scares me."

"You promise you'll be here? You won't leave me in this place alone?" I might be able to get through this if he can promise me that.

"If they'd let me, I'd go inside the operation room with you. Hold your hand and talk to you the entire time." He leans down. "But since they won't, I'll have to wait for you. I won't leave you here alone, promise. As soon as they release you, I'll take you home."

Gino kisses me then, another gentle kiss that takes my breath away. I do my best to soak it all in, so when the time comes to face what is coming, I can remember this moment.

Chapter Twenty-Seven

GINO

The Royals

It's been five days since I brought Ela with me to my home in Aragon. We spent the first few days in my place in Sevilla until she was well enough to travel. While she was in surgery, I made a few phone calls, knew it was better her family hear it directly from me than from those who report to them.

Okay, I made one call to Sir Edward, who handed the phone to Her Royal Highness Angela. Knowing her daughter as well as she does, she was worried about Gabriela being in the hospital. Offered to come and stay with her because she understood her daughter wouldn't be the best patient. Angela was surprised Crispin and I had dragged her inside of one without her throwing a huge fit and became concerned about how serious her injuries had to have been. Once I explained my plan to remain with her until she could get around, then to later, bring her back to Aragon with me to ensure she's following her doctor's orders, Angela immediately calmed. Gave me her blessing to do what I needed to do to help her daughter heal, even lock her up if necessary.

I thought I might have to do that, but so far, Ela's been behaving. Which discloses her pain level is higher than she's letting on. She hasn't complained about me strongarming her to sleep in my bedroom instead of one of the others. Maybe she protested at first, but she didn't fight me on it.

The first night we arrived at my house in Aragon, she had plenty to say. Even had questions about how a man in my position could afford such a large home. I'd chuckled a bit at her wording and then did my best to explain what I could.

"Are you skimming money off of us?" Ela questioned when I pulled up to the gate of the home Beni purchased for me. "Or is this payment for what you're doing on the side?"

"I'm not doing anything on the side." I punched in the code to open the gate. "My family owns this home. I'm living in it while I'm here, that's it."

It's not a lie. Beni used family funds to purchase the home. He's a Kelemen, one of my distant relatives. One my father trusted. I knew him as a boy. And he stayed in touch through my adopted father, Kyle Leblanc. He was one of a few who knew I was alive. And when I leave, I plan to gift this home to Kyle and my adopted mother, Melanie. A thank you for all they have done for me.

Ela studied the home carefully as I helped her out of my car. "I'm not buying that, but I'll let it slide for now."

I knew she was exhausted from the drive and that rest was what she needed most. With my hand on the small of her back, I guided her down the long corridor to the lift. Her eyes said what her mind was thinking, and all I could do was shrug. I'm aware that having a lift in a home said a few things about the home. All the Reyes homes have service lifts, they just don't use them much. I hadn't used mine until that moment. I guess I could have carried her up the stairs, but it would have been uncomfortable for her, so I'd chosen the lift instead.

We landed on the third level and the smirk on her beautiful face only grew.

"Just say it."

"I'm surprised, that's it. This place seems over the top." She stepped out and waited for me to show her the way.

"It is. My suite is this way." I touched her back and motioned to the right. "That's where we are heading."

"Is it the only suite on this floor?" she'd asked as we passed a couple of closed doors.

"No. There are two others, along with an office." I nudged her to keep moving. "I chose this floor because it also has the best view of the property, a safe room, and a private exit that isn't accessible unless you have the proper code."

"The proper code?" Ela tilted her head as her brows frowned.

I waved my hand at her as I shared a secret. "Only two hands will open it. Mine is one."

"Whose is the other?" she asked as I opened the last door at the end of the corridor. "Oh, wow."

"I told you it had the best view. You can admire it from the bed. Do you want to change?" My hands squeezed her shoulders from behind. "Come on, you can snoop around later after you've rested."

Ela was wearing leggings and a light pullover, so she headed straight for the bed. As she sat on it and kicked off her shoes, she glanced up at me. "You said two hands. Whose is the other?"

I helped her get comfortable, kissed her forehead, and tried not to give her an answer, but her face said she wanted one, and I was done denying her. "Yours."

She stared at me but said nothing.

"Sleep. We'll talk more later," I told her as I pulled a blanket over her. "I'll be just across the hall in my office."

That was five days ago.

We still haven't really talked. She slept in my bed while I tried to provide her space to heal. Only coming in when I was checking in on her to make sure she was comfortable. I wanted to crawl in the bed next to her, but knew if I did, I wouldn't be able to keep matters between us friendly. My desire would get us both in trouble, so I'd napped off and on in my office on the hard, uncomfortable couch in there.

I needed to leave today and return to work. While I knew she would be fine alone, I called in reinforcements and vowed to suffer the consequences later. My sister, the extra one I gained when I moved here, was more than willing to hang out with her. This was probably a huge mistake, Heidi often shared more than she should. And like most sisters, butted in and assumed everyone should be as happy as she was with her husband, Carl. She's also pregnant with their first child, has this idea that everyone needs to fall in love and have babies. While I appreciate her, I'm not sure Ela will.

"It will be fine, Gino." Heidi shoves me out the door. "I promise to be on my best behavior."

"That's what I'm afraid of." I plant my feet and try not to smile at the tiny thing, giving it all her might. Every time I look at her, I think of Giovanna, how they are close to the same age. I wonder if she's really alive or if that is only a rumor leaked to draw me out of hiding.

"Hi." Ela's voice vibrates off the walls. It's the first time she's come downstairs since I settled her in my room.

Heidi stops shoving me and makes a beeline for her. "Hello. I'm Heidi, Gino's sister. And you must be Ela."

I notice the moment my sister recognizes her. Hear it in her voice and see her demeanor change. "Gino Leblanc, why... I'm going to kill you."

Ela grins so big I think her face might crack. "I like her. Why haven't you introduced us sooner?"

"Cause he's a stupid blockhead." Heidi recovers quickly. "Seems we have a lot to talk about. Like why my brother didn't bother to tell me he was dating our Princess Gabriela."

"Is that what he told you? That we are dating?" Ela sits on the bench; she fatigues easily. "I don't think that's true."

"Oh. I guess I just assumed because he was taking care of you... I mean, I didn't know it was you. When he called and asked if I could come and keep his houseguest company, told me it was a woman, I just thought... So, you two are just... friends?" Heidi grins like she knows that is not at all true.

"Are we friends?" Ela narrows her eyes as she studies me. "We were more than that once, before he disappeared on me. I'm not really sure what we are, but we are *not* dating." She emphasizes the not.

I shake my head and walk over to her, lean down so we are now looking directly at each other. "I love you, Ela. I'm going to work. When I return tonight, we'll sit down and see if we can get on the same page. Please be nice to Heidi. And ignore her if she talks about how I was as a kid." Then I press my lips against hers and make sure to give her a kiss that cannot be mistaken as one between friends. "See you tonight."

"See you tonight." She whispers through the blush that now colors her cheeks. Then, under her breath, she admits, "I love you too."

I smile and sigh as I stand tall. When I turn, my sister is smiling as well. She may not have heard what Ela said, but she knows me. I don't show affection in front of others. Even as a teenager, I didn't kiss a girl in front of my family. I barely held a girl's hand. So she knows and maybe, just maybe, this will help me win Ela over to my side.

Chapter Twenty-Eight

GABRIELA

I've never gotten along with bubbly females. No judgment, but Heidi is giving me those vibes and I'm predicting it to be a very long day. I'm about to excuse myself, grab a cup of coffee, and then retreat upstairs to hide.

That's what I've been doing since arriving, hiding from the sexy male lurking around. Thankfully, he's been hiding as well. Sleeping in another room while I suffered in his. Not from the pains of my injury. I could manage those just fine. I was suffering from the deep-rooted pheromones imbedded in his sheets and room. If I'd had my vibrator with me, I'd have utilized it so much it would have burned out.

The last time I attempted to have sex was three years ago. What a disaster that had been. We were intoxicated. It was the only way I could stomach another man's touch, or so I'd presumed. Even pissed out of my mind, I'd not been able to tolerate it. When my date passed out on me, I'd slipped back on the minimal amount of clothing he stripped off, and hightailed it out of there. The only sex I had now was of my own accord, and it barely touched the surface.

Having the man my body desired only a room or two away, put me on edge. And I refused to give into temptation no matter how badly I wanted to. And I wanted it badly. I spent most of my days daydreaming about riding him until my lady parts couldn't take the abuse anymore.

I need to get out of here soon. I should go and stay with my mother until I am released to head back to Sevilla. Having to deal with her questions and hurt feelings about me not calling when this happened was better than this. Plus, I'm pretty sure Sir Edward has her preoccupied with this reunion they're enjoying. I might be able to fly under the radar for a few days.

Cup in hand, I turn to the smiling, bubbly face of Heidi. "I'm going to take this upstairs and—"

"How long have you and my brother been... friends?" She finds a pan and then opens the fridge to grab eggs and cheese and God knows what else. "I'll make you some breakfast, and if I'm still annoying you after, I'll let you hide out the rest of the day. It's just that Carl convinced me to give up my job and I've been bored out of my fucking mind for two weeks now."

"You're not annoying me." I lie and pray it sounds like the truth.

She tosses her head back and laughs. "I'm annoying myself. You don't think I know how crazy I sound? I'm like the overzealous girl back in school who finally got invited to a party and is now chatty and driving the popular crowd to drink more. I'm used to speaking to hundreds of people each day. Now the only people I see daily are Carl, our mail person, and my neighbor Ainsley—who is determined to make me one of *those moms*. I'll end up in the nut house soon if I don't figure out how to deal. See, annoying as fuck."

I may have misjudged her. "What did you do before?"

"I own a restaurant. So technically I didn't completely give up my job, I just stepped back to let someone else manage it. And this person is so amazing at doing the job. She doesn't even call me for the minor hiccups running a restaurant sees daily. She is probably doing a better job than I did, and once this little one comes, I'll be forced to let her continue doing it while I sit back and watch," Heidi informs me as she mixes up some sort of egg mixture. I'm not a great cook, so I'm not sure if it's something more than just scrambled eggs. "What do you do when you're not recovering or performing your princess duties?"

"First, I don't have any duties as a princess. Being the fourth born has its advantages." I smirk into my coffee cup, pleased with the truth in that statement. "So, I joined the military."

She pours the contents into the hot pan before she spins to look at me. "Wow. None of your brothers served, did they? That's impressive."

"Not active duty, no. They went through a summer boot camp as reservists. Father insisted. But that was as far as it ever went." Whatever she's cooking smells wonderful. "I've always loved the idea of being able to protect myself and those who couldn't. It's worked out better than I planned. Now I'm almost finished and soon I'll graduate and be given my first assignment."

"What does Gino think about that?" She adds some cheese and then folds it.

"It doesn't matter what he thinks. This is my life. My choice. He doesn't get a say in it. Not after taking off on me without so much as an explanation." When she starts to speak, I hold up my hand. "Look, I know he's your brother. And you will defend him even if he's wrong. I'd do the same with mine. But he's a chicken shit who once claimed he loved me the very same day he left. Burn me once shame on you. I'm not about to go through all that again. I'm not some naïve little girl. I've been through more than most, and I deserve some respect."

Plating what now looks like a delicious omelet, Heidi adds more cheese on top and slides it my way. "I agree with you completely. What I was going to say is I can't wait to watch Gino fall flat on his face, keeping up with you. You mess with him, and I love it."

I cut into the cheesy, tasty breakfast and nearly have a food orgasm. "Damn, this is good. So you own a restaurant. Are you also a chef?"

Heidi shrugs it off as if what she made is nothing special. "I can cook in the kitchen if they need me to. I still step in from time to time because it was my first love, what compelled me to get into the business. But we aren't talking about me. We're talking about you and my brother."

"There isn't much to talk about." I take another bite and hope she drops the subject.

Instead, Heidi goes a different route and offers me some insight on the man. "When Gino came to live with us, I was eight. He kept to himself, avoided me more than he did Bruno. I think I reminded him too much of the sister he lost." She takes a seat and grabs an apple. "It took him almost three years to show me he cared, that he even knew I existed."

I know little about his background. He's never shared it with me. And because I was too angry with him, I never took the time to see if I could dig something up. I'm soaking in as much as I can now, though.

"We were at our grandparents' farm. I climbed a tree and then became too afraid to climb back down. It was getting dark, and when I didn't return, the entire family started searching for me. Gino is the one who found me. He sighed audibly before ordering me to come down. When I started crying and informed him I was scared, he assured me I had nothing to be scared about, that he wouldn't let anything happen to me. Guided me down most of the way with a promise to catch me if I lost my footing. When I was to a point I just couldn't continue, he told me to jump. It took him a while to get me to agree, but his expression made me trust him, to take him at his word. So I jumped, and he caught me, and the moment I was in his grasp he squeezed me so tight I thought he was going to break me in half. I could feel the tears running down his cheeks into my hair as he went on about how I'd scared him and to never do that again. Promised to always be there to catch me no matter what, that I was his sister and he'd always love me like one." She wipes a tear from her cheek. "He carried me back to the house, and from that day forward, he's kept his promise."

Taking a deep breath she continues, "I know he has his secrets. What happened before he came to live with us was a big part of why he'd kept his distance. When he left without warning, I was so mad at him. My father would only tell us that one day we'd understand. That we had to let Gino do what he was born to do and support him while he did." The confusion and sadness shine in her eyes. "I'm trying, even though I want answers. Even though I had to watch him once again pull back from us when he returned, looking so unlike the brother I once knew."

My appetite disappears as I listen. Thankfully, I ate over half of what she made me. I've learned more in the twenty minutes we've been talking than all the years I've known the man who stormed into my life.

"So basically, what I'm saying is this. Don't write him off just yet. Let him explain if he is willing, and it seems like he might be. I know he cares, because you are the first woman I've ever seen him show affection toward or even brought around. But I also don't want you to let him off easily. Make him open up and let you in completely. Don't allow him to tell you half of the truth, demand he share it all. And once he does, if you still feel the same about him, please give him a chance to prove he's grown and can do better." Heidi pats my arm as she makes her sisterly plea. "Stubborn arsehole or not. He needs a good woman by his side."

I slowly stand, needing time to think about everything. She shared a lot with me and has gotten me thinking for sure. The stress isn't helping. I'm tired because my body is still healing. "I'm going to go lie down for a bit. I promise I'll give him a chance to explain, but I can't promise it'll make a difference."

She nods and stands, grabbing my dish. "That's all I ask. I'll be around if you need anything. Go rest. I hope we can talk again later."

I didn't get much rest. My mind was all over the place. I had trouble interpreting her father's explanation about doing what he was born to do.

What did that mean?

If I were home, I'd jump on my laptop and see what I could discover. Since I'm not, I can only pace the floor until I'm so worked up, the only way to calm me down is to make my escape.

Gino said that only two hands opened the private exit in this room. Time to determine if he was telling me the truth. Placing my hand on the sensor, I exhale when the door pops open. I take one more glance around the room before I step into the lightly dimmed staircase, escaping, hoping to get the answers I need.

Chapter Twenty-Nine

GINO

The Royals

My smart watch notifies me the second Ela activates the private exit. I'm surprised it took her this long to use it. Maybe it had more to do with the fact she knew I was otherwise occupied and couldn't go after her.

"Everything alright, Gino?" Her Royal Highness asks from her seat behind me while I drive.

It's been a crazy day. Something is brewing. It's in the air, but I can't put my finger on it. Everything seems to have calmed, but my training warns me otherwise. The holidays went by without a hitch, and now we are getting ready for the Constitutional Ball, the reason I'm driving Madam Angela all over Aragon. She's making the final arrangements, so the ceremony will be a successful one in a few weeks.

We're now heading back to Castile Vicente, where she lives. It eases Sir Edward's anxiousness when she works from home, rather than the palace. He can keep an eye on her at home better than he can anywhere else. And because he no longer has free access all over the palace after he resigned from the King's Guards, and she isn't required to always be there, she appeases him for now.

My job as her private body guard is to drive her where she needs to go. Stay by her side when she's not inside the palace. Although I have been granted access there as well, I am joined by one of the King's Guards. When she works from home, she's confined to the grounds with limited access to those who might pose a threat. It works best for me as well, because when she works out of her home office, it means I'm not required to constantly stand guard. I can work on other matters that require my attention. Today my focus will be tracking down the princess since she's made a run for it.

"It's fine, Madam," I lie as I tap my left hand against the steering wheel. Traffic isn't cooperating with me today. Too many citizens are taking advantage of the nicer than normal weather. It's been one of those years, the reason Ela was riding her baby more than she should this time of year.

"Then why did I just receive a text from Edward informing me not to worry if I hear my daughter has gone AWOL?" Her eyebrows furrow as she stares me down in the rearview mirror. "Did something happen I need to know about?"

"It was fine when I left this morning, or so I thought. My sister was supposed to be keeping an eye on her." I try hard to keep my voice level, but dammit if I can manage that. "We were going to speak when I returned later. I'm planning to find out what Heidi said that sent her running."

"I doubt she said anything. I'm sure it's Gabriela being herself and nothing else. You have to give her time, Gino. You hurt her very badly when you left. I've never seen her that way before. I know you had your reasons, but so did Edward."

She has always been a straight shooter, never not spoken her mind. I've heard some of the story surrounding her and Edward, but not all of it.

"And because my daughter is a lot like me, it means she'll come around when she's ready and not before. If you push her, she will only keep running. If you back down just a bit, feed her curiosity while also showing her you understand why she's upset, you'll get her to hear you through that thick wall she has built. Sometimes we have to work it out on our own. And while I understand how hard that is for men like you and Edward to accept, it isn't worth fighting against. I'll even speak with her once she comes to me, to see if I can help you."

I was going to say more when my phone rings. Speak of the devil. "Hello, Princess."

The partition rises between us as Her Royal Highness laughs while shaking her head. She knows how much her daughter hates that title and that I'm only doing it to provoke her. "Be nice, Gino. Pissing her off will not get you the results you are hoping for."

Ignoring my use of her title, Ela gets right to the point of her call. "I'll be staying with my mother while I heal. You can have your room back now. I'm sure the couch in your office has to be uncomfortable. Know that I'll be comfortable with her, safe, even."

"What happened? What did Heidi say?" I can't fix this if I don't know how. Fuck.

"Nothing really. Okay, not true. She told me how hurt she was when you left. Mentioned how your father explained she had to let you do what you were born to do, whatever that means." I hear the wheels inside of her head spinning fast. "What does that mean, Gino?"

"What does it sound like it means?" I know that isn't an answer and she'll probably call me out on it.

"You know what? Fuck you and the horse you rode in on." She's pissed and not holding back. "I don't need this."

"Hold up. This isn't a conversation I want to have over the phone. Can we please talk about it later, in person?" The stress inside is rising, and right now my focus should be on the job, not my love life. "I'll be at your mother's in fifteen minutes. Once she's settled, we can talk."

"Fine," she grumbles and hangs up.

I do my best to put that all aside. Getting my passenger home safely is what I need to focus on. Later, after I have passed her off to her overly protective man, I can hunt down my woman—even if she's not willing to admit she's mine—and try not to toss her over my shoulder and carry her back to my home. If anyone would understand, it would be Sir Edward. He's been dealing with these two for a very long time.

It's no surprise to find him waiting when we pull up. The expression he's wearing has me a little concerned. "Thank you for keeping my lady safe. I'll take over from here."

"Is Gabriela around?" Her Royal Highness asks before she accepts his kiss. "I thought she might need to talk."

Wrapping an arm around her waist, he draws her closer. "She does, but not to you. Stay out of it for now. I'll find us something to do to distract you if I need to." Turning my way, he continues. "She's taking a dip in the mineral pool. I had the doctor clear her first, since I wasn't sure she should. He said it was okay, if she felt up to it."

My brain immediately drifts to the first time I found Ela swimming. I doubt she's exposed like that now, but a man can dream. I make my way around to the back and step through the gate. The large hedges surrounding the pool are perfectly situated to keep anyone from seeing her. One reason the photos sent to Her Royal Highness of her swimming back here were so alarming.

My feet stop moving when Ela comes into view. I was right. This time she's wearing a bathing suit, barely one, but it is there. Meaning I won't have to poke out the eyes of any guards on duty who may have caught sight of her. The angry bruises still marring her skin after her accident do nothing to take away from her beauty. I can feel my dick hardening quickly while admiring her. He's so desperate for action and she is his all-time favorite place to get lost inside.

Fuck.

Her voice is huskier than normal. "Are you just going to stand there like a stalker?" It makes me wonder if she's been crying or sleeping.

I stroll in her direction and stop at the edge of the pool, looking down at her. "I don't keep trunks here. Plus, I'm not sure you should swim until you heal fully."

"The doctor cleared me. Edward insisted on it before he let me get in." The minx shrugs unfazed. She swims back a few, tugs on the stings of her top, releasing it, before she tosses it at me. It's a challenge to see how far she can push me. "Suits are optional."

I close my eyes and begin counting out loud when something wet hits me in the face. I don't need to open my eyes to know what it is. Brazen, as always, she's doing her best to see how far she can push me before I react.

The sexual tension at my house electrified the air. We fought it.

Stayed in our corners for five solid days, but it was there and now it seems she's done fighting. It's not the first time she's made the first move. I should say no, but I cannot deny her when she gets like this.

I have no more restraint where she's concerned. I don't even care that her mother and Sir Edward are somewhere inside. It isn't as if they don't know about us. I'm no longer interested in keeping this a secret, and it looks like she isn't either.

My dress suit, gun holster, and all the contents in my pockets are now lying on the chaise closest to me. Before I remove my briefs, I make eye contact and watch as she licks her lips when they drop.

I dive in and surface right next to her. "I thought we were going to talk?"

Snaking her arms around mine, she drags me to her, our bodies now touching. "We can talk later." Her lips land on mine, and I become lost.

I've missed her. I know we shouldn't be doing this right now, but fuck it. She's the one who started this, not me. I, however, am finishing it. I wanted to fuck her like this the first time I saw her floating in the spring, grip her waist and drive into her so hard she gasped.

"Are you sure?" I nip her lip and let my hands cup her tight arse. "Fuck, Ela. I'm dying here, baby. I need to sink my cock into your pussy before I expire."

She giggles, wraps her legs around my waist, while maneuvering her body until my dick is pressed against her entrance. "Do it. I haven't been fucked properly for way too long."

Fucked. I don't miss her words. She sees this as a fuck, nothing more and it hurts a little, but not enough for me to stop it. Nothing about this will be a fuck, even if it is hard and quick.

Holding her against me, I walk us to the edge until my back lands on the stones near the waterfall. I rock my dick against her clit to stimulate it while I ask, "How long has it been?"

She shakes her head and glances away. It's obvious she would rather not share that with me. Too bad. I need to know if I'm doing this to wash away another man's touch or reclaiming what is mine.

My hand releases her arse so I can grip her face and make her look at me. "How long?" I really hope she tells me what I need to hear.

Tears fill her eyes as she says the words that shatter me into a thousand pieces. "I've not been with anyone else, Gino. You ruined me." I can tell she hates admitting it, that she's angry about what that means.

I reach down to check her first and my finger slides in easily. Aligning myself, I slam into her so hard she calls out my name. It echoes around us like music to my ears. I don't stop or give her a chance to catch her breath. I would. I never want to hurt her or make it uncomfortable, but her eyes warn me not to stop, so I keep it up, loving her noises as I take us on a ride we won't forget anytime soon.

Right before we fall over the edge, I pause and wait for her to look at me. "I love you, Ela. I've not been with anyone else either. My heart, soul, and mind will forever be yours and only yours." And then I slam home one last time, sending us to the one place we've not visited in over four years. I'm home, and it is the only place I ever want to be.

We can't stay out here and reconnect like I'd love to do. There are too many people around for that. And while I know her mother will leave us alone, it feels wrong. So as soon as she's humming against my neck, I drag my still hard dick from her warmth and hold her in my arms. "We should have talked before doing that, Ela, but I must admit, I don't regret giving into temptation."

"Me either." She rests her head on my shoulder, more relaxed than she's been in days. "I needed to be fucked like that to help clear my mind."

Again, with the fucked. Why does it bother me so much to hear her use that term when I've used it myself? I believe it has to do with the fact I'm afraid she's purposely trying to keep the emotion out of it, and that hurts. Letting it go again. I do my best to enjoy the moment.

"Me too." I kiss the side of her cheek and we float around for several minutes, enjoying the aftermaths of a good orgasm while in the arms of a lover. "We really should get out so we can talk."

Tossing her head back, she falls under the water, spinning out of my hold, and swims for the stairs. I can only stare, watching the water roll off her curves. Her body is toned and powerful, sexy as fuck, and my cock springs back to life. I grip and squeeze him, trying to make it painful so he'll retreat.

After slipping her robe on, she announces over her shoulder, "I'm getting dressed. You should too. I'll meet you in the solarium. I'm hungry and probably should take another pain pill."

I gather my clothes and head for the pool house where there are towels. I'll probably jerk one off before putting my suit back on. Time to face the music and give this beautiful woman the answers she's been asking me to give for her for way too long now.

Chapter Thirty

GABRIELA

The Royals

I retreat to my room so I don't have a meltdown in front of Gino. He'd expect me to explain and I can't. I'm not even sure why I did what I did when he walked into the pool area. I can only claim temporary insanity.

He was staring at me with a hunger so strong I could feel it to my core. I was a needy bitch and tired of not getting to experience his touch all over me. It hadn't been my plan when I went for a swim to ease the stress, but nothing felt better in that moment than having him remind me why my body craved his so much.

Now I need to compose myself before talking to him. We have a lot to discuss. I expect real answers this time. I'm done only getting bits and pieces fed to me. It's time for him to tell me the entire story from start to finish.

His sister's words replay in my head on repeat. My brain won't let it go. If I'm being honest, I'm completely terrified of what they might mean. I've never been more afraid of the truth than I am right now. I've done my best to respect him, dug a little but when I came up empty, I left it. He said he'd explain, so now it's time for him to do just that.

Once dressed, I head to the solarium, where I'd asked my mother's staff to set up lunch. Like always, they followed through. Sandwiches, a small salad, and wine wait for us. Gino is already there, dressed in his power suit that enhances the body I admired only thirty minutes ago.

I give my head a good jostle so as not to get distracted again and head for the small table where our late lunch awaits us. "This looks good," I say as I sit down. "Are you going to join me?"

He grabs the wine bottle, opens it, and then pours some into each of our glasses before he takes his seat. I won't drink much, I'm still taking meds, and I know better than to mix the two.

Once we've both tasted it, he speaks, and I can only stare at him. He's not looking at me, he's gazing off into space while he recounts a story about a boy. One that is so unreal, I have trouble keeping up. It's one of secrets, deceit, and betrayal that ends in tragedy. I can't imagine a young boy watching in silence as his parents are being executed in cold blood. Witnessing something like that changes a person's soul forever. This young boy would surely grow into a very bitter and vengeful man.

"Hold up." I stand and walk over to him. Tears have filled his lovely eyes, and I know this person he's speaking about is someone he once cared for. I know I've heard the name before. "Are you telling me... is this boy, Simion, someone you know? A relative?"

"No." He looks directly into my eyes and shocks me with his next words. "I'm Simion. Or I was once him. The story I just told you is mine."

I knew I'd heard that name before.

Completely blown away, I sink to my knees and stare up at him. Hearing him recite the events of the absolute worst day of his life has my heart bleeding for him. I cannot even imagine watching my family being killed like that. Losing them all and then being dragged off by strangers to a land so far from the one I grew up in. Being placed in a home and given a new name, identity, and a backstory to keep me and those now raising me safe.

I know there's more, that he's leaving out some very important details, like who his parents were and why they were killed. But I can't take more right now. I rise and crawl into his lap, hold his face in my hands so I can wipe away the tears streaming down it. "I'm so sorry."

"It was a long time ago, Ela. I'm over it." He tries to tell me, even though he just shed so many tears while opening up.

I run my thumb along his wet cheek to prove a point. "You don't have to lie to me. That isn't something a person gets over. Is that why you left? Did you learn something and went back to settle the score? What can I do to help?"

Tilting his head back, he scoffs. "That's only the beginning of my life. There is so much more you have to understand first."

"Then tell me." I rake my fingers through his hair. "You said once I had a choice to make, so let me make it. Tell me what you've always been afraid to."

"I love you." His words come out broken. "Please keep that at the forefront of your mind. Don't assume my intentions were ever to drag you down with me. I never planned on allowing you to be a part of it, but you were so damn tempting. Always determined to break me, lead me down the path I knew would force us to decide what we were capable of being. No matter what you choose, Ela, I have come to understand that you were always meant to be mine. The woman who would help me know which path I am to follow. As long as you are by my side, I can survive anything."

"Would you just spit it out?" I swear I'm going to punch him if he doesn't start talking.

"Did you know I sat down with your father not long after my eighteenth birthday? We talked about you."

My confusion must show on my face because he nods. "Why? What would my father need to discuss... Wait? I was only eight then. Why would you talk about me?"

"I learned our fathers were once friends, or maybe they weren't friends, but men of like minds when it came to political matters. It wasn't a mistake, or by chance, I ended up in Hermosa Islas. I was always supposed to end up here so I could learn how to be a leader." He blinks a few times. "And marry the woman they had chosen for me."

Silence fills the room while I process what he's suggesting. Is he saying that our fathers made some kind of arrangement when I was just a baby? He was twelve when his parents were killed, meaning I was barely two. Why? What was the point in making such an arrangement?

I slide back and stand. I can't even believe I'm hearing him correctly. Is that why he was always looming around when I was a teenager? Was he hoping my mother would honor the agreement? Did he think I would or that my brothers would, even? Antonio made it clear, not long after he married Larkin, that he was abandoning that practice, found it barbaric.

I'm so confused. "Who are you? I mean... why would my father even agree to something like that unless your father and family brought something to the table? I was two, if that, when this all went down. Who in their right mind agrees to an arranged marriage when one of the offspring is so young? That sounds like a tale out of the dark ages."

"It does. Which is also why I told him to go fuck himself." He's now standing, staring at me, begging me to believe him.

"You told my father to go fuck himself?" I smirk. "I bet he took that well."

"He laughed at me. Said I had balls of steel to speak to a man in his position like that. Then explained an alternative plan, one he thought I might be more accepting of." Instead of coming my way, he turns and begins pacing the length of the solarium as he shares. "His offer was to take me under his wing and teach me what I needed to know, what my father couldn't. When the time arrived, he promised that this country I now called home would stand by my side and help me rebuild the kingdom that had fallen into the wrong hands. And when the time came for me to search for a wife, he didn't want me to ignore my father's understanding of what I would need. And because he knew it would be years down the road, he only suggested I keep an open mind and not hold two fathers' good intentions against you."

"Is that why?" I want to scream but don't. "Are you saying—"

"No! No. I was disgusted by the very thought. However, I was determined that you be given a choice in the matter. That when you became old enough to decide where your life was heading, that you not be forced to choose one you didn't want. I started looking out for you, keeping an eye on you. It may have backfired, put you on my radar as you grew older and started showing me how fierce you were. The older you got, the stronger you became, and the harder it was for me to keep my distance. And when I fell, I fell hard." He's on the other side of the room, so far away from me, but the way he's staring at me has me experiencing his touch, even from this distance. "You asked me who I am. I'm going to tell you and then I'm leaving you so you can think about it without me distracting you."

"What?" I storm toward him. "You're dropping a bomb on me and then just leaving? No!"

I'm half way there when his words stop me dead in my tracks. "I'm Simion Fenton Kelemen, the sole heir of Kosonia's royal family. I was a prince once, but the day my father died, I became a king. And the reason I left four years ago was to clear the way for me to return, so I could one day take my place as the leader my fallen country needs. Many believe I will become their King and lead them into a new world free of war. Or that was the plan they had for me, but now I'm not sure I can do it. I'm not confident I'm strong enough to face it alone. And unless you decide you will join me, I'm stepping away and will help Beni and Cezar find a more qualified leader."

Before I can stop him, he's gone. I'm left standing there stunned silent. That isn't possible. It's too crazy and someone has to be playing a cruel joke on me.

Except deep down I know. I have always known there was more to this man. My heart knew there was more and couldn't let him go. Even though I wanted to run, it would never allow me to do so, it was always drawn to his for good reason it seems. It's time to take a good solid look at my options and stop fucking around.

Chapter Thirty-One

GABRIELA

The Royals

I've holed up in my room for two days while struggling to figure out if the crazy tale Gino told me was true. There wasn't a lot out there about it, only a few older articles in the archives that mentioned the tragedy of his family. No mention of their being survivors. According to everything I read, his entire family, including the boy he claims to be, died after a group of rebels raided their home. Nothing more. Even though I'd dug deep, whoever was protecting him was doing a damn good job of it.

Dracul Kelemen, his uncle and his father's twin brother, found them. He called it a massacre and demanded justice for his brother's family. Swore to do whatever he had to do to hunt down those responsible and make them pay, blaming the rebellion. The war destroying his troubled country only escalated once he did that. This tragedy fueling those fighting with his uncle, offering a reasonable explanation on why the current government needed to wipe out those who were against them.

Convenient, since until then, the rebellion was growing and gaining power. Many claimed Dragos Kelemen was their leader, fighting with them not against. They accused Dracul of being the one responsible for this tragedy, allowing him to steal his brother's birthright and take his place on the throne once the war ended. These rebels labeled Dracul a conspirator. Each time a person spoke out against him or the current government, they disappeared or ended up in prison. A few killed in gruesome ways shortly after standing against those in charge.

It didn't take a genius to figure out why, and it was a sign that there was some truth to what the people were saying. The rebellion soldiers continued to fight this bloody war for over twenty years hoping one day to escape from under the corrupt government.

After reading that I need air, so I take a walk around the property. I'm feeling better each day. Soon I'll be well enough to return to Sevilla. I'll be placed on restricted duties, no physical activities for a few more months, but I'll be allowed to return to classes and support my classmates, my team. The only good thing about my accident was that it happened during a brief break, meaning I wasn't missing much. I could make up anything I needed to, shortly after released to do so. My graduation wouldn't be affected, and I'll receive my first assignment right beside my team. It won't hold them back, meaning we are on track to do what they were training us to do.

Sir Edward is in the garage messing with his car. The same one my mother has named James. Those two are almost sickening, the way they have so easily come together after all these years.

I'm happy for them. My mother deserves to be loved. Plus, I respect Sir Edward. He's always there when I need fatherly advice. I guess I know why now, since all this time he's been in love with her secretly. They even had a brief affair after my parents divorced. I have to wonder how different my life might have been if that had continued, if he'd had the valor to tell my father to fuck himself.

The thought of Gino saying those words to my father, King Ramon, makes me snicker. Which causes the man under the hood of his car, covered in grime, to glance up and find me lurking by the door.

"Bored?" He wipes off his brow. "Want to give me a hand?"

I jump at the chance. I'm not afraid of getting dirty. I work on my baby all the time, or I used to. Now it's in pieces somewhere and that makes me sad and angry all at the same time. Stepping into the extra pair of overalls hanging in his garage, I join Edward. "What are you doing?"

He hands me a wrench and points, motioning for me to tighten it.

"Just giving it a tune up and changing the oil. So, are you going to talk, or am I expected to pry it out of you?"

"There's nothing to talk about." I tighten the next bolt he points at. "Things with Mom going well?"

He points at something else as he hands me another tool. "It is. Are you going to tell me why Gino is once again avoiding you?"

"What do you know about his story? Do you know why he left the first time?" I watch him carefully. "Oh my God, you do. And you kept it from me. Why?"

His eyes meet mine. There's no remorse or guilt in them. "Because he asked me to let him share it with you when the time was right. And remember, it was my job for many years to know what others didn't. My charge wasn't to share that knowledge. Only if I suspected a threat, was I obligated to do so. Gino was no threat."

"You mean Simion was no threat?" I'm not even sure why I call him by his given name, not the name he has been using. It sounds foreign and isn't the name of the person I've fallen for.

Resting his forearms on the car, Edward shakes his head. "No, I mean Gino. That is the man we know. Although I also agree that the other side of him isn't a threat either, not to us at least. That man is a threat to those who wish him dead, though, so I'd be very careful calling him that. You could draw unwanted attention and put him and others in danger."

"Did you meet his father?" I ask after a few silent moments.

"Kyle? I know him well. Good man. One of our best Elite officers. I've worked with him several times." Edward grabs an oil pan and then slides under the car.

"Not Kyle. His other father." I see him peering up at me through the space between the engine. Which means I notice a slight hesitation, as if he's thinking if he should admit to it or not. "The truth. I've been lied to enough about all this. I want the truth."

"It was a long time ago, Gabby." He admits as he releases the oil plug. "Before Gino came here, even."

I spin the small wrench in my hand. "And you know why he was here, then, don't you?"

Sliding out from under the car, he sits up and shakes his head in disappointment. "Are you telling me you believe that the only reason Gino and you are together has to do with this meeting two men had over twenty-three years ago?"

I plop down on the bench and rest my elbows on my knees. "I want to believe it's not. I do. But even you have to admit, knowing that our fathers arranged it, plants a seed of doubt in my mind. He may not have noticed me had good old dad left well enough alone. I mean, seriously, who agrees to something like that? What kind of man thinks it's okay to offer his only daughter as a negotiation to bring two countries together? What does that say about them? And what does it reveal about us if we continue? Aren't we saying it's okay to do so? That it's okay for parents to pick the spouses of their children for the good of the nations?"

Edward chuckles as he rises and wipes off his hands on the rag in his pocket. "Gabby, Gino would have had to be a blind man not to notice you. I believe you are the one who put yourself on his radar by constantly sneaking out and forcing him to do his job and stop you."

"That's because he was watching me, because my father told him—"

"Your father did no such thing. I'm the one who asked him to help me keep an eye on you. I knew his background. The training he held. Once you moved into the palace with your mother, I understood I'd require an extra eye to keep you safe. He agreed, but wasn't thrilled about it." Edward smirks. "He actually tried to convince me it was a horrible idea. That it would be better to lock you in your room at night or even assign guards to sit by your door to make sure you stayed. But when he realized I wasn't budging, he accepted the assignment. Said he'd not be held responsible if he placed you in the dungeon and left you there. Thought that may be the only solution that would keep you from getting into trouble."

"He threatened to lock me in a dungeon?" I growl, completely prepared to go hunt his arse down and lock him in one now. "When was this?"

Sliding back under the car, he screws the plug back in place as he shares. "The night he confiscated your Ducati. He busted through my office door the next morning and told me I needed to assign more guards to your detail. Then he explained what happened. Afterward, he said the only way we could keep you from playing these stupid games was to lock you away each night in the old dungeon cells, maybe even put shackles on your ankles."

I huff and stomp my foot. "Did he also tell you he kissed me that night?"

A laugh echoes from beneath the car. "No. But I'm not surprised. Even back then, you two had this unexplainable connection. Like magnets drawn to each other. Except at that time you were flipped the wrong way. No matter how hard you tried, you couldn't get close enough without the negative force pushing you away. One of you had to turnabout and stop fighting against the pull. If I had to guess, I'd say it was Gino who finally lost the battle."

I remember it well. The day he found me in the spring and stopped being so damn stubborn about me running off. We spent six weeks together without the negative energy. That time had been long enough to bond us forever. But his disappearance flipped me back over, forcing me to push him away again.

"Want my advice?" Edward is pouring the new oil in his car. When I nod, he continues. "He's a good man. He tried to do the right thing, because at the time he felt it was best. You don't have to agree with that, of course. But here is what I see. I see how much you've grown since then. Know that you are a much stronger woman than you were before. In here and up here." He points to his heart and head. "I also know what you're doing in Sevilla. That had he shared who he was the first time, none of that would have happened. So maybe he was right. Maybe you weren't ready to know then. Perhaps you had a few more things to do before you could be what you both need you to be. Now you possess these skills that will help him in ways you couldn't before.

"What happens now, Gabby, is up to you. You can accept him for who he is and stand by his side. Or you can decide his life isn't for you, never was. But in the end, you have to also accept that the two men who orchestrated this so long ago, while they may have done it for selfish reasons, perhaps were only doing what God intended."

"My mother is wearing off on you," I grumble, standing and then wipe my hands on the overalls. "He told me if I didn't want to follow him, then he was walking away. That his life was with me, no matter what. That it was my choice. None of this feels like a choice, though."

Wrapping an arm around my shoulder, he kisses my head. "You already know what you have to do. So do it."

Do I?

I don't feel like I know. I feel like I'm the one who's standing at a crossroads and have no idea which road is the right path. Why do I have to choose? Why can't someone else tell me the path I'm supposed to follow?

I almost laugh. No one could ever do that. If someone tried, I'd most certainly choose the other one just to spite them.

Fucking hell, this really sucks.

Chapter Thirty-Two

GINO

The Royals

I stand off to the side and stare at the head table. The Constitutional Ball is tonight and I'm on duty. After the incident a few weeks ago at the opera house—where Her Royal Highness was shot at and the man who wanted her as his was killed—security is tight. We need to stay focused and alert. No more surprises.

But right now, my focus is not where it should be. Instead, it's on the man sitting next to my woman. One who was added to the official list a few days ago, against my objections. So now I'm standing here in my designated spot, staring, and doing my very best to remain calm.

Ela and I never got the chance to speak after the revelation of my true identity. I never planned on letting this much time pass, but when a madman sneaks past so many of us and almost accomplishes his goal, shit hits the fan. Everyone has been on high alert. The air holds an electric charge most of us can still feel. And that means long hours and not enough time to hash it out with her.

It was bad enough listening to her complaints about guards being more active in her life again. Knowing she wasn't wrong when she voiced how she was equally trained to handle any situation. That using them on her was taking resources off the problem at hand and wasteful, but Isaac, the new captain of the King's Guard, wasn't hearing any of it.

He was determined to get his boss, King Antonio, off his back. And since Ela wasn't ready to share her status as an Elite Force team member with her family, she had to live with his decision.

Why is Nico here in the first place? What evil scheme does he have up his sleeve?

Even as young boys, the two of us never got along. He was always up to no good and getting into trouble. We had our share of fist fights when he made comments about my little sister that were beyond inappropriate.

I fight a grin when I notice the way his nose sits a little crooked on his face. It goes well with the scar over his right eye. I put it there as well. My cousin hadn't learned the first time to keep his mouth shut, so I reminded him I didn't tolerate it when he mouthed off or was disrespectful.

The years haven't made him any smarter. He's still a piece of shit, only older, and from what I've noticed, a lot worse. The women he gets involved with learn very quickly what kind of monster he is. He may hide behind his tailored suits, money, and the title his father assigned him to lure them in, but his true colors shine, and he's left a trail of broken women behind who can't be fooled by a title.

His father, however, won't be equipped to clean up his mess this time. If he lays one finger on Ela, he'll no longer have a hand. I will cut it off. In fact, I'll do more than that. I'll chop him up slowly and send him back to his father piece by fucking piece. It would be my pleasure to make my uncle suffer the way I have all these years.

The only reason I'm still standing here is because I cannot reveal myself yet. If he saw me, he'd recognize me. Just like I recognized him when he walked into the pub where I was trying to enjoy a drink while in Kosonia. He'd not seen me seated in the dark corner where I shielded myself. But I'd gotten a full view of him, watched as he strutted in like he was the shit. The atmosphere changed as soon as he graced us with his presence. People became highly alert, a few discreetly left, others kept their heads down. I'd watched him approach a woman who clearly wanted nothing to do with him, witnessed him degrade her right there in front of everyone. It took all I had inside me to not kick his arse like I'd done several times before.

I did, however, follow him to the loo an hour later. He was alone. The men with him preoccupied, now acting like him. Idiots. I'd disabled the lights, locked the door, and had a man-to-man exchange with him.

"Do you know who I am?" He'd grunted as I shoved him hard against the urinal, dick still out, face now pressed into the piss covered wall.

I snarled in his ear. "You are Nico Sorin Kelemen."

"I'm Prince Nico, to be more accurate. Do you know what I could do to you for disrespecting me like this?" he spat out as he tried to fight me.

I flipped the knife open only inches from his face. "Prince? Well, damn. It seems I missed the ceremony promoting you."

"You're going to die." His words only made me laugh.

"I'm already dead. Hard to kill a man twice." I pressed the blade against his cheek. "All the lessons I once taught you and you never learned any manners. Perhaps now you'll be nicer to the ladies."

After I shoved a cloth napkin into his mouth to muffle his screams, I let the blade of my knife slice along his cheek. Then I took pleasure doing my best to make sure he could never use his dick to harm a woman again. He passed out from the pain and I slipped out the backdoor undetected. Leaving him disfigured and hopefully unable to father children.

Maybe that was cruel, but I don't think it was. Not after what I'd witnessed him do prior to our meeting in the bathroom. While his men stood guard, he dragged that woman off to a room. Her tear-stained bruised face and ripped clothes on display once he was finished. No. What I'd done was justice for her and all the other women he'd defiled over the years. Justice for my family as he sat in that room with his father and watched him put a bullet in my mother. That was justice, and I don't feel regretful.

Nico's arm slips behind Ela as he leans in to say something. His arm is only resting on her chair, but his eyes are roaming down her body, making my blood boil. He glides back when she stands. Then stands as well as if ready to follow, only to be dismissed. I can tell he's unhappy about it, but does his best to not show it. He's putting on a show, and I don't have time to figure out why that is tonight. The very reason I didn't want him here. He's a distraction I don't need. It's hard to focus on my job when I'm too busy watching him.

When Ela slips through the doors leading to the restrooms, I wave off her guard and follow instead. Her Royal Highness has Edward close by her side, so she's safe. He won't let her out of his sight and will understand me not wanting to let Ela out of mine.

Checking the handle to make sure it isn't locked, which I'm pleased to learn it's not, I push it open and lock it behind me. When I spin, I find her standing in the small space, staring at me. The dark green gown she has on makes my mouth water and has my eyes slowly scanning her delicious curves. I have to wonder how a woman uses the restroom in something that fits her form perfectly, hanging to the floor. Would it be easier to tug it up or pull it down?

Reaching under her left side, she tugs the zipper and lets out a deep breath. "I seriously hate all the hassle it takes to piss in a gown like this. Do you mind turning around?"

I cross my arms and shrug, not at all willing to look away. "I've seen it all before."

Or so I had thought. Tonight, I learn one thing I've never had the privilege of appreciating before. I learn where a woman hides her gun when dressed to kill.

Fuck me.

My head tilts upward to admire the ceiling, so I don't do something out of character. If I'm not careful, I'll have her bent over the sink with her hands pressed against the mirror while I take her from behind. Knowing she's armed is way sexier than it should be. My cock agrees and begins letting me know he has missed the half-naked fair maiden only a few strides away from him.

Just when I think it is safe to look, I discover it's not. Not only does she have a small caliber pistol shoved in her brassiere between her breasts, but she has a switchblade secured under her arm.

Running a hand down my face to distract my thoughts, I ask, "Are you enjoying yourself?"

Slipping back into her gown, Ela gazes up at me, unimpressed. "No. He's lucky he's my assignment, or he'd be long gone."

I blink, not sure I heard her correctly. Did she say her assignment? "I'm sorry. Could you repeat that?"

Turning toward the sink, she washes her hands. "You heard me.

Even though I still have a few weeks left before it becomes official, I'm working tonight."

"No." I'm not at all okay with that. "No."

Her eyes lock with mine in the mirror and I realize she's about to disagree with me. Ready to tell me her views on the matter when a loud pop explodes from the throne room. All thoughts of arguing this out leaves us and have our feet moving to find out what the fuck is going on.

Chaos has taken over as the sizeable crowd attempts to move all at once for the exits. My eyes land on the chandelier swaying above, all its lights no longer working. Odd, but not unusual. I've seen it happen a few times, but never have I seen all of them blow at once.

"Go with your guards to the secured location." I grab Ela's arm and hand her off to Zach. "Where is Prince Nico?" Bile rises in my stomach as I utter those words.

Zach places a hand on Ela's back as Yvette joins him. "He left shortly after she did. Went to the bar and sat down with his men to have a drink. Governors Hanson and Vons joined him."

Governor Hanson has been a thorn in this family's side for many years. He was very unhappy when Prince Esteban won the south seat after Collin's term ended. He's been grooming Governor Von, a first term new blood, pulling him over to his side of a political war. The fact they are meeting with my cousin bothers me. What are they plotting? And did they have something to do with what just happened?

Another loud pop pulls me out of my thoughts. A second chandelier's bulbs explode, sending sparks down on the crowd below them. Making them move faster to escape the unknown. It sounds like gunfire, so I don't blame them, but that has to be the plan, right?

Edward is next to me now. Panic on his usually stoic features. "Have you seen Angela?"

"Last I knew, she was with you?" I don't like this.

"Fucking hell. She ran to the bathroom. The one every other guest uses. Fuck. We thought it would be fine. Who would have predicted this? Fuck!" He's shoving his way through the crowd.

Before I can stop her, Ela is following after him. She's moving faster than we can, able to slither through the crowd and catch up to Edward rather quickly. They disappear outside, and even though I'm trying to make the crowd move for me, they aren't.

I walk out just in time to see Her Royal Highness emerge from the darkness, running. Who is she running from? I speak in my wrist to report it, when I spot Edward sprinting for her, Ela on his heels.

It happens in slow motion. Angela tripping and falling to her knees, her sister Cora is holding a gun behind her, ready to take the shot. Edward frozen, unable to move, knowing he's about to witness his worst fear come true.

It's Ela who acts when no one else can. She shouts over the crowd and warns her aunt to reconsider. Then, without so much as a hesitation, she fires the small caliber gun I saw earlier. The bullet hits her aunt in the shoulder, giving the other guards racing to the scene enough time to tackle her to the ground and secure her from doing more damage.

And while all this is interesting, it is the voice I hear behind me that worries me the most.

"Well, it seems the princess is quite handy with a gun. She might do just fine. Be the one I require standing by my side when the day comes for me to accept the throne. Not to mention I'll very much enjoy breaking her spirit and teaching her the proper way women are to act. She's been given way too many freedoms here, and it will be my pleasure training her how it should be. Now let's go and see if we can work out a deal that will give us both what we want." My cousin's voice isn't loud, but he's close.

I would turn around to see who he's talking to, but I don't want to risk him seeing me, recognizing me just yet. So that's what he's up to. He thinks he can somehow get Ela to agree to such an arrangement and then, once it's done, he plans to break her.

If she doesn't kill him when she learns of this plan, I will.

Chapter Thirty-Three

GINO

Chaos rained down after the incident at The Constitutional Ball. Everyone felt guilty and pointed fingers, unclear how something like that could even happen. After it calmed and the right people were punished or fired is when my life went up in flames.

I ended up resigning my position as a bodyguard for Darius' private protection company. I no longer had time to focus on anything other than the shit-show now taking place around me. All those words about me not moving forward without Ela by my side turned into another lie. My hand had been forced in the worst way, and now I was traveling back to Kosonia to smuggle out the woman I despised almost as much as my uncle.

It turns out Beni did something beyond stupid. He went behind my back and now Emoni, the traitor, is pregnant. I don't have time to question how it happened right now. All I know is if what he shared is true, then I need to help him get her out of there before anyone learns about her condition.

All those years of training have prepared me to handle a covert mission. There's no way I am allowing anyone else besides those I trust with my life to do this. I'm doing it with the help of the only people I fully trust—Darius, Stew, Hillary, Vincent, and Bruno. Hillary and Vincent are our decoys who work undercover for the King's Guard. They are excellent at what they do. The other men will help me clear the way to do what has to be done. Or more like clear the path for them, since they cannot catch me in Kosonia without raising a million red flags and compromising the mission.

We are all seated inside the home of one of Darius' associates just across the border. I hate I have to trust someone I don't know, but my faith in the Duke of Falcon is strong. He has proven his allegiance time and time again. One of the few people who knows my true identity and has kept that secret under lock and key. A friend to me and the crown I will one day wear.

The six of us are going over the plan, making sure there are no holes, and that we know what will happen should the unexpected occur. You must know the backup plans as well as you know the original. That way you can make quick decisions and get the job done. Thinking on your feet is never a good idea. That's how you get yourself killed or captured. Neither is an option on this mission.

The goal is to smuggle Emoni out of Kosonia, confirm her condition, and then take her back to Hermosa Islas without anyone knowing. And once she is by my side, she will remain there. No way am I letting her or anyone else spread more lies or try to harm an innocent. I will protect my family and its name with my life, even if that means keeping one more secret.

"Are you sure about this?" Darius leans back in his seat. "Before we risk all our lives, are you one hundred percent certain you've been told the truth this time?"

"No. Until one of our own can run a test, there will always be doubt. Would you trust anyone who told you such a tale?" I glare at Beni, who has been quiet as a mouse, knowing he's pushed me beyond my limits. "I mean, who steals from you like that without making you question everything? It was not his decision to make. I am the heir to the throne, and it was mine and mine alone. Not to mention, the woman he chose is an enemy. Why her?"

Hillary speaks up. "I'm guessing we won't know that until after we ensure she's safe. My question is why would she agree to something so absurd? Who would carry a child for someone when she didn't know why, exactly? My guess is she's in love with you and has been for a while now. She has an agenda of her own. Some women are manipulative like that. Those are the ones you need to watch carefully. She will turn on you if she thinks you will toss her to the side the moment this child is born."

I know this already. Emoni is a snake in the grass who will strike without warning. She has proven that once already. And it is why I will keep her close to me from now on. "I agree."

We all stare at each other for a long moment and then move quickly to get this show on the road. I have to stay behind because of who I am and the warning of what will happen should I step foot in Kosonia. The others depart to put the plan in motion, leaving Beni and me alone.

Beni looks at me with sympathy. "I know—"

"You know nothing. What you did is unforgivable. You've messed with my life, and you did so for selfish reasons." My voice is gruff and the tension in my body overwhelming.

"I did it to protect the regime." He lifts his head as if that is all he needs to say to make it okay.

"No. No, you did it to force my hand and make me choose this life over the one I could have had with Ela. You've made me look like a liar and a cheater. I wouldn't blame her for walking away and never looking back. And if that should be the case, then you've also sealed the fate of the people you claim you care about. If she is not by my side, then the kind of leader I am likely to become will not be the one you may want. Vengeance will be all I have to fall back on. I'll have no one to stand by me to be my voice of reason, and I'll only act on the bitterness that now poisons my heart and soul. Maybe you should have thought about that before you forced my hand." I shove my chair back and lean forward. "Leave me. I want to be alone."

As soon as the door closes, I walk to the desk and grab the cantor of dark liquid. I get the feeling I'll be drinking a lot more of this to numb the pain that now floods my veins. I should kill Beni for betraying me like he has. Publicly shoot him as a message. But that is not who I am. I'll save this rage for the true enemy lurking in the shadows, the dragon who has been haunting my dreams again at night. I can feel his breath on my neck, but I can't clearly see his face. It has me questioning if I'm missing something that has been right in front of me all along.

Chapter Thirty-Four

GABRIELA

The Royals

Weeks and then months passed quickly before things calmed again. My mother and Edward got married. I finished my training and went on a few out of the country (OTC) missions so my team would be ready when the time came.

Gino disappeared a few times in between without warning.

Meaning we still haven't taken the time to have a real conversation about us or the bomb he dropped on me. We've argued during the few occasions we've seen one another, all because he thought he could order me to stay far away from the business where Nico was involved. Demanding I reveal everything about why those in charge believe it is worth putting my life in danger by entangling me with his cousin. But when I ask the same questions, I get zero answers from him. He refuses to share why he keeps disappearing or why he's so against me being involved. Which means we get nowhere. We only fight until one of us ends up walking away before all hell breaks loose.

We are no better than we were, and each day that passes, I feel as if we're drifting further and further apart. He has once again stepped down from his job, no longer one of my mother's private guards. Shortly after he disappeared for the umpteenth time, he returned with a gorgeous, pregnant woman who looks at him with lust in her eyes. One who's staying at his home with him. One who has been glued to his side, accompanying him wherever he goes. I've tried not to make assumptions about why, but the mind has a way of going where you don't wish it to go.

My team and I are sitting down with our commanding officers for a briefing. We're lining up the details and getting ready for our first proper mission. The final team has five members: Peter, Ham, Iris, Beck, and myself. Our sixth member, Jae, was dismissed after an investigation into my accident revealed him as the asshat who ran me off the road. He's now cleaning toilets in prison while serving his sentence for the attempted assassination of a member of the royal family. No one misses him at all.

The five of us have completed four missions successfully, smaller ones that allowed us to work through some kinks. Now it's time to play with the big boys. Pull out all the stops and use my princess status to our advantage.

Our mission is rather simple. I've been invited to Kosonia to negotiate a truce between our countries. Since I was the royal who traveled there months ago to rescue one of our guards, they invited me back to be the negotiator. Or that's what those in charge are claiming to be the reason they want me to come. Intel discloses there is more to it than that.

The invitation is a setup. Typically, I'd not be allowed to go once something like that has been exposed. My brother would put a stop to it to protect me from being held captive inside a country in turmoil, because it's likely they would start making demands for my release. But I'm not just a princess, I'm a member of the Elite Force, a part of an exclusive covert team trained to know what to do in any situation. The request wasn't sent through normal channels. It was a personal invite from Nico to be his guest, where he has promised to be my guide and protector.

Political matters inside Kosonia are turning interesting. An announcement is expected soon where they'll introduce the next leader, who they hope will lead the country into a new era. Those watching predict it to be a natural born monarch who'll work side by side with the newly elected government. The new heads of state claim this person will stop the revolution threatening to break out again. Not everyone in Kosonia is confident this new government has their best interest in mind. The threat of war breaking out again is real.

Nico voiced it would help if he had a representative from an established monarch who could smooth the transition by showing our support. A country who is thriving with a natural born king and a group of elected officials working together. A country that has learned how to balance the powers and keep the peace for hundreds of years.

The problem Nico is having centers on the rumors about his family's rights to the throne. What he needs is for my family, who are known for honesty, to support his father when he announces Nico as the family's chosen one. The man the Kelemens believe this country should accept as the rightful heir.

I knew he wasn't telling me everything. That he's holding back and only feeding me information he thought would persuade me to agree. He's turning on the charm as well. Reminding me of how he accepted an invitation last minute to display an alliance. Now he's asking me to do the same.

Except the invitation he'd been sent hadn't come from the royal family. A few of our governors, who assumed they were being sneaky, invited him. What they were unaware of was by doing so, they were falling right into the trap set for them. It may have looked like I was taking the bait, but what I was really doing was finding my way in so we could take this family down. If I played my cards right, I could destroy the Kelemen family from the inside and reveal the truth of what they had done when the time was perfect.

Before our team meeting with our commanding officers' ends, we are interrupted. My brothers, Antonio and Esteban, walk in like only they can. They're not alone. The man who has been avoiding me struts in behind them. All three look as if they're ready to put a stop to this mission before it even begins.

I'm not having that, not this time. Standing, I take the initiative. "Gentleman, it's nice of you to finally join us."

Antonio shakes his head slightly walking over to an empty chair. "What's going on? Why is one of my former guards busting into my office and demanding I get my arse here to terminate whatever this is?"

Glaring over his shoulder, I notice Gino standing with a confidence that he'll get his way. He's been trying to convince those in charge to think of another way for months now. Pushing them to let my brothers handle this and keep me out of it.

Instead of explaining the mission, I take the folder in front of me and slide it across the table to Antonio. "Read that." I grab another from Iris and shove it toward Esteban. "You too. Read it and tell me it's a shitty plan and I might listen, or I might not."

Both take a seat and begin reading. I watch and wait, studying them closely, hoping to see what I want.

Only a few days ago everyone who needed to know was brought in on who Gino really was. Antonio knew most but not everything. Esteban was kept in the dark, like me and shocked about it. It explained why my eldest brother hadn't been against the two of us all this time, why he'd not fired Gino for fooling around with his little sister. And I'm a little pissed about that, but I'm letting it go for now.

The plan is not shitty at all, it's brilliant and they won't be able to deny it.

Gino's eyes lock with mine when I look up, and he tests me. "It's a shitty plan."

"You seem to be missing someone. Did she get sick of you already?" Even I can hear the bitterness in my voice.

"We're not here to discuss Emoni. We are here to discuss how this is a shitty plan." Gino steps forward and places his knuckles on the table as he leans toward me. "This is not happening. I won't allow it."

"You won't allow it? And you would be?" I slant forward in the exact same pose.

Smirking, he tries to shock me by openly sharing his thoughts with the rest of the room. "The man who will gladly toss you over his shoulder and lock you in one of those dungeons."

"I'd like to see you try." I lean closer, challenging him. "Someone has to do this. You can't. My brothers can't. Mother can't. Isabel is too young, although I don't think Nico would object. He seems to prefer them young. So that leaves me. He's too arrogant to admit I might be smarter than him, as is your uncle."

"No!" He slams his fist into the table, making it rattle. "It's my call, and I say absolutely no."

Antonio clears his throat before he speaks. "It's a good plan."

"No." Gino turns his angry gaze on the man he once worked for. "Would you allow Queen Larkin to do this? Or Princess Winifred?" His gaze lands on Esteban.

"If they were trained like Gabby has been, I'm not sure either would give us a choice." Esteban closes the folder and leans back in his seat. "If my wife had done this, came up with this plan, I'd have a few demands of my own. We'll talk later about how Gabby got into this unit without our knowledge. I'm not surprised, but damn."

"And your wives would tell you both to bugger off." I straighten and crack my neck. "Are you going to stop this? Have I wasted my time and the armed forces' who have trained me well to do missions like this? Or will you let those you trust to know what they are doing? Trust me to know that I can do this?" I'm speaking directly to Antonio now. No one else.

He flips through the pages and glances around the table while he decides. I'm certain he'll let Gino get his way, so I close my eyes, ready to object loudly when he speaks. "I'm letting those I trust decide. As long as they understand, should this go wrong, their jobs are on the line."

Each one of my commanding officers nod, and I watch Gino's face turn lethal. "Before I let that happen, I'll return home and do what I should have done the first time I was there."

"Get yourself killed?" I slap the table. "Because if you go back there, reveal you are there, they will throw your arse in jail, and this time they will kill you. Is that what you want? I thought we were in this together? I thought you told me I had a choice. Well, newsflash, my choice is this. I choose to stand by you, to take them down like this. Are you saying I no longer have that choice?"

He blinks and agitates his head, frustrated. "Things have changed since then. I can't protect both of you. I cannot be in two places at once. So no, you no longer have a choice."

"Well, then, I guess it's a good thing I'm free to make my own choices, isn't it? I don't need you to protect me. I'm more than capable of protecting myself. And if you think I'm going to just sit back and let you run off and get yourself killed, you're stupider than I thought." I turn and head for the door behind me as I address my team. "We have a plane to catch in seventy-two hours, I suggest you get your arses in gear and don't make me fucking wait."

I storm out of the room, not daring to stop to give him a chance to catch up with me. I almost make it out of there when a woman steps out of an office with four of Gino's men flanking her. I know they're his because I've seen them by his side these last several months. One is Beni. When his eyes meet mine, he at least has the decency to appear guilty. I'm not sure why, but I'm convinced it has to do with the woman standing next to him.

"Is that her?" I hear the woman ask the man closest to her.

I stop and extend my hand to introduce myself. "I don't believe we've properly been introduced. I'm Gabriela."

"Princess Gabriela," Beni corrects as his eyes turn downward.

Patting her swollen center, I immediately notice she's figured out that she knows more than I do. "He was never yours. I hear you refused to give him the heir he needs, which is why they came to me. What good is a princess if she refuses to help ensure the bloodline doesn't die?"

My palm collides with her cheek as tears threaten to spill from my eyes. She's not even shocked I slapped her. Our eyes lock. The hate she holds for me pisses me off more than anything. Her words cut me deep. I'm not so sure she knows my secret, but has overheard enough to understand what she's doing.

There was a time I thought if things worked out between Gino and myself, a medical miracle might be possible. But that was stolen from me as well. The study I entered reported the eggs I donated had a few issues they were concerned about. The chances of birth defects or complications would be high should I attempt to fertilize them. Once I learned of that, I'd went with my original plan. I demanded they destroy the rest as soon as the research was complete. A fire in the lab took care of it for me, making sure I didn't get the chance to change my mind.

"Emoni!" Gino works his way in between us. "Stop being a bitch. I thought I told you to wait for me. To stay put and out of trouble."

"Are you going to let her hit me like that? I'm carrying your child. A choice I made to..."

I use her tirade to get the hell out of there before I lose it completely. Not that I make it far once outside before I'm scooped up and tossed over broad shoulders.

"Put me down, now." My fist lands against his back. I'd kick him but the tosser has my legs secured tight. I could force him to set my feet on the ground if I wanted him to. I know how to get out of almost any hold, I just don't feel like fighting him right now. I want him to be willing to let me go for once.

He does, but not until we are in an area away from the eyes watching us. I could run or find my way out, again, but I don't. Instead, I drop and take a seat on the ground, crossing my legs. I sit there and wait.

Silence.

"Who is she?" I finally ask when I look up at him.

I can't read him as well as I once could. He's retreated again within himself. I thought we were past this, but it seems we've circled around one more time.

Fuck this.

Pushing myself up, I brush my pants off. "It doesn't matter. It's none of my business. You've made that clear by keeping me out of the loop. Message received loud and clear. So now I'm going to do the job I'm paid to do and—"

Gino lets out a resounding roar as he grips his hair. "This is so fucked up."

He's not wrong. "Yes, it is."

One of Gino's men approaches us. "Sir, I hate to interrupt."

"What now?" He turns and gives him the death stare. "What the fuck does she want now?"

"Just go. I have too much to do as it is. She clearly needs you, and I don't." I don't mean that. I need him so bad I ache for him, but I'm also very hurt at the moment, confused.

"This isn't over. I'm not done, and I'm not letting you think the worst." Gino follows his man when I nod but don't answer.

I've heard that before. I'm not holding my breath this time.

Chapter Thirty-Five
GINO

The Royals

How am I supposed to fix this when every time I turn around, another crisis is dropped into my lap? I can't. And this latest one makes me look like the biggest liar to ever walk the face of the earth. How can I explain something I myself have a hard time believing?

When Beni shared with me what he'd done behind my back, I saw red. How could he? How in the hell could the one man I trusted betray me in such a way? It was like being gutted and left to bleed out while the walls crashed in around me. He claimed it was for the good of the cause. That in order to prove my loyalty to the rebellion, who have been fighting for their freedom for so long, this was the only way.

He was wrong.

It was not the only way. What he'd done, however, forced me to act and keep yet another secret. I hate secrets. They only destroy the trust one has worked so hard to build. Nothing good has ever come from one, nothing.

I approach the vehicle Emoni is seated in and the have the urge to throw up. This woman is the most manipulative person I've ever met. I wouldn't be surprised if she thought by doing this it would force me to view her differently. It did, but not the way she'd hoped. When I look at her, all I see are lies, vengeance, and hate. All traits that disgusted me and have me watching her very closely, because I don't trust her at all.

It had me questioning Beni's sanity as well. Why would he pick the woman we know once betrayed us? The person who turned me in and sent me to the hell where I was certain I was going to die. My distrust is why she is here now. Until everything is confirmed and this war is over, she's not getting another chance to betray us again.

I'm having a hard time accepting any of it is real. That the one man I trusted with my life deceived me in the worst way possible. That he used my recovery from hell to get what he needed and then went behind my back to secure the future without asking for my permission to do so.

As soon as I'm close enough for her to grab my hand, she does. I try to yank it back as she places it on her swollen center. "Your son wants to remind you why I'm here and where your mind should be focused on now. She can never give you this. Refused to from what I've been told. Why waste your time with someone who refuses to help you get what is yours? You are the future, and he's your way of ensuring it does not die when you do."

My heart expands when I feel the baby inside her kicking. I'm so confused on why I have such an attachment to this child, when I suffer from pure hatred toward the mother. My child, who was put there without my knowledge, is growing inside my enemy. A woman who I know will stab me in the back the moment she realizes I'll never accept her for more. Never marry her. Never bring her into my inner circle. She will only ever be the mother to the child we now share. I'll never change my mind or walk away from the woman I love, not even in this fucked up situation.

How is that even possible? I mean, I know what these two did. Beni told me the doctor requested a sample of my semen to check for infection after what I'd been through. I'd not questioned it. I willingly supplied the specimen. That had been a mistake, one I regret. He'd kept it, saved it until the time was right, and then used it to create an heir behind my back.

For some reason, he'd considered Emoni as a suitable incubator. His reasoning was that she owed him after he'd saved her life. She'd come to him in dire shape after my cousin had used her to his advantage and later disposed of her. Which only made me distrust her more. If she was with my cousin, then this could all be a setup.

When Emoni agreed to help Beni with his deceitful plan, he claims she didn't know it involved me at first. He lured her in by telling her she could assist him by doing something that would change the world. Once she learned his plan somehow was linked with me, she hadn't hesitated to follow him into the darkness. And because she's a smart woman, it took her no time at all to put two and two together. She'd figured out I was someone important and used that to her advantage. I'm not sure she knows my true identity, but she knows I hold the keys to the kingdom. That the plan is for me to overthrow my uncle and take Nico's place.

Once informed of what Beni did, I immediately acted. There was no way I was letting Emoni out of my sight long enough for her to betray me again. I have to protect the child she carries, no matter what. That also means protecting the woman carrying it, keeping her from doing something stupid just to make a point. It forced me to put my plans with Ela on hold and had her assuming things that weren't true. Once Emoni learned of my infatuation with the princess, she demanded all my free time, making sure she held my full attention.

As soon as we return to my place, I retreat to the office on the third floor. It's where I spend most of my time. Here, I can be alone. The other floors are unrestricted for Emoni, but the third-floor office is off limits. She, under no circumstances, is allowed up there. Not just because it's where I plot my next move. But because I need at least one floor where I can think and focus on the task at hand.

My bedroom is also on that floor, but I found it difficult to stay there without my brain being overtaken by thoughts of Ela. I avoid it as often as possible. Only going in there to clean up and sometimes sleep. Not that I sleep much these days.

The knock on my office door three hours later brings my attention to how long I've been hiding out in here. Standing, I stalk toward it, expecting Emoni. She often breaks the rules and tries to coerce me out with food first. She's not above doing everything she can think of to persuade me to spend time with her. It never works. The last thing I want to do is to be around her, to look or listen to her while she spills more lies.

Throwing the door open, I state harshly. "What the fuck do you want now?"

It's not Emoni, though. It's Ela holding what looks like takeaway and a six pack of beer. She lifts them both as she speaks. "Truce?"

God, I miss her. I mean, like, really miss her. Not only the physical part we haven't gotten to enjoy since that unexpected fuck in the pool. I miss her. Talking to her. Being with her. I miss what she brings to my soul when it's just the two of us sitting around. It's something I never knew was possible until I met her, and I so very desperately want it back. I want her back.

I motion for her to come inside as I step back. "Something smells fantastic. What is it?"

My eyes follow her fine arse as she struts to the small table in the corner to set down the bag and beer. I can't help that my dick also notices. He's getting bored with my hand.

"Burgers and fries. Nothing better than greasy food and beer to clear the air, right?" Ela has two beers in her hand when she spins. "You said you wanted to talk. I'm tired of being the one who has to wait for you to come to me."

I take the beer and bring it to my lips, swallow, and let the cool liquid slide down my throat. While I do my best to enjoy the taste, I take in the sight of her as well. She's as gorgeous as I remember, more so, really. I'm so tired of fighting with her.

Taking a seat, Ela eats, and I join her, sitting in the chair across from hers. We eat while we stare at one another. No words are spoken. We drink the beer, eat the greasy food, and stare.

When she's had her fill and a few beers, she slouches back in her chair and kicks her feet to rest on the table. I shove the last bite in my mouth while I watch and try my best to read her thoughts.

She speaks first. "I'm not going to ask about your houseguest."

"You're not?" I wish she would.

"No." She picks on the label on the bottle of beer. "Not yet, at least."

"Emoni—"

"I'm not here to talk about her. That business clearly isn't going anywhere soon, so it can wait. We have other business, however, that can't." Ela looks up and the fire that burns behind her eyes is bright. "I thought we were in this together."

Spreading my legs, I rest my forearms on the table as I run a finger over the rim of my bottle. "So did I. But Ela, this plan of yours is dangerous. I know these men, and I've seen what they are capable of doing. It's unacceptable to allow you to put yourself in that kind of danger."

"But it's okay for you to put yourself in danger?" The calm tone of her voice alerts me she's thought about this and is ready to take it to the mats if necessary.

"It's my fight." I know the moment the words leave my mouth they were the wrong ones.

Her feet lift slowly as she straightens and pops her neck. "Well then. I guess I misunderstood when you shared your secrets with me before that shit with my mother hit the fan. My brain was all over the place, trying to figure it out. I can see where confusion might have set in and I heard what I wanted to hear, and not what you were actually saying."

I rub my forehead, undergoing the stress building again. "At the time when I shared that with you, that is what I said. Things have gotten way more complicated since then. Beni took a few matters into his own hands when he assumed I was about to walk away, forcing me to accept my fate. Making this now my fight to ensure no one else gets hurt because of what he has done."

"So, you no longer love me?" she asks softly, as if it's too much to think about.

"I love you. I will never stop loving you. But I cannot ask you or your family to do this. Blood will be shed, Ela. People will die on both sides of this conflict. The battle is not over, and the casualties will be devastating to all involved. I cannot in good conscious send you to the front lines knowing that. I've already lost more than one man can take." She has defiance in her eyes, warning me she will not back down, no matter how much I plead. "I will lock you in one of those dungeons if it comes to that."

I expected her to scream, not to laugh, but laughter falls from her mouth as she stands. "You may try, but you will never get a chance to do that. And thanks to you, I now have my brothers on my side. We had a pleasant chat after you left."

"What?" I fall back and shake my head in confusion.

"After you left, I found them still sitting in the conference room with my commanding officers. We sat down and put our heads together. Antonio demanded to know the details of the situation, which they shared with him. Esteban is the one who came up with a new plan. Both my brothers were very impressed I'd kept my Elite Force training from them. While they knew I was scheming something up, they hadn't assumed it to be that. Even though they too hate the idea of me being the one to carry this out, they agree no one else is capable of getting close enough to your family without raising suspicion. I came here as a courtesy to let you know, so what I have to share next doesn't shock you when it happens." She presses her lips together, and I know I won't like this one bit.

"When what happens?" The words fall from mine as I watch her walk toward the door. "What the fuck did you all decide that you felt I needed to know?"

Grabbing the handle, she stares me in the eye as she rips my heart from my chest. "I leave for Kosonia tomorrow. When I arrive, I'm having a meeting with your Uncle Dracul. My brother Antonio will be by my side. He'll suggest a union be the best way for us to show we support the Kelemen régime. After he agrees, we'll announce to the world that I have consented to marry the King of Kosonia once he accepts the throne."

I'm on my feet so fast the table moves and my chair hits the ground. "The fuck you will."

"I don't need your permission, Gino. I only thought it right to inform you, so you had time to ready yourself." Ela opens the door and walks out like she didn't just drop a fucking bomb in my lap.

Chapter Thirty-Six

GABRIELA

Ten days have passed since I dropped the bomb on Gino. In those ten days, a lot has happened. A weather front kept us grounded, delaying our mission. Gino has trampled around like a disgruntled child, making all these unnecessary demands. Not just to me, but also to Antonio.

He tried to drag my mother and Edward in as well. It didn't work. Edward knew as much as I'd been allowed to share. My mother learned about our plans a few days later when I sat down with her to explain my new job and what we were doing. She wasn't thrilled about my new career, but she supported me, trusted Antonio to not allow me to do something that would get me killed.

Could that happen? Could I die trying to help Gino get his country back? Sure.

But I could die tomorrow in a car crash, and that didn't stop me from getting in a vehicle. This was still happening. The only thing that has changed was those in charge have agreed to allow him to join us. Not in the meeting that involved his uncle, but on the trip. He was now a part of the team who worked behind the scenes. I wasn't so sure he'd be able to stay out of the thick of it, but that problem wasn't mine to handle. It was those in charge's problem, and they have assured me they know how to deal with Gino.

We're leaving tomorrow. I know this probably isn't the best idea. That I should read over the intel as it comes in, instead of showing up here once again to attempt to smooth things over. But I'm here to ensure that when this goes down, we're on the same page.

I ring the bell.

When his front door opens, I'm greeted by Emoni, who looks as if she's been crying. "He doesn't want to see you." She tries to shut the door in my face.

Tries but fails.

I let myself in and head for the stairs that lead to the third floor. My gut says he'll be in the same place I found him last time. The only reason I stop before I reach them is because Emoni is now screaming at me.

"You're going to get him killed. He's planning to march in there and give himself up just to keep you from marrying Nico." She actually hiccups, as if she cares about his life. I think it's all an act. "I've tried to talk some sense into him, but he refuses to listen to me. If you love him—"

Those words are the ones that have me spinning. "If I love him?"

Gino steps around the corner, a dark glass of liquid in his hand, shirt unbuttoned, and hair tousled. If I didn't know any better, I'd mistake his appearance as a just fucked one. Only I do know better. I know by his expression as he glares at the woman, yelling. "I thought I told you to find a place where I didn't have to look at or hear you. Yet here you are, lurking around like always. When are you going to get it through your thick head that I have never been or will ever be interested in you? Only one woman can make me happy, and she's lost her fucking mind."

"I can still change my mind." She crosses her arms boldly. "I can still walk away."

Gino slams back his drink and lets the glass fall to the floor. "You keep threatening to do that, Emoni, yet every chance you get you're trying to worm your way into my bed." Pointing at her rounded belly, he growls, "That may be my child you're carrying, but I did not put it there. And it doesn't change the fact that every time I look at you, all I see is your deception. I'm still not convinced it's mine. Nor have I figured out why you would agree to such a crazy scheme when you first thought I was only a rebel fighting for justice. None of it adds up. Nothing about any of this makes sense. The only person I trust is her, and she's about to annihilate me by walking straight into the lion's den."

Beni is now standing behind Gino, looking guilty. He steps around him to where Emoni is and gently grabs her arm to guide her down a hall. "Come on. This is not the time or place. Do you want to go back?"

I watch her body stiffen and stumble at his words. "You promised."

I know there is more to Emoni than I've been told, and I'll get to the bottom of it eventually. Something is off and I will not allow someone to hurt him more. He's suffered enough.

"Yet you cannot seem to stay out of trouble." He warns as he leads her out of my range of hearing, still talking and doing so in a tone I distinguish as the last straw.

Bending to pick up the tumbler he dropped, Gino speaks to me directly. "Why are you here? I thought you would be preparing for tomorrow's big day."

"Did you sleep with her?" I have to ask before I can let my mind focus on other things.

"No. Not when we first met over four years ago, and sure as hell not in the last six or so months to cause her condition." Gino makes his way to the bar, barely able to navigate a straight line. "Beni double-crossed me in the worst way. When I was in recovery, he convinced a doctor to collect my sperm and then kept it on hand so when the time came, he could use it."

I take the bottle of dark liquid he is about to pour and cap it. Grabbing two waters, I open them, handing him one while keeping the other for myself. "Are you saying he paid a doctor to do in-vitro on her? Why would he do that?"

His eyes are hollow as he looks into mine. "Because that's how this shit works. He was afraid I was going to walk away. My decision to choose you or the cause was not one he was willing to take a chance on. He took it to the extreme and made sure I had no choice but to fight for my birthright. It feels wrong, though. She should not be the one carrying my heir, yet it seems she is. I cannot be completely sure, though. She's refused to allow us to run any tests. Which is another reason I've not let her out of my sight since retrieving her. She's run off once already. If the child is mine, then it is my responsibility to protect it. Even if I hadn't been involved in the planning of it, I cannot take chances."

I have to wonder why Emoni would run unless she's intending to do something drastic. No wonder he's a big mess. I'm done being mad. I know it's time to let things go and for us to move forward. Together. "I believe you. If it is yours, I'll be here. Love this child as if it were my own."

Tears flood his dark eyes. "I'm sorry my life is so fucked up. I wish it weren't. I wish I could change it all and just be a man without this mess hanging over my head."

"My whole life I've wished to be anyone but who I am. You know what I've learned about wishing for that?" I lift my hand and run it over his hair and down his cheek. "It doesn't work."

I hate seeing such a powerful man so torn up about everything he has no control over. They've forced him to trust a group of men he never really knew, only to have one of them betray him. His life since his family died has been about surviving behind a curtain others constructed for him. Always trying to figure out who he can trust and what they want in return.

I appreciate how he feels. Until he came into my life, I only trusted my family. He hasn't even been granted that. The family he had left wanted him dead. But now he has me, and I won't allow him to believe I'm about to betray that trust or walk away from him.

"You know what else I've learned?"

He shakes his head slightly.

"That I was born into this life for a reason. Even though I've always hated it, there were details I wouldn't have learned had I been someone else. Things I needed to know, so when you stormed into my life, I'd be ready."

Taking a hold of his hand, I encourage him to stand. I lead him up the long staircase and am glad he's following without fighting. We land on the third floor and I drag him down the hallway to where his bedroom is.

"Why are we going to my bedroom?" He grunts behind me. "Ela, I'm only so strong. Resisting you has always been one of my greatest weaknesses."

"Ditto." I shove the door open and spin to face him. "Do you trust me?"

"It's not you I don't trust." Squeezing my hand, I see he's struggling to keep it together. "I'm afraid this will blow up in my face, and I'll be the one who pays the ultimate price. Once again, I'll be the one left behind to face my future alone."

Grabbing his face, I tug his closer to mine. "I'm never letting that happen. All this time, you were focusing on what you think I said, not what I actually said."

"You said that you and Antonio were meeting with my uncle to inform him you will marry my crazy cousin once he becomes king." His head tumbles forward as anger takes over his eyes. "I cannot allow that. He'll hold you to it, even if you're only saying it so you can get close enough to gain access to the information I need. It's a dangerous game."

"Most of what you said is correct, but not all. I said we would inform him I'll marry the next King of Kosonia. I never said I'd marry Nico. Tell me, Gino, who is the only man who has genuine claim to the throne? Your uncle doesn't. Your cousin doesn't, either. Nico could not claim it, not even if you died. Do you know why?"

I doubt he does. It took some digging to uncover all the secrets his family has been hiding.

"Did you know Nico isn't your uncle's son? It seems your aunt was sleeping with one of his men and ended up pregnant. And since no one knew it, no one bothered to question who Nico's father really was. The only reason we uncovered it was because of a medical record we came across. It stated that your cousin needed a blood transfusion after a bar fight. It revealed he was AB positive."

"So am I." Gino states, not understanding.

"I know. I'm A negative. Both are rare blood types. Your father was B and mother A. My mother is O and my father is B. Nico's mother is also both B, and since your uncle is your father's twin..."

A lightbulb goes off in his head. "Nico should be B as well."

"B or O, but there is no way for him to be AB unless..."

"One of his parents had A blood running through their veins."

"Exactly. And because Dracul didn't have other children with your aunt, once he dies, the next in line falls to the next surviving male relative from the same bloodline. Which would be a very distant relative, even I'm having trouble locating who that might be. It really would be easier if you just passed them down the line to the next relative, no matter the gender. But since your father and uncle only had sisters, it makes it a lot harder to follow."

Gino lips turn up into a smile, which I find odd.

"Why are you smiling?" I ask, not sure what he finds humorous about all this.

"This report you discovered. Did it explain where he lost so much blood that he required this transfusion?" He is almost giggling, and it's cute.

I nod. I had to read it three times when I came across it to make certain I was reading it correctly. "It stated that his male genital had nearly been severed. That it had to be reattached. Why do I get the feeling you know this already?"

"Did it say if he was able to use it?" Gino is way too interested in Nico's penis.

I grab his shirt that remains unbuttoned, displaying a chest I would love to sink my teeth into, and yank him to me. "I didn't read more. It wasn't my biggest concern. Perhaps if you ever get the chance, you can ask him yourself."

"The next time I see him will be when I put a bullet between his ears," Gino growls as he grabs my hips and yanks me forward. "Why are you telling me all this now? What are you saying, exactly?"

"I'm saying that the only man I plan to marry one day is you." I yelp when my feet leave the ground. I'm plastered against his hard chest as his hand delves into my hair to press my lips to his.

It has been too damn long since I've kissed this man. And this isn't just a kiss. It's a devouring, all-consuming, hold nothing back kind of kiss, where teeth clank together, tongues fight, and the air in your lungs burns because you refuse to stop and breathe. My back slams into the first hard surface, where I'm restrained while he rips my t-shirt from my body and tosses it somewhere behind us.

His lips finally leave mine and travel down my neck. Teeth scrap along my pulsing artery and clamp down on my collarbone, no doubt leaving a bite mark behind. It wouldn't be the first time I was forced to stare at his love bites left after a wild night of passion. He often wore a few of his own as well, because I believed in equality and turnabout is fair play.

"Gino." I moan his name as he clamps down on my tender nipple and then sucks hard. "Fuck. Gino. Yes. Please."

A phone rings in the background before we can go any further, stopping us.

"Fuck!" Gino groans as he sets my feet back on the ground.

"Who is calling you this time of night that you feel the need to stop?" I grumble as he tosses me my shirt.

Seizing my arm, he drags me behind him while I'm doing my best to slip it over my head. "Someone who's probably alerting me we have a problem. Story of my goddamn life."

"We?" I say, a little too excited about the fact he said we. "What kind of problem?"

Glancing over his shoulder, he grins, but only briefly. "One I wouldn't have had if you'd have told me everything from the start. I may have done something stupid to make sure you didn't end up married to the wrong man."

I should kick his arse for whatever that means, but right now I don't have time. I'll do it later after we figure out what's going on. Once we've figured out how to fix what he messed up.

Chapter Thirty-Seven

GINO

The Royals

I drag Ela down to my office where the burner phone I set up a few days ago is ringing. I connected it to my private cell so I wouldn't miss this. The ringing we heard that interrupted us was a call I couldn't ignore, no matter what, and the only business that would stop me from claiming her again.

Pointing to the chair in front of my desk, I grab the phone and place it on speaker, placing my finger over my mouth. She can listen, but she cannot speak. "Hello, Uncle."

Ela pauses her descent into the chair and an inferno burns behind her eyes.

"The man you're claiming to be has been dead for over twenty years. I buried him. Identified his body, along with the rest of his family, after rebels murdered them." Even I can hear the lies in his voice, and when I look up at Ela, I see she can as well.

"Funny, that's not how I remember it at all. I recall seeing you put a bullet in my mother before doing the same to my father." I keep my voice level. "You took everything from me. Now I'm going to take everything from you. Tell me, Uncle, when is the last time you've spoken with Nico?"

Silence echoes over the line for several minutes.

"You are playing a dangerous game. How do I even know you are who you claim to be?" I can hear his men in the background. One reports they are unable to reach my cousin. That he's not been in contact with them for several hours now.

I smile.

My men have been successful. Before this night is over, I'll once again come face-to-face with my cousin. He'll be lucky if he lives to see another day. I've been looking forward to this day since the day I watched my parents die. Some people don't deserve to live.

"You don't. Maybe I am Simion, and maybe I am not. Are you saying you're willing to risk Nico's life waiting for that kind of proof? You can save him. Or you can at least spare him for the time being. Eventually, I will kill him, that I can promise you. But if you follow my demands, he will live to see tomorrow, giving you a chance to make a few things right. So, what is it?" I hope he tests me. It would be my pleasure sending Nico's body back to him as a message I mean business.

Ela leans over so she can press the mute button. "What the fuck is wrong with you?"

Before I can respond, my uncle speaks. "What is it you want?"

I turn the mute off and lay it all out for him. "You have a meeting in the morning. Cancel it. Tell them something has come up and you no longer need their support."

"They won't believe me. This is something we've been working on for months now. Too many people are involved." If he thinks I'm stupid about how this shit works, he has another thing coming.

"Dear Uncle, I don't care. You can tell them to fuck off, if you wish. Inform them you never really were interested in their help to begin with. That you were only interested because you planned on using her against them. I don't blame you. The princess is very beautiful. I bet Nico was looking forward to violating her... oh wait. Can he still do that? I believe he had this mishap where he nearly sliced his dick off." I know I'm pushing my luck, but I do so love toying with him. "Or maybe he isn't the one who was eager about winning her. I believe you have always had a wandering eye and liked them young enough to be trained. Do you still like that, Uncle? Were you hoping to tie her to you, then forcing a union because of that?"

My girl is raging now. Did she not think about that being a part of this evil man's plans? While I know she cannot bear children, that isn't something others know. Men like my uncle will do whatever they want, even force themselves on a princess to gain power over others.

"You have five hours. If I don't hear from you before then, I'll send Nico back to you one piece at a time. Five hours." I don't wait for him to agree before I hang up.

"What the fuck, Gino? Are you trying to sabotage all the hard work so many people have put in just to get your way?" Ela's hands are gripping the arms of the chair so tight her knuckles are turning white. "My brother is going to be pissed when he hears about this."

"You gave me no other choice. I wasn't about to let you risk your life—"

"But you are prepared to risk yours? You trade mine for yours? That's stupid. No. No. That is not how it works. You don't get to decide how far I'm willing to go when you've not been completely upfront with me." Standing, she places her palms on my desk. "Do you really have Nico, or were you bluffing?"

I reach for my phone and find the photos one of my men sent a couple of hours ago. It's of Nico doing what he does best, being a complete prick and hitting on a woman who held no interest in him. Except this time the woman isn't your everyday female. She's a trained soldier. The last one was sent only moments ago. It is of him tied up, along with two of his men, in a concrete basement. All three haven't been hurt yet, just gagged and bound.

Ela stares at them, and I can almost see the wheels in her head spinning fast. "This could work."

"What could work?" I lean back and wait.

"Did you send these to your uncle yet?" She grabs a piece of paper off my desk and snags a pen, then scribbles something down. "Have you sent these to him yet?"

"No. I'll wait an hour before doing so. I want him to sweat it out first." I'm trying to figure out where she's going with all this.

Pulling out her phone, she presses the call button and lets it ring.

"You are worse than my men interrupting me at all hours of the night," Antonio grumbles.

"Well, excuse me, brother, but we have a problem. Gino has gone off to the nuthouse and done something. Which means we need to act now if we want to get ahead of this." She taps her pen against her lip.

"I'm listening." Antonio sounds more awake now.

"The documents you had made. Fax them to Dracul within the next hour. Send him an email to go with it." Looking down at the paper she reads what she wrote. "Did you get all that or do you need me to repeat it?"

I can hear amusement when he answers. "I got it, little sister. Are you sure? This could change the game drastically and have them acting."

"Gino's given him five hours to call this off. He's holding Nico for ransom if he doesn't. If we put pressure on him as well, he's going to have to make a choice. My guess is Nico was never the man he planned to announce as king. He was plotting to claim that title for himself." She writes something else down and smiles. "If you dangle a steak in front of a hungry lion, he will attack it without seeing the hunter who has been patiently waiting for him to leave his cave. Forgetting he was protected inside and act without thinking. When he acts, he exposes himself and opens the door for us. Do you understand?"

I'm shaking my head because this woman just might have a point. All this time we've been going about this separately, when we should have been putting our heads together.

"Oh, and Antonio." Ela's eyes glow when they find mine. "Send the other paperwork to Gino as well. We'll both sign it and fax it back to you as soon as we've finished. It's time to end this now. I'm done pussyfooting around."

"Are you sure he wants that?" Antonio laughs.

"Send the damn paperwork and then do what I told you to do. He'll either agree or I'll force him to agree." Ela smirks as she hangs up the phone and drops back down into her seat.

We sit opposite of each other, staring. What is it she thinks she can force me to do if I should protest? Our eyes never leave the others even when my fax machine comes to life.

"Do I even want to know what you have planned?" I stand and stroll over to it when it stops. "I'm not really sure I like you..."

My words end when my eyes land on the document last sent. I spin to find Ela down on one knee with the wickedest grin on her beautiful face.

"In order for you to prove who you are and for others to believe this is not some crazy scheme of revenge, you need a solid alliance. My family is willing to offer that to you. I know our fathers were doing this for selfish reasons, maybe I am too. The thought of you allowing any other woman to stand by your side has me seeing red. No one can protect you the way I can. No one else could stand by your side and understand what it's going to take to get you and your country through this. No one but me can claim to be doing so for no other reason than because I simply fell in love with you. All others would use you so they can hold a title. I hate the title, don't want it. But I'm eager to accept it if you're ready to offer it to me." She gathers her thoughts and lets out a breath. "Will you marry me, Gino? Will you make me your wife so we can stand together and take back what has always been yours?"

The papers drop to the floor as I tumble to my knees as well. "I'm supposed to be the one asking."

"I grew tired of waiting." She grabs my hands and brings them to her mouth. "A girl can only wait so long before she takes matters into her own hands."

I study her face while I do my best to recover. "If I decide to walk away, would you still choose to marry me?"

"Yes." She nods. "Do you want to walk away?"

Taking her face in my hands I shake my heads slowly. "I've learned too much to just walk away. I'm scared. Terrified actually. I'm not sure I'm the right man to do this, but I will not allow my uncle to continue to deceive those who have put their trust in him. It's time for me to make my father proud and be the man he intended me to one day become. I need you next to me, Ela. I cannot do this without you, that much I know. You calm the storm inside me like no one else can. It would be my greatest honor to be allowed to call you my wife."

Her lips fall on mine faster than I can get mine on hers. God, I love her. Everything about this woman does it for me. We kiss and hold one another like that until the sound of a phone ringing brings us back to the here and now.

It's the burner phone again. I didn't expect my uncle to call me so quickly. "Uncle, that was quick."

"Simion? Simion, is it really you?" I hear a woman ask me, one that sounds familiar.

"Who is this?" I lean back on my heels. "How did you get this number?"

The woman's voice cracks as she responds in hushed tones. "It's me, brother. Giovanna. He does not know who I am. I heard him talking and... I have to go. I'll call you again later. Take care, brother."

And like that she's gone.

Could it really be her? Is this a trick Dracul is playing, hoping to get me to react? What the fuck do I do now?

Chapter Thirty-Eight

GABRIELA

The room takes on a new ambiance the moment he answers the phone. All the color drains from his face when it ends seconds later. Gino stares at the rectangular device in his hand as if not sure what he should do next.

"Gino?" I brush my knuckles on his cheek. "Who was that?"

Eyes so distant glance up at me. The man who was ready to take on the world moments ago is gone. He's replaced by the boy he once was. I know this by the next words that come out of his mouth. "She said she was my sister."

"Heidi? Why would Heidi call you on that phone?" I tug it from his tight hold and see only one number displayed. It is the same one from earlier. Making me even more confused than before. "Why is Heidi with your uncle? Oh, no. Oh, Gino."

He's shaking his head frantically. "No, not Heidi. Giovanna. She said she was Giovanna."

Now I understand his shocked demeanor. He was told she died the same day his parents did. Shot and killed when the two of them tried to make their escape. How is this possible?

"Are you sure it's her?" I have to ask. I wouldn't put it past his uncle to try and trick him.

Still in shock, he admits. "I don't know."

I stand with the phone still in my hand and pull out my own. Time to call in my team and let them help us sort this out. We have a change in plans as it is. I was going to have to call them eventually.

I hate to be so nonchalant about the unfinished business we were discussing, but the sooner it is official, the better. Gathering the pile of papers scattered on the floor, I arrange them on the desk. While I send a message to my team to meet us here within the hour, I read the paperwork to make sure it's all in order.

I make one more call, knowing if I don't, I'll never hear the end of it.

"Gabriela? Is everything okay?" My mother does her best to keep her voice calm.

"For the most part, yes. But I have a request, or more like I know if I don't, you'll skin us both alive when we return." I take a seat in Gino's chair and look down at him, still seated on his knees. "Gino and I request that you and Edward come witness us signing our marriage certificate."

"Signing them? Did you two run off and get married? I thought—"

I interrupt her. "It is very complicated, mother. He did something that forced my hand. Now we need to get married so that when we return to Kosonia, he is protected under the laws of being a diplomat and spouse of a royal. Even that deranged government has laws that protect other diplomatic officials. So, for now, we are signing them to make it official. Later we'll have a proper ceremony, if that is what he wants."

Gino stands while I'm talking and reaches for my hand to tug me out of his chair. When he's seated, he tugs me back into his lap as he snickers at my last statement to my mother. "Do you not want a proper ceremony? Do you not wish to have a wedding where we exchange vows?"

I shrug because it's not something I've given much thought to doing before this crazy man. My plan was to remain single and never have to worry about putting a wedding together where I'd be the center of attention. The very thought makes my stomach sour.

He chuckles as he presses a kiss to my shoulder. "Maybe I've thought about that. Dreamed of you standing at the back of a long aisle dressed in a beautiful wedding gown. I stood there for as long as I could until my feet would no longer remain in my designated spot and I began walking toward you, meeting you halfway. Because that seems to be how this relationship works, meeting each other halfway so we don't have to face the unknown alone. Then standing there in front of everyone and declaring my unwavering love for you, where I promise to allow you to be a strong free-spirited woman who will never have to submit to me. Then kiss you until my knees go weak and I know if we don't stop, the crowd watching will get an unexpected display of our love."

My mother hums in my ear, and I swear I hear Edward encourage him to not let me off so easily. When he seems to be finished, Mother speaks. "Well, then. I guess you have something to think about when you return. For now, however, Eddie and I would love to be witnesses to you signing the proper documents. We'll see you within the hour. And Gabby?"

"Yes, mother?" I lean into him.

"I'm proud of you. This is where you belong. I know together the two of you will be amazing and change the world." I hear the sincerity in her voice.

"Thank you, Mom. Thanks for always being there for me. We have a huge battle ahead of us, but together we are stronger. I'll see you soon." I hang up and peer over my shoulder at the man who surprised even me.

"What?" He tightens his hold on me. "One of us has to be a romantic softy and give the people what they want."

I laugh as I shift in his lap, so I'm now straddling him. "Such a softy. My growly man who hid in the shadows all those years has a soft side. Who knew?"

He shrugs as the weight he's storing inside presses him down. "I'm sorry I cannot give it all to you right now. You deserve more than just an official signing of documents. I'm not even certain we'll be able to consummate our marriage with all this shit being thrown at us."

We can't have that now, can we? It's been way too long since I've had this man inside me. Perhaps this isn't the right time to take a break from the chaos and get lost in the one person we know gets us, but sometimes you have to make time.

I make the final decision and jump out of his lap, stride over to his office door, shut it, and secure the lock. As I spin, I yank my t-shirt over my head, reminding him of the fact I skipped the bra. I often chose not to wear one. They're restricting and since my boobs are tiny, I can get away with it. I slide my thumbs under the waistband of my leggings and step out of them as well. I'm left standing in a not so sexy pair of red boy shorts.

"Fuck me," Gino growls as he begins stripping. "God, Ela. How did I get so lucky? Get over here."

I step in front of him. His pants unbuckled and hanging open when he reaches for me to drag me close. One hand cups my firm arse and squeezes as the other skates into my hair and winds it around his fist.

Looking up at him, I let all my feelings spill from the inner depths of my soul. "I love you. I always thought I'd spend my life never knowing how that felt. I fought it. I tried my damndest to stay away and not let my heart get entangled with yours. But now that I've fallen, I can't imagine never experiencing this. I promise to always stand by you. To never leave you. To be there for you no matter what comes at us. To fight with you and for you. To devote myself to you completely from this day forward, and to never give up on making our lives an adventure worth taking."

Lifting me with his one arm, he places my arse on his desk and steps between my now open legs. "I love you. I was so determined to never drag another into my life that I almost missed out on this. I'm sorry I ran. I'm sorry I pushed you away and kept secrets. I promise no more secrets. We are in this together. I give you all of me and accept all of you. Together we will stand strong, never again alone, to face the challenges life will throw at us."

We rid the other of the clothes left on our bodies and come together as a united couple. It's not slow or easy. Gino drops to his knees and prepares me like only he can, encouraging my body to create the lubrication needed to accept his enormous cock. Without extra, it will be a challenge, but one I'm more than willing to suffer through.

I grab hold of his hard length and squeeze, forcing it to leak, and rub the moisture over the tip to help. As I slide closer, I settle him at my entrance and press my center against him. The head of his cock slips in and the burn that always follows is a little more than it has been before.

It's been months since I've used my vibrator. It just wasn't the same, and it left me unsatisfied and pissed that I couldn't find my release because this man ruined me completely.

"Okay?" Gino grunts as he works his way into me. Not fast, but not slow. "Fuck. You're so goddamn tight."

I arch my back and place my hands behind me, hoping to make it easier. "I swear you've somehow gotten bigger since the last time we did this. How is that possible?"

Tugging my hips closer to the edge, forcing me to almost lay back completely, he offers his philosophy on the matter. "Perhaps it's because I'm so backed up and swollen from not allowing myself any release. Fuck, Ela. This pussy of yours is squeezing the life right out of me. I'm going to blow before I get all the way in."

It might be a good idea if he did. At least then he'd have more lube to work with. So I tease him by bringing my hands to my breast and toy with my nipples, making them even harder than they once were.

Hot semen pulses inside of me, making it easier for him to channel his way in. "You little tease."

"Fuck me, Gino. Fuck me like it is the first time you've had the pleasure of fucking your wife. Fuck me so good that I'll feel you for hours later." I get my wish as his fingers dig into my hips and he slams into me. I'll wear his bruises later. My pelvis may even ache from the slamming of his against mine. I swear he's ripping me in half, and it feels amazing, the best erotic moment of my life. "Call me your wife."

Gino yanks me off his desk and falls into his chair behind him, still buried balls deep inside me. "Do you like that, wife?"

My eyes roll into the back of my head as he bends me back and sinks his teeth into my breast. "God, yes. Do all husband's fuck like this?"

Digging his fingers into my hair, he brings my mouth to his. "All I know is that your husband will. One day, he plans on tying you to his bed and having his way with you."

"Yes." I moan into his mouth. "Just understand turnabout is fair play."

One last hard thrust up and we both tumble over the edge of the hardest orgasms we've had. It leaves us breathless and limp.

"Ela?" Gino, my now husband, grumbles. "We should shower

before everyone shows up. I don't want you smelling of sex around all those men. You can only smell like sex when it's just us."

"Good thing you have a shower off your office," I mumble into his shoulder. "I think you may need to carry me there."

Grabbing my face, he holds it as he stares into my eyes and lets his deep emotions shine. "Gabriela Leblanc has a nice ring to it."

I think so too, but I have to ask because it seems, should we move forward, my name may not be Leblanc. "Are you not taking on your family name? Returning to the name you were given the day you were born?"

Running his thumb along my bottom lips, he smiles sadly. "I'll probably have to become Simion Kelemen legally, but I will also always be Gino Leblanc. Simion died with his family. Gino is the man I am now. That will never change."

Chapter Thirty-Nine

GINO

The Royals

I sit in my office and listen to Ela as she shares the new plan with her team. King Antonio has joined them. He showed up shortly after Sir Edward and Duchess Angela—once also known as Her Royal Highness, it changed after she remarried. They've informed me I no longer need to address them so formally now that I'm family. I'm not sure I'll ever be able to do that. Old habits are difficult to break.

Ham, the IT specialist, is sitting off to the side on his laptop, pounding away. I can tell he's listening intensely while doing some deep search. When he stops typing completely, I have to wonder why that is.

"What did you find?" Ela doesn't miss a beat.

"I'm not sure." He hits a few buttons, and the printer comes to life. "It could be nothing. How old would your sister be now?"

"Not quite thirty. Why?" I refuse to get my hopes up. I've been searching nearly five years for her now and have come up empty.

"Do you think you would recognize her if you saw her?" Ham flips his computer screen so I can see it.

All the air in my lungs disappear as my legs move. I cannot be absolutely certain; the photo isn't completely in focus. The woman is standing behind my uncle, posed like a guard. She has dark glasses and blends in well, like they have trained us guards to do. He flips through several. Each one, she's just out of focus, background noise.

We're all so focused on the screen, none of us are aware when Emoni joins until she speaks. "Why are you all staring at that woman? She's nobody. Dracul only keeps her around because it makes him look better having a few female guards. That one is a cold-hearted bitch. She killed another guard when he tried to take advantage of a young woman. Yet she did nothing to stop Dracul or Nico when they pranced other women around doing pretty much the same. Although Nico always watched her carefully, as if afraid she might snap. He didn't like her, but he knew his father did, which meant his opinion didn't matter."

Ela circles the room and approaches Emoni from behind. "How do you know all this?"

Emoni flinches, unaware that my wife—I love that word—has snuck up behind her. Her uneasiness has me watching closely. "I was his prisoner for a few years. Anna was assigned to me. Although she wasn't around all the time. Rumor had it she wasn't just a guard, but an assassin Dracul used to eliminate those who got in his way."

I sit on the edge of the desk always wanting to know this next question. "How did you escape?"

"I didn't. Dracul let me go." Emoni touches her stomach, her way of drawing my attention to it. "But not before his son got his hands on me. I thought Dracul was cruel. Nico is ten times worse. He can only get aroused when he... when he is inflicting pain. If you survived his attacks, you were lucky, they said. I didn't feel lucky."

Beck, another member of Ela's team, grabs our attention. "I'm not sure Anna is an assassin. It would be the first time I've met one."

"A female assassin?" Ela questions, unimpressed.

"No." He smirks as he looks around the room. "I've met a few of those. Thought we might be training one, even."

Ela rolls her lovely eyes as Emoni becomes more uncomfortable and takes a few steps back. "Then why don't you explain why you think she's wrong."

He flips his screen around and displays a clear photo. One of Anna without her dark glasses on. Another man is holding them in his hand as he runs his knuckles down the side of her face. One of her eyes is fused closed, the other pupil is blown as if permanently dilated. "A blind one. I guess she could be, but she'd have to get very close to her victims. Shooting them at long range wouldn't be possible. But as we all know, assassins don't have to all be shooters. Poison, a knife wound, a fall, or a broken neck can get the job done."

Emoni shares more as she stares at the screen. "Joel is the only man she ever let's get so close. I think they had a thing going on. I had no idea she was blind. I thought she just wore those glasses to look intimidating. She never used a cane or bumped into things like you might expect a blind person to do."

Ela shakes her head, irritated by that assumption. "She can probably see some from her one eye."

Iris, another team member, fills in more of the missing pieces. "Anna has only been with your... Dracul for a few years. She and Joel joined his organization around the same time."

I stare at the photo and try to determine if Anna looks familiar. Maybe a little. I'm guessing she's had some type of surgery, maybe plastic, to repair the damage to her eyes.

Could that have happened that night so long ago? Was that why they assumed her dead and left her? If so, who found her? Where has she been living all these years? Did another team find her, or was it the rebellion? Did they hide her from my uncle and then train her to kill? So many questions I won't have answers to until I can see her for myself.

"Why are you so interested in her?" Emoni seems to finally be catching on. "Who do you think she is?"

I still don't trust her. Her previous betrayal tells me she would do it again if ever given that chance. "We're only trying to learn all we can about what we will walk into when we return to Kosonia." It's the best and truest answer I can give her.

"Why are you so insistent about returning? There is a price on your head." She spins to my wife and glares at her. "It's because of you, isn't it? You have somehow convinced him to go back. Are you trying to get him killed?"

Ela's eyes lock with mine, and I can see we are both in agreement. She doesn't trust her any more than I do.

"I don't know what he sees in you." Emoni's voice turns angry.

"You're like every other princess I've ever met, hoping to somehow get that promotion and a better title. Willing to sacrifice anyone who gets in your way. Is he going to be the bait you dangle in front of Dracul? I'm not even sure why he hates him so much. I just know he does, has since you came to save him from that prison."

"Men like him don't like to be forced to give up a man like Gino. It makes them look weak in the eyes of those watching." Antonio responds this time. "But when I requested his return, he had no other choice but to do so. Gino is a very valuable man. One the world cannot afford to allow to rot away in a prison."

"Why is that, exactly?" Emoni wheels are spinning fast, putting two and two together. "Who is he? Who are you?" When no one replies, she only grows angrier. "Answer me! I deserve to know. Why is this child so important you feel the need to guard me twenty-four-seven, not even allowing me my privacy?"

"Yet you seem to somehow manage to have slipped up here without your guards." It isn't the first time she's done it. She's almost as good as another female in this room, almost but not quite. Unlike her counterpart, she hasn't yet figured out that we've implanted a tracker— that would never have happened to Ela. She'd have figured it out and removed it. It, along with all the others sewn into her clothes, just to make sure we never lost track of her. One can never be too careful when it comes to a traitor, and I have no doubt Emoni is just that.

Her guard is standing at the door now. He's been outside this entire time. I've instructed those guarding her to keep a close eye, but allow her to roam the grounds at will. She may have surprised us earlier, only because we were focused, but she wasn't going to learn anything we weren't willing to let her know. Had we been discussing something that sensitive, I'd have made sure to have secured the door, not left it wide open. I was constantly testing her, and she failed those tests regularly. My camera will tell us how long she stood outside before making her presence known.

"Miss Emoni, I believe this floor has been deemed off limits." He speaks as he steps inside. "We should not be disturbing them at this hour."

Shaking her head, she makes her exit, but not before having the last word. "Funny how no one cared until I began attacking your precious little princess. I'm not sure what you see in her. I mean seriously, she's so... plain, masculine, even. It makes me wonder if you're into men, the reason Beni felt the need for me to carry your child."

I've had it. "Apologize! Now!"

Whirling around, she stands her ground. "No. What are you going to do if I don't? Lock me in my room?"

I start to say more, but Ela holds up her hand to stop me. "It's fine. I don't need her to apologize. Nor do I require her approval."

"She does not get to speak to you like that." I square my shoulders. "No one gets to disrespect my wife like that."

That catches Emoni's attention. "Your what?"

"His wife." Ela grunts, not happy I let that slip. "You'll have to forgive my husband. He often has trouble keeping his mouth closed when he gets upset."

Before Emoni can ask more questions, her guard is leading her out of the room. Ela is staring at me, disappointed, but that is all soon forgotten when Beni steps into the room. One look in his direction and I know I won't like what he has to share with me. "What now?"

"We have a problem," he announces.

"Of course, we do." I'm so tired of problems.

Chapter Forty

GABRIELA

The room clears so the only people left are Gino, Antonio, and myself. The problem, Beni announced, was one only the three of us could handle. It seems Dracul wants to negotiate with Gino. Before doing so, he also has something he wishes to share.

He contacted Cezar, who was currently in Kosonia, to relay the message. It was one we couldn't ignore and required our immediate attention.

Antonio and I are only here so we can hear it firsthand. It will help us know how to move forward when we land in Kosonia later today. This may become a completely different mission if what he is claiming to be true. One I've been trained to do, but never considered I'd be asked to do so quickly.

Gino sits down in front of his computer as he dials the number Cezar provided. Using a secured line to ensure no one can track it. Ham was good at what he did and would be monitoring it the entire time, making certain no one could follow the trail. If he felt they were getting close, he'd disconnect the call. We couldn't afford to take chances.

While I can see what is happening, Dracul cannot see me or Antonio. We're watching from another screen with the sound disconnected. An older man who resembles the one before me appears.

His features are defined. Hard lines stand out where his brows frown, making him look as lethal as we know him to be.

Gino is seated just far enough back to cast a shadow, making it difficult to see him. He will reveal himself when the time is right, but not before. We have concluded his uncle already knows he exists, if Emoni was telling us the truth earlier.

I didn't trust that bitch. She's up to something. I could feel it all the way to my soul. I just couldn't put my finger on what that was yet. It felt odd that a woman would agree to carry a child without expecting something in return.

What had Beni promised her? She was clearly in love with Gino, that much I knew. I could see it in the way she looked at him. And a woman scorned is dangerous. She wasn't about to just walk away after the baby came if it was really Gino's. I'm not sure I blame her. It is, after all, her child as well. I know I'd do whatever I had to do to protect my child—not that I'll ever get the chance to have one.

"Where have you taken Nico?" His uncle wastes no time getting to the point of this call. "Do you think you can stop me by threatening me like that, Simion? If you hurt him, I will hurt her."

"Her?" Gino keeps his voice level. "I have no ties to your world any more. You stole them all from me years ago, Uncle."

A sadistic smirk grows on Dracul's face. "You are playing a dangerous game. Are you willing to risk the life of one of your last living relatives, just to prove your balls are bigger than mine?"

Now it's Gino's turn to scoff. "You are my closest last living relative. Am I wrong about that? So does that mean you will die? I might be inclined if that would be the end result. Your death is only a matter of time. One I've been looking forward to. I will cause it. Look into your eyes like you did my father's and watch you die, knowing you made a grave mistake, not making sure I died that day as well. Revenge, Uncle, is a dish best served cold."

Snapping his fingers, Dracul orders someone to step into view. It is the same woman we took notice of earlier. She's wearing the glasses, a blank face, even though there's a visible bruise on her right cheek. "All this time, a little spy has been hiding right in front of my eyes."

A spy? Does he not know who this woman is? Does he assume

Anna is only one of Gino's plants? If so, who is the relative he's threatening?

"I don't know her." Gino gives nothing away. "Time is ticking, Uncle. Are you willing to risk the life of your precious boy just to see if you can get me to flinch?"

A growl so evil roars through the speakers. "Anna? Can you believe my nephew is so stupid to not heed my warning? Should we tell him why it is best to respect your elders?"

Anna shrugs but doesn't speak. I can't get a read on her. It isn't until a young woman appears next to her, when I see something cross Anna's face, so slight that if one were not looking, they would've missed it. The young woman—Roma, Beni's daughter—has been crying. She looks scared, and her clothes are bloody.

"Do you recognize this one?" Dracul sneers as he stands and circles both women. "Do you know what I love most about my Anna?"

When Gino doesn't answer, he continues. "She has a gift. One I've only heard about, but have never had the privileged of watching. Should you decide to carry through with your plan to send me pieces of my son, I'll let her show you." He removes her glasses, and it is then Anna grows uncomfortable. "The fact she's legally blind makes it so much more fascinating. Maybe if you're lucky, you two can play. How good do you think you'd do wielding a sword? Could you kill her before she killed you? I have my doubts Miss Kelemen could."

Anna's entire body tenses when Dracul runs a finger down her chin, throat, and over the center of her body. She looks as if she would like to kill him, even though he seems not to notice. He's too busy fantasizing to catch on that he's pushing his luck.

Gino must notice, though, because he clears his throat before speaking. "Hate to interrupt you and your pet, but what is it you want, exactly? An exchange perhaps. Nico for Roma. It looks like I owe him a good beating, though. I'll make sure my men get on that soon. But if I notice one more bruise on her, I'll cut off his ear before returning him. Are we clear?"

Stalking back to the camera, Dracul leans closer. "Are you going to continue to hide in the shadows, boy? Or are you going to show your face so I can see for myself if you are a con?"

Leaning into the light, Gino reveals himself. Recognition shines on Dracul's face instantly. He may try to hide it, but I'm trained to notice the slightest tell that exposes a person's thoughts. "I suppose you could be my brother's son."

Gino tugs a chain out from under his shirt and lets the other man study it. "Do you remember giving this to me, Uncle? I've held on to it all these years as a reminder that one day I'd return it to you personally."

"My meeting with King Antonio could not be so easily dismissed. He's already on his way and it would be rude to turn him away this late in the game. I'll let him know we are no longer interested after we've talked. When we're done, I'll contact you with the details on where and when to meet me." Lies, all lies.

"You have twenty-four hours, Uncle. If I do not hear from you by then, I make no promises." He pauses for dramatic reasons. "Who am I kidding? I'll make you one. If you betray me, try to sway the princess and king into helping you, I'll come for you. I'll bring Nico with me in bags to feed the dogs as I march up to your home to do to you what you did to my family. I'm done playing games. It's time to end this once and for all."

He hangs up before his uncle can respond. His eyes find mine, and I recognize the pain in them.

Standing, I walk to him and take his face in my hands. "Nothing will happen to your cousin. I'll get her out of there, I promise."

He nods and looks over at my brother as he tugs my hand down and holds it tight in his grip. "It's not my cousin I'm worried about. Roma will do as she's told. Beni has prepared his family well. Anna is the one I'm concerned about. She won't leave until her mission is complete."

"What mission?" Antonio asks.

It's good to know I'm not the only person in the room who saw it. That my husband also recognized the signs those like us have been trained to see. "Emoni was right. Anna is a trained assassin. She's not been given the order to kill him yet. I'm not sure why. If she's been with him for a few years, she's had plenty of opportunities to have carried it out. For some reason, though, those she works with are waiting. They don't want him dead until they have the information they need."

Gino tugs me closer so he can wrap an arm around me. "Or until the true king returns to claim his birthright."

"Anna? Is she your sister?" Antonio asks as he stares at the photo we printed earlier.

"I still don't know. If she's not, then perhaps she knows my sister. Something about her feels familiar, but until I come face-to-face with her, I cannot say for sure." His fingers dig into my hips. "I'm coming with you, and I'm not taking no for an answer. My team and yours will work together. You two will distract Dracul, make him believe you'll do all you can to help him. While you do that, we will break into his place and finish this. I'll come to you when it is all said and done. This ends now. We've played his games long enough. Time to take him down."

Chapter Forty-One

GABRIELA

The Royals

We've been speaking with Dracul Kelemen for almost an hour now. He's an arrogant arse. I want to call him out on his bullshit, tell him to go straight to hell and forget about us forming an alliance. I can't, though, because if I do, he'll know something is off, and for now, he's buying everything we're selling.

My brother receives a phone call he insists he must take. It was all planned. As soon as we knew we had Dracul where we wanted him, we needed Antonio safe and out of danger. It was time for me to do my job, the one I'd been training for these last couple of years. I never thought I'd actually be called to carry out something like this, but I'll admit, this man deserves to be my first.

"Princess Gabriela, you truly are one very beautiful woman." My skin crawls at his words, but I fake a smile. "My son was right about you. You will fit into this family perfectly, be a great addition. The problem, however, is I'm not sure he's worthy of you."

I place a hand over my heart and feign to find him flattering. "Are you flirting with me, Dracul?"

He catches on quick and makes his move. Standing, he grabs the bottle of wine we've been enjoying and fills my glass before taking a seat. "Nico, I'm afraid, would never satisfy you. You need a man who knows his way around a woman. One who would take his time and savor you like the delicious treat you are."

As he's talking, his hand lands on my knee and begins slithering up. Thank God I wore pants today, not that it makes his touch any less sickening. He slides it up and pauses when he reaches my upper thigh, giving it a squeeze while he watches for my reaction. I pick up my wineglass and sip, ensuring I didn't break his fingers before it's time to do so.

"Older men have always fascinated me," I tell him, not lying, because it's true. Just not men old enough to be my father. That disgusts me. When his fingers brush the seam of my crotch, I grab his hand and carefully remove it. It would be so easy to snap his wrist. "But even I have standards, a limit where I draw the line. You're just too old for me. I'm not interested in a daddy figure, just a man old enough to know what he's doing."

This time, I stand, moving to the other side of the room. I sense him following me, like I expected. Men like him are so predictable. This is looking to be a lot more exciting than I'd first thought. He's giving me ample opportunity to set him up.

What disgusts me the most is I have to wonder how many helpless women he's done this too. Those who aren't trained to take a man down the way I am. Those who are forced to endure his advances and suffer the shame when they couldn't stop it from happening.

The nerve, this man has, making these advances with my brother nearby. The balls it takes to have the confidence he can do as he pleases, even to a woman of my status. It will be my pleasure showing him not all women are helpless creatures. I certainly am not.

He grips my right arm hard enough for me to realize there will be a mark later. "Perhaps you misunderstood, Princess. This isn't a request."

I gasp as he spins me, giving him the performance he desires. Playing the victim has never been easy for me. I'll never forget the first time a boy laid his hands on me like this. It was the same day my world changed and a certain man became the center of my universe.

Dracul shoves me up against the wall, holding my right hand above me. His other hand grips my throat, leaving my left unrestricted.

That was his first mistake.

Getting right in my face, the heat of his moist breath has me shrinking. "It always surprises me how the world has gone mad and allowed women to believe they have a say. You could've made this easier by simply agreeing. I'd have treated you with a modicum more respect, but now... now I'm taking what I want and there isn't a damn thing you can do about it."

Two things happen simultaneously.

The door to the room flies open, right as I'm forcing the tip of my switchblade into the seam of Dracul's slacks. I drag it along his sensitive bollocks with great satisfaction. He didn't see this as a threat when he started his attack. I press harder, feeling the material rip as the knife slices through the silk easily.

"You're late. I've got this under control," I report to the man brooding at the door.

Staring into my assailant's eyes, I press harder until I finish what I started. The blood drains from his face as it leaks from the deep wound along his crotch now trailing up making him flinch when I don't stop. Dracul's hold on me loosens as he drops to the floor in agonizing pain, squealing like a wounded animal.

"And if it weren't for the fact my husband has been waiting to finish you off for over twenty years, I'd do it myself. What's the matter Dracul? You don't like knife play? Too kinky for you? I was sure it would be a major turn on for you. It seems to be for me."

Sounding like an injured swine, he tilts his head back. Shock and confusion taking over his face. "Your husband? This man is your husband? He's a traitor. He won't make it out of here alive."

Gino kicks the door closed as he strides over to where Dracul is crumpled on the floor. "Hello, Uncle. I see you've met my wife. She's amazing, isn't she? Very talented with a knife. Hides it in the most peculiar places. Quick and efficient with it as well."

Grabbing his arm, he yanks Dracul to his feet and drags him to a chair. Once he's seated, he glowers down at him. "What were you doing that pissed her off so much she nearly unmanned you? She was only supposed to prick you with a needle to knock you out."

"You won't get away with this," Dracul weakly mutters while slowly bleeding out. His wound is deep, and if left unattended, he'll probably die in a few hours. "My men will kill you as soon as they realize you're here."

That makes us both laugh. His men have been taken care of. Those who are still alive have been secured properly. We're in control of this beautiful home now. Gino's men, alongside with our own, have this place locked down.

I walk over to his desk and pick up the phone. "We have a problem. It looks like Dracul needs a doctor. He's had a knife accident and is bleeding in a place a man rarely bleeds."

Peter grunts as he notifies me our medic is on the way. Lucky for Dracul, one of us is a trained field medic. Beck is good at his second job, but I'm not so sure he'll give two shits about being gentle when stopping the hemorrhage. Nor will he care about saving anything that a proper doctor might be concerned with. We stabilize him enough he'll make it to where we're heading next. He only needs to stay alive long enough for Gino to reveal his true identity to the right people and condemn his uncle to death.

"If you leave now, you may live," Dracul sputters through clenched teeth. "I'm a powerful man. Your husband is a wanted felon. If the authorities catch him, they'll shoot to kill. I've given them those orders, and my men don't ask questions."

Gino grabs the arm of the chair. "Your men are dead or severely wounded. Those still alive are only breathing to answer a few questions we have. Then I'll turn them over to the rebellion. Let them decide their fate. Tell me, Uncle, when I hand you over to them, what do you suppose they will do to you? Do you think they'll show you mercy? Or do you imagine they will slowly torture you in the same manner you have tortured those you've captured?"

"Fuck you!" He scowls. "I have loyal men all over this country. Your little bitch is dead as well. Princess or not, she'll be executed for daring to do this to me. I'm the future, their future."

Grabbing Dracul's shirt, Gino drags him closer. "Correction, Uncle, you were until I showed up. Now you are nobody. Well, that's not right either. You are two things. A murderer and a traitor. Do you know what they do with traitors in your country? They send them to hell."

"You should have died in that hell." Dracul is sweating now. His forehead has beads forming, dripping into his eyes, and rolling down onto the floor. I'm not sure it's only from the pain he is enduring, but also from the thought of being sent to hell. "If I'd have known who you were then, I'd have made certain of it."

"Nico is there now. I thought he might enjoy it," Gino informs his uncle so he can appreciate the fact his son is likely in agony and will die in the same place he sent his enemies. Even those in the hell my husband was forced to live weren't fans of Dracul. Most were there because he'd ordered them to be there. Later, he required them to do his dirty work while he held their own family's safety in the palm of his hands. "And unlike when they tossed me into the pits of hell, no one is paying for his protection."

"It's too bad your mother and father didn't play this game as well as you are," Dracul spits out. Before I can stop him, Gino punches his uncle so hard he loses consciousness.

I can't say I blame him. It's probably better this way. We'll get more done if we aren't arguing with his uncle the entire time. Now we need to regroup and get ready for what's coming next.

Chapter Forty-Two

GINO

The Royals

Desperate times call for desperate measures. Time is running out. My country is falling apart again and they need a leader to step up and take control. If it doesn't happen soon, a new revolution will break out and war will once again be upon us. We've seen enough war. I vow to keep it from happening. I'm done sitting back, watching as those who are supposed to be in charge let others control them.

Nothing like making an entrance when the world is watching. And right now, that is what the world is doing. Members of the elected government are about to announce the way Kosonia will govern. Those in charge expected my uncle to accept the throne and declare himself as king. But that isn't what is about to happen.

Beni set it all up. He invited the seven representatives of the council to his home so we could properly be introduced. One look at me was all it took for most of them. My resemblance to my father is undeniable. The DNA test, accompanied by the documents we presented, explained where I've been, along with a signed decree from my father with his verified signature—which he did before his death, when King Ramon and him planned my escape to Hermosa Islas. All three should have been enough, but it wouldn't be, and we knew they'd want more.

Which is why we dragged my uncle and Nico along for the last line of proof.

They didn't know where they were or that anyone was watching. Handcuffed to chairs in the dark, cold room, where they were being held as my prisoners, I let them unveil my story. To all of our surprise they did more than that. They spilled everything and opened the door wide for me.

"You will not get away with this," my uncle declares from his spot. He is in pain and looks like hell. "No one will believe you."

Ela joins me. She is very good at interrogation, something I learn quickly after taking my seat. "What is it you think no one will believe? Do you think they will question me or my account of how you were wounded? Or do you mean the story of how you've lied to them all these years? Which one is it, Dracul? Because both are going to be the legacy this country will remember you by."

Dracul says nothing, only glares at her.

Nico, however, rocks in his chair, straining to free himself. "I will kill you. Both of you. I begged him to let me execute you that night we raided your home."

Now it is my turn to speak. "What night?"

"You know what night. The night you ran like a scared little boy and escaped with your sister into the woods." Nico glares, exposing the evil that lives deep inside him. "She was going to be my reward. Had I killed you, I would have gotten to keep her. But you both disappeared into the darkness like ghosts. You're lucky, because had I found you, I'd have made it slow and painful. Made you watch me enjoy that little cunt before I ended you."

"Shut up, Nico. You don't know when to stop talking," Dracul orders, wincing when he moves wrong. "I swear, sometimes I have my doubts about you actually being my son."

"He's not," Ela proudly announces, stepping between them.

"What do you mean, he's not?" Dracul's face contorts as anger takes over. "That bitch."

Ela looks between the two of them. They really look nothing alike. "How did you not figure that one out? Do you not read medical records? Or is it you never shared with your father about the night you got your dick sliced off? I have to wonder how ironic it is that both of you appreciate what that feels like."

"I don't know what you're talking about." Nico lifts his crotch as if that says it all. "My dick is right here, Princess. Come over here and find out for yourself. And when I get out of here, I'm going to show you it works fine."

Withdrawing her switchblade from that hidden spot in the small of her back, Ela flips it open and steps closer. "Is that right? You think you can get the jump on me before I slice it off a second time? I promise I won't stop. I'll take your balls as well, shove them down your throat, then watch you choke on them."

He tries to headbutt her, but before he can, she kicks his chair over and her knife is strategically pressed against him. I almost feel sorry for the ass, almost. "You're lucky I need you alive, otherwise, I'd finish the job now and call it a successful day."

"Stop toying with him, Ela. He's already pissed himself. And like you said, we still need him." Confiscating the knife, I grab her face so I can kiss her. "You really have to stop showing off. Not all men find it as sexy as I do."

I pass the closed switch blade back to her before I step behind Nico and right his chair. Squeezing his shoulders hard enough to make him wince, I throw out a warning. "Threaten my wife like that again and she won't get the chance to feed your nuts to you. I'll bust them wide open and then break your pretty little neck. Just like I promised I'd do when we were kids. Do you remember that, cousin? Me promising to snap your neck if you laid one finger on my sister, after I broke each one slowly?"

"Fuck you, Simion. You aren't man enough to do it. You had to have your men ambush me and then tie me to a chair to obtain the upper hand. Why don't you untie me? Fight me like a real man?" Nico challenges, revealing my true identity by mistake.

"Don't lie, Nico. No one ambushed you. I believe a woman took you down, one you thought you were going to get the jump on." I lean forward and whisper in his ear to make sure he is paying attention. "Thank you for telling them my real name, cousin."

"Who?" He sounds confused for good reason.

"So, Uncle. Before we finish this game and I take back what has always been mine, anything you'd like to share with us?" I grab my chair and drag it in front of him. "Any last words before I end this once and for all?"

"You don't have the guts to do what I did. You won't kill me. You're too much like your father. Dragos' problem was he thought he could negotiate it out. It's why he ended up watching his wife die before I put one between his eyes. My biggest mistake was not making sure I killed you and Giovanna. If I had to do it all over again, I'd make sure to do it right."

I stand and straighten my shirt. Taking a few deep breaths, so I don't kill him before the pieces fall into place. I'd love nothing more than to put a bullet in his skull, then do the same to Nico. But I can't do that, not yet at least. Not while there are people watching.

We walk out of the room heads held high. I am now ready to take the next step necessary to secure my place as the new King of Kosonia.

I'm now standing behind the elected counsel while King Antonio speaks to the press gathered in the hall of the Capitol building. I listen to him explain how he is pleased to announce a united allegiance between our two countries. Revealing how he has agreed to offer military support along with financial aid to help Kosonia get back on its feet so it can become the powerful nation it once was. Then surprises everyone when he utters his final words before turning the podium over to the eldest member of the council.

"While we are sad to see our sister leave our country to join yours, we could not be prouder of her for following her heart. I know she will be a strong queen and stand firmly by your king's side, forever uniting our nations, and making us even stronger together." He doesn't stay to answer questions. Like the ruler he has always been, he says what he came to say and then exits.

It is now time for Kosonia's elected representatives to introduce their new king to the people. I took the oath shortly after I left my uncle, who was yelling we weren't done, we still had business that was unfinished.

My role won't be the same as Antonio's, not yet, at least. It'll take time to establish how this will work. I need to gain the respect of the people and those who will work with me. I'll have to prove myself as a leader they can trust first as I demonstrate I'll not tolerate traitors who wish me dead or want to overthrow this new régime. We need to display a united front while we clean up the trash.

"I know everyone has questions. In time, I'll answer those. We have been fighting for this moment for many years now. Ridding Kosonia of corruption and bringing back the régime that was dismantled by those who wanted to rule over us and not with us. We've learned some valuable lessons while fighting and praying for a leader who will heal the land. Legend told us he would bring with him a warrior who would strengthen him while showing us the way. King Dragos was the one many of us believed would be our hope, but his life was stolen, and left us in a state of confusion, distraught. Hope was lost.

"But I'm here to tell you what we thought was lost was only hidden. Two kings saw what we did not. They agreed to protect our hope until it was time for the chosen one to rise from the grave and show us the way. King Dragos had a son. We were told he died with him. He did not die and has returned to claim his rightful place.

"It is my honor to be the first to present to you the first King of the New Federation of Kosonia and the lost heir we have been waiting for. King Simion, who is accompanied by his wife and our new queen, Queen Gabriela."

The small crowd is quiet at first. But the moment they see me approaching, camera's click and they begin shouting questions.

Outside, the roar is louder. Those gathered start chanting. "Hale to King Simion and Queen Gabriela. God bless them and their reign."

I grab Ela's hand and lift it to my lips before I speak. "God bless Kosonia. I pray he will guide me and allow me to be the leader you require."

Cheers erupt.

"I know you're wondering why it has taken so long for me to return. Please realize you have always been in my heart and that I have been preparing for this day since I left. My first order of business as king will be to make Kosonia a safer place for all of us. Those who tried to keep me from returning will be punished. Those who stand in our way will suffer as well.

"There is a prison many of you call Hades. I spent almost a year inside, and its name serves it well. It will take time, but as of today we are closing it. We will find a better way to imprison those who require incarceration. Those inside will be evaluated and sent to facilities designed to keep them and everyone else safe. Those who work there will have to answer for the mistreatments they have bestowed upon its residents. We can and will do better."

Ela squeezes my hand to give me strength.

"I promise to be a king who listens to his people. One who does not rule over those God has put me in charge of, but lead them. With my lovely Queen's assistance, I know we can make Kosonia one of the strongest countries in the world. One we can be proud of. You have my word, and I vow to make my father, King Dragos, proud of the sacrifice he made. Thank you."

Chapter Forty-Three

GABRIELA

The Royals

This life is as draining as I expected it to be. If I didn't love my husband, I'd run for the hills and never look back. People in general drive me crazy, these people make me insane. Someone is always demanding there's an urgent issue that requires our immediate attention.

Mine, most of the time, is dealing with these snobby bitches who want my opinion on how we should decorate our new home. Those issues aren't on the top of my list of priorities. I didn't suffer through Elite Force training so I could pick out light fixtures, or décor no one but us will ever see. I didn't understand what was wrong with the way it is already. Why does it need sprucing up? Who the fuck cares?

I want to help my husband track down Anna. No one has seen her since we showed up at his uncle's a few weeks ago. Joel and she slipped away during the chaos and vanished.

The more we dug, the more we came to realize how easy it was for them to become ghosts while with his uncle. Blending in when they needed to, while other times it was as if they just disappeared. Not even being missed, just gone. Only to return a few days or weeks later, as if they had been around all along.

That wasn't normal. It meant they were involved in something bigger. That someone was helping them. But who?

I'm finally ready to steal a moment so I could talk with my team. I'm not sure how much longer they'll be mine. For now, I get to keep them, work with them while we dig through this shit show and clear out those whose agenda is to destroy everything Gino and I are working toward. So far, they've prevented five assassination attempts long before they became a serious problem. Too bad I'd been picking out curtains and upholstery instead of with them when they raided these home bases. That would have been so much more fun and kept my mood in high spirits.

I'm thinking of looking into hiring a stand-in, someone who can play my role as queen during the day so I can dance with my team. She can do all these duties I hate, like kissing arse, and leave the matters dealing with more serious issues for me. Is that too much to ask?

Mid-way through my meeting, Emoni uncovers my hiding place. A group of very well-dressed females, way too eager to talk with me, accompany her. Hiding out in my husband's office while he's gone isn't even safe anymore. Next time, I'm locking myself in one of the less used lavatories, we only have about thirty of them in this gigantic estate.

"There you are, Queen Gabriela." Emoni knows I abhor that title as much as I do Princess, the reason she always throws it out. "These ladies are here to discuss a ceremonial ball while getting to know you. Would you like to meet with them in here or somewhere else?"

Iris is seated next to me. She's the lucky one who gets to stick by my side. It was her or be assigned guards again. I opted for her to be my sidekick, and I think she hates my life as much as I do.

"Is it too late to change my mind about all this? I love the man, but he's really cramping my style." I flop back in my chair so un-lady like and wish I could throw a temper tantrum like I would have when I was five. "Can't this wait? I'm busy with more important matters. Do you honestly need me to plan some over the top ball I don't even want to attend, let alone plan?"

Emoni shakes her head and turns to the women, who are doing their best not to appear shocked by my outburst. "She's kidding. Her sense of humor is one of a kind. Why don't you follow this lovely maid to the library, and we'll join you soon? Don't worry ladies, soon we will discuss menus and guest lists while planning the best social event of the year."

That seems to get them moving again. Chatting it up while relocating to the other side of the house. I'm not going. I don't care what she says. I'm so done playing nice and feeling as if my skills are being wasted on things that don't matter. And yes, I get it's important to make nice and throw parties, but at the moment, there are way too many other critical issues that need to be dealt with.

"You don't deserve any of this." Emoni's arms are crossed as she voices her unsolicited opinions on me. "These people, they deserve so much better than you. You don't care about them. You're just here so you could get out from under your family and pretend to be a heroine. All you care about is you, and it won't take them long to figure that out. When they do, you'll ruin it for everyone. Turn this country against Simion and force him to choose. He won't choose you. He'll choose his country. I mean, what good are you, anyway? You've refused to grant him the one thing he needs. It's why they bade me to step in and provide him with the heir he requires. What good is a woman of your status if you won't do your job? I think there's more to it than that. I expect you can't give him an heir. That's why Beni came to me."

That hurt. I'm not going to lie. "What makes you so sure about that?"

"Oh, come on. Why else would they come to me? It doesn't take a genius to figure that out. I've been paying attention. Why haven't you conceived yet? You two have enough sex, yet nothing has happened. So, it makes me consider you're hiding something." Emoni grips the door frame.

"I'm not sure why Beni came to you. It's something I'm still trying to figure out." I watch her closely as she clutches the frame harder. She has over a month to go before the baby is due. "Are you okay?"

"I'm fine." The words barely leave her lips before she bends over and grabs her belly.

I may not like her or even trust her, but this baby she's carrying has done nothing wrong. And I'm not a completely cold-hearted bitch. I know there's so much more to the story than what she's telling any of us.

CHAPTER FORTY-THREE

Rising to my feet, I rush to her and hold her up. "You need to sit down."

Tears well up in her eyes as she lets me lead her to the closest chair. She's not faking this; something is seriously wrong.

"Breathe." I rest my hand on her leg. "Slow steady breaths. Iris, call the doctor."

"It's too early." Her sad, concerned eyes find mine. "I can't lose this baby. They will kill me if I do."

"No one is going to kill you. And you aren't losing this baby. Babies are born early every day. You're far enough along now. I'm certain even if it comes early, it will be fine. Let's let the doctor worry about that, okay?" I try to remain calm, but when I glance down at the floor, I see blood, bright red blood pooling under her. "Emoni, I need you to focus."

"Oh, God." She moans in pain again.

The good thing about being a royal is you have doctors on the ready at all times. Ridiculous, I know, but in moments like this I'm very happy we do. As soon as the doctor walks into Gino's office, he takes over. He has Emoni on the floor and is checking her over, doing whatever it is doctors do when women are in labor.

"I think the placenta has detached. We need to get the baby out now." He digs through his bag. "Emoni, I'm going to give you a shot. It's only a local. It will help, but you are definitely going to feel this."

"What can we do to help?" I watch in horror as he lifts her blouse and stabs a needle into her stomach. "What are you doing? I'm sorry, what's your name again? Are you even old enough to be a doctor?"

He glares at me as he pours what looks like alcohol over some tools and Emoni's stomach. "Dr. Kovac, I'm thirty-five. Been doing this for seven years now. OBGYN is my specialty. The reason Mr. Kovaloff hired me to begin with."

"You don't look thirty-five. Are you sure?" I stare at him as he shakes his head like he doesn't have time for this conversation, which he probably doesn't.

"I'm sure, Your Majesty." This arsehole would get punched for calling me that any other time, but right now I'll let it slide. "Now, if you don't mind, I need to concentrate. We need to get the baby out quickly or we could lose both of them."

He glances over at Iris, who is standing wide-eyed above us. "Grab Emoni. I need you to keep her steady while I do this. As soon as the baby is out, I'll inspect it to make sure it's okay. Get it breathing if necessary."

"It will be okay, Emoni." I rub her arm, hoping I'm not lying. "He's going to get the baby out first."

We watch in horror as he slices open her abdomen. Hear her screams before she passes out. That's probably better. I can only imagine how much that hurt. There is more blood, watery blood, before his hands disappear inside of her and he pulls out a small little person. I know something is wrong by the color of the baby's skin. It's bluer than it should be. After he takes a bulb looking thing and sucks crap out of the mouth and nose, he turns the little one over and starts stroking its back.

"Come on, little one." Dr. Kovac urges right as a soft cry emerges from the tiny body. "That's it. Good job. Breathe in some good air."

Iris' voice brings us back to Emoni and her frightful situation. "I think something's wrong. Emoni's body is shaking, like she's having a seizure."

"Shit." He looks over at me, and I don't even hesitate. I take the little person in my arms and cradle it close. "Grab a blanket and wrap her up. Shit. I need to clamp this off or her mother is going to bleed out. Shit. Shit. Shit."

I stand up and spot the throw I use when I'm vegging in here, hiding from the staff. Gino finds it amusing when he's home, especially when I pull it over my head and roll into a ball. I grab it and smile down at the now pink-skinned gray-eyed little girl staring up at me like she's pissed. I'd don't blame her. I'd be pissed too if someone snatched me from my warm cozy place without warning.

Dr. Kovac interrupts my thoughts. "How does she look? Is she more pink now than blue?"

"Yes." I glance up and see him working fervently. "Good. Fuck. Come on. Emoni. Work with me. No one dies today. Not on my watch, at least."

Fifteen minutes later he has her loaded on a stretcher the EMTs brought in. She's stable for now. They're rushing out and taking her to the hospital so they can hopefully save her life. Since the baby was okay when they first arrived, all focus remained on her mother.

"I can take her now." A female EMT approaches once the room has cleared. "We'll transport her. Have a doctor check her out once we get to the hospital."

"I'm coming with you. I'll hold her if you don't mind." I tighten my grip on the tiny little one, not ready to hand her over to a stranger. "Is her mother going to be okay?"

"It's hard to say. I've seen it go both ways." She leads Iris and me to the ambulance. Where I go, Iris follows, no exception.

When we step outside, a line of black SUVs comes to a stop and Gino jumps out before anyone can stop him. "What happened?"

I retell the story as quickly as I can while we settle in the back of the ambulance. He's staring at the bundle in my arms, rubbing his head. I see the confusion on his face as if he's not sure how he should feel about this little person.

"She's an innocent baby, Gino." I do my best to reassure him it's okay to feel something for her. I know I do. My protective instinct kicked in the moment I saw her.

"She?" He takes a finger and runs it over her small head. "I... I realize it's crazy. But damn, Ela, if I didn't know better, I'd say she looks a lot like you."

"Except I don't have gray eyes. It's just a coincidence. All babies look alike when they're first born." I stare at her again, thinking about my baby photos. I try not to cry. He's not wrong. But that is impossible.

"But my mother did." He informs me as he kisses my cheek. "Exactly like that."

If only it could be true. How crazy would that be? Really crazy. Impossible, really.

Chapter Forty-Four

GINO

The Royals

We've been in the NICU for a few hours now. Together, we've watched doctors perform tests to make sure this little angel will be fine. She's small, weighing a few ounces over five pounds. An oxygen tube is taped to her face. Several cords are attached to her chest to monitor her while she rests inside an open plastic crib with a lamp shining down on her. I've been told it's helping keep her warm and ward off jaundice, something she's likely to develop being so early.

A nurse walks in to check on her for what seems like the hundredth time. She has a cart full of little diapers and bottles. After she's checked the machines, she turns to the two of us looming close by. "Who wants to change her?"

"Change her?" I ask, clueless.

"Her diaper, Gino. I'll do it." Ela stands and smiles down at the sleeping beauty. "I used to change Isabel when she was a baby. Have had the pleasure of helping Larkin with Nicolette as well. Although, neither of them was this tiny, I hope I don't break her."

That makes the nurse laugh while handing the smallest diaper I've ever seen to my wife. "You won't break her, Your Majesty."

Taking it from her, Ela tries to not snap. "Call me Gabriela or even

Mrs. Leblanc. I know everyone is super excited about this royal title crap, but if I get my way, we will stop with all that nonsense. Only use it in very formal settings."

"You mean Kelemen?" The nurse passes her a few wet wipes.

"Yes. I'm still getting used to that new name. He's always been a Leblanc to me. I believe it will actually be Leblanc-Kelemen, but that is a mouthful. So, let's stick with Gabriela to keep it simple." Ela has the diaper off and replaced before I can even catch on to how to do it when my turn comes. "There. I bet that is so much better."

"You're a natural." The nurse smiles. "Now let's feed her. Do you want to do this... sir?"

"I'm good." I must look horrified because both women snicker as Ela scoops the tiny infant into her arms and carefully settles in the rocking chair. She's done this a few times already. The nurses showed her how. They said it was good for the baby to be held when possible. Human contact was very important, and Ela was willing to do what she had to do to make this little one's first hours in the world better.

Once she has her accepting the tiny bottle, my wife asks the same question she's been asking every time someone steps in. "Any word about how her mother is doing? I can't believe no one has heard anything yet. I realize they took her to a different hospital, but this is ridiculous."

"Nothing. I'm sorry. I promise as soon as we hear anything, I will let you know. It's odd, I agree. Usually someone has contacted us by now." The nurse does a few more tasks and then leaves us.

"I don't like this." Ela tells me once we are alone again. "I can't believe none of our men went with Emoni. Not even the ones assigned to her."

That's been addressed. My men are on it now. Someone should report to me soon. Just as I'm about to make another phone call, two of Ela's people join us. We have special permission to have more than the normal number of visitors allowed, but only a few. If I need to speak with a larger group, I'll have to leave and talk with them in one of the many private waiting rooms.

Iris and Beck step inside, and they look irritated. Before I can ask why, Iris speaks. "They've finally located the ambulance that was transporting Emoni."

"Thank god." Ela sighs as she glances down at the baby in her arms.

Beck shakes his head and I know we're about to learn something the two of us aren't ready to hear. "It was ambushed. The doctor and driver were shot in the head, both dead. The other EMT was also shot, but somehow survived. Emoni... because it took so long to locate them, didn't make it. According to the initial report, she bled out."

"I want traffic camera footage. How the fuck did this happen?" Ela's trying to keep her voice low, so she doesn't disturb the little one.

"Ham is already on it. He's actually the one who located the ambulance, even though Emoni's tracker wasn't working." Iris swallows, knowing neither of us will like this next bit of information. "What is even more strange is that it wasn't headed for any hospital. It was heading in the opposite direction, as if driving out of the city. We haven't figured out where yet, but we don't think they were real EMTs. Ham will figure it out. I'm not making excuses, but it was crazy at the house earlier. I'll admit the doctor was acting peculiar. He tried to get them to take the baby with them, remember? The other EMTs came a few minutes later, surprised to see another crew already there, then offered to transport the little one so the first could focus on Emoni. The first ones got the hell out of there quickly soon after that."

I have to ask, because it's been bugging me since I learned no one even bothered to follow them. "Where are her guards?"

Two guards have been glued to her side for months now. Why in the hell would they not at least take one of the SUVs and follow them to the hospital? It was odd and has been driving me crazy.

Beck's next words tell me so much more than I'm ready to hear. "Dead. We found one in a bathroom that is rarely used. The other was in Emoni's closet. Both shot in the head point blank."

I'm on my feet, ready to get to work. My job for so many years was dealing with shit like this. I know exactly what needs to be done, how to handle this type of intel. First, everyone in the family will be located and have trusted guards with them at all times. Once that is done, it's time to uncover the mole. I have always been very good at tracking down those problems. It was my second job, what Sir Edward counted on me for.

The very reason he hired me when Her Royal Highness had a stalker they needed eliminated.

There's only one problem.

I'm the family now. The one person, besides Ela, who those working for us have sworn to protect. Fuck that. I didn't gain all these skills so I could sit back and watch everyone else have all the fun.

"I know what you're thinking." My wife tries to keep the amusement out of her voice. "Sucks, doesn't it? Having to sit tight and let everyone else do the job you are confident you can do better."

I sigh and rake my fingers through my hair. "Fuck. This is stupid."

She nods in agreement. "It is. Iris, tell Ham what we need. We may be stuck here while everyone else does their best to locate this arsehole, but that doesn't mean we have to do it quietly. There are plenty of other ways for us to help. I'm done sitting around playing house and pretending all I'm capable of doing is picking out ugly curtains. It's time we show those who work for us how much more we can accomplish when the two of us put our heads together. You with me, Gino? Ready to rock the boat and go off script?"

Throwing my head back, wearing the biggest fucking grin, I laugh. "Hell yeah. Time to show them who they are messing with. I was born ready, and so were you."

"You bet your arse I was." Ela glances down at the little girl sleeping in her arms and brings her head to her lips. "What the hell are we going to do about her? I mean... she's an orphan now. Motherless, and we still don't know if you're the father. This is so fucked up, Gino. I have this sick suspicion in my gut that her life is in danger as well. I'll do whatever I have to do to make sure nothing happens to her, give my own life for hers, even. She is an innocent baby, never once asked for this."

I walk over and kneel in front of them. "We will know soon enough about her paternity. Your team sent it off to the lab Falcon recommended. I don't trust anyone here yet, which is why I reached out to him." One hand on my wife's knee, I lift the other to place on top of the little one's head. "No matter what we discover, I agree. She'll need a family to look out for her. If we can't be that for her, then we will find one where she'll grow up loved and safe."

Ela's eyes are misty as they lift to meet mine. "I never thought I'd be a mom, Gino. But fuck, I think I might want to be hers. No one could protect her better than us. Love her, even. My heart belonged to hers the instant I watched the doctor pull her from Emoni's stomach. It latched on and has only become more attached as the seconds tick by. I'm the only person she's bonded with since the moment she entered this world."

My heart tightens at the thought of us being allowed to keep this little one. To claim her as ours and raise her to be a strong, independent woman, just like the one holding her. "If that is what you want, I'll make it happen. She needs a name."

Running her fingers over her sweet little face we have now claimed as ours, she thinks. "It should to be a powerful one with meaning. She's going to be a force to be reckoned with."

"Just like you," I tease, but agree. "Emersyn means fearless and strong."

"I like it. Do you like it, little one? Do you want your name to be Emersyn?" I swear the sweet girl smiles as she sinks further into Ela's arms. "Okay then, Emersyn it is. Emersyn Grace Leblanc-Kelemen. A very strong name for a little princess who will one day rule this world."

"I bet she hates being a princess as much as her mother," I say without thinking, but once the words are out, I know them to be true. Ela is now Emersyn's mother, will forever be her mother.

Tears stream down her cheeks as she holds our daughter closer. "And as her mother, I will do my best to let her know why God chose her as one. Teach her to be true to herself first, but to remember, not everyone is privileged enough to be given such a title. To wear it proud and be the best damn princess she can be."

While we wait for the others to return, we bond as a family. This little girl is going to change everything, and as her father, I will protect her always. This is my family, and no one is threatening it ever again.

Chapter Forty-Five

GABRIELA

The Royals

The first thing we do before we go after those responsible is to make sure Emersyn is safe. There are only a few people I trust enough to watch out for her.

My mother and Edward are at the top of that list. She flew in as soon as I called. They arrived with a full team capable of transporting a newborn safely back to Hermosa Islas. I fear if Emersyn stays here, she'll have a target on her. I don't know this country well enough to charge anyone with her life. And while it kills me to send her so far away, I understand it is for the best.

"Gabriela, she'll be fine." My mother reassures me as I check her carrier is properly fastened to the plane's seat. "I do have some experience with infants born before their time."

"I know. Why is this so hard? She's not even mine, yet I feel so attached to her." I fall against my mother as she tugs me close. "I was never meant to be a mother. We both know this."

That makes my mother snicker. "You believed that, not me. I always knew you'd one day be someone's mother. You don't have to birth a child to feel connected to them. Look at Larkin and her parents. Three people could not be any closer. She was always meant to be their daughter. Emersyn was always meant to be yours and Gino's as well.

How's he doing? I know he feels violated, knowing those he trusted betrayed him to create her."

"He held her and cried once they affirmed it." I will forever remember that moment.

Gino is so torn about how this all came to be. He feels like those he counted on most took full advantage of him and went behind his back. Dragged so many others into this mess and eventually cost Emoni her life. We are still putting the pieces together, but it's not looking so great for those he once believed were on his side. He held his daughter, his flesh and blood, and swore to allow no one to cause her that same pain.

"No one will get near her. You have my word, Gabby." Edward takes the seat next to Emersyn. "Your mother and I will keep her safe for both of you. Now go. Your husband needs you. This is the job you were born to do. It's time to stand tall together and stop those who think they know better."

I kiss my mother and Edward on their cheeks. "Thank you."

Giving one last lingering kiss on the forehead of my daughter, I turn and leave before I change my mind. I have a job to do. One only I am capable of doing.

My heart feels as if it is being torn from my chest when the plane takes off. It only makes me that much more determined to get this shit taken care of so I can bring her back and start our lives as a family. I find it crazy to know that something so small and innocent can change everything.

"We should get moving," Iris reminds me. "No need to draw attention. Everyone believes you are all together at the safe house. Time to get back so we can set the trap."

I climb into the passenger seat and try to get my head back in the game. We've learned a few important details these last forty-eight hours.

Those responsible killed the guards at the house moments after Emoni went into labor. No one noticed them not with her, because she could roam the grounds unrestricted. Her tracker made it easy for them to keep a close eye, but that had been disabled sometime during the day. By whom and when no one knows yet.

Dr. Kovac, we've uncovered, was often involved with those who sold infants on the black market. Worked with some very shady individuals and a fugitive in surrounding countries. The first EMTs were his men, and the ones who shot the guards. We haven't been able to figure out if Emoni going into labor was a coincidence or a result of something he did.

We do, however, know Cezar hired him, which has me questioning everything. There is no way the doctor fooled him. It took Ham less than ten minutes to expose it all. My team is working hard now to run background checks on every single person associated with Cezar. What we've discovered is disturbing on so many counts. For far too long, it seems Cezar has had his own agenda. Power can often blur the lines for those hoping to gain it. Too many times, it's like a poison that slowly darkens the soul.

There was a reason Gino kept his uncle and cousin alive. While it would have been his greatest pleasure to kill them, he knew executing them meant too many secrets died with them. Until he unveiled as many as he could, they were alive and safe, courtesy of my brother, in Hermosa Islas' maximum security facility under pseudo names in solitary confinement. We weren't taking any chance of escape or the possibility of someone murdering them before this was resolved. They would die once everything has settled. Pay for the crimes they were guilty of. Made an example of when the time to do so felt right, not before.

It's late. Without the bustle of the others working with us, the house quieted. Gino and I are in the office reading reports, trying to figure out our next move. Iris knocks before she steps inside, and we react immediately. She has company. It's surprising someone got the jump on her. The fact they could get past our security is alarming.

The ghosts we've been chasing these last couple of days are showing off again. Neither flinch when our guns are drawn, ready to take them out. They only stand there waiting for us to calm down and ask the right questions.

"How did you get in here?" Gino stares at the woman he's been curious about since he received that phone call. "Who are you?"

"Do you mind?" Anna shows us her hands, void of any weapons. "If we wanted to do you harm, don't you think we would have killed your guards first? We only wish to talk. Shed some light on your current situation before moving on."

"Forgive me if I seem a little untrusting at the moment." Gino keeps his weapon on Joel as he steps closer.

Mine is firmly on Anna. "Iris, pat her down."

Lifting her hands, Anna shows her irritation. "There's a knife in the small of my back. I have another along my rib cage. No gun. I like my knives better. I need to be close to my victims so I can sense them, feel the life leave when I take them down."

Gino removes a gun and knife from Joel, tucks them in the back of his pants. "He's clean now."

Holding the weapons Anna told us about, Iris signals she is now, too.

I'm still not ready to drop mine. "Why don't you two have a seat before you explain why you're here?"

Joel lifts his hands and steps behind Anna. "Ten paces. You should be able to tap it with your toe."

"Thank you." Anna turns her head, smiling, before she moves and takes a seat on the couch. "As I'm sure you have figured out, my eyesight isn't the best."

My husband stares at the stunning woman. He's not admiring her like most men I'm sure do. She is beautiful, even with the scar that trails down one of her cheeks. Her hair is cut very short, a wash and go style, with some wave to it. Very similar to Gino's wavy hair. It is as black as his with a tint of red when she turns just right.

"Are you her?" Gino finally asks after a long moment of silence. "I need to know."

Joel reaches over and takes Anna's hand. His touch seems to encourage her, offering some peace even. "You mean am I Giovanna? I was once. I am no longer. That little girl died shortly after her family did. Just like you're no longer Simion. He also died. Those close to you call you Gino. My name is Anna. This is Joel. His family, or more like his grandparents, raised me. He has been there for me through the years, helped me find my way."

"He's more than that." I watch her lips turn upward.

"He is. We've been together as a couple since I turned eighteen."

Anna squeezes Joel's hand. The love they have for each other shining bright.

"Did you lose your eyesight after being shot?" Gino cannot take his eyes off her. The slight tilt of his head tells me he isn't buying her story. I'm not sure why.

"No." Reaching up, she absentmindedly touches her chest and rubs it. "I lost it a few years later when Uncle Dracul's army burned the home where I was living."

So we can fully appreciate the extent of the damage Anna removes her glasses. Numerous scars mar her eyes. Some appear like burns; they are rough and angry.

Joel reaches up and runs his knuckles along her jaw. "A Molotov cocktail those assholes threw inside hit the wall above her bed. The hot liquid splattered and landed on her face, burning her eyes. One so bad they could not save it. The other was damaged from the shrapnel they shoved inside. She can see shapes, shadows, but not much else. The doctors did everything they could. My grandfather hired the best plastic surgeon he could afford to make sure her face remained as flawless as always. She is still the most beautiful woman I've ever laid eyes on. Inside and out."

"How do you know Dracul was the one involved?" Gino's anger is building. I can feel it. "Did he learn who you were?"

Anna shakes her head slowly. "No. Plastic surgery altered my face enough to make me look nothing like our mother. He once said something about my mannerisms being familiar, but dropped it quickly.

"Joel's family is part of a secret society sworn to protect the integrity of the régime and those born into it. It is an organization going back thousands of years, connecting royal families all over the world. They don't take it lightly. It's their job to make sure these families remain strong and true. Anyone who dares to destroy the integrity is exposed or terminated or both. I'm part of this family now. One of their soldiers who has learned ways to get close to those who are a threat and eventually eliminate such threats."

"Yet you let Dracul and Nico live. Why is that, exactly? You had plenty of chances to expunge them and stop all of this." I have a hard time believing her tale. A secret society, seriously? Those are legends passed down through the years. There is no such society, not one I've heard of.

"You're right. But the thing is, we had to wait until we knew for certain Simion was alive. Our father and your father were smart men. They did an excellent job keeping him hidden, only allowing a few he trusted to never spill the secret they held. Although it now seems they too have a few secrets, ones that need exposed and then eliminated." Anna doesn't even flinch at the suggestion of taking a life and I have to wonder if she'd also kill a child.

"I'll not let you touch her. She is an innocent." I aim my pistol at them. "I'll kill both of you first."

"You misunderstand." Joel stands placing his body between my gun and Anna. "Killing a child is the last thing we would ever do. When we ambushed the ambulance, we did so to keep them from executing her, thinking she was with them. Surely you understand what some of them believe to be important. Why Emoni didn't allow you to test the paternity or why she revealed the child she was carrying was your son?"

Anna stands and forces Joel out of the way. "They had one chance to get to her. The plan was to abduct Emoni before the baby was born and then replace it with a boy. Later mislead you once again if necessary."

"DNA would have proven him not to be Gino's," I point out, knowing we would have demanded a test.

"Or it would be used to prove he wasn't who he claimed to be, allowing another to step in and take his place. Shining doubt on all of this and causing what you're building to fall before he could win the people over." Anna's revelation explains so much. "Who do you think would benefit if you and Dracul were both gone? Who would rise up and take over? Who do the people trust, because so far no one has given them a reason not to?"

Gino and I look at each other as realization slaps us in the face. "Cezar Kovaloff. All this time he has been playing both sides. That much we've figured out, but why?"

"He is the one who first betrayed father. Fed Dracul the intel that forced his hand and sent him to our house all those years ago. He never expected father to have a backup plan. Never thought you'd be smart enough to get us out of there. Didn't realize Joel's family was also close by that night, ready and waiting. Father knew we couldn't escape together. That it would be more dangerous if we were together, easier to track. But separately, he could hide us. You inside a kingdom that could protect you, while also teaching you what he could not. Me with a family sworn to protect the régime and keep it pure and whole." Anna pauses as if letting him absorb all that before dropping the next bomb.

"The dragon you are hunting is not Uncle Dracul. The dragon whose head you need to cut off is the one hiding in plain sight. The one who believes he's about to rain fire and brimstone down, destroying us all. It is time to show him otherwise. This is why father separated us, so we could be stronger when it was time for us to reunite. Are you with us, brother? Are you ready to end this once and for all?"

Gino steps toward Anna and extends his hand to her. When she accepts it, they stand there as emotion takes over. Yanking her into his arms, he wraps them around her shoulders, and they both fall apart. All these years, they believed the other was dead. I cannot imagine what it must be like to find out the lies you were told so you could come together and be stronger.

"We can talk more about this later." Gino wipes his face and reaches for my hand. "It seems we need to figure out the best way to slay the dragon before he sees us coming."

Chapter Forty-Six

GINO

The Royals

All this time, I've been surrounded by the enemy and didn't even realize it. My uncle wasn't the only adversary hoping to extinguish my family.

Why Cezar didn't just kill me, blame Uncle Dracul or even Nico, made no sense. There had to be more behind his reason that required me to take the throne before he took me down. But what was it?

I didn't want to believe Beni was involved, but how could he not be? Cezar and he worked closely together, and I find it difficult to expect that all these years he'd not once stumbled upon the truth. Was he that blinded by the régime being restored, that he couldn't see the forest for the trees? Couldn't feel the heat of the dragon's breath on his neck as the fire behind Cezar's deceit got hotter, ready to spill out of him and burn everything in his path?

We called a meeting and spread a few lies of our own. Ela's team summoned reinforcements. Antonio sent a few of his guards to join us, those I've worked with, who knew me and how I operated. Darius Falcon even joined us, blending his men in like he's so very good at doing. We've reassigned Cezar's men, sent them on a mission that would help us determine whose side they were on. Those who failed would suffer the same fate as Cezar. It was time to sever the dragon's head and become the man my father always hoped I'd be.

Beni and Cezar join me in the office of my family home, the one we've been living in since taking the throne. Ela is pacing the floor, displaying how frustrated she is. The reason behind her frustration will be expressed as a lie, but the rest is very real.

As soon as they're inside, Stew follows behind and closes the door. Stew and I worked together while protecting Her Royal Highness. I trust him to know my thoughts and with both our lives. He takes his place at the door, standing exactly like he often did back in the day when he protected Esteban.

Cezar does a quick survey of the room. "Who are these men? Where are the men I assigned to you? What's going on?"

I glance up from what I'm doing and motion for them to take a seat. "I sent your men on a task that only they could do. Ela asked her brother for a few extra guards. These men have our best interest at heart. We know we can trust them fully."

"What kind of tasks?" Cezar unbuttons his suit jacket and takes a seat. "Why is your wife so jumpy?"

Ela paces my way and stands behind me. "I'm restless because it seems we have a mole amongst us."

Cezar's only response is to raise his bushy eyebrows, while keeping his face void of emotion. He is good, I'll give him that.

"Someone has kidnapped the child, stolen her right from under our noses." I lean back and place my hand on Ela's. "Do you have any idea who it could be and why they would do this?"

Beni's head snaps to the left and before he can even think, he speaks. "Did you know about this?"

"Why would he know about it? It's not public news. Unless?" Ela releases my shoulder and makes her way around the front of my desk.

Cezar's eyes follow her, but he doesn't flinch. "He only meant, did one of my guards tell me? Isn't that right, Beni?"

Leaning her backside against the corner, she crosses her arms as she studies him very closely. She waits for him to show something, and when he shifts slightly, she turns to Beni. "Is that what you meant?

Think very carefully about your answer. If one hair on that sweet, innocent head is harmed, I'll be the person to avenge her."

"I only meant... I mean... Yes. Yes, that is what I was referring to. Why would someone kidnap her? Please tell me you have a lead so we can send our men to find her." Beni isn't very good at this game. His forehead and his upper lip have beads forming of sweat. "You should have informed us. Sitting here discussing it seems pointless. We need to gather a team. Cezar, let's go so we can do that now."

He begins to stand when my next words have him dropping back into his seat. "Tell me this. Did you actually think you could switch one baby for another and I'd never know?"

"What are you talking about?" Beni turns an awful shade of pale. He knows the gig is up and his goose is cooked. "Why would we do that? The whole reason we went behind your back was to help you produce an heir. One who could carry on tradition."

"This is where it gets confusing." I stand and step around my desk to join my wife, leaning next to her so I can look down on these two traitorous men. "If the child had been a boy, what would you have done? Why not kill me when you learned who I was all those years ago? Why did you not let me die in that prison and call it a day? What was the point of keeping me alive, if in the end you only wanted me dead and gone?"

Beni starts to speak, but Cezar cuts him off. "I have my reasons."

"Please share them with me now." My grip on the desks tightens so I don't launch myself at him and wrap my hands around his neck. "It's the one thing I cannot figure out."

"The child—heir—was not my idea. It was never in my plans. Beni did that one all on his own. He still believes in the cause, that it is best to bring back the régime and restore all its power. Loyal to the end, never once doubting you were the answer to all our prayers." Cezar's face turns an ugly red and his hatred for me shines bright. "You were to be the last living heir, and you were to die the kind of death that would end all their hopes and dreams. Once I destroyed the precious Kelemen name, I would rise from the ashes your family left behind and give them no other reason than to appoint me as their Czar."

Ela doesn't miss a thing. "Don't you mean king?"

"A king is not the same as a Czar. A Czar is the ultimate leader. He takes no prisoners and rules with an iron fist. My mother is Russian and it is time to bring that heritage back to power." Cezar's fierce eyes display what a fool he is if he thinks that would ever happen.

"My uncle was supposed to kill me." I try to put the missing pieces together.

"Your uncle or Nico. I didn't care which one. But you were smarter than I ever gave you credit for. I did not expect her family to accept you and take you in as their own. Ramon was never meant to die early, and when the time came, I was sure we could manipulate him into giving you up. I was so close. His son, however, couldn't be so easily persuaded. And when you displayed your loyalty to him by stopping an attempt on his life, I had to come up with a new plan. One that would be much harder to achieve. I would've killed you sooner, but the news that your sister had also survived changed things again. Locating her has been more problematic. She's like a ghost I know is there but cannot see."

Ela straightens and steps forward, making Cezar fall a little farther back in his chair. "My father would have eaten you alive. If he were still living, the wrath he rained down on you would be tenfold."

"Your father would have sold you to the highest bidder. He was as eager to gain power as me. And a barren princess isn't worth her weight in gold, only good enough to fuck and dispose of later." Cezar dares to speak to her like that, and they may just be his last words.

I don't wait for Ela to recover from the vile filth spilling from his lips. My reaction is quick. I have him in my grasp so fast he doesn't even have a chance. My hands are around his throat as I lift him from his chair and feel him struggling to breathe. "A person's value has nothing to do with any of that. She's more valuable than anyone in this fucking room, myself included. The worth she brings to others, her kindness, her strength, her heart of gold, her beautiful mind, they all make her a priceless treasure someone like you could never understand. Now tell me why before I squeeze the life right out of you and watch you die a slow painful death."

His hands squeeze mine as he tries to loosen my grip. "Because your father stole my life, took what should have been mine. Your mother."

I close my eyes as I drop his arse into the chair and hear him cough as he sucks in air. "You did all this because he took my mother from you?"

"She was promised to me." He coughs. "Mine. She was to meet me, not him. And the moment he saw her, he decided otherwise. I've plotted my revenge ever since. I only wish I'd been there to watch them both die."

My mother told us the story about how she met my father. It was at a function where she was being introduced to those interested in her hand. She was eighteen and not excited about being forced to play along, but loyal to her family, she agreed. An hour into it she was ready to bail, thought of sneaking out through the kitchen and stomaching the wrath of her father later. Just as she was about to slip away a tall handsome male approached her, cutting off her exit. She was pissed at first, ready to dismiss him, but then he spoke, and it was as if her soul knew the suitor and demanded her to stay. They fell in love almost instantly, married a year later, and I was born on their second anniversary. They truly loved each other. Chose the other person, something unheard of for people in their positions, even then. Love was a rare thing. Loyalty to the régime was always what brought powerful couples together, not the other way around.

"That isn't the only reason though, is it?" Anna steps out of her hiding place. "Tell them the truth. The entire ugly truth. I can hear the lie in your voice. A secret you are holding onto, perhaps."

"I believe you two have met Anna. She's shared a few interesting private conversations between Cezar and Dracul that she sat in on. What you didn't know, what my uncle was even unaware of, is that Anna is my long-lost sister," I share, never once taking my eyes off either man.

Beni smiles slightly. He always loved Giovanna, spoiled her. "How did I not figure that one out?"

Anna doesn't seem as excited about being reunited. "Don't pretend you were ever looking. You had an agenda. To bring Simion home. You never once thought about what might happen once you did. Never considered what the consequences would be. You trusted the wrong people. Refused to admit it, even. Tried to make amends by going behind their backs and practically destroying everything. Your carelessness almost cost another innocent life."

Turning back to Cezar she addresses him now. "One advantage of losing my sight is that I have to rely on my other senses. I've always known there was more, I just could never figure out what that was. Your voice fluctuates whenever you discuss Dragos or Dracul. It's slight, but for someone like me, it's a tell, one that warns me to keep my guard up whenever you're around. So why not explain why that is and stop pretending you're our ally."

He stares at her for a long moment. Anger takes over his face as he squares his shoulders and shocks the hell out of all of us. "I am also their brother."

Chapter Forty-Seven

GINO

The Royals

The room goes silent. So silent that the sound of a chopper overhead draws all our attention. It's dark outside and the cover of night is to these subversives' advantage. Had it been day, we would have seen the attack and been able to take shelter.

One look at Cezar and I realize he's somehow behind this. The smirk on his face gives him away. But it fades just as quickly when he watches it take position outside the large window and hover. Perhaps he thought they were here to rescue him, not take him out along with the rest of us.

Two armed men lean out and fire rapidly into the window. Thankfully, it's bulletproof glass, which only helps us long enough to run for cover. That many bullets won't be stopped for long. As soon as I grab Ela, I dive to the left with her in my arms, and behind us glass shatters. I don't give her the chance to protest. I stand and shove her inside the bathroom, intending to be a part of this—whatever this is. My plans get sabotaged when a large body appears behind me and shoves me inside as well.

"Get in the shower and don't you dare think of leaving this room until I come for you." Stew grabs the handle and slams it closed.

I'm standing there gaping at the steel-reinforced door, unable to believe this is now my fate. Being shoved inside a damn safe room and left to wait while the others deal with the crisis beyond the door.

Equally annoyed is my wife, who takes my arm and tugs me behind her as she does what Stew ordered us to do. "It's fun, isn't it? Being forced to not get in the middle of the battle all because of who you are."

"It fucking sucks balls," I grumble as I step inside the small space and wish we were in here for other reasons. "This could be so much more enjoyable if we were in here to have fun."

"Yes, it could. We'll have to try it out later when this shit cools down." A frown develops on her lovely face. "Do you really think Cezar was telling the truth?"

"I don't know what to believe anymore." My head slams back into the tile wall, the stress weighing heavily on my shoulders. "Why would he lie about that?"

"I'm not sure he would. I assume he was about to share all the gory details when hell broke loose. What a fucking mess." Ela leans into me, and I can't help but wrap my arms around her. "We'll uncover the truth one way or another, Gino. I promise you that."

A loud explosion rocks the house. It's in the distance but close enough we feel it. My best guess is it's the helicopter crash landing. Probably when the pilot faced return fire, he got the hell out of there, but did so too late.

The gunfire that was background noise only moments ago has stopped. There's a lot of shouting. Men yelling in Russian as well as English and Spanish. The more familiar ones are louder and soon it ends.

"How long do they expect us to stay holed up in here?" I'm getting extremely antsy. "This is ridiculous."

My wife chuckles against my chest. "Preaching to the choir, honey. If you hadn't shoved me inside this bathroom, we'd be out there having some fun. Instead, we are forced to wait it out in here until one of them deems it safe enough for us to come out."

I untangle her from my body so we can get out of this room. "Well, fuck that. I'm not some helpless royal who doesn't understand how to take care of himself."

"Be careful. I'm not either, but you assumed I was. Always have."

My wife steps behind me, and the look she's giving warns me to tread lightly.

Grabbing her face, I draw her close. "I know that now. Old habits, okay. Forgive me for acting first before thinking. I'll remember to do better next time."

"No, you won't. You'll do it again and will also be stuck inside with me. It sucks but tis the price we pay for being the top dog they believe will save them and lead this country into a better way of life. I blame you."

After I kiss her smart mouth, I spin and grab the door handle. Gun in hand, I pray it opens. Thankfully, it does. The room is a chaotic mess. Glass everywhere. Splintered wood where the bullets tore into every visible surface. I count three bodies on the floor, only one I recognize.

Beni was a man who thought he could make this country a better place. He tried, but he also let the dream get in the way of capturing the dragon lurking behind the mask. Now he has paid the ultimate price for freedom, his life. I vow not to let his dream die with him.

Stew, along with a few other guards, step over the mess and toward me. "What did I tell you?"

I glare at him as I demand a report. "Tell me Cezar didn't get away."

Not impressed with my demands, he shakes his head. "Anna wasn't about to let that happen. She's one crazy bitch. Sorry, but she is. While you acted like the rest of us and took cover. She walked right up to him and dragged his arse out of the chair, knife to his throat, and forced him to watch it play out from behind the bookcase. He didn't go unscathed, a few bullets nicked him but he'll live. So will she. I've seen nothing like it. Unreal is what it was. Rounds flying all around us and she somehow walks right through them, not getting more than a few scratches, mostly from the glass when it shattered behind her."

Ela's fist lands on my chest as she grumbles. "Dammit. I would have loved to see that. No more shoving me out of the action. The next time you do, I'm taking my wrath out on you while we wait it out."

Stew tries his best to hold back a smirk. "Be careful. I can't have either of you getting hurt on my watch. I have a reputation to uphold. And for the record, Your Majesty, if he'd not have done it, I would have.

Then after you were safe. I'd have carried his arse inside and dumped him next to you."

"You think I'd let you do that?" I grab Ela's waist and stop her from moving. There is too much glass and other debris, and I'm not about to let her walk through it.

"No. I would have knocked you out first, which is why I'd have to carry you." He smirks and then laughs when I toss Ela over my shoulder, protesting. "And you'd have bickered just like that."

"What the hell? Put me down, you big brute." Ela slaps my back.

"Hush." I smack her sweet arse. "I don't want you getting cut or catching dysentery."

She pinches my side hard. "Dysentery? Seriously? I don't think I can catch that walking through a room destroyed by bullets. Now set me down."

I do, but only because we're outside the war zone. Stew leads us down the hall to a room guarded by more of our men. Cezar is loudly protesting about something happening inside.

When we open the door, Anna is leaning against the wall opposite him while one of our medics patches him up. I seriously kind of expected her to be torturing him, was hoping to assist her if I'm being honest.

"Leave us," I order a few minutes later. "He'll not bleed out, correct? His wounds can wait to be cleaned and dressed. We need answers, and I don't have time to play games."

Cezar glares at me, but remains silent. How did I never see the hatred this man held for me? I always took his more solemn demeanor to be just how he was. I never suspected it to be his way of disguising how much he'd wished me dead.

"So, you're my uncle? Am I really expected to believe this? That no one ever put two and two together?"

He only stares at me. Well, that's until a knife flies across the room, missing his head by a breath, then he seems to find his voice. "What the fuck was that for?"

I kind of thought Ela would be the one to speak, but I was wrong. It's Anna. "Well, damn, I missed. I guess I can try again. I always enjoyed throwing these little daggers, doing my best to hit my target from this distance."

Ela speaks now, and I know then these two are going to be trouble for many years to come. "Me too. Let me have one of those. Let's see if I can do better."

Before I can get a word out to stop her, a knife flies across the room and lands on the opposite side of Cezar, just barely missing him. "You fucking bitch. I should have killed you when I had the chance. Both of you."

Anna straightens and moseys over to the wall to retrieve the daggers. Once she has them in her hand, she gets in his face. "Probably should have. Your mistake. Now why don't you tell my brother what he wants to know before one of these lands right here?" She presses the tip of one against the center of his forehead. "It probably won't kill you, but fuck, it will hurt."

"You are nothing more than a whore. You don't have the guts to..." the painful squeal that follows his words has us jumping.

"Don't I?" Anna has thrust one dagger into his hand resting on the armrest, pinning it there. "Now speak before I decide to see if I'm as skilled with a knife as our queen. I hear she castrated poor Uncle Dracul. I always assumed a man would bleed out, but I guess not. Shall we test my theory?"

Sweat streams down his face as he grits his teeth. "I'm your uncle. My mother had an affair with your grandfather. When she told him she was pregnant, he sent her away. Banished her. My father found her, took her in, and because of the bad blood between families, he raised me to hate all that should have been mine. What is that saying? Keep your friends close and your enemies closer. Watching each one of you fall was to be the best revenge. Taking it all from them was to be my reward for never getting the acknowledgement I was also one of them. It's always the bastard child who takes down the beloved. Every king that ever ruled was destroyed from the inside, a forgotten heir they assumed was worthless. What they never once realized is that hatred is the most powerful obsession a person can have inside them. It allows one to destroy everything in his path without giving a fuck who gets hurt in the process."

I can only laugh because I know exactly what he means. Hatred pushed me all these years. I was willing, am prepared, to take out anyone who stole my family from me. The only difference is that I'm only willing to eliminate those involved. I don't wish to harm the innocent.

"This ends now. This vendetta you have against me, my family, ends." I say it as if my words are enough to make it happen.

Cezar throws his head back and laughs. "The only way it will end is when I'm no longer alive and capable of destroying you. I will never give up. No matter where you ship me off to, I'll find a way."

It happens almost in slow motion. Ela must see it at the same time I do. Because we both lunge forward to stop her, but she's fast, and it is done.

"Those were the words I was waiting for you to say so I could finish it. I guess your death will do." Anna shoves the knife in his heart farther. "Any last words?"

Cezar stares down at the knife piercing his chest, unable to speak.

"No? Good, because I was tiring of your voice." Then she twists it, to ensure the job is done, before pulling it out. "May your soul go straight to hell."

Chapter Forty-Eight

GABRIELA

The Royals

I can only stand there as I watch Anna take control and end Cezar's life. His body slumps forward as blood drips down the handle wedged deep inside his chest. If he were any other person, I might feel an ounce of sadness. The only thing I feel is relief.

The man's eyes told me all I needed to know. He would continue to do everything he could to destroy my husband, us. I never felt comfortable around him. Something always put me on edge when he was in the room. I guess there was an excellent reason for that.

"Why did you do that?" Gino is now pacing the room.

No one else is inside with us. Joel and Stew are standing guard to make sure no one disturbs us.

Anna steps away from Cezar, leaning her back against the wall. Her voice may be steady, but her body is anything but. It's then I notice the red blood soaking her shirt.

"Fuck." I rush to her side and lift it slowly. "Why didn't you say anything?"

"Because there wasn't time to worry about something so..." Her legs give way, and she collapses into me. "Maybe it's worse than I first predicted."

Gino takes her from me and scoops her into his arms. "Oh, no you don't. I just found you, you will not die."

While he carries her, I open the door for him. "We need a doctor right now."

Joel's eyes widen, and if I'd any doubts about his feeling for this woman, I no longer would. "Anna, I swear. You promised you wouldn't do this shit anymore. You're more important than some damn mission."

After Gino places her on the table of our dining room so the doctor can do her thing, Joel grabs Anna's hand. We watch as the doctor examines her wound. "It's a through and through. Once I stitch her up, she should be fine."

"See, I'll be fine." Anna does her best to relax. "Plus, now it's all over and you don't have to worry about me putting myself in danger anymore."

Joel and Gino seem to find that funny, but Joel is the one to speak first. "I'll believe that when I see it."

Gino lays a hand on the other man's shoulder. "We should probably keep these two far away from each other. If what happened in that room is any indication of the trouble they can get into, it would be safer for everyone."

"What?" Anna and I try to play innocent.

"We were just practicing our knife throwing skills." Anna starts to laugh but winces and grabs her side. "And I was doing what I had to do, brother. His blood could not be on your hands. I had my orders. Once he revealed his true intent, I was to take the target out and end the threat. If I hadn't done it, she would have. Maybe not today, but soon. She maybe your queen and wife, but her job does not differ from mine. We are both trained assassins who only kill when there is no other way. Tell me I'm wrong."

She's not. They'd given me the same order a few days ago. The moment we uncovered the person responsible, I had permission to eliminate them. I was still a member of the Elite Forces, and my team's objective was to exterminate all threats. This was a unique case. Cezar not only threatened Hermosa Islas, but an ally who was also under the protection it stood for. One way or another, Cezar was going to die.

"That's what I thought," Anna says as the drugs the doctor gave her a few moments ago kick in, causing her words to slur. "I'll let you all decide how to spin his death. Seems we could use his attack on this lovely home against him. No one would question that he got caught in the battle. Or you could even... even reveal his double cross. I think doing that would gain you friends you desperately need. He isn't as well-admired as he likes everyone to believe."

She fades quickly after that, and we leave them so we can talk in private. Stew has so many questions and is surprised when we share what went down. It's not every day a guard is forced to deal with this kind of attack. All the training you hoped you never have to put into use becomes way too real.

Covering up what took place would be easy. We could call Cezar a casualty of an attack on the family and be done with it. But that seems deceitful and wrong. So instead, we go with the truth, or a version of it. The truth seems too farfetched and something no one would truly believe. One of Gino's advisors will release it in a statement when he also announces the royal family being forced into hiding until it is safe.

Once the day is over, Gino and I are escorted to a plane and on our way back to my home country. Right now, we need to get as far away from the fallout and check on the little girl who stole our hearts. We'll return in a few days or weeks, once the dust has settled. Take our place as the leaders of a new nation that is ready to end the war they have been driven to undergo for so long.

It won't be easy. We'll have to stand strong together and display a united front for this to work. I never wanted this title or job, but I now understand that this is my destiny. That my suffering and struggles taught me a few lessons I'd not have learned if my life had been different. I may not fully understand what the people I serve have been through, but I can empathize with them. Be the queen they call for me to be, a fearless warrior who will fight for the freedom each one of them deserves.

Chapter Forty-Nine

GINO

The Royals

We've been back in Hermosa Islas for two days. My country is ready for our return, but before we can do that, we need to ensure it's safe for all of us. Plus, it's nice to not feel the pressure surrounding us while we bond as a family.

The moment we stepped off the plane, Angela and Edward greeted us. It was clear Ela's mother understood the need for her to hold Emersyn. For her to make sure the little one was fine and doing well. The way my wife brought our daughter to her chest and cradle her tight, kissed her dark hair and whispered how much she missed her, told me all I needed to know about the family we were building.

We quickly learned that a baby was a lot of responsibility. Neither of us had been prepared for what it actually meant. I'd been so focused on the world around me I'd not stopped to think that the child Emoni was carrying could be mine. Nor had I taken the chance to consider what being a father meant, or even what it meant to be a parent. And Ela had never once let her mind ponder on what being a mother would be like. She'd given that dream up a long time ago.

"Are all parents this exhausted at the end of the day?" I ask as she sits on our bed while giving Emersyn her last bottle before bedtime.

"Shh. She's fighting it," Ela whispers as we watch our little princess' eyes grow heavy. "She is one stubborn little girl. Why do I feel we will constantly have to be on our toes?"

I run my knuckles along Emersyn's sweet cheek and catch a smile from the angel I never expected. "Because we are her parents, and this is payback. My mother told me one day I'd understand why she worried so much."

"Mine too." Ela grins over at me. "Is it wrong I'm excited about all that?"

I shake my head as I tug her into my side. "No. I just hope we don't screw her up. That we provide her with a life where she can freely become whatever she wants to be. I mean, besides being the first queen who will be expected to rule."

"She'll hate it. I have no doubt about that. But eventually she will understand why God chose her instead of someone else. And together we'll do our best to help her. This adventure is new to all of us. None of us thought we'd one day actually be here."

Once Emersyn is asleep, I take her from her mother's arms and place her in the bassinet. Neither of us are ready for her to sleep where we can't watch over her. Silly? Maybe it is. But after all the shit we've faced since she came into this world, we don't care.

After I make sure I secure the door and the system to this floor is on, I take Ela's hand and tug her to her feet. Tired or not, we need a shower to wash the day away.

When I go to kiss her neck as she undresses, she laughs. "I think I have puke in my hair. I know I have it caked down my back. You might want to wait until I've washed it off. God, that feels nice, though."

I step back and yank my own stained t-shirt over my head. I also have baby spit up on me. A few joys of parenthood I refuse to complain about. Until it was forced on me, I'd been determined not to be a father, but in the days since becoming one, I have to wonder why that is. I love it all. The interruptions when she is hungry, bored, tired, or needs to be changed, helps me see the bigger picture. It reminds me life is more than just the day-by-day routines we get caught up in. It's the little things we should focus on more. The memories we will cherish one day when those we once had to watch, like an eagle, grow up and venture out into the world. I'd been required to mature faster than I should have, so I'm determined to slow it down as much as I can and treasure every second.

Scooping my sexy wife into my arms, I carry her inside the shower. My need to cherish her is great as well. I fought that connection longer than I should have. If I'd have only been honest with her in the beginning, we could have enjoyed this life sooner. I'll never take her for granted again.

Once we've washed away the day, no longer smelling like sour milk, I draw her into my arms. My body forgets how exhausted it is and decides it has enough energy to get lost inside of hers.

"Yes." Ela moans as my fingers tease her sweet spot. "I love how my body reacts to your touch."

"As do I," I whisper against her shoulder before I sink my teeth into her flesh. She will have a mark there in the morning, scold me later for it. The thought of that only makes me sink my teeth in harder. If I'm going to get scolded, I might as well make it worth the trouble.

Her nails dig into my thigh, leaving behind half-moons and scratch marks as she drags them upward. "Two can play that game."

I spin her around and slam her into the glass wall behind us. "I'm fucking you against this wall. You need to keep it down so you don't wake Emersyn."

Digging her fingers into me, she brings my lips to hers. "Then you had better swallow my screams."

That's exactly what I do. After I lift her, encourage her legs to wrap around my waist, I swallow all her cries as I slam into her. I don't let up. This isn't an easy, slow fucking. This one is hard and brutal, making us both feel how much our love is a force so strong we cannot always control it.

Breathless and limp, I finish and make sure we're clean again. Then I help her slip on a clean t-shirt of mine before carrying her into our bedroom and falling into bed with her. Exhaustion takes over again, but not before I smile and thank God for the life he's granted me. He knew what I required, who I needed, and that the little girl sleeping only a few steps away from us also was an important part of the plan. I vow then to do my best to make certain both the girls in my life remain strong, fearless warriors, always ready for what life throws at us.

Epilogue

GABRIELA

The Royals

"Mom, why do I have to wear this stupid dress? Can't I dress like Steven?" Emersyn stomps into my room like only a ten-year-old can, where I'm getting ready for the annual ball.

My daughter is so much like I was. She loves to climb trees, ride horses, go for a swim in the pond, wearing only her underwear and t-shirt. She would rather play with frogs and snakes than attend a formal ball where she's obliged to dress up and smile while everyone fawns over her.

Spinning to see what the problem is, I try not to laugh. She looks like a true princess, which is what is making her so unhappy. "If I have to wear a dress, so do you."

"But you like wearing them. Daddy goes all crazy and kisses you in that way that makes me want to throw up." Emersyn pretends to gag. "Plus, Rosa said I can't wear my hair in pigtails tonight. She said I have to leave it down and let all these wild curls free."

Rosa is our nanny. She helps us with the children while Gino and I work. We hired her shortly after we returned to Kosonia. While I hated needing help, I could not do everything I wanted to and be a full-time parent. We only used her during the hours we were focused on other things. Our evenings and weekends are for family, and we do our very best to keep it that way.

Our son, Steven, comes running in and tries to sneak past his sister and behind me. Gino is fast on his tail, with a smaller version of a tux that matches his, draped over his arms.

"I don't want to wear the money suit." He shouts while trying to hide. "Why can't I just wear my jeans and t-shirt? That thing is itchy."

When Emersyn was three, Gino and I decided we wanted another child. She brought us so much joy and we loved her and wished for her to have a sibling. Just because we couldn't have children of our own didn't mean our child wasn't out there somewhere. He was, and we found him a year later.

One of the young girls who worked in the palace discovered she was pregnant. I spotted her crying in the garden one day, unsure how she was going to take care of a child. I listened to her. At only sixteen, she knew there was no way she could care for a baby and give it the life it deserved. I talked to Gino, and later we sat down with her and offered to adopt her child. She cried again, and while it was hard, she agreed. This time, I took a more supportive role. Became a friend of the young girl, took her to all her appointments, became her birthing coach, even. We are still very good friends and she visits regularly, is a huge part of our family. But is more like an aunt to Steven, and very happy to play that role. He knows who she is, the woman who gave birth to him, because I think it's important for him to not be confused about any of it. I am his mother. Gino is his father. Emersyn his sister. A family is what one makes, not the blood that runs through their veins.

My husband growls. "Steven, we don't have time for this. Aunt Anna and Uncle Joel will be here soon. Jordy is going to be dressed in a monkey suit as well. You two can match."

"Can I have ice cream?" He is our negotiator, never misses a moment to get what he wants out of us.

I reach behind me and pick him up. I almost laugh when I notice the superhero underwear he will sport under his little man tux. My father would never have allowed that. I, however, couldn't care less and love that at least a part of him can be a little boy and that we don't force him to be only a prince. Our children are being raised differently from how my brothers and I were. We want them to learn what it takes to be a leader one day, but we also prefer them to have a choice. And at ten and five, wearing superhero underwear is an option every little one should get to have.

"Yes." I kiss his chubby little face. "I bet you look as handsome as daddy in it."

Both kids make a face.

Gino hands me Steven's suit as he steps up to our daughter and inspects her dress closely. "You're growing up way too fast, sunshine. I'm not sure I like it. Soon I'll be required to strap my sword onto my side so I can scare off the boys."

Emersyn blushes at the compliment. "Boys are gross, Dad."

Picking up a brush, he combs her hair. He has always been very hands on, learned how to do hair, even. "I'm reminding you of that in a few years."

While I dress Steven, he gathers her hair in a fancy updo and steals one of my decorative barrettes and clips it into her hair. "You hate your hair down, but I think this will work. How about you?"

"I get to wear one of Mommy's special hair pieces?" she asks as she studies her reflection in the mirror.

"You promise to be careful with it?" Gino straightens it a little. "I don't see why not, if you are careful."

She nods and even dances around a little, showing us how her dress twirls when she spins fast. "I guess dressing up isn't totally awful."

The kids hear Rosa announce the arrival of Jordy and take off.

Gino steps up behind me as I finish putting on my jewelry. "You look as stunning as always. When we return tonight, I'm ripping this dress off you so I can find out what you're wearing underneath it."

"You don't look so bad yourself." I walk out of the room and head down the stairs before I share. "I'm not wearing anything under it."

My feet hit the bottom step before I turn. Gino has paused at the top and is now doing his best to control his breathing. Even after ten years of marriage, I can sometimes surprise him. I mean, it's not the first time I've gone without, but when he knows, it drives him insane.

Before the night is over, I'll be dragged off into some corridor so he can have his way with me. That may have been my plan all along. These things are so boring it will give me something to look forward too.

If you enjoyed the story of Gabriela & Gino, I ask you leave me a review on Amazon, Goodreads, or BookBub. Reviews are important and help others know they too should read this book.

I have several books available listed in the back of this book. Please check them out.

Thank you and Happy Reading!!!!

Bonus Chapter

FEARLESS WARRIOR

Do you want more of Gino & Gabriela?

I have a bonus chapter available to those who sign up for my newsletter. Don't worry if you are already signed up, it won't double your subscription, only update any changes. Click the link below to download their royal wedding.

https://dl.bookfunnel.com/dv8dmah84m

The Duke

FALCON GLOBAL NOVELLA

One kiss was all it took...

All I want is my freedom. All my father wants is to chain me to the highest bidder. I have one last opportunity to live on my terms before my choice is taken from me.

Darius Falcon, also known as The Duke, enters my world. He's an arrogant prick who won't take no for an answer. Refusing to change course once he sets his sights on me. Too bad he won't get to keep me for more than a week.

Then one day he materializes from the shadows to save me from a monster. It's then I wonder if now is my chance to take control of over my future. Maybe when you wish upon a hunk, dreams really do come true.

Only Available to Newsletter Subscribers.
https://dl.bookfunnel.com/xn53pw0g4o

Acknowledgments

I would like to take the time to thank all of you for supporting me on this incredible journey. This series started on the dreams of a little girl who played princess daily. She would dress up and ran around my house looking for her prince. If it weren't for that sweet little angel, who has grown into a wonderful young woman, Suddenly Enthroned may never have been written. So thank you for helping both of our our dreams come to life.

To all you who have been a part of my team for several years now, thank you. My books are now better because of you. There are too many names to list, but you know who you are and each one has made my life easier. My books the very best they can be because you helped me.

To my family who allows me to spend hours hidden in a room or with my EarPods in and never complains. You have supported me since this journey to becoming an author started, and as my fan base grew have cheered me on. I love you so much. Life wouldn't be as fun without the three of you by my side. We have so many more new adventures coming our way and I can't wait to face them together.

One more. I'd like to thank my talented daughter Megan for drawing the map of Hermosa Islas. She took my idea and brought it to life. You are the reason this series came to be, so it means that much more you took your time and contributed. I cannot wait to see where your talents will take you one day. I love you so much.

Remember dreams are what this world is build on. You just have to be brave enough to take the first step.

Be brave.

* Updated 04/20/24

Also by C. R. Riley

<u>Crystal Lake Series</u>

Facing the Storm

Uncharted Waters

Light in the Shadows

When the Fog Lifts

<u>Life Series</u>

The Good Life

A Transformed Life

<u>Love of the Game</u>

Sneaky Quarterback

Tight End Comeback

Scoring the Birdie

Fielder's Choice

Catcher's Interference

<u>Kohl Family Series</u>

Untouchable

Unbreakable

Unforgettable

Unavoidable

Undeniable

<u>The Royals</u>

Suddenly Enthroned

Unexpected Princess
My Noble Fight
Her Royal Highness
Fearless Warrior

About the Author

Contemporary romance author C. R. Riley is celebrated for creating worlds and characters that don't always follow the rules, including those she futilely tries to set herself. But the best characters always find a way around them, often surprising her with their willingness to make each and every journey unique, if not emotionally satisfying.

Her Kohl Family series has been called the perfect epitome of contemporary romance with a twist of the unexpected. The characters tackle tough topics while making you fall in love with them, and despising those baddies who deserve it. Each story is a unique standalone. That cares over in her Modern-Day Royals series, which features characters who are unlike any royal put to the page before. And of course, combining her love of football and baseball she adds a steamy sports romance, Love of the Game which follows a family of athletes on their separate journeys to find true love.

You can find all her romantic and out-of-the-ordinary series on Amazon and free in Kindle Unlimited. Never miss a new project update or book release by signing up for her newsletter or follow her on social media, accounts listed below.

I'd love to hear from you and do my best to personally answer emails. crriley@crrileyauthor.com